DOUBLE
DEXTER

JEFF LINDSAY

DOUBLE DEXTER

A NOVEL

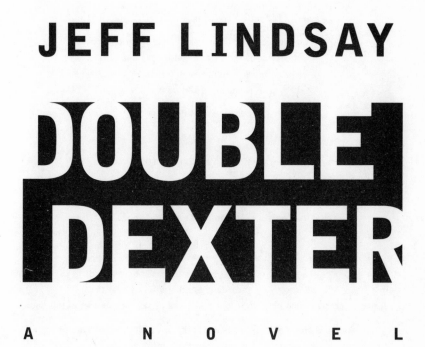

First published in Great Britain in 2011 by Orion Books,
an imprint of The Orion Publishing Group Ltd
Orion House, 5 Upper Saint Martin's Lane
London WC2H 9EA

An Hachette UK Company

1 3 5 7 9 10 8 6 4 2

A CIP catalogue record for this book is
available from the British Library.

ISBN 978 1 4091 1350 8

Printed in Australia by Griffin Press

The Orion Publishing Group's policy is to use papers that are natural,
renewable and recyclable products and made from wood grown in sustainable
forests. The logging and manufacturing processes are expected to
conform to the environmental regulations of the country of origin.

www.orionbooks.co.uk

For Hilary, as ever

Acknowledgments

My very great thanks to Samantha Steinberg, one of the nation's top forensic artists and the author of *Steinberg's Facial Identification Catalog* and *Steinberg's Ethnicities Catalog*, who provided a technical review of the manuscript.

And special thanks, as always, to Bear, Pookie, and Tink, who remind me why I bother.

DOUBLE DEXTER

ONE

OF COURSE THERE ARE CLOUDS. THEY TAKE OVER THE SKY and hide that pulsing swollen moon that is clearing its throat above them. The slow trickle of its light is there—but any possible glimmer is hidden, invisible behind the clouds that have rolled in low and bloated and so very full. Soon the clouds will open up and pour down a heavy summer rain, so very soon, because they, too, are full of what they must do, full to the point of bursting, so very full that they, too, must work to hold back the flood that absolutely must come, and soon.

Soon—but not now, not yet. They must wait, too, swelling with the power of all that is growing in them, the true and blinding current of what will come, of what *must* come when it is right, when it is beyond necessary and into the true shape of this moment, when it forges the real and necessary skeleton of *now*—

But that time is not yet here, not yet. And so the clouds glower and bunch and wait, letting the need build, and the tension grows with it. It will be soon; it has to be soon. In only a few moments these dark and silent clouds will shatter the silence of the night with the unbearable bright omnipotence of their might and blast the darkness into flickering shards—and then, only then, the release will come.

The clouds will open up and all the tension of holding in so much weight will flow out in the pure bliss of letting go, and the clean joy of it will pour out and flood the world with its oh-so-happy gift of light and liberation.

That moment is near, so tantalizingly close—but it is not yet. And so the clouds wait for that just-right moment, growing their darkness, swelling even bigger and heavier with shadow, until they absolutely must let go.

And here below, in the lightless night? Here on the ground, in the stark pool of shadow these clouds have made with their moon-sheltering sky-hogging sulkiness? What can this be, over there, skyless and dark, sliding through the night so very full and ready and waiting, just like the clouds? And it *is* waiting, whatever its dark self might be; it waits tense and coiled and watching for that perfect moment to do what it will, what it must, what it has always done. And that moment skitters closer on little mice feet as if it too knows what must come and fears it, and feels the terror of the stalking moment of rightness that is even now pattering up close, closer—until it is right there behind you, looking at your neck and nearly tasting the warm flutter of those tender veins and thinking, *Now*.

And a shattering blast of lightning shreds the dark night and shows a large and soft-looking man scuttling across the ground, as if he, too, has felt the dark breath so close behind. Thunder booms and lightning flashes again and the figure is closer, juggling a laptop and a manila folder as he fumbles for keys and disappears into darkness again as the lightning ends. One more burst of lightning; the man is very close now, clutching his burden and holding a car key in the air. And he is gone again in black stillness. There is sudden silence, a complete hush, as if nothing anywhere is breathing and even the darkness is holding its breath—

And then there comes a sudden rush of wind and a last hammer of thunder and the whole world cries out, *Now*.

Now.

And all that must happen in this dark summer night begins to happen. The skies open up and let go of their burden, the world begins to breathe again, and here in the newly wet darkness other tensions flex and uncoil so very slowly, carefully, reaching their soft sharp tendrils out toward the fumbling, clownlike figure now scrabbling to unlock his car in this sudden rain. The car's door swings open, the laptop and folder thump onto the seat, and then the soft and doughy man slides in behind the wheel, slams the door, and takes a deep breath as he wipes the water from his face. And he smiles, a smile of small triumph, something he does a lot these days. Steve Valentine is a happy man; things have gone his way a lot lately and he thinks they have gone his way again tonight. For Steve Valentine, life is very good.

It is also almost over.

Steve Valentine is a clown. Not a buffoon, not a happy caricature of inept normality. He is a real clown, who runs ads in the local papers and hires out for children's parties. Unfortunately, it is not the bright laughter of childish innocence that he lives for, and his sleight of hand has gotten somewhat out of hand. He has been arrested and released twice when parents pointed out to the police that you don't really need to take a child into a dark closet to show him balloon animals.

They had to let him go both times for lack of evidence, but Valentine took the hint; from that point on nobody has complained—how could they? But he has not stopped entertaining the children, certainly not. Leopards do not change their spots, and Valentine has not changed his. He just got wiser, darker, as wounded predators do. He has moved on into a more permanent game and he thinks he has found a way to play and never pay.

He is wrong.

Tonight the bill comes due.

Valentine lives in a run-down apartment building just north of Opa-locka airport. The building looks at least fifty years old. Abandoned cars litter the street in front, some of them burned-out. The building shakes slightly when corporate jets fly low overhead, landing or taking off, and that sound interrupts the constant white noise of traffic on the nearby expressway.

Valentine's apartment is on the second floor, number eleven, and it has a very good view of a rotting playground with a rusting jungle gym, a tilting slide, and a basketball hoop with no net. Valentine has put a battered lawn chair on the balcony of his apartment, placed so he has a perfect view of the playground. He can sit and sip a beer and watch the children play and think his happy thoughts about playing with them.

And he does. He has played with at least three young boys that we know about and probably more. In the last year and a half small bodies have been pulled from a nearby canal on three occasions. They had been sexually abused and then strangled. The boys were all from this neighborhood, which means that their parents are poor and probably in this country illegally. That means that even when their children were killed they had very little to say to the police—and that makes their children perfect targets for Valentine. Three times, at least, and the police have no leads.

But we do. We have more than a lead. We *know*. Steve Valentine watched those little boys at their games on the playground, and then he followed them away into the dusk and taught them his own very final games and then he put them into the murky trash-filled water of the canal. And he went satisfied back to his decrepit lawn chair, opened a beer, and watched the playground for a new little friend.

Valentine thought he was very clever. He thought he had learned his lesson and found a better way to live out his dreams and make a home for his alternative lifestyle and there was nobody smart enough to catch him and make him stop. Until now he has been right.

Until tonight.

Valentine had not been in his apartment when the cops came to investigate the three dead boys, and that was not luck. That was part of his predator's cleverness; he has a scanner for listening to police radio traffic. He knew when they were in the area. It would not be often. The police did not like to come to neighborhoods like this one, where the best they could hope for was hostile indifference. That is one reason Valentine lives here. But when the cops do come, he knows about it.

The cops come if they have to, and they have to if Somebody calls 911 to report a couple fighting in apartment eleven on the second floor, and if Somebody says the fight ended suddenly with the sound of screaming terror followed by silence, they come quickly.

And when Valentine hears them on his scanner, coming to his address, to his apartment, he will naturally want to be sure he is somewhere else before they get here. He will take any material he has that hints at his hobby—and he will have some material, they always do—and he will hurry downstairs and out into the darkness to his car, thinking that he can drive away until the radio tells him that things have calmed down again.

He will not think that Someone would bother to look up his car's registration and know that he drives a light blue twelve-year-old Chevrolet Blazer with CHOOSE LIFE! plates on it and a magnetic sign on the door that says, PUFFALUMP THE CLOWN. And he will not think that Something might be waiting for him in the backseat of this car, hunched down carefully into the shadows.

He will be wrong about both of those things. Someone does know his car, and Something does wait silently hunkered down on the floor of the dark backseat of the old Chevy, waits while Valentine finishes wiping his face and smiling his secret smile of small triumph and finally—*finally*—puts the key in the ignition and starts the engine.

And as the car sputters into life, the moment comes, suddenly, *finally*, and Something roars up and out of the darkness and snakes a blinding-fast loop of fifty-pound-test nylon fishing line around Valentine's doughy neck and pulls it tight before he can say anything more than, "Guck—!" and he begins to flail his arms in a stupid, weak, pitiful way that makes Someone feel the cold contemptuous power running up the nylon line and deep into the hands holding it. And now the smile has melted from Valentine's face and flowed instead onto ours and we are there so close behind him that we can smell his fear and hear the terrified thumping of his heart and feel his lack of breath and this is *good*.

"You belong to us now," we tell him, and our Command Voice hits him like a jolt of the lightning that crackles outside now to punctuate the darkness. "You will do just what we say and you will do it only when we say it." And Valentine thinks he has something to say about that and makes a small wet sound and so we pull the noose tight, very tight, just for a moment, so he will know that even his breath belongs to us. His face goes dark and his eyes bulge out and he raises his hands to his neck and his fingers scrabble madly at the noose for a few seconds until everything goes dark for him and his hands slide down into his lap and he slumps forward and begins to fade away and so we ease up on the noose because it is still too soon, much too soon for him.

His shoulders move and he makes a sound like a rusty ratchet as he takes in one more breath, one more in the quickly dwindling number of breaths he has left to him, and because he does not yet know that the number is so very small he takes another quickly, a little easier, and he straightens up and wastes his precious air by croaking, "What the fuck!"

A string of nasty mucus drips from his nose and his voice sounds cramped and raspy and very irritating and so we pull once more on the noose, a little more gently this time, just enough so he will know that we own him now, and he very obediently gapes and clutches at his throat and then goes silent. "No talking," we say. "Drive."

He looks up and into the rearview mirror and his eyes meet ours for the very first time—only the eyes, showing cool and dark through the slits cut in the sleek silk hood that covers our face. For just a moment he thinks he will say something and we twitch the noose very gently, just enough to remind him, and he changes his mind. He looks away from the mirror, puts the car in gear, and drives.

We steer him carefully south, encouraging him now and then with small tugs on the noose, just to keep that one thought in his mind that even breathing is not automatic and will not happen unless we say so, and he is very good for most of the trip. Only one time at a stoplight does he look back at us in the mirror and clear his throat and say, "What are you—where are we going?" and we pull very hard on his leash for a long moment and let his world go dim.

"We are going where you are told to go," we say. "Just drive, and do not talk, and you might live a little longer." And that is enough to make him behave, because he does not yet know that soon, so very soon, he will not *want* to live a little longer, because living as he will come to know it is a very painful thing.

We steer him carefully along side streets and into an area of battered newer houses. Many of them are empty, foreclosed, and one of them in particular has been selected and prepared and we drive Valentine to this place, down a quiet street and under a broken streetlight and into an old-fashioned carport attached to this house and we make him park the car at the back of the carport, where it cannot be seen from the road, and turn off the engine.

For a long moment we do nothing except hold the noose and listen to the night. We push down the rising gurgle of the moon-music and the soft compelling rustle of inner wings aching to open wide and take us up into the sky, because we must be very careful. We listen for any sound that might stalk unwelcome into our night of need. We listen, and we hear the lash of the rain and the wind, and the splash of water from the carport's roof and the rattle of the trees as the summer storm moves through them, and nothing else.

We look: The house to our right, the only house that could see into this carport, is dark. It is empty, too, like the house where we have parked, and we have made certain that there is no one there either, and we silently reach out along the street, listening, carefully tasting the warm wet wind for the scent of any other thing that might see or hear—and there is nothing. We breathe in, a deep and beautiful breath filled with the taste and smell of this marvelous night and the terrible-wonderful things we will soon be doing together, just us and Puffalump the clown.

And then Valentine clears his throat, trying so very hard to do it softly, quietly, trying to clear away the tight sharp pain of the line around his neck and somehow make sense of the impossible thing that is happening to special, wonderful him—and the sound of it grates on our ears like all the awful clatter of a thousand cracking teeth and we pull hard on the noose, hard enough to break skin, hard enough to squeeze out forever the whole idea of making any sound ever again, and he arches back against the seat with his fingers scrabbling feebly at his throat for just a second before he slumps down into bulge-eyed silence. And we get rapidly out of the car, open the driver's door, and pull him out onto his knees on the shadowed pavement of the carport.

"Quickly now," we say. We loosen the line so very slightly and he looks up at us with a face that says the whole concept of *quickly* is fading away from him for all time and as we see this new and wonderful awareness grow in his eyes we tighten the leash just enough to bring home to him the truth of that thought and he lurches up off his knees and trundles ahead of us through the jalousied back door and into the darkness of the empty house. And now we have him in his new home: the last place he will ever live.

We lead him into the kitchen and stop to let him stand for a few silent seconds and we stay close behind him with a taut hand on his noose and he clenches his fists and then wiggles his fingers and then he clears his throat again. "Please," he whispers, in a ruined voice that has already gone on ahead of him into death.

"Yes," we say with all our calm patience lapping at the edges of a wild shoreline of joy—and it may be that he thinks he hears some hope in that smooth anticipation because he shakes his head, just a little bit, as if he could persuade the tide to go backward.

"Why," he croaks. "It's, it's, just . . . why?"

We pull the line very tight around his throat and watch as his breath stops and his face goes dark and he drops once more to his knees and just before he goes off into unconsciousness we loosen the line, just a little bit, just enough for a small cloud of air to roll into his lungs through his ravaged throat and bring him back up into his eyes, and we tell him all of it, with full and joyful truth. "Because," we say. And then we pull the noose tight again, tighter, very tight, and we watch happily as he slides down the long slope into airless sleep and flops over onto his now-dark-purple face.

We work quickly now, arranging everything just right before he can wake up and spoil things. We get our small bag of toys and tools from the car and pick up the manila folder he dropped onto the car's seat and we go quickly back to the kitchen with these things. Very soon Valentine is taped in place on the counter with his clothing cut away and his mouth sealed shut and around him we have arranged the pretty photos we found in his folder, lovely shots of small boys at play, laughing at a clown in a few of them, in others simply holding a ball or riding a swing. And three of them are placed oh-so-carefully in just the right place so he *has* to see them, three simple portrait shots taken from the newspaper stories of three small boys who had been found dead in a canal.

And as we finish making everything just right, just the way it has to be, Valentine's eyelids flutter. For a moment he lies still, perhaps feeling the warm air on his naked skin and the tight unyield-ing duct tape holding him motionless, and perhaps wondering why. Then he remembers and his eyes slam open and he tries impossible things, like breaking the duct tape or taking large breaths or scream-ing out of a carefully sealed mouth loud enough for anyone else in his receding world to hear. None of this can happen, not ever again, not for him. For Valentine, only one small thing is possible at all, only one unimportant, meaningless, wonderful, necessary thing, and now it will start to happen, *now*, whatever futile flopping struggles he might try.

"Relax," we say, and we put a gloved hand onto his bare and heav-ing chest. "Soon it will all be over." And we mean *all* of it, everything, every breath and blink, every leer and chuckle, every birthday party and balloon animal, every hungry trip into the dusk in the wake of a small and helpless boy—all over, forever, and soon.

We pat his chest. "But not too soon," we say, and the cold hap-piness of that simple truth floods up through us and into our eyes and he sees it and perhaps he knows for sure and perhaps he still feels stupid impossible hope. But as he melts back onto the counter in the tight unbreakable grip of the tape and the stronger need of this delirious night, the beautiful music of the Dark Dance begins to rise around us and we go to work, and for Valentine all hope washes away forever as that one essential thing begins to happen.

It starts slowly—not tentative, not out of uncertainty, not at all, but slowly so it will last. Slowly to draw out and relish each well-planned well-rehearsed often-practiced stroke and bring the clown *slowly* to the point of final understanding: a clear and simple insight into how it ends for him, here, now, tonight. *Slowly* we paint for him a true portrait of how it must be, stroking strong dark lines to show that this is all there will ever be. This is his very last trick, and now, here, tonight, he will slowly, carefully, meticulously, slice by slice and piece by piece, pay the toll to the happy bridge keeper with the bright blade, and *slowly* cross that final span into an unending darkness that he will soon be very willing, even very anxious, to join, because by then he will know that it is the only way out of the pain. But not now, not yet, not too soon; first we have to get him there, get him to the point of no return and just beyond it to where it is oh-so-clear to him that we have arrived at the edge and he can never go back. He must see that, understand that, absorb that, accept it as right and necessary and immutable, and it is our happy task to take him there and then point back to the border at the edge of the end and say, *See? This is where you are now. You have crossed over and now it all ends.*

And so we go to work, with the music rising around us and the moon peeking in through a rift in the clouds and chuckling happily at what it sees, and Valentine is very cooperative. He pitches and hisses and hurls out muffled squeals as he sees that what is happening can never be undone, and it is happening so very thoroughly to rapidly disappearing *him,* Steve Valentine, Puffalump the clown, the funny happy man in whiteface who really and truly loves kids, loves them so much and so often and in such a very unpleasant way. He is Steve Valentine, party clown, who can take a child through the whole magic rainbow of life in one dark hour, all the way from happiness and wonder into the final agony of hopelessly fading sight and the dirty water of a handy canal. Steve Valentine, who was far too clever for anyone ever to make him stop or prove what he has done in a court of law. But he is not in a court of law now, and he never will be. Tonight he lies upon the bench in the Court of Dexter, and the final verdict gleams in our hand, and there is no access to court-appointed lawyers where he is going and no appeal will ever be possible.

And just before the gavel falls for the very last time we pause. A small and nagging bird has perched on our shoulder and chirped its troubled song: *Cher-wee, cher-woo, it must be true.* We know the song and we know its meaning. It is the song of the Code of Harry, and it says that we have to be sure, have to be certain that we have done the right thing to the right person, so the pattern will be complete and we can finish with pride and joy and feel the satisfied rush of fulfillment.

And so at the place where breath comes slow and very hard for all that is left of Valentine and the final light of understanding is in his red and swollen eyes, we pause, lean over, and turn his head to face the pictures we have placed around him. We rip up one corner of the tape on his mouth and it must hurt, but it is such a very small pain compared to what he has been feeling for so long now that he makes no sound at all beyond a slow hiss of air.

"See them?" we say, shaking his wet slack chin and turning his head to make sure he sees the pictures. "See what you have done?"

He looks, and he sees them, and a tired smile twitches onto the uncovered part of his face. "Yes," he says, in a voice that is half-muffled by the tape and shattered by the noose but still sounds clear when he sees. He is drained of hope now, and every taste of life has faded from his tongue, but a small and warm memory tiptoes across his taste buds as he looks at the pictures of the boys he has taken away. "They were . . . *beautiful*. . . ." His eyes wander over the pictures and stay there for a long moment and then they close. "Beautiful," he says, and it is enough; and we feel so very close to him now.

"So are you," we say, and we push the tape into place over his mouth and go back to work, winding up into well-earned bliss as the climax of our sharp symphony blares up out of the cheerful growing moonlight, and the music takes us higher and higher until finally, slowly, carefully, joyfully, it comes to its final triumphant chord and releases everything into the warm wet night: everything. All the anger, unhappiness and tension, all the cramped confusion and frustration of the everyday pointless life we are forced to trudge through just to make *this* happen, all the petty meaningless blather of trying to blend with bovine humanity—it is all gone, all of it shooting up and out and away into the welcoming darkness—and with it, trailing along like a battered and beaten puppy, all that might have been left inside the wicked, tattered husk of Steve Valentine.

Bye-bye, Puffalump.

TWO

WE WERE CLEANING UP AND FEELING THE SLOW AND tired contentment creeping into our bones as we always did, a smug and satisfied laziness at being done and done well with our very happy night of need. The clouds had rolled away and left a cheery afterglow of moonlight and we felt much better now; we always feel better afterward.

And it may be that we were not paying quite as much attention as we should have to the night around us, wrapped as we were in our satisfied cocoon—but we heard a noise, a soft and startled breath, and then the whispered rush of feet, and before we could do any more than turn toward it, the feet ran toward the back door of the darkened house, and we heard that door bump shut. And we could only follow and stare through the door's glass jalousies in silent all-consuming dismay as a car parked at the curb leaped into life and sprinted away into the night. The taillights flare—the left one dangles at an odd angle—and we can only see that it is an old Honda, some uncertain dark color, with a large rust stain on the trunk that looks like a metallic birthmark. And then the car races out of sight and a cold and acid knot tightens in the pit of our stomach as the impossible, dreadful truth burns up inside us and pours out panic like the bright and awful blood from a newly opened wound. . . .

We have been seen.

For a long appalling minute we just stare out the door, rocked by the endless echoes of that unthinkable thought. *We have been seen.* Someone had come in, unheard, unnoticed, and they had *seen* us as we really were, standing drained and contented over the half-wrapped leftovers. And they had very clearly seen enough to recognize the odd-shaped pieces of Valentine for what they were, because whoever it was had left in a lightning-fast panicked gallop and vanished into the night before we could do more than take a breath. They had *seen*—they might even have seen our face; in any case they had seen enough to know what they were looking at, and they had raced away to safety—and probably to call the police. They would be calling right now, sending patrol cars to scoop us up and put us away—but here we stood, frozen into dumb astonished inaction, gaping and drooling at the place where the taillights had disappeared, stuck in stupid incomprehension like a child watching a familiar cartoon dubbed into a foreign language. *Seen* . . . And at long last, the thought gives us the jolt of fear we need to galvanize us into action, kick us into high gear, and send us racing through the last stages of cleanup and out the door with the still-warm bundles of all we have done this once-fine night.

Miraculously, we make it away from the house and off into the night and there are no sounds of pursuit. No sirens wail their warning; no squealing tires or crackling radios rip the darkness with their threats of Descending Doom for Dexter.

And as I finally, tensely, vigilantly made my way out of the area, the blather-headed numbness of that single shattering thought came back and roiled through me like the never-ending rattle of waves on a rocky beach.

We had been seen.

The thought stayed with me as I disposed of the leftovers—how could it not? I drove with one eye on the rearview mirror, waiting for the blinding burst of blue light to flare at my bumper and the brief harsh *whoop!* of a siren. But nothing came; not even after I ditched Valentine's car, climbed into mine, and drove carefully home. Nothing. I was left entirely at liberty, all alone, pursued only by the demons of my imagination. It seemed impossible—someone had *seen* me at play, as plainly as it was possible to be seen. They had looked at the carefully carved pieces of Valentine, and the happy-weary carver standing above them, and it would not take a differential equation to arrive at a solution to this problem—A plus B equals a seat in Old Sparky for Dexter, and someone had fled with this conclusion in perfect comfort and safety—but they had not called the police?

It made no sense. It was crazy, unbelievable, impossible. I had been *seen*, and I had walked away from it consequence-free. I could not really believe it, but slowly, gradually, as I parked my own car in front of my house and just sat for a moment, Logic came back from its too-long vacation on the island of Adrenaline, and I sat hunched over the steering wheel, and communed once more with sweet reason.

All right, I had been seen *in flagrante iugulo* and had every right to expect that I would be instantly outed and arrested. But I hadn't been, and now I was home, evidence disposed of, and nothing remained to tie *me* to the happy horror in the abandoned house. Someone caught a very quick glimpse, yes. But it had been dark in there—probably too dark to make out my face, especially in one brief, terrified glance, with me turned half away. There was no way to connect the shadowy figure holding the knife with any actual person, living or dead. Tracing the license plate of Valentine's car would only turn up Valentine, and I was reasonably sure he would not answer any questions, unless somebody was willing to use a Ouija board.

And in the incredibly unlikely event that my face was recognized and a wild accusation was made against me, they would find no evidence at all, only a man with a sterling reputation as a member of the Law Enforcement Community who could certainly stand on his dignity and scoff at these absurd allegations. Absolutely no one in their right mind would believe that I could possibly have done anything of the kind—except, of course, for my very own personal nemesis, Sergeant Doakes, and he had nothing at all on me except suspicion, which he'd had for so long that it was almost comforting.

So what remained? Aside from a dubious dark and partial glimpse of my features, what could anyone possibly have seen that might prove awkward to my ambitions for remaining at liberty?

The wheels and levers in my mighty brain clicked, whirled, and spat out their answer: Absolutely Nothing.

I could not possibly be connected to anything that some shadowy, frightened someone had seen in a dark abandoned house. It was an inescapable conclusion, pure deductive logic, and there was no way around it. I was home free, and I would almost certainly remain that way. I took a very deep breath, wiped my hands on my pants, and went into my house.

It was quiet inside, of course, since it was so very late. The sound of Rita's gentle snoring drifted down the hall to me as I peeked in at Cody and Astor; they were asleep, unmoving, dreaming their small and savage dreams. Farther down the hall, into my bedroom, where Rita lay fast asleep and Lily Anne was curled up in her crib—wonderful, improbable Lily Anne, the one-year-old center of my new life. I stood looking down at her and marveling, as always, at the soft perfection of her face, the miniature beauty of her tiny fingers. Lily Anne, the beginning of all that is good about Dexter Mark II.

I had risked all that tonight. I had been stupid, wildly thoughtless, and almost paid the price—capture, imprisonment, never again to cradle Lily Anne in my arms, never to hold her hand as she tottered through her first steps—and, of course, never again to find some well-deserving friend like Valentine and take him out to the Dark Playground. It was far too much to risk. I would have to lie low and be very well behaved until I was absolutely sure I was in the clear. I had been *seen*; I had brushed up against the flowing skirts of that old whore Justice, and I could not take that chance again. I must drop Dark Dexter's Delights and let my Dex Daddy disguise morph into the real me. Perhaps this time it would be a permanent hiatus; did I really need to take such awful risks just to do these dreadful-wonderful things? I heard a soft and sated chuckle of mockery rise from the Dark Passenger as it slithered down into rest. *Yessss, you do,* it hissed with sleepy satisfaction.

But not for a while; tonight would last, would have to last; I had been seen. I climbed into bed and closed my eyes, but the brainless worries of capture scurried back into my mind. I batted at them, swept them away with the broom of logic; I was perfectly safe. I could not be identified, and I had left no evidence anywhere that could ever be found, and reason insisted that I had gotten away with it. All was good—and even though I still did not quite believe it, I finally drifted off into anxious, dreamless sleep.

Nothing that happened at work the next day gave any indication that there was anything at all to worry about. Things were quiet in the forensics lab of the Miami-Dade Police Department when I arrived at my job, and I took advantage of the morning stupor to fire up my computer. A careful check of last night's duty logs revealed that no frantic call for help had come in with reference to a maniac and a knife in an abandoned house. No alarm had sounded, no one was looking for me, and if it had not happened by now it was not going to happen at all. I was in the clear—so far.

Logic agreed with the official record; I was perfectly safe. In fact, Logic said this to me countless times over the next few days, but for some reason my lizard brain would not listen. I found myself hunched over at work, raising my shoulders against a blow that never fell—that I *knew* would never fall, but I anticipated it anyway. I woke up at night and listened for the sounds of the Special Response Team scuffling into place around the house. . . .

And nothing happened; no sirens came in the night. No knock on the door, squeal of bullhorn, demands that I come out with my hands up—nothing at all. Life steamed along on its well-oiled tracks, with no one calling for Dexter's head, and it began to seem like some cruel invisible god was taunting me, mocking my watchfulness, sneering at my pointless apprehension. It was as if the whole thing had never happened, or my Witness had been consumed by spontaneous combustion. But I could not shake the thought that something was coming to get me.

And so I waited, and my jitters grew. Work became a painful test of endurance, sitting at home each night with my family was an annoying chore, and in short, all the zing and zest had fled from Dexter's life.

When the pressure builds too high, even volcanoes boil over, and they are made of stone. I am made of slightly softer stuff, and so it should have been no surprise when I finally erupted after three days of waiting for a blow that never fell.

My day at work had been particularly stressful for no real reason. The main corpse of the day was a floater, a badly decomposed thing that had probably been young and male and had apparently been standing on the wrong end of a large-caliber pistol when it fired. A retired couple from Ohio had found it when their rented pontoon boat ran over it. The floater's silk shirt had gotten tangled in the boat's propeller, and the man from Akron had suffered a small, nonfatal heart attack when he leaned over to clear the prop and saw the rotting face staring back up at him from the end of the motor's shaft. Peekaboo: Welcome to Miami.

There was a great deal of jollity among the cops and forensics geeks as this scenario became known, but the warm glow of camaraderie failed to penetrate Dexter's bosom. The gruesome jokes that would ordinarily bring forth my best fake chuckle seemed like fingernails on a chalkboard, and it was a miracle of self-control that I simmered silently through the moronic hilarity for ninety minutes without setting anyone on fire. But even the most trying experiences must end, and since there was no blood left on the body after so much time in the water, there was really no call for my particular expertise, and I was finally released to return to my desk.

I spent the rest of the workday on routine paperwork, snarling at misplaced files and seething at the stupidity of everyone else's report writing—when did Grammar die? And when it was finally time to go home I was out the door and in my car before the last stroke of the hour rang out.

I found no cheer in the casual bloodlust of the evening traffic. For the first time I found myself honking my horn, returning the upraised middle fingers, and raging at delay along with all the other frustrated drivers. It had always been obvious that everyone else in the world is painfully stupid; but tonight that truly grated on my nerves, and when I finally arrived home I was in no mood to pretend I was glad to be back with my little family. Cody and Astor were playing Wii, Rita was giving Lily Anne a bath, all of them performing their empty, oblivious dumb show, and as I stood inside the front door and looked at the profoundly annoying idiocy of what my life had become, I felt something snap, and rather than smashing furniture and laying about me with my fist, I flung my keys on the table and stalked out the back door.

The sun was just starting to set, but the evening was still hot and very humid, and after three steps into the yard I already felt beads of sweat blooming on my face. They felt cool as they rolled down my cheeks, which meant that my face was hot—I had flushed with an alien rage, a feeling that almost never took me over, and I wondered: What was going on in the Land of Dexter? Of course I was on edge, waiting for an inevitable apocalypse, but why should that suddenly blossom into anger, and why should it be directed at my family? The dull and anxious interior muck I'd been mired in had suddenly erupted into rage, a new and dangerous thing, and I still did not know why. Why did I feel this steaming wrath growing out of what was no more than a few small and harmless examples of human stupidity?

I crossed the patchy brownish grass of our yard and sat at the picnic table, for no real reason except that I had come out here and so I thought I should *do* something. Sitting wasn't much as an activity and it didn't make me feel any better. I clenched and unclenched my fists and then my face, and I pulled in another hot, damp breath. It didn't calm me down, either.

Dull, petty, pointless frustrations, the very stuff of life, but they had built to a point where I was falling apart. Now more than ever I needed to stay icy calm and in complete control; someone had *seen* me. Even now he might be on my trail, pitter-pattering closer and bringing with him Dexter's Destruction, and I needed to be at my absolute Mr. Spock–logical best—anything less would be fatal. And so I needed to know whether this flight of angry passion was some final unraveling of the carefully woven artistic tapestry that is Dexter, or merely a temporary tear in the fabric. I took one more large hot breath and closed my eyes to listen as it steamed through my lungs.

And as I did, I heard a soft and reassuring voice over my shoulder, telling me that there *was* an answer, and really and truly it *was* very simple, just this one more time, if only I would listen for a single moment to the voice of clear and thrilling reason. I felt the breath inside me chill into a frosty blue mist and I opened my eyes and looked behind me, through a gap in the tree above me, over the top of the neighbor's hedge and off into the darkening horizon, where these silky words were floating down from a giant yellow-orange burbling happy moon, just now drifting up over the rim of the world and sliding into the sky to hover like the fat and happy friend from a childhood holiday. . . .

Why wait for him to find you? it said. *Why not find him first?*

And it was a lovely, seductive truth, because I was good at two simple things: hunting my prey and then disposing of it. So why not do those things? Why couldn't I be proactive? Jump into the databases with both feet, find a list of every old, dark-colored Honda in the Miami area with a dangling taillight, and track them down one at a time until I found the right one, and then settle the whole thing once and for all by doing what Dexter does best—clean, simple, and fun. If there was no Witness, there was no threat, and all my problems would melt away like ice cubes on a summer sidewalk.

And as I thought about that and breathed in again, I could feel the dim red tide recede completely, and my fists unclenched, and the flush drained out of my face as the cool and happy light of the moon blew its gentle feather breath across me, and from the shadowy corners of my inner fortress a silken purr uncoiled, agreed, chuckled encouragement, and told me oh-so-clearly, *Yes, indeed. It really is just that simple. . . .*

And it was; all I had to do was spend some time on the computer, find a few names, and then slip away into the night, casually stroll off into darkness with a few harmless props—no more than a roll of duct tape, a good blade, and some fishing line. Find my Shadow, and then lead him gently away to share with me the small pleasures of a fine summer evening. Nothing could be more natural and therapeutic: a simple unwinding, a carefree interval to untie all the unreasonable knots, and the end of an unjust threat to all I held dear. It made such good sense, on so many levels. Why should I let anything stand in the way of life, liberty, and the pursuit of vivisection?

I breathed in again. Slowly, soothingly, the seductive purr of this simple solution whispered through me, stropping its fur on my interior legs and promising me utter contentment. I looked up into the sky; the bloated moon gave me one more beguiling simper, an invitation to the dance tinged with the promise of endless regret if I should be stupid enough to say no. *Everything will be fine*, it hummed to me with a rising tempo and a delightful blend of major chords. *Better than fine—blissful.* And all I had to do was be myself.

I had wanted something simple—here it was. Seek and slice, and an end to all strife. I looked up at the moon, and it looked back fondly, beaming at its favorite student, who had at last worked through the problem and seen the light.

"Thank you," I said. It didn't answer, except with one more sly wink. I took another cool breath, stood up, and went back into the house.

THREE

THE NEXT MORNING I WOKE UP FEELING BETTER THAN I had in days. My decision to take a proactive path had released all the unwanted anger I'd been wallowing in, and I jumped out of bed with a smile on my lips and a song in my heart. Of course, it was not the kind of song I could share with Lily Anne, since the lyrics were a little too sharp for her, but it made me happy. And why not? I was no longer simply waiting for something bad to happen; I was going to leap into action and *make* it happen—even better, happen to someone else. That was much more to the point; I was meant to be a stalker, not a stalkee, and accepting that this was my lot in life was bound to make me more content. I hurried through breakfast and managed to get to work a little early in order to get right at my new research project.

The lab area was empty when I got there, and I sat down at my computer and called up the DMV database. I had spent my morning drive thinking about how to construct a search for the phantom Honda, so there was no need to ponder and dither. I called up a list of all Honda sedans more than eight years old and sorted them by the owner's age and location. I was quite certain that my Shadow had been under the age of fifty, so I quickly discarded anyone older.

Next, I sorted for vehicle color. I could only say with certainty that the car was a darkish color; one very quick look at it racing away was not enough to be more specific. In any case, age, sunlight and the salty Miami air had done their work on the car and it would probably be impossible to say what color it was even if I looked at it under a microscope.

But I knew it was not light colored, so I pulled up all the dark-painted cars from the first search and tossed out the rest. Then I did one final sort for location, throwing away anything on the list registered to an address more than five miles away from the house where I had been seen. I would start with the assumption that my Witness lived somewhere nearby, in the South Miami area; otherwise, why would he be there, instead of Coral Gables or South Beach? It was a guess, but I thought it was a good one, and it immediately cut two-thirds of the entries from my list. All I needed was one quick glance at each car, and when I saw one with the dangling taillight and distinctive rusty birthmark on its trunk, I would have my Witness.

By the time my coworkers began to wander into the lab, I had compiled a list of forty-three old, dark-colored Hondas registered to under-fifty owners in my target area. It was a little daunting; I clearly had my work cut out for me. But at least it was my work, on my terms, and I was confident that I could get this done quickly and efficiently. I put the list into an encrypted file labeled "Honda," which sounded innocent enough, and e-mailed it to myself. I could call it up on my laptop when I got home and go right to work.

And as if to prove that I was finally moving in the right direction, a mere two seconds after I sent myself the list and brought my computer back to its official home screen, Vince Masuoka came in carrying a white cardboard box that could only be pastry of some kind.

"Ah, Young One," he said, holding up the box. "I have brought you a riddle: What is the essence of the moment but as fleeting as the wind?"

"All that lives, Master," I said. "Plus, whatever is in the box."

He beamed at me and opened the lid. "Snatch the cannoli, Grasshopper," he said, and I did.

Over the next few days I slowly, carefully, began to check the names on the list after work. I started with the ones closest to my house; these I could check on foot. I told Rita I needed exercise, and I jogged through the area in ever-widening circles, just another Normal Guy out for a run without a care in the world. And in truth, I began to feel as if I might really be back on the path to a worry-free life. The simple decision to take action had halted my fretting, stilled my churning bosom, and smoothed my furrowed brow, and the thrill of the hunt put the spring back in my step and brought a very good fake smile to my face. I fell back into the rhythms of Normal Life.

Of course, normal life for a forensics geek in Miami is not always what most people think of as *normal*. There are workdays when the hours are very long and filled with dead bodies, some of them killed in startling ways. I have never lost my sense of wonder at the endless ingenuity of human beings when it comes to inflicting fatal wounds on their fellow creatures. And as I stood in the rain one night almost two weeks after Valentine's Night, on the shoulder of I-95 at rush hour, I marveled again at this infinite creativity, because I had never before seen anything like what had been done to Detective Marty Klein. And in my small and innocent way, I was very glad that there was something new and noteworthy about Klein's exit, because Dexter was Drenched.

It was the dark of the moon, and I stood in the rain, in a cluster of people blinking at the lights of rush-hour traffic and the huddled police cars. I was soaked and hungry, with frigid water dripping from my nose, my ears, my hands, rolling down the neck of my useless nylon windbreaker, into the back of my pants, soaking into my socks. Dexter was very, very wet. But Dexter was at work, too, and so he must simply stand and wait and endure the endless babble of the police officers—officers who can comfortably take all the time they want to repeat the same pointless details, because they have been thoughtfully provided with bright yellow rain suits. And Dexter is not actually a police officer. Dexter is a forensics geek, and forensics geeks don't get bright yellow rain suits. They must make do with whatever they might have flung in the trunk of their car—in this case a flimsy nylon jacket that couldn't protect me from a sneeze, let alone a tropical downpour.

And so I stand in the rain and soak up cold water like a semihuman sponge while Officer Grumpy tells Officer Dopey one more time how he saw the Crown Vic pulled off onto the shoulder and went through all the standard procedures, which he repeats out loud again as if reading them from the manual.

And worse than the tedium, worse than the chill spreading through his bones and deep into his very center, Dexter must stand in all this dripping rain-soaked misery and maintain an expression of shocked concern on his face. This is never an easy expression to get right, and I can't really summon the urgency tonight, wallowing as I am in my blank misery. Every two minutes I find the necessary expression slipping away, replaced by a more natural look of soaking-wet annoyed impatience. But I fight it off, rearrange my features to the appropriate mask, and soldier on in the dark, wet, and endless evening. Because in spite of my cloudy disposition, I need to get it right. We are not looking at some nasty little drug dealer who got what he deserved. This is no headless wife caught in unfaithful performance by a temperamental husband. The body in the Crown Vic is one of us, a member of the fraternal order of Miami cops. At least, it seems to be, from what we can tell by glancing casually through the car's windows at the shapeless blob inside.

And it is shapeless, not because we cannot see it clearly through the windows—unfortunately, we can—and not because it has slumped down into a relaxed sprawl and curled up with a good book—it hasn't. It is shapeless because it has, apparently, been hammered out of its formerly human shape, slowly, carefully, and thoroughly bludgeoned into a blob of shattered bones and bruised flesh that no longer resembles even a little bit anything that might be called a person, let alone a sworn officer of the law.

Of course, it is terrible to do such a thing, even worse to do it to a cop, a peacekeeper, a man with a badge and a gun whose only purpose in life is to stop such things from happening to everyone else. Squishing a cop like that, so slowly and deliberately, is an extra-awful affront to our well-ordered society, and it is a dreadful insult to every other brick in the thin blue wall. And we all feel outrage—or at the very least, we present a reasonable facsimile. Because this kind of death has never been seen before, and even I can't imagine who, or what, could have done it this way.

Someone, or something, has spent a tremendous amount of time and energy smashing Detective Marty Klein into a glob of jelly—and worse still, outrageous beyond measure, they've done it at the end of a long day's work, when dinner is waiting. No punishment is too severe for the kind of animal who would do this, and I truly hoped that terrible justice would be served—right after dinner and dessert, over a cup of dark coffee. Possibly with a small biscotti or two.

But it's no good; the stomach growls, and Dexter is drooling, thinking of the sublime pleasures of Rita's cooking that wait for him at home, and therefore not keeping his facial muscles locked into the required expression. Someone is bound to notice and wonder why Detective Klein's dreadfully battered corpse would make any-one salivate, and so with a major effort of my iron will, I realign my face again and wait, pointing my somber scowl at the puddle of rain growing around my sopping shoes.

"Jesus," says Vince Masuoka, suddenly materializing at my side and craning his neck to see past the yellow rain suits and into the car. He wore an army surplus poncho and looked dry and contented and I wanted to kick him even before he spoke. "It's unbelievable."

"Very close to it," I said, marveling at the iron control that keeps me from attacking him for his ninny-hood.

"That's all we need," Vince said. "A maniac with a sledgehammer and a hard-on for cops. Jesus."

I would not have brought Jesus into the discussion, but naturally I'd had the same thoughts as I stood there turning into a small piece of Florida's aquifer. Even when someone was beaten to death, we had never before seen it done so savagely, so thoroughly, and with such maniacal focus. Among all the annals of Miami crime fighting this was unique, unmatched, brand-new, never seen before—until this evening, when Detective Klein's car had appeared on the shoulder of I-95 at rush hour. But I saw no point in encouraging Vince to make any more witless and obvious remarks. All clever conversation had washed out of me in the steady flow of the rain pouring into my clothing through my flimsy jacket, so I just glanced at Vince and then returned to concentrating on maintaining my solemn face: furrow the brow, turn down the mouth—

Another car slid to a halt beside the patrol cars already parked there on the shoulder, and Deborah got out. Or to be more formally

correct, Sergeant Deborah Morgan, my sister, and now lead investi-
gator on this new and dreadful case. The uniformed cops glanced
at Debs; one of them did a double take and nudged the other, and
they moved aside as she stalked over to look inside the car. She was
shrugging on a yellow rain jacket as she walked, and that did not
endear her to me, but she was, after all, my sister, so I just nodded at
her as she passed, and she nodded back. And her first word seemed
carefully chosen to reveal not merely her command of the scene, but
a picture of her true inner self as well. "Fuck," she said.

Deborah looked away from the mess in the car and turned her
head toward me. "You got anything yet?" she said.

I shook my head, which caused a small waterfall to roll down the
back of my neck. "We're waiting for you," I said. "In the rain."

"Had to get the sitter," she said, and shook her head. "You should
have worn a poncho or something."

"Gosh, I wish I'd thought of that," I said pleasantly, and Debs
turned back to look at the leftovers of Marty Klein.

"Who found it?" she said, still staring through the Crown Vic's
window.

One of the officers, a thick African-American man with a Fu
Manchu mustache, cleared his throat and stepped forward. "I did,"
he said.

Deborah glanced at him. "Cochrane, right?"

He nodded. "That's right."

"Tell me," she said.

"I was on routine patrol," Cochrane said. "I spotted the vehicle in
its present location, apparently abandoned on the shoulder of Inter-
state 95, and recognizing that it was an official vehicle, I parked my
patrol unit behind it and called in the tag. Receiving confirmation that
it was indeed a police vehicle signed out to Detective Martin Klein,
I exited my patrol vehicle and approached Detective Klein's vehicle."
Cochrane paused for a moment, possibly confused by the number of
times he had said "vehicle." But he just cleared his throat and plowed
on. "Upon arriving at a point where I could make a visual surveillance of the interior of Detective Klein's vehicle I, uh—"

Cochrane stumbled to a stop, as if he wasn't sure what the correct word might be in report-ese, but the cop beside him snorted and

supplied the missing word. "He hurled," the other cop said. "Totally lost his lunch."

Cochrane glared at the other cop, and harsh words might have been spoken if Deborah had not called the men back to their purpose. "That's it?" she said. "You looked inside, threw up, and called it in?"

"I came, I saw, I blew chunks," Vince Masuoka muttered beside me, but happily for his health Deborah didn't hear him.

"That's it," Cochrane said.

"You saw nothing else?" Debs said. "No suspicious vehicle, nothing?"

Cochrane blinked, apparently still fighting the urge to punch his buddy. "It's rush hour," he said, and he sounded a little testy. "What's a suspicious vehicle in this mess?"

"If I have to tell you that," Debs said, "maybe you should transfer to code enforcement."

Vince said, "Boom," very softly, and the cop beside Cochrane made a choking sound as he tried not to laugh.

For some reason, Cochrane didn't find it quite so amusing, and he cleared his throat again. "Lookit," he said. "There's ten thousand cars going by, and they're all slowing down for a look. And it's raining, so you can't see anything. You tell me what to look for and I'll start looking, all right?"

Debs stared at him without expression. "It's too late now," she said, and she turned away, back to the blob in the Crown Vic. "Dexter," she called over her shoulder.

I suppose I should have known it was coming. My sister always assumed that I would have some kind of mystical insight into a crime scene. She was convinced that I would know instantly all about the sick and murderous freaks we encountered after one quick glance at their handiwork, merely because I was a sick and murderous freak myself. And so every time she was faced with an impossibly grotesque killing, she expected me to provide the name, location, and social security number of the killer. Quite often I did, guided by the soft voice of my Dark Passenger and a thorough understanding of my craft. But this time I had nothing for her.

Somewhat reluctantly, I sloshed over to stand beside Deborah. I hated to disappoint my only sister, but I had nothing to say about this.

It was so savage, brutal, and unpleasant that even the Passenger had pursed its glove-leather lips with disapproval.

"What do you think?" Deborah said to me, lowering her voice to encourage me to speak frankly.

"Well," I said, "whoever did this is off-the-charts insane."

She stared at me as if waiting for more, and when it was clear that no more was coming, she shook her head. "No shit," she said. "You figured that out by yourself?"

"Yes," I said, thoroughly annoyed. "And after only one quick glance through the window. In the rain. Come on, Debs, we don't even know yet if that's really Klein."

Deborah stared inside the car. "It's him," she said.

I wiped a small tributary of the Mississippi River off my forehead and looked into the car. I could not even say for sure that the thing inside had ever been a human being, but my sister sounded quite positive that this amorphous glob was Detective Klein. I shrugged, which naturally sent a sheet of water down my neck. "How can you be sure?"

She nodded at one end of the lump. "The bald spot," she said. "That's Marty's bald spot."

I looked again. The body lay across the car's seat like a cold pudding, neatly arranged and apparently intact, unpunctured. There were no visible breaks in the skin and no apparent blood spill, and yet the pounding Klein had taken was total, terrible. The top of the skull was perhaps the only part of the body that had not been shattered, probably to avoid ending Klein's life too quickly. And sure enough, the fringe of greasy hair around the bright pink circle of bare skin did look a lot like what I remembered about Klein's bald spot. I would not have sworn an oath that it truly was, but I was not a real detective like my sister. "Is this a girl thing?" I asked her, and I admit I said it only because I was wet, hungry, and annoyed. "You can tell people apart by their hair?"

She glanced at me, and for one terrifying moment I thought I had gone too far and she was going to attack my biceps with one of her ferocious arm punches. But instead, she looked over to the rest of the group from Forensics, pointed at the car, and said, "Open it up."

I stood in the rain and watched as they did. A shudder seemed to go through the whole group of watchers as the car door swung open; this was a *cop* who had died this way, one of *us*, so terribly hammered into oblivion, and all of the watching cops took this as a very personal affront. But worse than that, somehow we were all quite sure it would happen again, to another one of us. Sometime soon, this frightful pounding would fall once more on one of our small tribe, and we could not know who, or when, only that it was coming—

It was the dark of the moon, and a dark time for Dexter; there was dread spreading through the ranks of all Miami cops, and in spite of all this fearsome unease Dexter stood dripping and thinking only one dark thought:

I missed my dinner.

FOUR

I

T WAS PAST TEN WHEN I FINISHED, AND I FELT AS IF I HAD
been standing underwater for the last four hours. Even so, it
seemed like a shame to head for home without checking some of
the names on my list. So I cruised slowly past two of the more distant
addresses that were more or less on my way. The first car was parked
right in front of the house; its trunk was unblemished and I drove
past.

The second car was under a carport, hidden by shadows, and I
could not see the trunk. I slowed to a crawl, and then nosed into
the driveway as if I was lost and merely turning around. There was
something on the trunk—but as my lights hit it, it moved, and the
fattest cat I had ever seen raced away into the night. I turned the car
around and drove home.

It was past eleven when I parked in front of my house. The light
was on over the front door, and I got out of my car and stood just
outside the small circle of light it cast. The rain had finally stopped,
but there was still a low bank of dark clouds filling the sky, and it
reminded me of the night almost two weeks ago when I had been seen,
and an echo of unease clattered through me. I stared up at the clouds,

but they did not seem intimidated. *We made you wet*, they sneered, *and you're standing there like a schmuck while your whole body puckers.*

It was true. I locked my car and went inside.

The house was relatively quiet, since it was a school night. Cody and Astor were asleep, and the late news muttered softly from the TV. Rita dozed on the couch with Lily Anne tucked onto her lap. Rita did not wake up when I came in, but Lily Anne looked up at me with bright and wide-awake eyes. "Da," she said. "Da da *da!*"

She recognized me right away, a brilliant girl. I felt a few of the interior clouds roll away as I looked at her happy little face. "Lily-willy," I replied with all the great seriousness required for the occasion, and she chortled back.

"Oh!" Rita said, jerking awake and blinking at me. "Dexter—are you home? I didn't," she said. "I mean, you're out so late. Again."

"Sorry," I said. "All part of the job."

She looked at me for a long moment, doing no more than blinking, and then she shook her head. "You're soaking wet," she said.

"It was raining," I told her.

She blinked a few more times. "It stopped raining an hour ago," she said.

I couldn't see why that mattered, but I am full of polite clichés, so I just said, "Well, it just goes to show."

"Oh," Rita said. She looked at me thoughtfully again and I began to feel a little self-conscious. But she finally sighed and shook her head. "Well," she said, "you must be very— Oh. Your dinner. It was getting so— Are you hungry?"

"Starving," I said.

"You're dripping on the floor," Rita said. "You'd better change into some dry clothes. And if you get a cold . . ." She waved a hand in front of her face. "Oh, Lily Anne—she's wide-awake." She smiled at the baby, that same mother-to-child smile Leonardo tried so hard to capture.

"I'll get changed," I said, and I went down the hall to the bathroom, where I put my wet clothes in the hamper, toweled off, and put on some dry pajamas.

When I came back, Rita was crooning and Lily Anne was gurgling, and although I didn't really want to interrupt, I had some important things on my mind. "You said something about dinner?" I said.

"It was getting very— Oh, I hope it didn't get all dried out, because— Anyway, it's in a Tupperware, and— I'll just microwave the here, take the baby." She jumped up off the couch and held Lily Anne toward me, and I stepped in quickly and grabbed my baby, just in case I had not heard Rita correctly and she really did mean to microwave the child. Rita was already moving in the direction of the kitchen as Lily Anne and I sat back down on the couch.

I looked down at her: Lily Anne, the small and bright-faced doorway into Dexter's newfound world of emotions and normal life. She was the miracle that had brought me halfway into humanity, just by the pink and wonderful fact of her existence. She had made me *feel* for the first time, and as I sat and held her, I felt all the fuzzy sunrise thoughts that any mere mortal would feel. She was almost one year old, and already it was clear that she was a remarkable child.

"Can you spell 'hyperbole'?" I asked Lily Anne.

"Da," she said happily.

"Very good," I said, and she reached up and squeezed my nose to show me that the word had been too easy for a highly intelligent person such as herself. She gave my forehead an openhanded smack and bounced a few times, her way of asking politely for something a little more challenging, perhaps involving movement and a good sound track, and I obliged.

A few minutes later, Lily Anne and I had finished bouncing through two verses of "Frog Went A-Courtin' " and were already working out the final details to a unified field theory of physics when Rita came bustling back into the room with a fragrant and steaming plate in her hand. "It's a pork chop," she said. "I did the Dutch oven thing, with mushrooms? Except the mushrooms at the store were not very— So anyway, I sliced in some tomatoes and a few capers? Of course, Cody didn't like it— Oh! And I forgot to tell you," she said, putting the plate down in front of me on the coffee table. "I'm sorry if the yellow rice is a little—but the dentist said? Astor is going to need braces, and she's completely . . ." She fluttered one hand in the air and started to sit. "She said that she would rather— Damn, I forgot the fork, just a minute," she said, and raced back into the kitchen.

Lily Anne watched her go, and then turned to look at me. I shook my head. "She always talks like that," I told her. "You get used to it."

Lily Anne looked a little unsure. "Da da *da*," she told me.

I kissed the top of her head. It smelled wonderful, a combination of baby shampoo and whatever intoxicating pheromone it is that babies rub into their scalps. "You're probably right," I said, and then Rita was back in the room, putting a fork and a napkin down beside the plate, lifting Lily Anne up out of my arms, and settling down beside me to continue the saga of Astor and the Dentist.

"Anyway," she said. "I told her it's just for a year, and a lot of other girls— But she has this . . . Has she told you about Anthony?"

"Anthony the asshole?" I said.

"Oh," Rita said. "He's not really an— I mean, she says that and she shouldn't. But it's different for a girl, and Astor is at the age— It's not too dry, is it?" she said, frowning at my plate.

"It's perfect," I said.

"It is dry; I'm sorry. So I thought maybe if you would talk to her," Rita finished. I truly hoped she meant talk to Astor and not the pork chop.

"What do you want me to say?" I asked her around a mouthful of very tasty but slightly dry pork chop.

"That it's perfectly all right," Rita said.

"What, braces?"

"Yes, of course," she said. "What did you think we were talking about?"

Truthfully, I was often not quite sure what we were talking about, since Rita usually managed to combine at least three simultaneous subjects when she spoke. Perhaps it came from her job; even after several years with her, I only knew that it involved juggling large numbers, converting them to different foreign currencies, and applying the results to the real estate market. It was one of life's wonderful puzzles that a woman smart enough to do that could be so completely stupid when it came to men, because first she had married a man addicted to drugs who beat her savagely, beat Cody and Astor just as badly, and finally committed enough unpleasant and illegal acts that he had been tucked away in prison. And Rita, free at last from the long nightmare of marriage to a drug-addled demon, had danced happily into marriage with an even worse monster: Me.

Of course, Rita would never know what I really was, not if I could help it. I had worked very hard to keep her blissfully ignorant of the true me, Dexter the Dark, the cheerful vivisectionist who lived for the purr of duct tape, the gleam of the knife, and the smell of fear rising up from a truly deserving playmate who had earned his ticket to Dexterland by slaughtering the innocent and somehow slipping through the gaping cracks in the justice system. . . .

Rita would never know that side of me, and neither would Lily Anne. My moments with new friends like Valentine were private—or they had been, until the terrible accident of the Witness. For a moment I thought about that, and the remaining names on my Honda list. One of those names would be the right one, had to be, and when I knew which one . . . I could almost taste the excitement of taking and taping him, almost hear the muffled squeals of pain and fear. . . .

And because my mind had wandered onto my hobby, I committed the dreadful felony of chewing Rita's pork chop without tasting it. But happily for my taste buds, as I pictured the Witness thrashing against his binds, I bit down on the fork, which jolted me out of my pleasant reverie and back to dinner. I scooped the last mouthful of yellow rice and one caper onto my fork and put it in my mouth as Rita said, "And anyway, it isn't covered by the insurance, so— But I should have a nice bonus this year, and braces are very— Astor doesn't smile very much, does she? But maybe if her teeth . . ." She paused suddenly, waved a hand, and made a face. "Oh, Lily Anne," she said. "You really do need a diaper change." Rita got up and took the baby away down the hall to the changing table, trailing an aroma that was definitely not pork chop, and I put down my empty plate and settled back onto the couch with a sigh: Dexter Digesting.

For some strange and very irritating reason, instead of letting the cares of the day slip away into a fog of well-fed contentment, I slid headfirst back into work and thought about Marty Klein and the dreadful mess that was his corpse. I hadn't really known him well, and even if I had I am not capable of any kind of emotional bonding, not even the rough and manly kind so popular at my job. And dead bodies don't bother me; even if I had not been occasionally involved in producing them, looking at them and touching them is part of my job. And although I would rather not have my coworkers know it, a dead cop is no more disturbing to me than a dead lawyer. But a corpse like this one, so completely hammered out of human shape . . . it was very different, almost supernatural.

The fury of the pounding that had killed Klein was completely psychotic, of course—but the fact that it had been so thorough, and had taken such a very long time, was far beyond normal, comfortable, homicidal insanity, and I found it very disturbing. It had required remarkable strength, endurance, and, most frightening by far, a cool control during the whole wild process so as not to go too far and cause death too soon, before all the bones were broken.

And for some reason, I had the very strong conviction that it was not a simple and relatively harmless single episode in which some-body had slipped over the line and gone postal for a few hours. This seemed like a pattern, a way of being, a state that was permanent. Insane strength and fury, combined with a clinical control—I could not imagine what kind of creature was capable of that, and I didn't really want to. But once again I had the feeling we would find more squashed cops in the near future.

"Dexter?" Rita called softly from the bedroom. "Aren't you com-ing to bed?"

I glanced at the clock by the TV: almost midnight. Just seeing the numbers made me realize how tired I was. "Coming," I said. I got up from the couch and stretched, feeling a very welcome drowsiness come over me. It was clearly sleepy time, and I would worry about Marty Klein and his awful end tomorrow. Sufficient unto each day is the evil thereof; at least, on the very good days. I put my plate in the sink and went to bed.

From far away in the dim, wool-packed world of sleep I felt an uneasy sensation elbowing its way into my head and, as if in answer to a vague but demanding question, I heard a loud and explosive roaring sound—and I was awake, my nose dripping from a powerful sneeze. "Oh, lord," Rita said, sitting up beside me. "You caught a cold from all that— I knew you were going to— Here, here's a tissue."

"Tanks," I said, and I sat up in bed and took the tissue from her hand and applied it to my nose. I sneezed again, this time into the tissue, and felt it disintegrate in my hand. "Ohggg," I said, as the slime dripped onto my fingers and a dull ache rolled into my bones.

"Oh, for heaven's— Here, take another tissue," Rita said. "And go wash your hands, because— Look at the time, it's time to get up anyway." And before I could do more than raise the new tissue to my face, she was up and out of the bed, leaving me to sit there dripping and wondering why wicked fate had inflicted this misery on poor undeserving me. My head hurt, and I felt like it was stuffed with wet sand, and it was leaking all over my hand—and on top of everything else, I had to get up and go to work, and with the way my head was rolling sluggishly through the fog I wasn't sure I could even figure out how.

But one of the things Dexter is truly good at is learning and following patterns of behavior. I have lived my life among humans, and they all think and feel and act in ways that are completely alien to me—but my survival depends on presenting a perfect imitation of the way they behave. Happily for me, ninety-nine percent of all human life is spent simply repeating the same old actions, speaking the same tired clichés, moving like a zombie through the same steps of the dance we plodded through yesterday and the day before and the day before. It seems horribly dull and pointless—but it really makes a great deal of sense. After all, if you only have to follow the same path every day, you don't need to think at all. Considering how good humans are at any mental process more complicated than chewing, isn't that best for everybody?

So I learned very young to watch people stumbling through their one or two basic rituals, and then perform the same steps myself with flawless mimicry. This morning that talent served me well, because as I staggered out of bed and into the bathroom, there was absolutely nothing in my head except phlegm, and if I had not learned by rote what I was supposed to do each morning I don't think I could have done it. The dull ache of a major cold had seeped into my bones and pushed all capacity for thinking out of my brain.

But the pattern of what I do in the morning remained: shower, shave, brush teeth, and stumble to the kitchen table, where Rita had a cup of coffee waiting for me. As I sipped it and felt a small spark of life flicker in response, she slid a plate of scrambled eggs in front of me. It might have been the effect of the coffee, but I remembered what to do with the eggs, and I did it very well, too. And as I finished the eggs, Rita dropped a pair of cold pills in front of me.

"Take these," she said. "You'll feel much better when they start to— Oh, look at the time. Cody? Astor? You're going to be late!" She refilled my coffee cup and hustled off down the hall, where I heard her rousting two very unwilling children out of their beds. A minute later Cody and Astor thumped into their chairs at the table, and Rita pushed plates in front of them. Cody mechanically began to eat right away, but Astor slumped on her elbow and stared at the eggs with disgust.

"They're all runny," she said. "I want cereal."

All part of the morning ritual: Astor never wanted anything Rita gave her to eat. And I found it oddly comforting that I knew what would happen next, as Rita and the kids followed the every-morning script and I waited for the cold pills to kick in and return to me the power of independent thought. Until then, no need to worry; I didn't have to do anything but follow the pattern.

FIVE

THE PATTERN HELD TRUE WHEN I GOT TO WORK. THE SAME officer sat at the desk and nodded at my credentials; the same people crowded into the elevator as I rode to the second floor. And waiting for me in the coffeepot was apparently the same vile bilge that had been there since the dawn of time. All very comforting, and out of gratitude I actually tried to drink the coffee, making the same horrified face as I sipped. Ah, the consolation of dull routine.

But as I turned away from the coffee machine into what should have been empty space, I found an object in my path, so very close to me that I had to lurch to a stop—which naturally caused the venomous brew in my cup to slop all over the front of my shirt.

"Oh, shit," said the object, and I looked up from the scalding ruin of my shirtfront. Standing before me was Camilla Figg, one of my coworkers in Forensics. She was thirtyish and square, kind of drab and usually quiet, and at the moment she was blushing furiously, as she often seemed to do when I saw her.

"Camilla," I said. I thought I said it quite pleasantly, considering that my shirt was relatively new and because of her it was probably going to dissolve. But if anything, she turned an even darker red.

"It's only I'm really sorry," she said in a staccato mutter, and she looked to both sides as if seeking a way to escape.

"Perfectly all right," I said, although it wasn't. "The coffee is probably safer to wear than to drink."

"I didn't anyway you know want what," she said, and she raised a hand, either to grab her words back from the air or to brush the coffee off my shirt, but instead she wobbled the hand in front of me, and then ducked her head. "Very sorry," she said, and she lurched away down the hall and around the corner.

I blinked after her stupidly; something new had broken the pattern, and I had no idea what it meant or what I should have done. But after pondering for a few pointless seconds, I shrugged it off. I had a cold, so I didn't have to try to make sense of Camilla's bizarre behavior. If I had said or done something wrong, I could say it was just the cold pills. I put the coffee down and went to the restroom to try to save a few scraps of fabric from my shirt.

I scrubbed with cold water for several minutes without really removing the stain. The paper towels kept falling apart, leaving dozens of small wet crumbs of paper all over the shirt without affecting the stain. This coffee was amazing stuff; perhaps it was part paint or fabric dye—that would explain the taste. I finally gave up and blotted my shirt dry the best I could. I left the restroom wearing my semi-wet stained shirt and headed for the lab, hoping I might get some sartorial sympathy from Vince Masuoka. He was generally quite passionate and knowledgeable about clothing. But instead of receiving condolences and advice on stain removal, I walked into a room absolutely overflowing with my sister, Deborah, who was following Vince around and apparently hectoring him about something as he tried to work on the contents of a small evidence bag.

Leaning on the wall in one corner was a man I didn't know, about thirty-five, with dark hair and a medium build. No one offered to introduce him, and he was not pointing a weapon of any kind, so I just walked past him and into the lab.

Debs looked up at me and gave me the kind of warm and loving greeting I have come to expect from her. "Where the fuck have you been?" she said.

"Ballroom dancing lessons," I said. "We're doing the tango this week; would you like to see?"

She made a sour face and shook her head. "Get in here and take over from this moron," she said.

"Great, now I'm a moron," Vince grumbled, and nodded at me. "You see how smart *you* are with Simone Legree halfway up your ass."

"If it's only halfway up, I can see why you're upset," I said. "Can I assume that there's been some development in the Marty Klein case?" I asked Debs politely.

"That's what I'm trying to find out," Deborah said. "But if ass-wipe can't get his ass in gear, we'll never know."

It occurred to me that Debs and Vince both seemed to be dwelling on "ass" this morning, which is not really the way I prefer to start my day. But we all need to show tolerance in the workplace, so I let it slide. "What have you got?" I said.

"It's just a fucking wrapping paper," Vince said. "From the floor of Klein's car."

"It's from some kind of food," the stranger in the corner said.

I looked at the man, and then back at Deborah with a raised eyebrow. She shrugged.

"My new partner," she said. "Alex Duarte."

"Oh," I said to the man. *"Mucho gusto."*

Duarte shrugged. "Yeah, right," he said.

"What kind of food?" I asked.

Deborah ground her teeth. "That's what I'm trying to find out," she said. "If we know where he ate before he died, we got a good chance to stake it out and maybe find this guy."

I stepped over to where Vince was poking at a wad of greasy white waxed paper in an evidence bag. "All that grease," he said. "There's gotta be a fingerprint. I just wanted to look for it first. Standard procedure."

"Asshole, we already got Klein's fingerprints," Deborah said. "I want the killer."

I looked at the congealed grease through the plastic of the evidence bag. It had a reddish brown tinge to it, and although I don't usually hang on to food wrappers long enough to be certain, it looked familiar. I leaned over and opened the bag, sniffing carefully. The cold pills had finally dried my nose, and the smell was strong and unmistakable. "Taco," I said.

"Gesundheit," said Vince.

"You're sure?" Deborah demanded. "That's a taco wrapper?"

"Absolutely," I said. "Can't miss the smell of the spices." I held up the bag and pointed out a tiny yellow crumb on one corner of the waxed paper. "And right there, that has to be a piece of the taco shell."

"Tacos, my God," said Vince with horror. "What have we come to?"

"What," Duarte said. "Like from Taco Bell?"

"That would have a logo on the wrapper, wouldn't it?" I said. "Anyway, I think their wrappers are yellow. This is probably from a smaller place, maybe one of those lunch wagons."

"Great," Deborah said. "There must be a million of those in Miami."

"And they *all* sell tacos," Vince said very helpfully. "I mean, *yuck*."

Deborah looked at him. "You're a total fucking idiot, you know that?" she said.

"No, I didn't know that," Vince said cheerfully.

"Why tacos?" Duarte said. "I mean, who eats fucking tacos? I mean, come on."

"Maybe he couldn't find empanadas," I said.

He looked at me blankly. "Empa-what?" he said.

"Can you find out where it came from?" Debs said. "You know, like analyze the spices or something?"

"Debs, for God's sake," I said. "It's just a taco. They're all pretty much the same."

"No, they're not," Deborah said. "These tacos got a cop killed."

"Killer tacos," Vince said. "I like that."

"Maybe it's a hangout," I said, and Deborah looked at me expectantly. I shrugged. "You know, sometimes word gets around, like the burgers are great at Manny's, or the *medianoche* at Hidalgo is the best in town, or whatever."

"Yeah, but these are *tacos*," Vince said. "I mean—seriously."

"All right, so maybe they're cheap," I said. "Or the girl who makes them is wearing a string bikini."

"I know a lunch wagon they do that," Duarte said. "This very nice-looking woman, she wears a bikini? They go around to construction sites, and she does big business, believe me. Just from showing her boobs."

"I can't believe you assholes," Debs said. "Why does it always end up about tits?"

"Not always. Sometimes it's ass," Vince said, cleverly bringing ass back into the conversation one more time. I began to wonder if there was a hidden camera, with a smirking game-show host handing out a prize every time we used the word.

"We could ask around," Duarte said. "See if any of the other detectives are talking about a great taco place."

"Or great tits," Vince said.

Deborah ignored him, which should have made him grateful. "Find out what you can from the wrapper," she said, and then she turned away and hustled out of the room. Duarte straightened up, nodded at us, and followed her out.

I watched them go. Vince blinked at me, and then bustled out of the room, mumbling something about reagent, and for a moment I just sat there. My shirt still felt damp, and I was very peeved with Camilla Figg. She had been standing right behind me, much too close for safety, and I could think of no reason for that kind of proximity. Even worse, I really should have known it when somebody got that near to my exposed back. It could have been a drug lord with an Uzi, or a crazed gardener with a machete, or almost anything else as lethal as a cup of that wretched coffee. Where was the Passenger when you really needed him? And now I was sitting in a chilly lab wearing a wet shirt, and I was pretty sure that would not help my already fragile health. Just to underline the point, I felt a sneeze coming on, and I barely got a paper towel up to my nose before it erupted. Cold pills—bah, humbug. They were worthless, like everything else in this miserable world.

Just before I melted into a dripping heap of mucus and self-pity, I thought of the clean shirt hanging behind my desk. I always kept one on hand in case of a work-related accident. I took it off the hanger and put it on, tucking the damp, coffee-spattered shirt into a plastic grocery bag to take home. It was a nice shirt, a beige guayabera with silver guitars on the hem. Perhaps Rita would know a magic trick to get the stains out.

Vince was already back in the lab when I returned, and we went right to work. And we really tried our very best. We ran every test we could think of, visual, chemical, and electronic, and found nothing that would bring a smile to my sister's face. Deborah called us three times, which for her showed wonderful self-control. There was really nothing to tell her. I thought it was very likely that the wrapper held a taco and came from a lunch wagon, but I certainly couldn't have sworn to it in a court of law.

At around noon the cold pills wore off and I began to sneeze again. I tried to ignore it, but it's very difficult to do really high-quality lab work while holding a paper towel to your nose, so I finally gave up. "I have to get out of here," I said to Vince. "Before I blow my nose all over the evidence."

"It couldn't hurt the tacos," he said.

I went to lunch alone, at a Thai restaurant over by the airport. It's not that looking at old taco wrappers had made me hungry, but I have always believed that a large bowl of spicy Thai soup fights a cold better than anything else, and by the time I finished my soup I could feel my system sweating out the unhealthy molecules, forcing the cold out through my pores and back into the Miami ecosphere where it belonged. I actually felt a great deal better, which made me leave a tip that was slightly too large. But as I walked out the door and into the afternoon heat, the entire front of my skull exploded with an enormous sneeze, and the accompanying ache kicked at my skeletal system as if someone was tightening vise grips on all my joints.

Happiness is an illusion—and sometimes so is Thai soup. I gave up and stopped at a drugstore to buy more cold pills. This time I took three of them, and by the time I got back to the office the throbbing in my nose and my bones had subsided a little bit. Whether it was the cold pills or the soup, I began to feel like I might be able to handle any routine pain the day might throw at me. And because I was more or less prepared for something unpleasant to happen, it didn't.

The rest of the afternoon was completely uneventful. We worked on, using all our massive skill on what was really rather flimsy evidence. But by the end of the day, the only thing I'd found out was that

Masuoka disliked all Mexican food, not just tacos. "If I eat that stuff, I get really bad gas," he told me. "Which really has a negative impact on my social life."

"I didn't know you had one," I said. I had the crumb from the taco shell under a microscope in the vain hope of finding some tiny clue, while Vince was examining a grease spot on the wrapper.

"Of course I have a social life," he said. "I party almost every night. I found a hair."

"What kind of party is that?" I said.

"No, there's a hair in the grease," he said. "For partying, I shave all over."

"Way too much information," I said. "Is it human?"

"Yeah, sure," he said. "A lot of people shave."

"The hair," I said. "Is it a human hair?"

He frowned into his microscope. "I'm gonna guess rodent," he said. "Another reason I don't eat Mexican food."

"Vince," I said, "rat hair is not a Mexican spice. It's because this came from a sleazy lunch wagon."

"Hey, I don't know; you're the foodie," he said. "I like to eat some-place where they have chairs."

"I've never eaten one," I said. "Anything else?"

"Tables are nice," he said. "And real silverware."

"Anything else in the *grease*," I said, winning a very tough strug-gle against the urge to push my thumbs deep into his eye sockets.

Vince shrugged. "It's just grease," he said.

I had no better luck with the taco crumb. There was simply noth-ing there to find, except that it was made of processed corn and con-tained several inorganic chemicals, probably preservatives. We did every test we could do on-site without destroying the wrapper and found nothing significant. Vince's verbal wit did not leap magically to a higher level, either, and so by quitting time my mood had not really burbled up into steady good cheer. If anything, I felt even meaner than I had that morning. I fended off one last telephone attack from Deborah, locked up the evidence, and headed for the door.

"Don't you want to go for tacos?" Vince called as I hit the door.

"Go jump up your ass," I said. After all, if there really was a prize for saying "ass," I deserved a shot at it.

SIX

I DROVE HOME THROUGH THE USUAL RUSH-HOUR TRAFFIC, A nerve-jangling crawl of aggressive lane jumping and near collisions. A pickup truck was on fire on the shoulder of the Palmetto Expressway. A shirtless man in jeans and a battered cowboy hat stood beside it, looking almost bored. He had a large tattoo of an eagle on his back and a cigarette in one hand. Everyone slowed to look at the smoldering pickup, and behind me I could hear a fire truck, siren shrieking and horn blasting as it tried to get through the dawdling gawkers. As I edged past the burning truck my nose began to drip again, and by the time I got home some twenty minutes later, I was sneezing, one good skull-splitting blast every minute or so.

"I'b hobe!" I called out as I walked through the door, and a roar of something that sounded like rocket fire answered me; Cody was already at the Wii, working dutifully to destroy all the evil in the world with a massive artillery attack. He glanced up at me, and then quickly back to the TV screen; for him, it was a warm greeting. "Where's your mom?" I asked him.

He jerked his head toward the kitchen. "Kitchen," he said.

That was always good news; Rita in the kitchen meant something wonderful was on the way. Purely out of habit, I tried to sniff the aroma, which turned out to be a very bad idea, since it tickled my sinuses and launched me into a debilitating multiple sneeze that nearly brought me to my knees.

"Dexter?" Rita called from the kitchen.

"Ah-*choo*," I answered.

"Oh," she said, appearing in the doorway wearing rubber gloves and holding a large knife in her hand. "You sound awful."

"Thag you," I said. "Why glubs?"

"Glubs? Oh, gloves. I'm making you some soup," she said, and she waved the knife. "With those Scotch-bonnet peppers, so I have to— Just in *your* soup, because Cody and Astor won't eat it that way."

"I hate spicy food," Astor said, coming down the hall from her room and plopping down on the couch next to Cody. "Why do we have to have soup?"

"You can have a hot dog instead," Rita said.

"I hate hot dogs," Astor said.

Rita frowned and shook her head. A small lock of hair flopped down onto her forehead. "Well," she said, rather forcefully, "you can just go hungry then." And she pushed the hair off her forehead with her wrist and went back into the kitchen.

I watched Rita go, mildly surprised. She almost never lost her temper, and I could not remember the last time she had said something like that to Astor. I sneezed, and then went and stood behind the couch. "You could try a little harder not to upset your mom," I said.

Astor looked up and then hunched away from me. "You'd better not give me your cold," she said, with very convincing menace.

I looked at the top of Astor's head. Part of me wanted to smack her on the head with a carpentry tool. But the other part of me realized that disciplining a child in such a forthright and vigorous manner was generally not encouraged in our society, a society I was trying to fit into at the moment. And in any case, I could hardly blame Astor for showing the same kind of cranky meanness I was feeling myself. Even Rita seemed to be feeling it. Perhaps some toxic chemical was falling with the summer rain and infecting all of us with a sour attitude.

So I simply took a deep breath and walked away from Astor and her towering sulk, heading into the kitchen to see if my nose might be working well enough to smell the soup brewing. I paused in the doorway; Rita was standing at the stove with her back to me. A cloud of fragrant-looking steam rose up around her. I took one step closer and sniffed experimentally.

And, of course, that made me sneeze. It was a wonderful sneeze, very loud and vigorous, with a full, beautiful tone. It apparently startled Rita, because she jumped several inches straight up and dropped a wineglass she had been holding, which shattered on the floor beside her. "Damn it!" she said, another surprising outburst. She looked at the puddle of wine spreading toward her shoe, and then looked at me. To my very great surprise, she blushed. "It was only . . ." she said. "I just thought, while I was cooking. And then you scared me," she said.

"Sorry," I said. "I just wanted to smell the soup."

"Well, but really," she said, and then she lurched toward the hallway and raced back clutching a broom and dustpan. "Go check on the baby," she told me as she bent to clean up the broken glass. "She might need a diaper change."

I watched Rita for a moment as she swept up the mess. Her cheeks were bright red and she avoided looking at me. I had the very strong impression that something was not right, but no matter how hard I gawked and blinked I got no clue to what it was. I suppose I was hoping that by staring long enough I might get some indication of what had just happened—perhaps subtitles would appear, or a man in a lab coat would hand me a pamphlet explaining things in eight languages, possibly with diagrams. But no such luck; Rita remained hunched over, blushing and sweeping shards of glass through the puddle of wine and into the dustpan, and I still had no idea why she, and everyone else, was acting so strangely today.

So I left the kitchen and went to the bedroom, where Lily Anne was lying in her crib. She was not quite awake, but she was fussing, kicking one leg and frowning, as if she, too, had caught whatever it was that had made everyone else peevish. I leaned over and felt her diaper; it was very full, pushing outward against the fabric of her little sleepy suit. I picked her up and moved her to the changing table, and she woke up almost immediately. It made changing the diaper a bit harder, but it was nice to have the company of somebody who wasn't snarling at me.

When she was changed I took her into my little study, away from the sulking and the video violence of the Wii in the living room, and I sat at my desk with Lily Anne on my lap. She played with a ballpoint pen, tapping it on the desk with commendable concentration and an excellent sense of rhythm. I pulled a tissue from a box on the desk and blotted at my nose. I told myself that my cold would go away in a day or two, and there was no reason to blow it up into anything more than a minor inconvenience. Besides, everything else was fine, lovely, happy, with metaphorical birds flocking around me and singing twenty-four/seven. My home life was close to perfect, and I was keeping it in a very nice balance with my job. Very soon I would track down the one small cloud on my horizon, and then I would get a free, extra playdate, which would be pure bonus bliss.

I took out my Honda list and laid it on the desk. Three names crossed off. At my present deliberate pace, several more weeks of searching. I wanted to get it all done immediately, cut right to the cutting, and I bent closer to study the list, as if some telltale clue might be hidden between the lines. As I leaned in Lily Anne tipped over and tapped at the paper with her pen. "Na na *na*!" she said, and of course she was right. I had to be patient, deliberate, careful, and I would find him and flense him and everything would be fine—

I sneezed. Lily Anne flinched, and then picked up the paper, waved it at my face, and threw it jerkily onto the floor. She turned to me and beamed, very proud of herself, and I nodded at her wisdom. It was a very clear statement: *No more daydreaming. You and I have work to do.*

But before we could begin to restructure the tax code, a beautiful sound floated down the hall to us.

"Dexter? Children?" Rita called. "Dinner is ready!"

I looked at Lily Anne. "Da," she said, and I agreed. We went to dinner.

The next day was Friday, which was just as well. It had not been a pleasant workweek, and I would be thoroughly glad to put it behind me and have the weekend to sit at home and murder my cold. But first, there were the last few hours of my job to suffer through.

By midday I'd gone through six cold pills and half a roll of paper towels, and I was working through the second half of the roll when Deborah came into the lab. Vince and I had reached the point where there was nothing else we could think of to do with the taco wrapper, and since he refused to draw straws for the privilege of telling Deborah, I'd been forced to make the call to give her the news that we'd come up blank. And three minutes later, here she was, striding into our lab like avenging fury.

"Goddamn it," she said before she was even all the way in the room, "I need something from you!"

"Maybe a sedative?" Vince suggested, and for once I thought he was right on the money.

Deborah looked at him, and then at me, and I wondered whether I could make it to the bomb shelter in time. But before my sister could inflict any grievous bodily harm, there was a scuffling sound at the door, and we all turned to look; Camilla Figg stood in the doorway. She stared at me, blushed, looked around the room, and said, "Oh. I didn't even sorry." She cleared her throat, and then scurried away down the hall before anyone could decide what she'd said or what to do about it.

I looked back at Deborah, expecting her to resume her eruption. But to my surprise she did not reach for her weapon, or even wind up to throw a blistering arm punch. Instead, she took a deep breath and visibly calmed herself down. "Guys," she said, "I got a really bad feeling about this guy. This psycho that smashed up Marty Klein."

Vince opened his mouth, presumably to say something he thought of as witty. Deborah looked at him, and he thought better of it and closed his mouth.

"I think he's going to do it again, and soon," Debs said. "The whole force thinks so, too. They think this guy is some kind of spook, like Freddy Krueger or something. Everybody is freaking out, and everybody is looking at me to find the killer. And all I got is just this one small lead—a crappy little taco wrapper." She shrugged and shook her head. "I know it's not much, but it's what there is, and I . . . Please, guys—Dex—isn't there something else you can do? Anything?"

There was real need in her face, and it was clear that she was really and truly pleading with us. Vince looked at me with a very uncomfortable expression. He was not good at sincerity, and it obviously made him too nervous to speak, which meant it was my problem. "Debs," I said, "we'd like to catch this guy, too. But we've hit the wall. The wrapper is standard, from a restaurant supply place. There's not enough left of the tacos to say anything except that they were tacos, and even that I couldn't swear to on the stand. No prints, no trace evidence, nothing. We don't have any magic tricks," I said, and as I said "magic tricks" the image of a clown secured to a table with duct tape popped into my mind. But I pushed the happy memory firmly out of my head and tried to concentrate on Deborah. "I'm sorry," I said, and my sincerity was no more than half-artificial, which was pretty good for me. "But we've done everything we can think of."

Deborah looked at me for a long moment. She took another deep breath, looked at Vince, and then shook her head slowly. "All right," she said. "Then I guess we just wait for him to hit again, and hope we get lucky next time." And she turned away and walked out of the lab at about one-quarter the speed she'd come in.

"Wow," said Vince in a hushed voice when Deborah was gone. "I've never seen her like that." He shook his head. "Very scary," he said.

"I guess this really bothers her," I said.

Vince shook his head. "No, it's her; she's changed," he said. "I think motherhood has made her all mushy inside."

I could have said that she was not nearly as mushy as Detective Klein, but that might have hit the wrong note, and anyway it was true. Deborah had softened since the birth of her son, Nicholas. The child had been a parting gift from Kyle Chutsky, her live-in boyfriend of several years who had vanished in a fit of low self-esteem. Nicholas was a few months younger than Lily Anne, and a nice enough little chap, although next to Lily Anne he did seem to be a bit slow and not nearly as attractive.

But Deborah doted on him, which was natural enough, and she really had seemed to mellow around the edges since his arrival. Still, I would almost rather have seen the old Debs and suffered one of her terrifying arm punches than see her so visibly deflated. But even her new sensitivity couldn't get cheese from a stone; there truly wasn't anything we could do that we had not already done. A taco wrapper from the floor of a car is not a lot to go on; that was all we had, and wishing for more wouldn't make it appear in front of me.

I spent the rest of the day turning the problem over in my head, trying to think of some neat and clever angle to make the wrapper yield more information, but I came up empty. I am good at my job, and I do have a certain amount of professional pride. I would also prefer to see my sister happy and successful. But there was just no way to take things any further than we had done. It was frustrating, and very bad for my sense of personal worth, and it added to my general feeling that life was a mangy dog that was badly in need of a hearty kick.

By five o'clock I was quite happy to slip away from the frustration and tension, and head for a relaxing and recuperative weekend at home. Traffic was worse than usual; after all, this was Friday night. All the usual violence and anger were there, but there was a festive edge to it, as if people had saved all the energy left over from the workweek and were putting it into causing as much mayhem as possible on the way home. On the Dolphin Expressway a tanker truck had rammed into the back end of a van from a retirement village. They had only been going five miles per hour, but the back of the van still crumpled a bit, and it had plowed forward into a fifteen-year-old Toyota with only one regular tire and three doughnuts on it.

I crawled past in a long, slow line of cars, most of them filled with people cheering as the tanker's driver yelled at the four men in the Toyota and a flock of terrified old people from the van huddled together on the shoulder. Traffic ground to a dead stop, then slowly started up again. I saw two more fender-benders before I got off onto Dixie Highway. But somehow, through a combination of skill, life-long practice, and blind luck, I made it home without serious injury.

I parked my car behind a two-year-old SUV that was already in front of the house; my brother, Brian, was here for his every-week Friday-night dinner with the family. It was a custom we had gotten used to over the last year, after he had turned up and apparently wanted nothing more than to be with me, his only living relative. He had already bonded with Cody and Astor, since they knew him for what he was—a cold and empty killer, like me—and they wanted to be just like him. And Rita, showing the same solid good judgment about men that had led her to marry two different monsters, ate up Brian's horribly fake flattery and thought he was wonderful, too. And as for me? Well, I still had trouble believing that Brian did not have some secret motive for hanging around, but he was my brother, after all, and family is family. We don't get to pick our kin. The best we can hope for is to survive them, especially in my family.

Inside the house, Lily Anne was in her playpen next to the couch, where Brian was sitting with Rita, deep in very serious conversation. They looked up at me as I entered, and for some reason I thought Rita looked a little guilty when she saw me. It was impossible to read Brian, of course. He certainly couldn't feel guilt, and he merely gave me his large and very fake smile of greeting, like always. "Greetings, brother," he said.

"Dexter," Rita said, and she jumped up and came over to greet me with a quick hug and a peck on the cheek. "Brian and I were just talking," she said, probably to reassure me that they had not been performing amateur brain surgery on the neighbors.

"Wonderful," I said, and before I could say more I sneezed.

Rita jumped back and managed to avoid most of the spray from my nose. "Oh," she said. "Here, I'll get some tissues." And she vanished down the hall toward the bathroom.

I blotted my nose with my sleeve and sat in the easy chair. I looked at my brother, and he looked back at me. Brian had recently landed a job with a large Canadian real estate conglomerate that was buying up homes in South Florida. My brother was charged with approaching people whose houses were in foreclosure and encouraging them to leave right away. In theory, this was done by offering them "key money," usually around fifteen hundred dollars, to walk away and let the corporation take over and resell the property. I say "in theory" because Brian seemed very prosperous and happy lately, and I was almost certain that he was pocketing the key money and using less conventional means of emptying the houses. After all, if someone is running out on a mortgage, they generally want to disappear for a while—and why shouldn't Brian help them do a more thorough job of it?

I had no proof, of course—and it was none of my business how my brother conducted his social life, as long as he showed up at the house with clean hands and good table manners, which he always did. Still, I hoped he had abandoned his flamboyant recreational style and was being careful.

"How's business?" I asked him politely.

"Never better," he said. "They may say the market is recovering, but I haven't seen it yet. It really is a good time to be me in Miami."

I smiled politely, mostly to show him what a really *good* fake looked like, and Rita hustled back in with a box of tissues.

"Here," she said, thrusting the box at me. "Why don't you just keep the box with you, and— Oh, damn it, there's the timer," she said, and she vanished again, into the kitchen this time.

Brian and I watched her go with very similar expressions of bemused wonder. "A really lovely lady," Brian said to me. "You are very lucky, Dexter."

"Don't let her hear you say that," I said. "She might think you sound envious, and she does have single friends, you know."

Brian looked startled. "Oh," he said. "Silly me, I hadn't thought of that. Would she really try to, ah . . . I think the expression is, 'fix me up'?"

"In a heartbeat," I assured him. "She thinks marriage is man's natural state."

"And is it?" he asked me.

"There is much to be said for domestic bliss," I said. "And I am quite sure Rita would love to see you try it."

"Oh, dear," he said, and he looked at me thoughtfully, running his eyes over my entire frame. "Still," he said, "it seems to agree with you."

"I suppose it must seem like it," I said.

"Do you mean it *doesn't* agree with you?" Brian asked, arching his eyebrows up high on his forehead.

"I don't know," I said. "I guess it really does. It's just that lately—"

"Lights seem dimmer, tastes are all duller?" he asked me.

"Something like that," I admitted, although in truth I could not tell if he was merely mocking me.

But Brian looked at me very seriously, and for once he did not seem to be faking his expression, nor the thoughts behind his words. "Why don't you come along with me some night very soon?" he said softly. "We'll have a Boys' Night Out. Rita couldn't possibly object."

There was absolutely no mistaking what he meant; aside from the fact that he only had one form of recreation, I knew that he had long dreamed of sharing a playtime with me, his only living relative, who had so much in common with him—we were brothers of the blade as well as in blood. And truthfully the idea was almost unbearably compelling to me, too—but . . . but . . .

"Why not, brother?" Brian said softly, leaning forward with genuine intensity on his face. "Why shouldn't we?"

For a moment I simply stared at him, frozen between lunging at his offer with both hands and thrusting him away from me, probably with one hand to my brow and a loud cry of, *Retro me, Brianus!* But before I could decide which choice to jump at, life intervened, as it usually does, and made the decision for me.

"Dexter!" Astor yelled from down the hall, with all the fury of a very cranky eleven-year-old girl. "I need help with my math homework! Now!"

I looked at Brian and shook my head. "You'll excuse me, brother?" I said.

He settled back into the sofa and smiled, the old fake smile again. "Mmm," he said. "Domestic bliss."

I got up and went down the hall to help Astor.

SEVEN

ASTOR WAS IN THE ROOM SHE SHARED WITH CODY, HUNCHED over a book at the little hutch that served them both as a desk. The expression on her face had probably started life as a frown of concentration, and then evolved into a scowl of frustration. From there it had been just a short jump to a full-blown menacing glare, which she turned on me as I came into the room. "This is *bullshit*," she snarled at me with such ferocity that I wondered whether I should get a weapon. "It doesn't make any sense at all!"

"You shouldn't use that word," I said, and rather mildly, too, since I was quite sure she would attack if I raised my voice.

"What word, *sense*?" she sneered. "'Cause that must be a word they forgot in this stupid book." She slammed the book closed and slumped down in the chair with her arms crossed over her chest. "Bunch of crap," she said, looking at me out of the corner of her eye to see whether she would get away with "crap." I let it go and went to stand next to her.

"Let's take a look," I said.

Astor shook her head and refused to look up at me. "Useless dumb crap," she muttered.

I felt a sneeze coming on and fumbled out a tissue, and still without looking up she said, "And if I get your cold, I swear." She didn't tell me what she swore, but from her tone it was clear that it wouldn't be pleasant.

I put the tissue in my pocket, leaned over the desk, and opened the book. "You won't get my cold; I took a vitamin C," I said, still trying for a winning note of lighthearted and tolerant reason. "What page are we on?"

"It's not like I'll ever have to know this stuff when I'm grown up," she grumbled.

"Maybe not," I said. "But you have to know it now." She clamped her jaw and didn't say anything, so I pushed a little. "Astor, do you want to be in sixth grade forever?"

"I don't wanna be in sixth grade *now*," she hissed.

"Well, the only way you'll ever get out of it is if you get a passing grade. And to do that you have to know this stuff."

"It's *stupid*," she said, but she seemed to be winding down a bit.

"Then it should be no problem for you, because you're *not* stupid," I said. "Come on; let's look at it."

She fought it for another minute or so, but I finally got her to the right page. It was a relatively simple problem of graphing coordinates, and once she calmed down I had no problem explaining it to her. I have always been good at math; it seems very straightforward compared to understanding human behavior. Astor did not seem to have a natural gift for it, but she caught on quickly enough. When she finally closed the book again she was a lot calmer, almost contented, and so I decided to push my luck just a bit and tackle another small item of pressing business.

"Astor," I said, and I must have unconsciously used my I'm-a-grown-up-here-it-comes voice, because she looked up at me with an expression of alert worry. "Your mom wanted me to talk to you about braces."

"She wants to ruin my life!" she said, hurtling up into an impressive level of preteen outrage from a standing start. "I'll be hideous and no one will look at me!"

"You won't be hideous," I said.

"I'll have these huge steel *things* all over my teeth!" she wailed. "It is *so* hideous!"

"Well, you can be hideous for a few months now, or hideous forever when you're grown up," I said. "It's a very simple choice."

"Why can't they just do an operation?" she moaned. "Just get it over with, and I'd even get to miss school for a few days."

"It doesn't work that way," I said.

"Doesn't work at *all*," she said. "They make me look like a *cyborg* and everybody will laugh at me."

"Why do you think they'll laugh at you?"

She gave me a look of amused contempt that was almost adult. "Weren't you ever in middle school?" she said.

It was a good point, but not the one I wanted to make. "Middle school doesn't last forever," I said, "and neither will the braces. And when they come off, you'll have great teeth and a terrific smile."

"What do I care; I've got nothing to smile about," she grumbled.

"Well, you will," I said. "When you're a little older, and you start to go to dances and things with a really great smile. You have to think of it in a long-term kind of way—"

"*Long*-term!" she said angrily, as if now I was the one using bad words. "The *long* term is that I'll look like a *freak* for a whole year of middle school and everybody will remember *that* forever and I'll always be That Girl with Huge Awful Braces even when I'm forty years old!"

I could feel my jaw moving, but no words were coming out; there were so many things wrong with what Astor had said that I couldn't seem to pick one to start on—and in any case she had walled herself into such a high tower of miserable anger that whatever I said would just set her off again.

But luckily for my reputation as an urbane negotiator, before I could say anything and have it slammed back down my throat, Rita's raised voice came floating down the hall. "Dexter? Astor? Come to dinner!" And while my mouth was still hanging open, Astor was up and out the door and my little encouraging chat about braces was over.

I woke up again on Monday morning in the middle of an enormous sneeze and feeling like a Turkish weight lifter had spent the entire weekend squeezing every bone in my body. For that one confused moment between waking and sleeping I thought the psycho who had hammered Detective Klein into a limp pudding had somehow gotten into my bedroom and worked me over while I slept. But then I heard the toilet flush, and Rita hurried through the bedroom and down the hall toward the kitchen, and normal life lurched up onto its feet and stumbled on into another day.

I stretched, and the ache in my joints stretched with me. I wondered whether the pain could make me feel empathy for Klein. It didn't seem likely; I'd never been cursed with that kind of weak emotion before, and even Lily Anne's transformational magic couldn't turn me into a soft-shelled empathy feeler overnight. It was probably just my subconscious playing connect-the-dots.

Still, I found myself dwelling on Klein's death as I got up and went through my morning routine, which now included sneezing every minute or so. Klein's skin had not been broken; a remarkable amount of force had been used on him, but there had been no blood spilled at all. It was my guess—and the Passenger hissed its agreement—that Klein had remained conscious as every bone in his body had been shattered. He'd been awake and alert for every smash and crunch, every agonizing smack of the hammer, until finally, after a very impressive period of agony, the killer had done enough internal damage to allow Klein to slip away into death. It was much worse than having a cold. It didn't sound like a lot of fun—especially not for Klein.

But in spite of my distaste for the method, and the Dark Passenger's contempt, I really did start to feel the limp fingers of empathy tickling at the inside of my skull—empathy, yes, but not for Klein. The fellow feeling that sent small tendrils curling into my thoughts was all for Klein's executioner. It was totally stupid, of course—but nonetheless I began to hear a niggling little whisper in my inner ear that my only real objection to what had been done to Klein was the use of the wrong tools. After all, hadn't I made sure that Valentine, too, stayed awake to feel every moment of my attention? Of course, Valentine had earned it with his habit of molesting and killing young boys—but were any of us truly innocent? Maybe Detective Klein had been a tax cheat, or a wife beater, or perhaps he had chewed food with his mouth open. He might have deserved what the so-called psycho had done to him—and really, who was to say that what I did was any better?

I knew very well that there was a great deal wrong with that unpleasant argument, but it stayed with me anyway, a discontented murmur of self-loathing in the background as I ate my breakfast, sneezed, got ready for work, sneezed, and finally took two cold pills and headed out the door, sneezing. I couldn't shake the absurd notion that I was just as guilty—perhaps far more so, since Klein was the only victim of this killer so far, and I had fifty-two glass slides tucked away in my rosewood souvenir box, each with its single drop of blood representing a departed playmate. Did that make me fifty-two times as bad?

It was completely ridiculous, of course; what I had done was totally justified, sanctified by the Code of Saint Harry, and beneficial to society, aside from being a great deal of fun. But because I was so wrapped up in navel-gazing, it was not until I crawled off U.S. 1 to merge onto the Palmetto Expressway that the insistent sibilance of self-preservation finally broke through my egotistical fog. It was just a quiet hiss of warning, but it was persistent enough to get my attention, and as I finally listened to it, it solidified into a single, very definite thought.

Someone is watching me.

I don't know why I was certain, but I was. I could feel the gaze in a nearly physical way, almost as if somebody was trickling the razor-sharp point of a knife along the back of my neck. It was a sensation as definite and inarguable as the heat from the sun; someone was watching me, specifically *me,* and they were watching me for some reason that did not have my best interests at heart.

Reason argued that this was Miami at morning rush hour; almost anyone might stare at me with distaste, even hatred, for any reason at all—maybe they didn't like my car, or my profile reminded them of their eighth-grade algebra teacher. But whatever Reason said, Caution argued back: It didn't matter *why* someone was watching me. It only mattered that they *were.* Someone was watching me with mischief in mind, and I needed to find out who.

Slowly, oh-so-casually, I looked around me. I was in the middle of an exceptionally normal crush of morning traffic, indistinguishable from what I drove through every morning. To my immediate right there were two lanes of cars: a battered Impala, and beyond it an old Ford van with a camper roof. Behind them was a line of Toyotas, Hummers, and BMWs, none of them appearing to be any more menacing than any of the others.

I looked ahead again, inched forward with the traffic, and then slowly turned to look to my left—

—and before my head had turned more than six inches, there was a screech of tires, a chorus of blaring horns, and an old Honda accelerated off the Palmetto's on-ramp, down the shoulder, and back onto U.S. 1, where it squealed north, slid through a yellow light, and vanished down a side street, and as it went I could see the left taillight dangling at an odd angle, and then the dark birthmark stain on the trunk.

I watched it go until the drivers behind me began to lean on their horns. I tried to tell myself that it was pure coincidence. I knew very well how many old Hondas there were in Miami; I had them all on my list. And I had visited only eight of them so far, and it was very possible that this was one of the others. I told myself that this was just one more idiot changing his mind and deciding to drive to work a different way this morning; probably someone had suddenly remembered that he'd left the coffeepot on, or left the disk with the Power-Point presentation at home.

But no matter how many good and banal reasons I thought up for the Honda's behavior, that other, darker certainty kept talking back, telling me with calm and factual insistence that whoever had been driving that car, they had been staring at me and thinking bad thoughts, and when I had turned to look at them they had rocketed away as if pursued by demons, and we knew very well what that really meant.

My breakfast began to churn in my stomach and I felt my hands turn slick with sweat. Could it be? Was it remotely possible that whoever had *seen* me that night had found me? Somehow tracked me down and learned my license number, long before I found them—and now they were following me? It was wildly, stupidly unlikely—the odds against it were monumental; it was ridiculous, impossible, totally beyond the bounds of belief—but was it possible?

I thought about it: There was no connection between Dexter Morgan, Boy Forensics Whiz, and the house where I had been seen with Valentine. I had gone to and from the house in Valentine's car, and I had not been followed when I fled. So hunting along my back trail was impossible: There wasn't one.

That left either magical powers or coincidence, and although I have nothing at all against Harry Potter, coincidence got my vote. And to make it a little more likely, that abandoned house had been only a little more than a mile from where the Palmetto Expressway intersects U.S. 1. I had already assumed that he lived in the same area—and if he did, he would almost inevitably drive to work along U.S. 1 and quite likely up onto the Palmetto, too. Work for most people started at roughly the same time every day, and everyone in this area drove to work along the same road. That was painfully obvious; it was what caused the perpetual traffic jam at this time each morning. So it was not as wildly coincidental as it had seemed at first. In fact, it was even *likely* that if we both repeated the same drive at the same time long enough, sooner or later he would see my car, and even me.

And he had. Once again, he had seen me, and this time he'd had an opportunity to study me at length. I tried to calculate how long he might have been staring. It was impossible; traffic had been stop-and-go, with an emphasis on stop that had lasted for almost two minutes. But it was pure guesswork to decide how long he had known it was me. Probably only a few seconds; I had to trust my alarm system.

Still, it was long enough to note the make and color of my car, write down the plate number, and who knows what else. I knew very well what I could do with only half that much information—it was entirely possible that with just the plate number he could find me—but would he? So far he had done nothing but flee in terror. Was he really going to look me up and then plant himself outside my door with a carving knife? If it was me, I would have—but he was not me. I was exceptionally good with computers, and I had resources that weren't available to most people, and I used them to do things that no one else did. There is only one Dexter, and he was not it. Whoever this was, he could not possibly be anything like me. But it was just as true that I had no idea what he was like, or what he might do, and no matter how many different ways I told myself that there was no real danger, I couldn't shake the illogical fear that he was going to do *something*. The voice of calm reason was battered into silence by the screams of pure panic that had taken over my brain. He had seen me again, and this time I was in my workaday secret identity, and that made me feel more naked and helpless than I could remember.

I have no memory of driving up onto the Palmetto and continuing my morning commute, and it was pure blind chance that I was not flattened like a wandering possum by the raging traffic. By the time I got to work, I had calmed down enough to present a reasonably convincing facade, but I could not shake that steady trickle of anxiety that was once again burbling up on the floor of my brain and leaving me just on the edge of panic.

Luckily for the tattered shreds of my sanity, I didn't have long to dwell on my own petty concerns. I had not even settled into my morning routine when Deborah came steaming in to distract me, with her new partner, Duarte, trailing along behind.

"All right," she said, as if she was continuing a conversation we'd already been having. "So the guy has to have some kind of record, right? You don't just suddenly do something like that out of nowhere, and nothing before it."

I sneezed and blinked at her, which was not a very impressive response, but since I was mired in my own worries it took me a moment to connect with hers. "Are we talking about whoever killed Detective Klein?" I said.

Debs blew out an impatient breath. "Jesus shit, Dex, what did you *think* I was talking about?"

"NASCAR?" I said. "I think there was a big race this weekend."

"Don't be an asshole," she said. "I need to know about this."

I could have said that "asshole" might better describe somebody who charged into her brother's office first thing Monday morning and didn't even say "gesundheit" or ask how his weekend had been—but I knew very well that my sister had no tolerance for suggestions on workplace etiquette, so I shrugged it off. "I guess so," I said. "I mean, something like what he did, that's usually the end of a long process that started with other things, and . . . you know. The kind of thing that gets you noticed."

"What kind of thing?" Duarte said.

I hesitated; for some reason, I felt a little bit uncomfortable, probably because I was talking about this stuff in front of a stranger—generally speaking, I don't really like to talk about it at all, even with Debs; it seems a little too personal. I covered the pause by grabbing a paper towel and blotting at my nose, but they both kept looking at me expectantly, like two dogs waiting for a treat. I was on the spot, with no real choice but to go on. "Well," I said, tossing the paper towel into the trash, "a lot of the time they start with, you know, pets. When they're young, just twelve years old or so. And they kill small dogs, cats, like that. Just, um, experimenting. Trying to find what feels *right*. And, you know. Somebody in the family, or in the neighborhood, finds the dead pets, and they get caught and arrested."

"So there's a record," Debs said.

"Well, there might be," I said. "But if he follows the pattern, he's young when he does that, so he goes to Juvie. So the record is going to be sealed, and you can't just ask a judge to give you every sealed case file in the system."

"Then give me something better," Deborah said urgently. "Give me something to work with here."

"Debs," I protested, "I don't *have* anything." I sneezed again. "Except a cold."

"Well, shit," she said. "Can't you think up some kind of hint?"

I looked at her, and then at Duarte, and my discomfort grew and mixed with frustration. "How?" I said.

Duarte shrugged. "She says you're like some kind of amateur profiler," he said.

I was surprised, and a bit upset, that Debs had shared that with Duarte. My so-called profiling talent was highly personal, something that grew out of my firsthand experience with sociopathic individuals like myself. But she *had* shared it; that probably meant she trusted him. In any case, I was on the spot. "Ah, well," I said at last. "*Más o menos*."

Duarte shook his head. "What is that, yes or no?" he said.

I looked at Debs, and she actually smirked at me. "Alex doesn't speak Spanish," she said.

"Oh," I said.

"Alex speaks French," she said, looking at him with hard-edged fondness.

I felt even more uncomfortable, since I had made a social blunder by assuming that anybody with a Cuban name who lived in Miami would speak Spanish—but I also realized that this was one more clue to why Debs liked her new partner. For some reason, my sister had taken French in school, too, in spite of the fact that we grew up in a city where Spanish was used more widely than English, and French was no more useful than lips on a chicken—it didn't even help her with the city's growing Haitian population. They all spoke Creole, which was only slightly closer to French than Mandarin.

And now she had found a kindred spirit, and clearly they had bonded. I am sure a real human being would have felt a warm glow of affectionate satisfaction at my sister's newly happy work situation, but this was me, and I didn't. All I felt was irritation and discomfort. "Well, *bonne chance*," I said. "But even speaking French to a judge won't get him to unseal a juvenile record—especially since we don't even know *which* record."

Deborah lost her annoying fond look. "Well, shit," she said. "I can't just wait around and hope I get lucky."

"You may not have to," I said. "I'm pretty sure he's going to do it again."

She just looked at me for a long moment, and then she nodded. "Yeah," she said. "I'm pretty sure he will." She shook her head, looked at Duarte, and walked out of the room. He followed right behind her, and I sneezed.

"Gesundheit," I told myself. But it didn't make me feel any better.

EIGHT

OVER THE NEXT FEW DAYS I PICKED UP THE PACE OF MY Honda hunt. I stayed out a little later each evening, trying to squeeze in just one more address, driving when it was too far to walk. I went home only when it was too dark to see any longer, trudging past the family tableau in the living room and into the shower without speaking, a little more frustrated every evening.

On the third night of my enhanced search, I walked in the front door, very sweaty, and realized that Rita was staring at me, her eyes running over me as if she was searching for a blemish, and I stopped in front of her. "What?" I said.

She looked up at me and blushed. "Oh," she said. "It's just late, and you're so sweaty, I thought— It's nothing, really."

"I was jogging," I said, not sure why I felt like I was on the defensive.

"You took the car," she said.

It seemed to me that she was paying far too much attention to my activities, but perhaps this was one of the little perks of marriage, so I shrugged it off. "I went over to the track at the high school," I said.

She looked at me for a very long moment without saying anything, and there was clearly something going on in there, but I had no idea what it might be. Finally, she just said, "That would explain it." She stood up and pushed past me into the kitchen, and I went to my hard-earned shower.

Perhaps I just hadn't noticed it before, but each evening when I came in after my "exercise," she would watch me with that same mysterious intensity, and then head into the kitchen. On the fourth night of this exotic behavior, I followed her and stood silently in the kitchen doorway. I watched as she opened a cupboard, took out a bottle of wine, and poured herself a full glass, and as she raised it to her lips I backed away, unobserved.

It made no sense to me; it was almost as if there was a connection between my coming home sweaty and Rita wanting a glass of wine. I thought about it as I showered, but after a few minutes of musing I realized that I didn't know enough about the complex topics of humans and marriage, and Rita in particular, and in any case I had other worries. Finding the right Honda was far more important, and even though it was something I *did* know a lot about, I wasn't getting that done either. So I put the Mystery of Rita and the Wine out of my mind as just one more brick in the wall of frustration that was forming all around me.

A week later my cold was gone, and I had crossed many more names off my list, enough of them that I was beginning to wonder whether it wasn't a waste of precious time. I could feel hot breath on the back of my neck, and a growing urgency to do before I was done to, but that got me no closer to finding my Witness than anything else I tried. I was more jittery with each day, and with each dead-end name I crossed off my list, and I actually began to bite my fingernails, a habit I had dropped in high school. It was annoying, and added to my frustration, and I began to wonder whether I was starting to fall apart under the strain.

Still, at least I was in much better shape than Officer Gunther. Because just when Marty Klein's brutal murder had settled into a kind of background hum of nervousness on the force, Officer Gunther turned up dead, too. He was a uniformed cop, not a detective like Klein, but there was no doubt at all that it was the handiwork of the same killer. The body had been slowly and methodically pounded into a two-hundred-pound bruise. Every major bone had been broken with what looked like exactly the same patient routine that had been so successful with Klein.

This time the body was not left in a police cruiser on I-95. Officer Gunther had been carefully placed in Bayfront Park, right beside the Torch of Friendship, which seemed more than a little ironic. A young Canadian couple on their honeymoon had found the corpse as they took a romantic early morning stroll: one more enduring memory of a magical time in Our Enchanted City.

There was a feeling of something very close to superstitious dread running through the small knot of cops when I got there. It was still relatively early in the day, but the air of quiet panic on-site had nothing to do with the lack of coffee. The officers on the scene were tense, even a bit wide-eyed, as if they had all seen a ghost. It was easy to see why: To dump Gunther here, so publicly, did not seem like something a human being could get away with. Biscayne Boulevard in downtown Miami is not the kind of private and secluded spot where your average psychotic killer might normally stroll by and drop a stiff. This was an amazingly public display, and yet somehow the body was here, and apparently it had been here for several hours before it had been discovered.

Cops are normally oversensitive to that kind of direct challenge. They take it as an insult to their manhood when someone flaunts the law with such flamboyant exhibitionism, and this really should have stirred up all the righteous wrath of an angry police force. But Miami's Finest looked like they were filled with supernatural angst instead of fury, almost as if they were ready to throw away their weapons and call the Psychic Hotline for help.

And I admit it was a bit disturbing, even to me, to see the corpse of a cop so carefully puddled on the pavement beside the Torch. It was very hard to understand how any living being could stroll through one of the city's busiest streets and deposit a body that was so clearly and spectacularly dead, without being seen. No one actually suggested out loud that there were occult forces at work—at least, not that I overheard. But judging by the look of the cops in attendance, nobody was ruling it out, either.

My real area of expertise is not the Undead, though; it's blood spatter, and there was nothing in that line here. The killing had obviously happened somewhere else and the body had merely been dumped at this lovely and well-known landmark. But I was sure my sister, Deborah, would want my insight, so I hovered around the edges and tried to find some obscure and helpful clue that the other forensics wonks might have missed. There wasn't a great deal to see, aside from the gelatinous blob in the blue uniform that had once been Officer Gunther, married, father of three. I watched Angel Batista-No-Relation crawl slowly around the perimeter, searching meticulously for any small crumb of evidence and, apparently, finding none.

There was a bright flash of light behind me, and, somewhat startled, I turned around. Camilla Figg stood a few feet away, clutching a camera and blushing, with what seemed to be a guilty expression on her face. "Oh," she said in her jerky mutter. "I didn't mean the flash was on but I had to sorry." I blinked at her for a moment, partly from the bright blast of the flash and partly because she had made no sense at all. And then one of the people stacked up at the perimeter leaned over and took a picture of the two of us staring at each other, and Camilla jerked into motion and scuttled away to a small square of grass between the walkways, where Vince Masuoka had found a footprint. She began to refocus her camera on the footprint, and I turned away.

"Nobody saw anything," Deborah said as she materialized at my elbow, and on top of the unexpected explosion from Camilla's flashbulb, my nerves responded instantly and I jumped as if there really was a ghost on the loose and Debs was it. As I settled back to earth she looked at me with mild surprise.

"You startled me," I said.

"I didn't know you could startle," she said. She frowned and shook her head. "This thing is enough to give anybody the creeps. It's like the most crowded public area in the city, and the guy just pops up with a body, drops it by the Torch, and drives away?"

"They found it right around dawn," I said. "So it was dark when he dumped the body."

"It's never dark here," she said. "Streetlights, all the buildings, Bayside Market, the arena a block away? Not to mention the goddamned Torch. It's lit up twenty-four/seven."

I looked around me. I had been here many times, day and night, and it was true that there was always a very bright spill of light from the buildings in this neighborhood. And with Bayside Marketplace right next to us and American Airlines Arena just a block away, there was even more light, more traffic, and more security. Plus the goddamned Torch, of course.

But there was also a line of trees and a relatively deserted belt of grass in the other direction, and I turned to look that way. As I did, Deborah glanced at me, frowned, and then she turned around to look, too.

Through the trees and beyond the stretch of park on the far side of the Torch, the morning sun blazed off the water of Biscayne Bay. In the middle of the near-blinding glare a large sailboat slid regally across the water toward the marina, until an even larger motor yacht powered past it and set it bobbing frantically. A half thought wobbled into my brain and I raised an arm to point; Deborah looked at me expectantly, and then, as if to signal that we really were in a cartoon, another camera flash came from the perimeter, and Deborah's eyes went wide-open as the idea blossomed.

"Son of a bitch," Deborah said. "The motherfucker came by boat. Of course!" She clapped her hands together and swiveled her head around until she located her partner. "Hey, Duarte!" she called. He looked up and she beckoned him to follow as she turned and hurried away toward the water.

"Glad to help," I said as my sister raced away to the seawall. I turned to see who had taken the picture, but saw nothing except Angel with his face hovering six inches over a fascinating clump of grass, and Camilla waving to somebody standing in the crowd of gawkers who were two-deep at the yellow crime scene tape. She went over to talk to whoever it was, and I turned away and watched as my sister raced to the seawall to look for some clue that the killer had come by boat. It really did make sense; I knew very well from a great deal of happy personal experience that you can get away with almost anything on a boat, especially at night. And when I say "almost anything," I mean much more than merely the surprising acts of athletic immodesty one sees couples performing out on the water from time to time. In the pursuit of my hobby I had done many things on my boat that narrow minds might find objectionable, and it was quite clear to me that nobody ever sees anything. Not even, apparently, a psychotic and semisupernatural killer lugging a completely limp but rather large dead cop around the Bay and then up over the seawall and into Bayfront Park.

But because this was Miami, it was at least possible that somebody had, in fact, seen something of the sort, and simply decided not to report it. Maybe they were afraid it would make them a target, or they didn't want the police to find out they had no green card. Modern life being what it is, it was even possible that there was a really good episode of *Mythbusters* on TV and they wanted to watch the end. So for the next hour or so, Debs and her team went all along the seawall looking for that Certain Special Someone.

Not surprisingly—at least, not to me—they didn't find him or her. Nobody knew nothin'; nobody saw nothin'. There was plenty of activity along the seawall, but it was morning traffic, people getting to work in one of the shops in Bayside, or on one of the tour boats tied up by the wall. None of this crowd had been keeping watch in the dark of the night. All those people had gone home to their well-earned rest, no doubt after a full night of staring anxiously into the darkness, alert for every danger—or possibly just watching TV. But Deborah dutifully collected names and telephone numbers of all the night security personnel and then came back to me and scowled, as if it was all my fault because she had found nothing and I was the one who had made her look for it.

We stood on the seawall not far from the *Biscayne Pearl*, one of the boats that provided tours of the city by water, and Deborah squinted along the wall toward Bayside. Then she shook her head and started to walk back toward the Torch, and I tagged along.

"Somebody saw something," she said, and I hoped she sounded more convincing to herself than she did to me. "Had to. You can't lug a full-grown cop onto the seawall and all the way up to the Torch and nobody sees you."

"Freddy Krueger could," I said.

Deborah whacked me on the upper arm, but her heart really wasn't in it this time, and it was relatively easy for me to stop myself from screaming with pain.

"All I need," she said, "is to have more of that supernatural bullshit going around. One of the guys actually asked Duarte if we could get a *santero* in here, just in case."

I nodded. It might make sense to bring in a *santero,* one of Santeria's priests, if you believed in that sort of thing, and a surprising number of Miami's citizens did. "What did Duarte tell him?"

Deborah snorted. "He said, 'What's a *santero?*' "

I looked at her to see if she was kidding; every Cuban-American knew *santeros.* Odds were good there was at least one in his very own family. But of course, they hadn't asked Duarte in French, and anyway, before I could pretend to get the joke and then pretend to laugh, Debs went on. "I know this guy's a psycho, but he's a live human being, too," she said, and I was relatively sure she didn't mean Duarte. "He isn't invisible, and he didn't teleport in and out."

She paused by a large tree and looked up at it thoughtfully, and then turned back around the way we'd come. "Lookit this," she said, pointing up at the tree and then back to the *Pearl.* "If he ties up right there by the tour boat," she said, "he's got cover from these trees most of the way to the Torch."

"Not quite invisible," I said. "But pretty close."

"Right beside the fucking boat," she muttered. "They *had* to see something."

"Unless they were asleep," I said.

She just shook her head and then looked toward the Torch along the line of trees as if she was aiming a rifle, and then shrugged and began to walk again. "Somebody saw something," she repeated stubbornly. "Had to."

We walked back to the Torch together in what would have been comfortable silence if my sister hadn't been so obviously distracted. The medical examiner was just finishing up with Officer Gunther's body when we got there. He shook his head at Debs to indicate that he'd found nothing interesting.

"Do we know where Gunther had lunch?" I asked Deborah. She stared at me as if I had suggested we should strip naked and jog down Biscayne Boulevard.

"Lunch, Debs," I said patiently. "Like maybe Mexican food?"

The light came on and she lurched over to the ME. "I want stomach contents from the autopsy," I heard her say. "See if he ate any tacos recently." Oddly enough, the ME looked at her without surprise, but I suppose if you have worked with corpses and cops in Miami long enough you are very hard to surprise, and a request to search for tacos in a dead officer's stomach was mere routine. The ME just nodded wearily, and Deborah stalked off to talk to Duarte, leaving me to twiddle my thumbs and think deep thoughts.

I thought them for a few minutes, but I didn't come up with anything more profound than the realization that I was hungry, and there was nothing for me to eat here. There was also nothing for me to do; no blood spatter at all, and the other geeks from Forensics had things well in hand.

I turned away from Gunther's body and looked around the perimeter. The usual crowd of casual ghouls was still there, standing in back of the tape in a jostling bunch as if they were waiting to get into a rock concert. They were staring at the body and, to their credit, one or two of them actually tried very hard to look horrified as they craned their necks to see. Of course, most of the others made up for it by leaning forward over the tape to get a better picture with their cell phones. Soon the pictures of Officer Gunther's smooshed corpse would be all over the Web, and the whole world could join together and pretend to be appalled and dismayed in perfect harmony. Isn't technology wonderful?

I hung around and made helpful suggestions for a little while longer, but as usual, no one seemed to care about my thoughtful insights; real expertise is never appreciated. People would always rather muddle along in their own dim, blundering way than have someone else point out where they were going wrong—even if that other person is clearly brighter.

And so it was that at an hour depressingly far beyond lunchtime, an underappreciated and underutilized Dexter finally got bored enough to hitch a ride back to the land of real work waiting for me in my little cubbyhole. I found a friendly cop who was headed that way. He just wanted to talk about fishing, and since I do know something about that, we got along very nicely. He was even willing to make a quick stop along the way for some Chinese takeout, which was certainly a very chummy gesture, and in gratitude I paid for his order of shrimp lo mein.

By the time I said good-bye to my new BFF and sat down at my desk with my fragrant lunch, I was beginning to feel like there might be some actual point to this patchwork quilt of humiliation and suffering we call Life. The hot-and-sour soup was very good, the dumplings were tender and juicy, and the kung pao was hot enough to make me sweat. I caught myself feeling rather contented as I finished eating, and I wondered why. Could I really be so shallow that the simple act of eating a good lunch made me happy? Or was something deeper and more sinister at work here? Perhaps it was the MSG in the food, attacking the pleasure center in my brain and forcing me to feel good against my will.

Whatever it was, it was a relief to be out of the dark clouds that had been clustered around my head for the past few weeks. It was true that I had some legitimate worries, but I had been wallowing in them a little too much. Apparently, however, one meal of good Chinese food had cured me. I actually caught myself humming as I tossed the empty containers into the trash, a very surprising development for me. Was this real human happiness? From a dumpling? Perhaps I should notify some national mental health organization: Kung pao chicken works better than Zoloft. There might be a Nobel Prize waiting for me for this. Or at least a letter of thanks from China.

Whatever my lighthearted mood was really all about, it lasted almost until quitting time. I had gone down to the evidence room to return a few samples I'd been working with, and when I came back to my little cubbyhole I found a large and unpleasant surprise waiting for me.

My surprise was about five feet, ten inches, two hundred pounds of African-American anger, and it looked more like an exceptionally sinister insect than a human being. He was perched on two shiny prosthetic feet, and one of the metal claws he had for hands was doing something to my computer as I walked in.

"Why, Sergeant Doakes," I said, with as much pleasantness as I could fake. "Do you need help logging onto Facebook?"

He jerked around to face me, clearly not expecting me to catch him snooping. "Nyuk ookig," he said quite clearly; the same amateur surgeon who had removed his hands and feet had taken out his tongue, too, and having a pleasant conversation with the man had become nearly impossible.

Of course, it had never been easy; he had always hated me, always suspected what I was. I had never given him any reason to doubt my carefully manufactured innocence, but doubt it he did, and always had—even before I had failed to rescue him from his unfortunate surgery. I had tried, really I had: It just hadn't quite worked out. To be fair to me, which is very important, I did get *most* of him back safely. But now he blamed me for the amputations as well as many other unspecified acts. And here he was at my computer, and he was "Nyuk ookig."

"Nyuk?" I repeated brightly. "Really? Are you a fan of the Three Stooges, Sergeant? I never knew. Nyuk nyuk nyuk!"

He glared at me with even more venom, which added up to an impressive amount, and he reached down to the desk for the small notebook-size artificial-speech device he carried around. He punched in something, and the machine called out in its cheerful baritone, "Just! Looking!"

"Of course you are!" I said, with real synthetic good cheer, trying to match the bizarre happiness of his voice machine. "And no doubt doing a wonderful job of it! But unfortunately, you are accidentally looking on my private computer, in my private space, and technically speaking, that's kind of against the rules."

He glared at me some more; really, the man had become completely one-note. Without taking his eyes off me he punched in something new on his speech machine and after a moment it called out, in its unlikely and happy voice, "I will! Get! You! Someday! Maa-ther. Fucker!"

"I'm sure you will," I said soothingly. "But you'll have to do it on your own computer." I smiled at him, just to show there were no hard feelings, and pointed in the direction of the door. "So if you don't mind?"

He pulled a large breath of air in through his nostrils, and then hissed it out again through his teeth, all without blinking, and then he tucked the speech machine under his arm and stomped out of my office, taking the tatters of my good mood with him.

And now I had another reason for uneasiness. Why had Sergeant

Doakes been looking on my computer? Obviously, he thought there was something incriminating to find—but what? And why now, on my computer, of all things? There could be absolutely no legitimate reason for him to look at my computer. I was reasonably sure he had no knowledge of or interest in IT. Since the loss of his limbs he had been given a desk job out of pity, so he could serve out his last few years and qualify for a full pension. He'd been working at some kind of useless administrative thing in Human Resources; I didn't really know or care what.

So he had been here, in my space, on my computer, strictly as a part of his private program to Demolish Dexter—but right here at work? Why? As far as I knew, he had always confined his attempts to "get" me to general surveillance, and he had never actually snooped through my things before. What had brought on this new and unwelcome escalation? Had he finally slipped over the line into a kind of hostile insanity, permanently focused on me? Or did he really have some reason to think he was onto something specific, and he had a chance to prove me guilty?

It seemed impossible, on the face of it. I mean, of course I really am guilty, of many somethings, all of them lethal and very enjoyable and technically not quite legal. But I was extremely careful, I always cleaned up nicely afterward, and I could not imagine what Doakes thought he might come up with. I was fairly sure that there was nothing there to find.

It was puzzling, and very unsettling. But at least it jolted me out of my stupid good cheer and back into general gloominess again. So much for Chinese food: Half an hour later you're grumpy again.

Deborah, however, was even grumpier when she slouched into my office as I was getting ready to go home.

"You took off early," she said, "from the Torch." And she made it sound like she was accusing me of stealing office supplies.

"I had to go to *work*," I said, and I did what I could to match her surly tone.

She blinked. "What the hell has gotten into you lately?" she said.

I took a breath, more to stall for time than because I needed air. "What do you mean?"

She pursed her lips, cocked her head to one side. "You're jumpy all the time. You snap at people. Maybe a little distracted? I don't know. Like something's bothering you."

It was a very uncomfortable moment for me. She was right, of course, but how much could I tell her? Something *was* bothering me; I was convinced that someone had *seen* me and recognized me, and now I had caught Sergeant Doakes looking at my computer. It was nearly impossible to connect the two things in any way—the idea of some anonymous witness to Me at Play teaming up with Doakes to get me was ludicrous—but taken together, the two separate things had knocked me for a very uneasy loop. I was in the grip of illogical emotions, and I was not used to that at all.

But what could I say to her? Debs and I had always been close, of course, but that was partly because we *didn't* share our feelings with each other. We couldn't; I didn't have any, and she was too ashamed of hers to admit she had them.

Still, I had to say something, and when I thought about it, she was probably the only one in the world I could really talk to, unless I was willing to shell out a hundred dollars an hour to talk to a shrink, which seemed like a very bad idea; I would either have to tell him the truth about myself, which was unthinkable, or make up some plausible fiction, which was certainly a waste of good money that might be put toward Lily Anne's medical school tuition.

"I didn't know it showed," I said at last.

Debs snorted. "Dexter. This is me. We grew up together; we work together—I know you better than anybody else in the world. To me, it shows." She raised an eyebrow encouragingly. "So what is it?"

She was right, of course. She *did* know me better than anyone else—better than Rita, or Brian, or anybody I had ever known, with the possible exception of Harry, our long-dead dad. Like Harry, Deborah even knew about Dark Dexter and his happy slashing, and she had come to terms with it. If ever there was a time to talk, and a person to talk to, it was now, with her. I closed my eyes for a moment, and tried to think of how to begin. "I don't know," I said. "It's just that, um . . . a few weeks ago, when I was—"

Deborah's radio squawked, a loud and rude electronic belch, and then it said quite clearly, "Sergeant Morgan, what is your twenty?" She shook her head at me and held her radio up.

"This is Morgan," she said. "I'm in Forensics."

"You'd better come down here, Sergeant," a voice said over the radio. "I think we found something you need to see."

Deborah looked at me. "Sorry," she said. She pushed the button on the radio and said, "On my way." Then she got up and started for the door, hesitated, and turned back to me. "We'll talk later, Dex, okay?"

"Sure," I said. "Don't worry about me." Apparently it didn't sound as pitiful to her as it did to me; she just nodded and hurried out the door. And I finished closing up shop for the night and then headed to my car.

NINE

THE SUN WAS STILL BRIGHT IN THE SKY WHEN I GOT HOME. It was one of the very few benefits of summer in Miami: The temperature may be ninety-seven, and the humidity well over a hundred percent, but at least when you got home at six o'clock, there was still plenty of daylight left, so you could sit outside with your family and sweat for another hour and a half.

But, of course, my little family did no such thing. We were natives; tans are for tourists, and we preferred the comfort of central air-conditioning. Besides, since my brother, Brian, had given Cody and Astor a Wii, they hadn't left the house at all except by force. They both seemed unwilling to leave the room where the thing sat, for any reason. We'd had to make some very strict rules about using the Wii: They had to ask first, and they had to finish their homework before they turned it on, and they could play with it no more than an hour a day.

So when I came into the house and saw Cody and Astor already standing in front of the TV with their Wii controllers clutched tightly in their hands, my first question was automatic. "Homework all done?" I said.

They didn't even look up; Cody just nodded, and Astor frowned. "We finished it at after-school," she said.

"All right," I said. "Where's Lily Anne?"

"With Mom," Astor said, frowning deeper at my continuing interruption.

"And where's Mom?"

"Dunno," she said, waving her controller and jerking spasmodically with whatever was happening on the screen. Cody glanced at me—it was Astor's play—and he shrugged slightly. He almost never said more than three words at a time, one small side effect of the abuse he'd received from his biological father, and Astor did most of the talking for both of them. But at the moment she seemed uncharacteristically unwilling to talk—probably a continuing miff over impending braces. So I took a breath and tried to shake off my growing irritation at both of them.

"Fine," I said. "Thank you for asking, yes, I did have a hard day at work. But I already feel a lot better, now that I'm here nestled in the warm bosom of my family. I've enjoyed our little chat very much."

Cody gave a funny little half smirk and said, very softly, "Bosom." Astor said nothing; she just gritted her teeth and attacked a large monster on the screen. I sighed; as comforting as it may be to some of us, sarcasm, like youth, is wasted on the young. I gave up on the kids and went to look for Rita.

She wasn't in the kitchen, which was a very large disappointment, since it meant she was not busily whipping up something wonderful for my dinner. There was nothing burbling on the stove, either. And it wasn't leftover night; this was very puzzling and a little bit troublesome. I hoped this didn't mean we were going to have to order pizza—although it made the kids happy, it simply could not compete with even the most casual of Rita's efforts.

I went back through the living room and down the hall. Rita was not in the bathroom, and not in the bedroom, either. I began to wonder whether Freddy Krueger had grabbed her, too. I went to the bedroom window and looked out into the backyard.

Rita sat at the picnic table we'd put up under a large banyan tree that spread its branches over nearly half our backyard. She was holding Lily Anne on her lap with her left hand and sipping from a large glass of wine with the right. Other than that, she seemed to be doing absolutely nothing except staring back at the house and slowly shaking her head. As I watched she took a gulp of wine, hugged Lily Anne a little tighter for a moment, and then appeared to sigh heavily.

This was very strange behavior, and I had no idea what to make of it. I had never seen Rita act like this before—sitting alone and unhappy and drinking wine—and it was disturbing to see her doing it now, whatever the reason might be. It seemed to me, however, that the most important point was that, whatever Rita was doing, she was not cooking dinner, and that was just the sort of dangerous inaction that calls for prompt and vigorous intervention. So I wound my way back through the house, past Cody and Astor—still happily killing things on the TV screen—and on out the back door into the yard.

Rita looked up at me as I came outside and she seemed to freeze for a moment. Then she hurriedly turned away, put her wineglass down on the picnic table's bench, and turned back around to face me. "I'm home," I said, with cautious good cheer.

She sniffled loudly. "Yes, I know," she said. "And now you'll go get all sweaty again."

I sat next to her; Lily Anne had begun to bounce as I approached, and I held out my hands for her. She launched herself toward me and Rita passed her over to me with a tired smile. "Oh," Rita said, "you're such a *good* daddy. Why can't I just . . ." And she shook her head and snuffled again.

I looked away from Lily Anne's bright and cheerful face and into Rita's tired and unhappy one. Aside from a runny nose, she also seemed to have been crying; her cheeks were wet and her eyes looked red and a little swollen. "Um," I said. "Is something wrong?"

Rita blotted at her eyes with the sleeve of her blouse and then turned around and took a large sip of wine. She put the glass back down again, behind her, and faced me once more. She opened her mouth to say something, bit her lip, and looked away, shaking her head.

Even Lily Anne seemed puzzled by Rita's behavior, and she bounced vigorously for a moment, calling out, "Abbab bab *bab*!"

Rita looked at her with a small, tired smile. "She needs a fresh diaper," Rita said, and before I could respond to that, Rita sobbed: just one small sob, and she strangled it off for the most part so that it might almost have been a hiccup, but I was very sure it was a sob. It seemed like overreacting to a dirty diaper.

I am not comfortable with emotions, partly because I do not have them and so I generally don't understand where they come from and what they mean. But after years of careful study and a great deal of practice I had learned to cope when others displayed them, and I usually knew the correct response when a human being was in the grip of strong feelings.

In this case, however, I admit I was helpless. Going by the book, a woman's tears generally called for comfort and reassurance, no matter how phony—but how could I apply either of those things if I didn't know what was causing Rita's crying fit? I looked at her carefully, searching her face for some clue, and found nothing; red-rimmed eyes and wet cheeks, yes, but unfortunately no one had scrawled a message on her face outlining a cause and a course of treatment. And so, sounding almost as awkward as I was beginning to feel, I stuttered out, "Uh, are you . . . I mean, is something wrong?"

Rita sniffled again and wiped her nose on her sleeve. Once more she seemed about to say something truly momentous. Instead, she just shook her head and touched the baby's face with a finger. "It's Lily Anne," she said. "We have to move. And then you."

I heard those terrifying words, "It's Lily Anne," and for just a moment the world got very bright and spun around me as my brain was filled with an endless list of terrible maladies that might be attacking my little girl. I clutched my baby tightly and tried to breathe until things steadied down again. Lily Anne helped out by swatting at the side of my head and saying, "Abah-a-*bah!*" The clout to my ear brought me back to my senses and I looked back at Rita, who apparently had no idea that her words had sent me into a full-scale tizzy. "What's wrong with Lily Anne?" I demanded.

"What?" Rita said. "What do you mean? There's nothing— Oh, Dexter, you're being so— I just meant, we have to move. Because of Lily Anne."

I looked at the happy little face of the child bouncing on my lap. Rita was not making sense, at least not to me. How could this perfect little person force us to move? Of course, she was my child, which raised a few terrifying possibilities. Perhaps some vagrant strand of wicked DNA had surfaced in her and the outraged neighborhood was demanding her exile. It was a horrible thought, but it was at least possible. "What did she do?" I said.

"What did she— Dexter, she's only a year old," Rita said. "What could she possibly *do*?"

"I don't know," I said. "But you said we have to move because of Lily Anne."

"Oh, for God's sake," she said. "You're being completely . . ." She fluttered a hand in the air, and then she turned around again and took another gulp of wine, bending over the glass and shielding it from me, as if she didn't want me to know what she was doing over there.

"Rita," I said, and she slapped the glass down onto the bench and turned back toward me, swallowing convulsively. "If nothing is wrong with Lily Anne, and she didn't *do* anything wrong, why do we have to move?"

She blinked, and then wiped the corners of her eyes with her sleeve. "That's just . . ." she said. "I mean, because look at her." Rita gestured at the baby, and it seemed to me that her motor skills were not quite what they should have been, because her hand bumped clumsily against my arm. She jerked the hand back and waved at the house. "Such a little house," she said. "And Lily Anne is getting so big."

I looked at her and waited for more, but I waited in vain. Her words did not add up to anything I could understand, but they were apparently all I was going to get. Did Rita really think that Lily Anne was growing into some kind of gigantic creature, like in *Alice in Wonderland,* and soon the house would be too small to contain her? Or was there some hidden message here, possibly in Aramaic, that would take me years of study to decipher? I have heard and read many suggestions about what it takes to make a marriage work, but at the moment what mine seemed to need most was a translator. "Rita, you're not making any sense," I said, with all the gentle patience I could fake.

She shook her head, just a little bit sloppily, and scowled at me. "I'm not drunk," she said.

One of the few eternal truths about humans is that if someone says they aren't sleeping, they're not rich, or they're not drunk, they almost certainly are. But telling them so when they deny it is thankless, unpleasant, and sometimes dangerous. So I just smiled understandingly at Rita. "Of course you're not," I said. "So why do we have to move because Lily Anne is getting so big?"

"Dexter," Rita said. "Our little family is *all* getting so big. We need a bigger house."

A small light flickered in my mighty brain and then came on. "You mean we need a house with more room? Because the kids are growing up?"

"Yes," she said, slapping her hand on the picnic table for emphasis. "That's exactly right." She frowned. "What jid you think I meaned?"

"I had no idea what you meaned," I said. "But you're sitting out here—and you're *crying.*"

"Oh," she said, and she looked away, and once more she blotted clumsily at her face with her sleeve. "It doesn't seem like right now." She looked at me and quickly looked away again. "I mean, you know, I'm not soopit. Stooper." She frowned, and then said very carefully, "I'm. Not. Stupid."

"I never thought you were," I said, which was actually true: amazingly scatterbrained, yes, but not stupid. "Is that why you're crying?"

She looked at me very hard, and I was just beginning to get uncomfortable when her eyes glazed over a little, and she looked away.

"It's just hormones," she said. "I didn't want anyone to see."

I skipped over the image of anyone seeing her hormones and tried to focus on the heart of the matter. "So there's nothing wrong with Lily Anne?" I said, still not quite sure that everything was exactly what it should be.

"No, no, of course not," Rita said. "It's the *house* too small. Cody and Astor can't share a room forever, because you know," she said. "Astor is getting to that age."

Even without really knowing what specific age she meant, I thought I understood. Astor was growing up, and she couldn't share a room with her brother forever. But even so, aside from the fact that I was used to this house and didn't really want to move away from it, I had a few practical objections. "We can't afford a new house," I said. "Especially not a bigger one."

Rita waggled a finger at me and squinted playfully through one eye. "You have not been paying attention," she said, working very hard to make each word distinct.

"I guess not."

"There are lots of wonderful opportoonies," she said. "Toon-a-nitties. Damn." She shook her head, and then closed her eyes tightly. "Oh," she said. "Oh, lord." She breathed heavily for a moment and swayed so that I wondered if she was going to fall off the bench. But then she took an extra-deep breath, rolled her head in a half circle, and opened her eyes. "Foreclosures," she said carefully. "Not a new house. A foreclosing houses." She smiled loopily, and then jerked around and hunched over the wineglass again; this time she drained it.

I thought about what she said—or at any rate, I thought about what I thought she had said. It was true that South Florida was littered with bargain real estate right now. No matter how much the economy was officially improving everywhere else, Miami was still full of people who were in over their heads on a bad mortgage, and many of them were simply walking away, leaving the bank holding the worthless paper as well as the overpriced house. And quite often the banks, in turn, were anxiously unloading the houses for a fraction of the original price.

I knew all this very well from a general and somewhat disinterested standpoint. Lately the whole subject of foreclosure and bargain houses was on everybody's lips, much like the weather. Everyone talked about it, and the media were full of stories and discussions and panels with dire warnings. And closer to home, even my own brother, Brian, was happily employed dealing with this same phenomenon.

But to go from this theoretical awareness of foreclosure into the very real idea of taking personal advantage of it took a moment of adjustment. I liked living where we were, and I had already given up my comfy little apartment to do so. Moving again would be difficult and uncomfortable and inconvenient, and there was no guarantee at all that we would end up someplace better, especially with a house that had been abandoned in despair and anger. There might be holes kicked in the roof, and wiring ripped out—and at the very least, wouldn't there be bad karma to deal with?

But once again, Lily Anne proved that she saw things a little more clearly and shrewdly than her dunderheaded father. As I wrestled with all the concepts of foreclosure and moving and personal inconvenience, she cut right to the heart of the matter with an insight that was sharp and compelling. She bounced three times on her powerful little legs and said, "Da. Da da *da.*" And for emphasis, she reached out and pulled on my earlobe.

I looked at my little girl, and I came to a decision. "You're right," I told her. "You deserve your own room." I turned to Rita to tell her what I had decided, but she had leaned back against the edge of the table and closed her eyes again, and her head was swaying gently, her mouth open and her hands clasped in her lap.

"Rita?" I said.

She jerked upright and her eyes popped open wide. "Oh!" she said. "Oh, my God, you scared me."

"I'm sorry," I said. "About the house?"

"Yes," she said, and she frowned. "Brian says— Oh, I hope you don't mind," she said, and she looked a little bit guilty. "I talked to *him* first? Because, you know, his job." She fluttered a hand again and it bumped against the edge of the table. "Ouch," she said.

"Yes," I said, with soothing encouragement. "You talked to Brian. That's good."

"It *is* good," she said. "He Is Good. He knows really what ups. Wha's up. With houses. Right now, I mean."

"Yes, he does."

"He's going to help us," she said. "Find, find . . ."

"Find a house," I said.

Rita shook her head slowly and then closed her eyes. I waited, but nothing happened. "I'm sorry," she said at last, very softly. "I think I need to go lie down." She got up from the bench; the empty wineglass fell to the ground and the stem snapped off, but Rita didn't notice. She stood there, swayed for a moment, and then meandered back into the house.

"Well, then," I said to Lily Anne. "I guess we're moving."

Lily Anne bounced. "Da," she said firmly.

I stood up and carried her into the house to make a telephone call; it looked like it was pizza night after all.

TEN

THE NEXT MORNING WHEN I GOT IN TO WORK, THERE WAS A lab report from the medical examiner's office waiting on my desk. I glanced through it briefly and then, when I saw what it was, I sat down and read it with real interest. The report gave the results of the autopsy on Officer Gunther, and if you threw out all the technical jargon, it said several significant things. First, blood pooling in the tissue indicated that he had been lying facedown for several hours after death—interesting, since he had been faceup when his body was found by the Torch of Friendship. It probably meant our psycho had killed Gunther in the late afternoon, then left him stashed all alone somewhere until dark. Sometime in the night he had recovered his sense of camaraderie and moved the body to the Torch of Friendship.

There were several pages detailing the massive trauma to Gunther's assorted organs and limbs, adding up to the same picture we'd gotten from Klein. The report did not speculate, of course; that would have been unprofessional and possibly a little too helpful. But it did state that the damage had been caused by an object that was probably made of steel and possessed a smooth, oblong striking surface about the size of a playing card, which sounded like some kind of large hammer to me.

Once again, the condition of the internal organs confirmed what the exterior tissue indicated: The killer had worked very hard to keep Gunther alive as long as possible, while carefully breaking every conceivable bone with deliberate and vicious force. It didn't seem like a very pleasant way to die, but then, on reflection, I couldn't think of a single way to die that was pleasant—certainly nothing I had ever tried. Not that I'd really looked for anything of the kind; where would the fun be in a pleasant death?

I flipped through the report until I came to a page that had been highlighted with fluorescent yellow marker. It listed the contents of Gunther's stomach, and half of the list had been colored in a solid bright yellow, almost certainly by Deborah. I read it and I didn't need the highlighting to find the significant part. Among the other nasty things swimming around in his guts, Gunther had eaten something containing cornmeal, iceberg lettuce, ground beef, and several spices, chief among them chili powder and cumin.

In other words, his last meal had been a taco, just like it had been for Klein. For both their sakes, I hoped they were really good tacos.

I had barely finished reading the report when my desk telephone rang, and using my vast and all-seeing psychic powers I determined that it was probably my sister calling. I picked up the receiver anyway and said, "Morgan."

"Did you read the coroner's report?" Deborah demanded.

"Just finished it," I said.

"Stay put," she said. "I'll be right there."

Two minutes later she walked into my office carrying her own copy of the report. "What did you think?" she said, sliding into a chair and waving the pages.

"I don't like his prose style," I said. "And the plot seems very familiar."

"Don't be an asshole," she said. "I got a briefing in a half hour, and I need to have something to say to everybody."

I looked at my sister with some little annoyance. I knew very well that even though she could face down an angry and well-armed mob of cocaine cowboys, or bully around large thuglike cops twice her size, she fell to pieces when she had to speak in front of any group containing more than two people. That was fine, even a little bit endearing, since it was rather nice to see her humbled from time to time. But somehow, her terrible stage fright had become my problem, and I always ended up writing the script for her presentations—a completely thankless job, since she fell apart anyway, no matter how many great lines I wrote for her.

But here she was; she had come all the way down to my office for once, and she was asking nicely, for her, so I really had to help out, no matter how much I resented the idea. "Well," I said, thinking out loud. "So it fits the same pattern, all the bones broken, and the tacos."

"I got that," she snapped. "Come on, Dex."

"The interval between kills is interesting," I said. "Two weeks."

She blinked and stared at me for a moment. "Does that mean something?" she said.

"Absolutely," I said.

"What?" she said eagerly.

"I don't have a clue," I said, and before she could lean over and hit me I added, "But the differences must mean something, too."

"Yeah, I know," she said thoughtfully. "Gunther's in uniform; Klein is a detective. He gets left in his vehicle; Gunther gets dumped by the goddamned Torch. By boat, for Christ's sake. Why?"

"More important," I said, "why does the other stuff stay the same?" She looked at me oddly. "I mean, yeah, the MO stays the same. And they're both cops. But why these two specific cops? What is it about the two of them that fit the killer's pattern of need?"

Debs shook her head impatiently. "I don't really give a shit about the psychological stuff," she said. "I need to catch this psycho motherfucker."

I could have said that the best way to catch a psycho motherfucker is by understanding what makes him a psycho motherfucker, but I doubted that Deborah would be very receptive to that message right now. Besides, it wasn't really true. Based on my years of experience in the business, the best way to catch a killer is by getting lucky. Of course, you don't say that out loud, especially if you're talking to the evening news. You have to look serious and mention patient and thorough detective work. So I just said, "What about the boat?"

"We're looking," she said. "But, shit, do you know how many boats there are in Miami—even if you only count the legally registered ones?"

"It won't be his. It was probably stolen in the last week," I said helpfully.

Deborah snorted. "Almost as many," she said. "Shit, Dexter, I got all the obvious stuff covered. I need an actual idea here, not more dumb-ass chatter."

It was true that I had not been in the best of moods lately, but it seemed to me that she was moving rapidly past the boundaries of how to speak when begging someone else for help. I opened my mouth to make a crushing remark and then, out of nowhere, an actual idea hit me. "Oh," I said.

"What," she said.

"You don't want to find a stolen boat," I said.

"The fuck I don't," she said. "I know he wouldn't be stupid enough to use his own boat, even if he had one. He stole one."

I looked at her and shook my head patiently. "Debs, that's obvious," I said, and I admit I might have been smirking slightly. "But then it's also obvious that he wouldn't hang on to that boat afterward. So you don't look for a stolen boat; you look for—"

"A *found* boat!" she said, and she clapped her hands together. "Right! A boat that was abandoned somewhere for no reason."

"It had to be somewhere he had a car stashed," I said. "Or even better, someplace he could *steal* a car."

"Goddamn it, that's more like it," Debs said. "There can't be more than one place in town where a boat turned up and a car got stolen the same night."

"A quick and simple computer search to cross-reference it," I said, and the moment the words were out of my mouth I wanted to jam them back in and slide under my desk, because Deborah knew almost as much about using a computer as she did about ballroom dancing. I, on the other hand, must modestly admit to something verging on expertise in that area, and so anytime the word "computer" came up in conversation, my sister automatically made it my problem. And sure enough, she bounced to her feet and whacked me playfully on the arm.

"That's great, Dex," she said. "How long will it take you?"

I looked around the room quickly, but Debs was standing between me and the door, and there was no emergency exit. So I turned to my computer and went to work. Deborah jiggled around anxiously like she was jogging in place, which made it very hard to concentrate, until finally I said, "Debs, please. I can't work with you vibrating like that."

"Well, shit," she said, but at least she stopped hopping up and down and perched on the edge of a chair instead. But three seconds later, she started rapidly tapping her foot on the floor. Clearly there was no way to keep her still, short of flinging her out the door or finding what she wanted. Since she had a gun and I didn't, flinging was too chancy, so with a heavy and pointed sigh I went back to my search.

Less than ten minutes later, I had it. "Here we go," I said, and before I got out the final syllable Deborah was at my elbow, leaning in anxiously to see the screen. "The pastor of St. John's Church on Miami Beach reported his car stolen this morning. And he's got a new twenty-one-foot Sea Fox at his dock."

"A fucking church?" Deborah said. "On the *Beach*, for God's sake? How did he get the boat in there?"

I pulled up a map on-screen and pointed. "See, the church is right here, by this canal, and the parking lot is on the water." I ran my finger along the canal from the church and out into the bay. "Ten minutes across the water to Bayfront Park and the Torch."

Deborah stared for a moment, then shook her head. "It doesn't make any fucking sense at all," she said.

"It does to him," I said.

"Well, shit," she said. "I'd better get Duarte and get out there." And then she straightened up and ran for the door without a single word of thanks for my arduous eight minutes of labor. I admit I was a bit surprised—not that my very own sister had failed to display gratitude, of course. That would be too much to expect. But normally she would have dragged a reluctant Dexter along with her for backup, leaving her partner to count paper clips. But this time it was Dutiful Dexter left behind, and Debs had gone to find her new French-speaking partner, Duarte. I supposed that meant she liked working with him, or maybe she was just being more careful with her partners now. Her last two had been killed on the job while working a case with her, and I'd heard more than one cop muttering that it was very bad luck to work with Sergeant Morgan, since she was obviously some kind of black widow or something.

Whatever the case, there was really nothing to complain about. Debs was actually doing things the way she was supposed to for once, working with her official partner instead of her unofficial brother. And that was fine with me, because it truly was dangerous to hang around with her when she was at work; I had scar tissue to prove it. And it wasn't my job to run around in the big, bad world dodging slings and arrows and, apparently, hammers. I didn't need the adrenaline; I had real work to do. So I just sat and felt unappreciated for a few minutes, and then went back to doing it.

Just after lunch, I was in the lab with Vince Masuoka when Deborah rushed in and dumped a large hammer on the counter in front of me. I guessed from the loud thump that it weighed about three pounds. It was in a big plastic evidence bag, and a film of condensation had formed on the inside surface of the bag, but I could still see that it was not an ordinary carpenter's hammer, and it did not quite look like a sledgehammer, either. The head was round and blunt at both ends, and it had a yellow, well-worn wooden handle.

"All *right*," Vince said, peering in over Deborah's shoulder. "I always wanted to get hammered with you."

"Go piss up a stick," Debs said. It was not up to her usual high standards in a put-down, but she said it with considerable conviction, and Vince scuttled away quickly to the far corner of the lab, where his laptop sat on a counter. "Alex found it," Deborah said, nodding at Duarte as he trickled in the door. "It was lying in the parking lot at that church, St. John's."

"Why would he drop his hammer?" I said, poking carefully at the plastic bag to see better.

"Right here," Debs said, and I could hear barely suppressed excitement in her voice. She pointed through the plastic to a spot on the handle, just above where the yellow color was partially faded away from use. "Lookit," she said. "It's cracked a little bit."

I bent over and looked. On the worn wooden handle, just barely visible through the misted bag, was a hairline crack. "Wonderful," I said. "Maybe he cut himself."

"Why is that wonderful?" Duarte said. "I mean, I'd like to see the guy hurt, but a little cut? So what?"

I looked at Duarte and very briefly wondered if some malignant personnel computer always assigned to Debs a partner with the lowest possible IQ. "If he cut his hand," I said, carefully choosing one-syllable words, "there might be some blood. So we can get a DNA match."

"Oh, yeah, sure," he said.

"Come on, Dex," Deborah said. "See what you can get from it."

I pulled on gloves and took the hammer out of its bag, placing it carefully on the counter. "Unusual kind of hammer, isn't it?" I said.

"It's called a club hammer," Vince said, and I looked at him. He was still sitting on the far side of the room, hunched over his laptop. He pointed to an image on the screen. "Club hammer," he repeated. "I Googled."

"Very appropriate," I said. I leaned over the handle of the hammer in question and carefully sprayed on some Bluestar. It would reveal any trace of blood, no matter how small. With any luck, there might be just enough for me to get a blood type or DNA sample.

"They use it for demolition, mostly," Vince went on. "You know, like knocking out walls and things?"

"I think I remember what demolition means," I said.

"Cut the shit," Deborah said through her teeth. "Can you get anything from it or not?"

Deborah's hands-on management style seemed more profoundly annoying than usual, and I thought of several stinging remarks to slap her back into her place. But just as I was about to let fly with a really good one, I saw a dim smudge on the hammer's handle, brought out by the Bluestar. "Bingo," I said.

"What," Deborah demanded, and she was suddenly so close to me I could hear her teeth grinding.

"If you'll take your foot out of my pocket, I'll show you," I said. She hissed out a breath, but at least she did back up a half step. "Look," I said, pointing at the smudge. "It's a trace of blood—and even better, it's also a latent fingerprint."

"Pure dumb luck," Vince said from his stool across the lab.

"Really?" I said. "Then why didn't *you* find it?"

"What about DNA?" Deborah said impatiently.

I shook my head. "I'll try," I said. "But it's probably too badly degraded."

"Run the print," Deborah said. "I want a name."

"And maybe a GPS reading?" Vince said.

Deborah glared at him, but instead of ripping him into small and bloody shreds she just looked back at me and said, "Run the print, Dexter," and then she turned around and whirled away out of the lab.

Alex Duarte straightened up as she hustled past him. *"Au 'voir,"* I told him politely.

He nodded. *"Mange merde,"* he said, and he followed Deborah out the door. His French accent was much better than mine.

I looked at Vince. He closed his laptop and stood up. "Let's run it," he said.

We ran it. As I had thought, the bloody smudge was too badly degraded to get any kind of usable DNA sample, but we did get a picture of the fingerprint, and after computer enhancement the image was clear enough to send to the Integrated Automated Fingerprint Identification System with some hope that we might get a match. It was a national database of felons' fingerprints, and if our hammer-loving friend was in it, a name would pop out, and Deborah would get him.

We sent the print in, and then there was nothing to do but wait for the results. Vince scurried away on some other errand, and I just sat for a few minutes. Deborah seemed excited, and as close to happy as she got on the job. She was always very upbeat when she thought she was closing in on a bad guy. For just a second I almost wished I had feelings, so I could get that kind of positive surge of purpose and fulfillment. I never got any sort of glow from my work, just a kind of dull satisfaction when things went well. My only real sense of happy self-affirmation came from my hobby, and I was trying not to think about that right now. But that slender file at home in my study contained three names. Three very intriguing candidates for oblivion, Dexter style, and pursuing any one of them would almost certainly relieve my feelings of low self-worth and bring a bright synthetic smile to my face.

But this was not the time for that, not with an unknown Witness closing in on me, and the entire police force on edge over the untimely and unpleasant demise of Klein, and now Gunther. Every cop in the greater Miami area would be working each shift with extra diligence in hopes of becoming the Hero of the Day, the cop who caught the killer, and although all that extra watchfulness would make the streets temporarily a little safer for most of us, it would also make things a little too risky for a Dexter Dalliance.

No, a recreational side trip was not the answer, not in this climate of frenzied, hostile police vigilance. I had to find my Witness, and until then just resign myself to being paranoid, grumpy, unhappy, and unfulfilled.

But when you came right down to it—so what? From what I could learn by watching my fellow inhabitants of this vale of tears, everybody else was just as wretched at least two-thirds of the time. Why should I be exempt merely because I had an empty heart? After all, even though Lily Anne made being human thoroughly worthwhile, there were bound to be less rewarding aspects of personhood, and it was only fair that I should have to suffer through the bad parts, too. Of course, I had never been a big believer in fairness, but I was clearly stuck with it for now.

My sister, however, was not. Just as I was concluding that everything was horrible and it truly served me right, she burst into my office like the Charge of the Light Brigade. "Have you got anything yet?" she said.

"Debs, we just sent it off," I said. "It's going to take a little time."

"How long?" she said.

I sighed. "It's one partial print, sis," I said. "It could take a few days, maybe up to a week."

"That's bullshit," she said. "I don't have a week."

"It's a huge database," I said. "And they get requests from all over the country. We have to wait our turn."

Deborah ground her teeth at me, so hard I could almost hear enamel flaking off. "I need the results," she said through a clenched jaw, "and I need them *now*."

"Well," I said pleasantly, "if you know a way to make a database hurry up, I'm sure we'd all love to hear it."

"Goddamn it, you're not even trying!" she said.

I will freely admit that nine times out of ten, I would have had a little more patience with Deborah's patently impossible request and rotten attitude. But with things as they were lately, I really didn't want to knuckle my forehead and leap into worshipful compliance. I took a deep breath instead and spoke with audible patience and steely control. "Deborah. I am doing my job the best I can. If you think you can do it better, then please feel free to try."

She ground her teeth even harder, and for a moment I thought the canines might splinter and burst through her cheeks. But happily for her dental bill, they did not. She just glared at me instead, and then nodded her head twice, very hard. "All right," she said. And then she turned around and walked rapidly away without even looking back at me to snarl one last time.

I sighed. Perhaps I should have stayed home in bed, or at least checked my horoscope. Nothing seemed to be going right. The whole world was slightly off-kilter, leaning just a bit out of its normal axis. It had a strange and mean tint to it, too, as if it had sniffed out my fragile mood and was probing for further weakness.

Ah, well. If only I'd had a mother, I'm sure she would have told me there would be days like this. And the kind of mother who could say that with a straight face would probably have added, *An idle mind is the devil's playground.* I certainly didn't want to upset Hypothetical Mom, and I didn't want to go on the swing set with Satan either, so I got out of my chair and tidied up the lab.

Vince stuck his head in a minute later and watched me with puzzled concentration as I wiped down the counter with some cleaner and paper towels. He shook his head. "Such a neatnik," he said. "If I didn't know you were married, I would wonder about you."

I lifted a small stack of case files off the counter. "These all need to be filed," I said.

He held up a hand and backed away. "My back is acting up again," he said. "No heavy lifting, doctor's orders." And he disappeared down the hall. Dexter Deserted—but it fit the general trend of recent events, and I was sure I would get used to it sooner or later. In any case, I managed to finish cleaning up without bursting into tears, which was probably the best I could hope for, the way things were going.

ELEVEN

I WAS JUST SITTING DOWN TO DINNER THAT NIGHT WHEN MY cell phone began to chime. It was leftover night, which was not a bad thing at our house, since it allowed me to sample two or three of Rita's tasty concoctions at one sitting, and I stared at the phone for several seconds and thought very hard about the last piece of Rita's Tropical Chicken sitting there on the platter before I finally picked up my phone and answered.

"It's me," Deborah said. "I need a favor."

"Of course you do," I said, looking at Cody as he pulled a large helping of Thai noodles out of the serving dish. "But does it have to be right now?"

Debs made a sound somewhere between a hiss and a grunt. "Ow. Yeah, it does. Can you pick up Nicholas from day care?" she said. Her son, Nicholas, was enrolled at a Montessori day-care center in the Gables, although I was reasonably sure he was too young to count beads. I had wondered whether I should be doing the same for Lily Anne, but Rita had pooh-poohed the idea. She said it was a waste of money until a child was two or three years old.

For Deborah, though, nothing was too good for her little boy, so she cheerfully shelled out the hefty fee for the school. And she had never been late to pick him up, no matter how pressing her workload—but here it was, almost seven o'clock, and Nicholas was still waiting for Mommy. Clearly something unusual was afoot, and her voice sounded strained—not angry and tense as it had been earlier, but not quite right, either.

"Um, sure, I guess I can get him," I said. "What's up with you?"

She made the hiss-grunt sound again and said, "Uhnk. Damn it," in a kind of hoarse mutter, before going on in a more normal voice, "I'm in the hospital."

"What?" I said. "Why, what's wrong?" I had an alarming vision of her as I had seen her in her last visit to the hospital, an ER trip that had lasted for several days as she lay near death from a knife wound.

"It's no big deal," she said, and there was strain in her voice, as well as fatigue. "It's just a broken arm. I just . . . I'm going to be here for a while and I can't get Nicholas in time."

"How did you break your arm?" I asked.

"Hammer," she said. "I gotta go—can you pick him up, Dex? Please?"

"A hammer? For God's sake, Deborah, what—"

"Dexter, I gotta go," she said. "Can you get Nicholas?"

"I'll get him," I said. "But what—"

"Thanks. I really appreciate it. Bye," she said, and she hung up.

I put down my phone and saw that the whole family was staring at me. "Set one more high chair for dinner," I said. "And save me that chicken breast."

They did save me the chicken, but it was very cold by the time I got back to the house with Nicholas, and all the Thai noodles were gone. Rita immediately grabbed Nicholas from me and took him away to the changing table, cooing at him, and Astor trailed along behind to watch. I'd had no further calls from Deborah, and I still had no idea how she had managed to break her arm with a hammer. But I could only think of one hammer in the news this week, so I had a very strong suspicion that she had somehow caught our psychotic club-hammer killer.

It didn't really make sense. The ID on the fingerprint could not have come back yet—there was no way it could have worked its way through all the layers of ossified bureaucracy in just a few hours—but as far as I knew that was the only lead. Besides, she would never do something insanely risky without me along to take the hit for her, and cornering a homicidal psycho with a hammer certainly fit in the category of "risky."

Of course, she'd never had a partner she really trusted to back her up before, and she seemed to be bonding with Alex Duarte, probably in French. And she was certainly free to work with her new partner instead of with me. Nothing could be more natural—it was even suggested by regulation, and it didn't bother me, not in the slightest. Let Duarte stick his neck in the noose instead of me. To be perfectly frank, I was a little bit tired of being her sidekick on every single perilous bust, and it was high time she stood up on her own two feet and stopped leaning on me.

After Rita put the children to bed, she sat beside me for a little while, until she began to yawn hugely. Very shortly afterward, she gave me a peck on the cheek and tottered off to bed herself. I stayed up with Nicholas, waiting for Deborah to come and claim him. He was not a bad baby, not at all, but he didn't seem nearly as clever as Lily Anne. His little blue eyes didn't have the same intelligent gleam in them, and it seemed to me that, from a purely objective point of view, his motor skills were not as advanced as hers had been at the same age. Maybe there was nothing to the Montessori thing after all. Or maybe he was just a slow learner—and there was really nothing actually wrong with that. After all, perfection is far from universal, and there could be only one Lily Anne. Nicholas was still my nephew, and allowances must be made for children less gifted.

So I sat on the couch with Nicholas in chummy silence after everyone else went to bed. I fed him a bottle, and then shortly after that I changed his diaper. As soon as I took off the wet one, he began to pee straight up into the air, and it took all my considerable skill to dodge the stream. But I got him safely rediapered and, thinking that the soothing drone from the TV might encourage him to fall asleep, I turned on the set and sat back down on the couch with him.

And there was Deborah, all over the TV screen, accompanied by flashing lights and the urgent, ultraserious voice-over of the local news anchor. The picture showed my sister cradling her left arm as the emergency med techs helped her onto a stretcher and slapped an inflatable cast on her arm. She was talking the whole time to Duarte, clearly giving him orders on something or other, while he nodded and patted her on the uninjured shoulder.

And as the anchor finished a horrible, run-on sentence about Deborah's true grit and heroism, even pronouncing her name correctly, the picture made a jump cut to another gurney as two uniformed cops followed it into the ambulance. On this stretcher a large, square-faced man strained against his bonds. His shoulder and stomach were seeping blood, and he was shouting something that sounded obscene, even without sound. Then two studio portraits appeared on the screen, Klein and Gunther, side by side in their formal pictures. The anchor's voice got very somber, and he promised to keep me updated as the story developed. And in spite of the way I felt about TV newspeople, I had to admit that this was a lot more than my sister had done.

Of course, there was no reason she should update me. She was not her Dexter's keeper, and if she was finally beginning to realize that, so much the better. So I was completely content, not at all miffed with my sister, when she showed up at last to claim her child. It was almost midnight when she finally arrived, and Nicholas and I had watched several more news bulletins, and then the lead story on the late news itself, all pretty much repeating that first tiresome bulletin. Heroic officer injured while catching cop killer. Ho-hum. Nicholas showed no sign of recognizing his mother when she appeared on television. I was quite certain that Lily Anne would have known me, whether on TV or anywhere else, but that did not necessarily mean there was anything actually wrong with the boy.

In any case, Nicholas seemed glad enough to see Debs in person when I opened the front door and let her in. The poor child didn't know yet that he couldn't fly, and he tried to wing his way out of my arms and into hers. I fumbled and clutched and almost dropped him, and Deborah grabbed him awkwardly into a tight grip with her one good arm. The other, her left, was in a cast and hung from a sling.

"Well," I said. "I'm surprised to see you in public without an agent."

Deborah was nose-to-nose with Nicholas and talking nonsense syllables to him in a soft voice while he chuckled and squeezed her nose. She looked up at me, still smiling. "What the hell does that mean?" she said.

"You're all over the TV," I told her. "The network's biggest new star. 'Heroic detective sacrificing her limbs to catch psychotic cop killer.' "

She made a frustrated face. "Shit," she said, apparently unconcerned about corrupting the morals of young Nicholas with potty talk. "The goddamned reporters wanted interviews, and pictures, and a fucking bio—they're everywhere, even in the ER."

"It's pretty big news," I said. "The guy was making everybody very jumpy. Are you sure you got the right psycho?"

"Yeah, it's him," she said happily. "Richard Kovasik. No question about it." She nuzzled Nicholas again.

"How did you find him?" I said.

"Oh," she said without looking up. "I got a match back from IAFIS. You know, on the fingerprint."

I blinked, and for a moment I couldn't think of a single thing to say. In fact, what she'd said was so unlikely that I found it very hard to remember how to speak at all. "That's not possible," I blurted out at last. "You can't get a match on a partial in six hours."

"Oh, well," she said. "I pulled a few strings."

"Deborah, it's a national database. There aren't any strings to pull."

She shrugged, still smiling at Nicholas. "Yeah, well, I had one," she said. "I called a friend of Chutsky's, inside the Beltway. He got them to hustle it through for me."

"Oh," I said, which I admit was not terribly witty, but it was just about all I could come up with under the circumstances. And it added up; Chutsky, her departed boyfriend, had many connections in all the Washington organizations with three letters for their names. "And, um, you're absolutely positive it's the right guy?"

"Oh, yeah, no question," she said. "There were a couple of possible matches, you know—it was just a partial print—but Kovasik was the only one with a history of psychotic violence, so it was kind of a no-brainer. And he even works for a building demolition company up in Opa-locka, so the hammer's a match, too."

"You took him down at his job?" I said.

She smiled, half at the memory of the arrest and half at Nicholas, who was doing nothing more interesting than staring at her with adoration. "Yeah," she said, touching the baby's nose with her finger. "Right across the street from Benny's."

"What were you doing at Benny's?" I said.

"Oh," she said without looking up. "It's almost five o'clock, and we got the match on the print, but he's listed as transient, and we got no place to look for the guy. Kovasik," she added, in case I had already forgotten the name.

"Okay," I said, brilliantly concealing my impatience.

"So Duarte is like, 'Five o'clock, let's stop for a beer.' " She made a face. "Which is a little hard-core for me, but he's the first partner I've had that I can stand."

"I noticed," I said. "He seems very nice."

She snorted; Nicholas flinched a little at the sound, and she cooed at him for a second. "He's not *nice*," she said. "But I can work with him. So I say fine, and we stop for a beer at Benny's."

"That explains it," I said. And it did; Benny's was one of those bars that was unofficially For Cops Only, the kind of place that would make you very uncomfortable if you wandered in without a badge. A lot of cops stopped there on their way home from work, and some of them had even been known to pop in for a quick unauthorized snort during working hours—a stop that would never be logged in. If Klein and Gunther had gone to Benny's right before they were killed, it would explain why there was no record of where they had been when they were killed. "So we pull up in front," she said, "and there's this taco wagon parked across the street. And I don't even think about it until I hear this kind of *boom* from the old office building over there. And then I look again and I see the sign, 'Tacos,' and I think, No fucking way."

I was a little bit irritated. It was very late, and either I was too tired to follow her story, or it really wasn't making sense. "Debs, is this going somewhere?" I said, trying not to sound as peevish as I felt.

"A *boom*, Dexter," she said, as if it was the most obvious thing in the world. "Like from a *hammer*. Hitting a wall?" She raised her eyebrows at me. "Because they are tearing out the insides of the building across the street from Benny's," she said. "With hammers and a taco wagon out front." And at last I began to understand.

"No way," I said.

She nodded her head firmly. "Way," she said. "Totally way. They got a couple of guys working in there, ripping out the walls, and they are using these big hammers."

"Club hammers," I said, remembering what Vince had called them.

"Whatever," Deborah said. "So Duarte and I go over there, just thinking it's totally impossible but we gotta check it out? And I barely get my badge out when this guy just goes nuts and comes at me with his hammer. I shoot him twice and the son of a bitch still swings the goddamned thing and gets me on the arm." She closed her eyes and leaned against the doorframe. "Two slugs in him and he would have swung it again and crushed my head if Duarte hadn't Tasered him."

Nicholas said something that sounded like, "Blub-blub," and Deborah straightened and shifted her baby's weight awkwardly in her arm.

I looked at my sister, so tired and yet so happy, and I admit I felt a little envious. And the whole thing still seemed unreal and incomplete to me, and I couldn't really believe it had happened without *me*. It was as if I had put only one word in a crossword puzzle and someone else finished it when I turned my back. Even more embarrassing, I actually felt a little bit guilty that I hadn't been there, even though I wasn't invited. Debs had been in danger without me, and that felt wrong. Completely stupid and irrational, not at all like me, but there it was.

"So is the guy going to live?" I said, thinking it would be a shame if he did.

"Shit, yes, they even had to sedate him," Deborah said. "Unbelievably strong, doesn't feel pain—if Alex hadn't gotten the cuffs on him right away he would have hit me again. And he shook off the Taser in, like, three seconds. A total psycho." And with a smile of tired fulfillment, she hugged Nicholas tighter, pushing his little face into her neck. "But he's locked up safe and sound, and it's over. It's him. I got him," she said, and she rocked the baby back and forth gently. "Mommy *got* the *bad* guy," she said again, more musically this time, like it was part of a lullaby for Nicholas.

"Well," I said, and I realized that it was at least the third time I'd said "well" since Deborah arrived. Was I really so flustered that I couldn't even manage basic conversation? "You caught the Hammer Killer. Congratulations, sis."

"Yeah, thanks," she said, and then she frowned and shook her head. "Now if I can only make it through the next couple of days."

It might have been that the painkillers were making her incoherent, but I didn't know what she meant. "Is your arm painful?" I said.

"This?" she said, holding up the cast. "I've had worse." She shrugged and then made a terrible face. "No. It's Matthews," she said. "Fucking reporters are making a big deal of it, and Matthews is ordering me to play along because it's fucking great PR." She sighed heavily, and Nicholas said, "Blat!" quite distinctly and hit his mother's nose. She nuzzled him again and said, "I fucking *hate* that shit."

"Oh. Of course," I said, and now it made sense. Deborah was totally inept with public relations, departmental politics, routine ass kissing, and any aspect of police work that didn't involve finding or shooting bad guys. If she'd been even half-good at dealing with people, she'd probably already be Division Chief at the least. But she wasn't, and here she was again in the middle of a situation that called for fake smiles and bullshitting, two talents that were as alien to her as a Klingon mating dance. Clearly she needed a warning from someone who knew the steps. Since Nicholas couldn't even say his own name, that left me.

"Well," I said cautiously, "you're probably going to be in the spotlight for a couple of days."

"Yeah, I know," she said. "Lucky me."

"It wouldn't hurt to play the game a little, Debs," I said, and I admit that I was getting a little cranky now, too. "You know the right words: 'The entire Miami-Dade team did outstanding work in their tireless effort to apprehend this suspect—' "

"Fuck it, Dex," she snapped. "You know I can't do that kind of crap. They want me to smile at the camera and tell the whole fucking world how great I am, and I never could do that shit and you know it."

I did know it, but I also knew that she would have to try again, which meant she was probably in for a couple of rough days. But before I could think of something really smart to say on the subject,

Nicholas began to bounce again and say, "Ba ba ba *ba!*" Deborah looked at him with a tired smile and then back at me. "Anyway, I'd better get my little buddy to bed. Thanks for picking him up, Dex."

"Dexter's Day Care," I said. "We never close."

"I'll see you at work," she said. "Thanks again." And then she turned for the door. I had to open it for her, since she only had one good arm and that was full of Nicholas. "Thanks," she said again—a third time in less than a minute, which was certainly a record for her.

Deborah trudged to her car, looking as tired as I had ever seen her, and I watched as Duarte climbed out from behind the wheel and opened the back door for her. She fumbled Nicholas into a car seat, and Duarte held the passenger door as she got in. Then he closed it, nodded to me, and climbed in behind the wheel.

I watched as they drove away. The whole world thought Debs was wonderful right now because they believed she had caught a dangerous killer, and all she wanted was to get on with catching the next one. I wished she could learn to exploit a moment like this, but I knew she never would. She was tough and smart and efficient, but she would never learn to lie with a straight face, which was a real killer for any career.

I also had a niggling little feeling that at some point in the next few days she would need a little PR skill, and since she didn't have any, that would make it a case for the public relations firm of Dexter and Dexter, Spin Doctors to the Stars.

Naturally—it always ended up being my problem, no matter how much it actually wasn't. I sighed, watched as Deborah's car disappeared around the corner, and then I locked the door and went to bed.

TWELVE

THE MEDIA FRENZY THAT DEBORAH'S BIG ARREST GENERATED was bigger than anyone had anticipated, and for the next few days Deborah was a very reluctant rock star. She was deluged with requests for interviews and photographs, and even in the relative security of police headquarters she was not safe from people stopping her to tell her how wonderful she was. Of course, being Deborah, the attention did not please her. She turned down all the invitations from the media, and she tried very hard to disengage herself from the workplace well-wishers without showing them any actual hostility. She didn't always succeed, but that was all right. It made the other cops think that, on top of being spectacular, she was modest, gruff, and impatient with bullshit—which was actually true, for the most part—and it added even more luster to the growing Morgan Legend.

And somehow, some of the shine even reflected onto me. I had helped Deborah solve her cases often enough, usually with my special insight into things as they really are—wicked, and quite happily so—and just as often I had been beaten, bullied, and battered in the process. Never once in all those times had I ever received so much as a casual pat of thanks on my bruised back—but now, the one time I had done absolutely nothing, I began to get credit. I had three requests for interviews from reporters who had suddenly come to believe that blood spatter was fascinating, and I was invited to submit an article to the *Forensic Examiner.*

I turned down the interviews, of course—I had worked very hard to keep my face out of public view and saw no reason to change now. But the attention continued; people stopped me to say nice things, shake my hand, and tell me what a good job I had done. And it was true enough; I usually do a very good job—I just hadn't done it *this* time. But suddenly I was the target of far too much unwelcome attention. It was disconcerting, even annoying, and I found myself flinching when the phone rang, ducking as the door opened, and even chanting the classic mantra of the clueless: *Why me?*

Tragically, it was Vince Masuoka who finally answered that lame question. "Grasshopper," he said, shaking his head wisely, on the morning when he overheard me turning down *Miami Hoy* for the third time. "When temple bell rings, crane must fly."

"Yes, and one apple every eight hours keeps three doctors away," I said. "So what?"

"So," he said, with a sly semismile, "what did you expect?"

I looked at him and he smirked back; he seemed to have some actual point in mind, as much as he ever did, so I gave him a more or less serious answer. "What I expect," I said, "is to be ignored and unrecognized, laboring on in solitude at my unique level of unmatchable excellence."

He shook his head. "Then you gotta get a new agent," he said. "Because your face is all over the blogosphere."

"My what is where?" I said.

"Lookit," Vince said. He scrabbled at the keyboard of his laptop for a moment, and then turned the screen to face me. "It's you, Dexter," he said. "A superman shot. Very studly."

I looked at the screen and had a moment of almost hallucinogenic disorientation. The computer showed a Web site with a red and dripping headline that said, "Miami Murder." And under that was a photo of a male model in a heroic pose in front of the Torch of Friendship—at the scene where Officer Gunther's body had been discovered. The model looked commanding, brilliant, and sexy—and he also looked an awful lot like me. In fact, to my astonishment, it *was* me, just as Vince had said. I was standing beside Deborah and pointing toward the waterfront, and she had an expression of eager compliance on her face. I had no idea how someone had managed to capture the two of us frozen in these completely uncharacteristic expressions, and somehow make me look so very *studly* in the process—but there it was. And even worse, the caption to the picture said, "Dexter Morgan—the *real* brains in the Cop-Hammer case!"

"It's a really popular blog," Vince said. "I can't believe you haven't seen this, 'cause everybody else in the world has."

"And *this* is why everybody suddenly thinks I'm interesting?" I said.

Vince nodded at me. "Unless you have a hit single I didn't know about?"

I blinked and looked at the picture again, hoping to find that it had gone away, but it hadn't. And as I looked I felt my stomach churn with something that was very close to fear. Because there was my face and my name and even my job all together in one convenient package, and the first thought that popped into my brain was not, *Oh, boy, I look studly.* Instead it instantly gave a shape to the anonymous unease I had been feeling, and it looked like this:

What if my unknown Witness saw the pictures? My name was right there with my face, along with my job—practically everything but my shoe size. Even if he had not traced my license plate or tracked me before, this would give him everything he needed. This was not even a matter of putting two and two together; it was looking at four. I swallowed, which was not as easy as it should have been, since my mouth was suddenly dry, and I realized that Vince was staring at me with a strange look on his face. I searched for something witty and forceful to say and finally settled on, "Oh. Um—shit."

Vince shook his head and looked very serious. "Too bad you're not still single," he said. "This would *so* get you laid."

It seemed more likely that it would *so* get me arrested and executed. I had always been very careful to avoid publicity of any kind; it was far better for someone with my recreational tendencies to stay anonymous as much as possible, and until now I had managed to keep my face out of public view. But here it was, apparently splashed across the blogosphere, and there was nothing I could do except hope that my Witness was not a reader of the Miami Murder blog. If my picture had really spread as much as Vince said, maybe I should also hope he lived under a rock—and a rock without an Internet connection at that. There was no way to cover myself; this was public nudity, pure and simple. Worse still, there was absolutely no way out; I just had to wait for all the attention to go away when things calmed down.

Things did not, in fact, calm down right away, not as far as the Cop-Hammer case was concerned—but happily enough, things did move on away from me. The details of the case began to pour out into the mainstream media. A few photographs of the bodies appeared online—originating at Miami Murder, of course, but the newspapers got hold of them, as well as some very graphic descriptions of what had been done to Klein and Gunther. Public interest shot up several notches, and when the exciting conclusion leaked out, the newspaper and TV talking heads found the headline just too good to ignore— "Working Mom Puts Psycho Killer in Time-out!"—and the press stampede for Deborah left me far behind in the dust, and made me wonder if my sister had actually been one of the Beatles and forgotten to mention it.

Debs really was a much better story than me, but, of course, she wanted no part of it. And, of course, the reporters assumed that meant she was holding out for money, which made her even less eager to talk to them. Captain Matthews had to order her to accept one or two requests for interviews with the national media; he considered it his primary job to maintain a positive public image, for himself and the department, and nationally televised interviews do not grow on trees. But Deborah was clearly uncomfortable, awkward, and terse on camera. So Captain Matthews quickly decided that Debs as PR maven was a bad idea, and concentrated on trying to get his own manly face on TV instead. TV was not terribly interested, however, in spite of the captain's truly impressive chin, and after a week or so the requests for Deborah died out and our happy nation moved on to the next Incredibly Fascinating Story: an eight-year-old girl who had climbed halfway up Mount Everest all by herself before getting frostbite and losing her leg. The interviews with her proud parents were particularly compelling—especially the mother weeping at the expense of a new prosthetic leg every six months as the girl grew—and I made a mental note to be certain not to miss their reality show in the fall.

At about the same time the press moved on, the rest of the police force got tired of telling Deborah how terrific she was, too, especially since her thank-yous were growing very close to vicious. One or two of the other detectives even began to make the kind of sarcastic remarks that a suspicious mind might assume were tinged with envy. In any case, the congratulations and praise at work dried up and the force returned to the routine brutality of life on the job as Miami's Finest. The tense, haunted-house atmosphere seeped out of the department, and things settled back into their old comfortable workday rut once more, with Debs happily back out of the spotlight and working on routine stabbings and beheadings again. Her broken arm didn't seem to slow her down too much, and Alex Duarte was always at her side on the job if she needed a hand, literal or figurative.

For my part, I crossed off a few more names on the list, but it was all happening with nightmare slowness now, and I could do nothing but plod on. I knew something terrible was about to happen, and that I would be on the receiving end. My Witness absolutely *had* to know who I was now. I had been identified by name, with a picture, and it seemed to me that it would have to be only a matter of time before those two hard facts crashed together, with Dexter in between. I moved through my day with the horrible uneasy feeling of being observed by hostile eyes. I couldn't see any sign that I was, no matter how hard and long I stared around me, but the feeling would not go away. No one was staring intently at me when I was out in public, although I imagined that I could feel his eyes on me everywhere. I didn't *see* anything out of the ordinary anywhere, not even once, but I *felt* it. Something was coming my way, and I knew I wouldn't like it when it got here, not at all.

The Dark Passenger was just as disturbed; it seemed to be pacing endlessly back and forth, like a tiger in a cage, but it offered no help and no suggestions, nothing but more unease. And my near-constant feeling of creeping dread stayed with me over the next few days. At home I found it almost impossible to keep up my mask of cheerful daddyhood. Rita had not mentioned hunting for a new house again, but it might have been because some kind of crisis involving euros

and long-term-bond yields had come up at her job, and she was suddenly too busy to do anything about it, although she still found time
to give me odd, disapproving looks, and I still had no idea what I had
or hadn't done.

It also fell to me to take Astor to the dentist to get her braces, a trip
that did not delight either one of us. She still considered the whole
idea of braces as a kind of personal Apocalypse, designed by a venge-
ful world to force her into social death, and she sulked for the entire
drive. She would not speak at all, all the way to the dentist, which
was very unusual for her.

And on the trip home, with brand-new shiny silver bands on her
teeth, she was just as silent, but more aggressively so. She glowered
at the scenery, snarled at the passing cars, and none of my clumsy
attempts to cheer her up got anything out of her except some very bitter glares and two simple declarative sentences: "I look like a *cyborg*,"
she said. "My life is *over*." And then she turned to look out the side
window of the car and would say no more.

Astor sulked, Rita stared and crunched numbers, and Cody
maintained his normal silence. Only Lily Anne knew that something
was wrong. She tried very hard to bring me out of my funk, distracting me with numerous rounds of "Old MacDonald" and "Frog Went
A-Courtin'," but even her great musical talent brought no more than a
temporary fading of my deep disquiet.

Something was coming; I knew it, and I couldn't stop it. It was
like watching a piano fall from a tall building and knowing that in
just a few seconds there is going to be a huge and terrible crash and
there is nothing you can do but wait for it. But even though this piano
was entirely in my head, I still found myself bracing for the shattering
din when it inevitably hit the pavement.

And then one morning I arrived at work to find that my piano
wasn't imaginary after all.

I had just settled into my chair with a cup of toxic sludge dis-
guised as coffee. No one else was around yet, so I turned on my
computer to check my in-box. It was all junk—a departmental memo
advising us all that the new departmental dress code did *not* permit
guayaberas, a note from Cody's Cub Scout leader reminding me to
bring snacks next week, three offers from online Canadian pharma-

cies, two notes suggesting some highly improper and rather personal activities, a letter from my attorney in Nigeria urging me to claim my huge inheritance, and an invitation for me to submit a blog on blood spatter to a homicide fan site. For just a moment I allowed myself to be distracted by the idea of writing for a Web site for murder groupies. It was absurd, bewildering, and weirdly attractive, and I could not stop myself from taking a quick peek. I opened the e-mail.

My screen went briefly blank, and for two heartbeats I felt panic; had I let in some kind of virus? But then a flash-graphics file started up, and a bright red glob of animated blood went *splat!* across the screen. It dripped down toward the bottom edge, looking realistic enough to make me feel deeply uneasy. Dark letters began to form in the awful red mess, and as they slowly spelled out my name I felt a sick jolt of dread run through me, which did not get any better when the screen suddenly flashed a blinding blast of light and then, in huge black letters, *GOTCHA!*

For a moment I could only stare at the screen. The words began to fade, and I could feel my entire life fading away with them. I was Got; it was all over. Who it was, what they were going to do—it didn't matter. Dexter was Done.

And then a paragraph of text appeared, and with a sick numb helplessness, I began to read it.

"If you're like me," it said, "you like murder!"

All right, I really am like you; what's your point?

It went on:

> There's nothing wrong with that—you'll find lots of
> other people who feel the same way! And just like
> you, they love living here in Miami, where there's
> always a new case to follow! Until now it's been
> too hard to keep up with the latest in local homicide.
> But now, there's a simple way to do just that!
> Tropical Blood is an exciting new online magazine
> that offers you an insider's look at all kills on the
> current casebook—all for just $4.99 a month! This
> special rate is only for our founding subscribers! You
> must join now, before the price goes up!

There was more, but I didn't read it. I was somewhere between relief that this was mere spam, and anger that it had put me through such a very bad moment. I deleted the e-mail, and as I did my lap-top gave a muted *bong!* announcing one more e-mail, a note with the one-word title "Identity."

I moved the mouse to delete this one, too, but I hesitated for just a moment. It made no sense at all, but the timing seemed magical—one arriving as I deleted the other. Of course, it wasn't connected, but there was a kind of wondrous symmetry to it. So I opened it. I assumed it would be an advertisement for some amazing new prod-uct that would protect me from identity theft, or possibly enhance my sexuality. But that word, "identity" . . . it had been on my mind as I wrestled with the question of my Witness. I had been thinking about his identity and whether he knew mine, and now this same word in the subject line had tweaked the memory. It was a stupid, almost nonexistent connection, but it was there, and I could not stop myself from taking a quick peek. I opened the e-mail.

A page of single-spaced writing appeared on my screen, under a large stylized heading that said "Shadowblog." The letters of the headline were printed in a gray, semitransparent typeface, and under them was a shadowy mirror image of the letters done in faint red. There was no name below it, just a URL: *http://www.blogalodeon.com/ shadowblog.*

Oh, joy and bliss: I had made it onto some anonymous two-bit blogger's mailing list. Was this the price of my newfound fame? To be assailed by every semiliterate twinkie with a keyboard and an opin-ion? I didn't need this, and once more I moved the mouse to delete the e-mail—and then I saw the first sentence and everything went cold and very still.

And now I know your name, it said.

For an endless moment I just stared at that sentence. It was irra-tional nearly to the point of clinical brain death, but for some reason I was convinced that the sentence referred to me, and it had been written by my Witness. I stared, and I may even have blinked once or twice, but other than that I did nothing. Finally I became aware of a distant pounding, and realized it was my heart, reminding me that I needed to breathe. I did, closing my eyes and giving the oxygen a moment to get up to my brain and whip a few thoughts into action. The first thought was an order to calm down, followed by a very logical reminder that this was, after all, only a spam e-mail and it could not possibly be about me or from my Witness.

And so I took another breath, found it to be good, and opened my eyes. The sentence was still there; it still said, "And now I know your name," and there was still a page of writing under it. But I was very proud to discover that I had yet another calm thought, which was that looking at this page would very quickly prove that the blog had nothing to do with me. All I had to do was read one or two sentences to see that I was being a paranoid idiot, and I could go back to sipping calmly from my cup of vile coffee.

So I moved my eyes down to the second line and began to read.

Since I saw you that night in the foreclosed house your face has been stuck in my head. I have seen it everywhere, awake and asleep, and I can't shove away that picture of you standing over a heap of raw red meat that had been a human being just a few minutes before. Even you have to know it is so fucking wrong—*! And I keep thinking—who the fuck are you? Or maybe* what the fuck—*are you even human? Can someone that does that really get away with walking around in the real world, buying groceries and talking about the weather?*

I ran from you. I ran from just the sight of you doing what you were doing. But that picture ran with me, and I know I should have done something, but I didn't, and I could not get it out of my head.

And because I ran from you, it seems like I started seeing you everywhere. My whole life I never see you even once, and now you pop up every time I step out the door. I see you with your kids, or out there in the street with your job, and I can't stand it anymore.

I'm not stupid. I know it's not an accident, because that kind of coincidence is just impossible. But I didn't want to think about what it meant, because if I did I would have to do something about it. And I kept thinking I wasn't ready for that. I mean, my divorce, on top of all the other shitty stuff that keeps happening to me. It seemed like it was all too much, and to have to deal with you, too—forget it.

And then I see your picture, and it has your name and your job. Your job. I'm thinking, Holy Christ, he's a fucking cop? Talk about brass balls. How does he get away with that? And I know right off, no fucking way can I do anything about a guy like you who's a cop, too.

But I can't stop thinking about it, and the more I think the more I keep shoving it away, because I've already got way too many problems to have to deal with your kind of shit, too. And it just buzzes around and around in my head until I think I'm going to totally freak and I want to run for it, but there's no place to run, and I can't avoid dealing with you anymore because now I know who you are and where you work, and I got no more excuses, and it just piles up and whirls around in my head and it's making me fucking nuts—

And then all of a sudden it's almost like a switch going on in my brain. Click. And I can almost hear a voice saying, You are looking at this all wrong. Like the Priest used to say, every stumbling spot is really a stepping-stone if you look at it right. And I think, Yeah.

This is not another problem. This is an answer.

This is a way to make all the other bullshit mean *something, to finally bring it all together. And I may not know exactly how to do it just yet, but I know it's right, and I know I can do this.*

And I will *do this. Soon.*

Because now I know your name.

Somewhere down the hall I heard a door slam shut. Two voices called to each other, but I couldn't hear the words, and I wouldn't have understood them if I did, because there was only one thing in the entire world that meant anything:

He knew my name.

He had seen the pictures online, with my name on them, and he had put that together with what he had Witnessed me doing with Valentine. He *knew* me. He knew who I was and he knew where I worked. I sat there and tried to be calm and think of the right thing to do about this, but I could not get beyond that one wild, world-shattering thought. He knew me. He was out there and he could destroy me at any moment. I didn't have the faintest notion of who he was, but he knew me and he could expose me whenever he wanted to and there didn't seem to be a whole lot I could do about it.

And what was that about seeing me with my kids—was he threatening Lily Anne? I could not allow that—I had to find some way to get to him and stop him. But how could I, when I'd been trying to find him for two weeks and failing?

I scanned the blog again, looking for any clue that might tell me who he was, just some tiny hint of a way out of this nightmare, but the words had not changed. Still, on second reading, I saw that he had not written anything that might reveal me to anyone else. I was at least safe from that. So what was he really threatening? A physical attack on me or my family? He wrote about "dealing with" me, and I had no idea what that meant, but I didn't like the sound of it. And there, at the end, he said he didn't know yet exactly what to do—that could mean anything, and I couldn't rule out a single thing until I knew more about who he was.

I needed to find a clue the way a drowning man needs air, and I had nothing but this single page of blather. But wait: It wasn't technically blather; it was a *blog*. That implied that it was a semiregular thing, and if there were other postings, one of them might reveal something useful.

I copied the URL at the top of the page, pasted it into my browser's window, and went to the Web address. It was one of the sites that allowed anybody to post a blog for free, and Shadowblog was just one of thousands. But at least there were other entries, one every few days, and I scanned them all as quickly as I could. The very first one opened with, "Why does everything always turn to shit?" It was a fair question, and it showed a little more insight into life than I expected. But that still told me nothing about him.

I read on: Most of it was a rambling, unfocused whine about how nobody appreciated him, ending with his decision to start this blog to help him figure out why. It ended with, *I mean, I don't get it. I walk into a room and it's like they can't even see me, like I'm not real to anyone else, no more than a fucking shadow. So I'm calling this the Shadowblog. . . .* Very touching and sensitive, a true existential call for human contact, and I very much wanted to make contact as quickly as possible. But first I needed to know who this was.

I read more postings. They covered a period of over a year, and they seemed increasingly angry, but they were all anonymous, even the ones that mentioned the writer's divorce from someone he referred to only as "A." He wrote very bitterly about the fact that she wouldn't get off her ass and get a job and still expected him to give her alimony to pay for everything, and he couldn't afford two places so even though they were divorced now, he had to live under the same roof with her. It was a very touching portrait of lower-middle-class anguish, and I'm sure it would have melted my heart, if only I had one.

A's refusal to work seemed to make him madder than anything else; he wrote passionately about responsibility and the fact that not doing your Fair Share was just plain Evil. That led him to a series of observations about Society in general and the "assholes" who refused to "follow the rules like the rest of us have to." From there he rambled on into several tedious rants about Justice, and people getting what they deserved, and his apparent belief that the world would be a much better place if only everyone in it was more like him. Altogether, it was a portrait of someone with anger-management issues, low self-esteem, and a growing frustration with a world that refused to acknowledge his sterling qualities.

I read more. I hit a section of a half dozen entries in which he went on at great length about growing problems with "A"—and I really did sympathize, but why couldn't he use real names? It would make things so much easier. But, of course, then he would have used my name, too, so I guess it balanced out. I worked forward through the blogs. They were all the same sort of grouchy, self-involved drivel, until I came to an entry headed, "Snap!" I recognized the date at the top; it was the day after my rendezvous with Valentine. I stopped scanning and began to read.

> So it was just too much with "A," just one bitchy crack too many about how I couldn't even make decent money, which is a laugh since she can't make ANY. But it's like, no, you're the man, you're supposed to. And I look at her sitting there in a house where I pay the bills, and I buy the groceries, and she doesn't do shit! She won't even clean up properly! And I look at her and I don't see lazy and bitchy anymore, I see Evil with a capital E, and I know I can't take any more of this shit without doing something about it and I have to get out before I do it. So I take her Honda, just to piss her off,

and I drive around for a while, just chewing on my teeth and trying to think. And after maybe an hour, I'm up in the Grove and all I got is a sore jaw and a nearly empty gas tank. I really need to just sit somewhere and think what to do, like maybe Peacock Park or some-place, but it's raining, so I circle back south. The closer I get to home, the madder I get, and when I turn on Old Cutler some asshole in a new Beemer cuts me off. And I think, That's it, that fucking does it, and I can almost hear *something go* snap *inside. And I put the pedal down and go after him, and it's like, Dude, wake up: He's in a new Beemer and you're in a beat-to-shit old Honda. And he's totally gone in about three seconds, and I'm even madder. I turn down the street where I thought he went, and there's no sign. And I cruise for a few minutes, thinking, What the hell, maybe I'll get lucky. But there's nothing. He's totally gone.*

And then I see this house. It's totally trashed, another foreclosed place. Some dumb asshole ripping off the bank and raising the rates for the rest of us. I slow down and look, because there's an old Chevy kind of hidden in the carport, like he's still in there, living for free, while I bust my ass making payments.

I park the car, and I go around to the side door by the carport, and I slip inside. I don't know what I was thinking or what I would have done, but I know I was pissed off. And I hear something in the next room, and I sneak to the doorway and peek—

The counter. There's a hand lying there. A human hand.

But it's not attached to anything. This doesn't make sense.

And right next to it that's a foot, also not attached. And other parts, too, and oh holy shit that's the head right there on top, eyes wide-open and looking right at me and all I can do is stare back—

And something moves and I see this guy standing there, totally calm, just cleaning up and looking like no big deal, another day at the office. And he starts to turn toward me—and I see his face—

The Priest used to try to scare us with these pictures of the Devil. Horns and red face and evil stare—but this guy is scarier, because he's just so fucking ordinary-looking and real *but so totally fucking* evil *and really, really happy about that, and about being there with this chopped-up body.*

And now he's turning to look at me—

It's too much. Something just popped and I was in the car and hauling ass out of there before I even knew I was moving. And I'm almost all the way home before I think, Why didn't I do something? Even if it was only just calling the cops? It pisses me off to think I'm being a wuss, like maybe they're all right about me being nothing but a fucking shadow. I should have done something. I should still do something.

But what?

In a very strange way, it was fascinating to read a description of Dark Dexter at play. A little creepy, perhaps, and not very flattering—"Ordinary-looking"? *Moi?* Surely not. But other than that, it wasn't terribly helpful in providing clues to the blogger's identity.

I moved on to the later blogs. One of them described seeing me in the grocery store—the Publix nearest to my house, no less—and how he had slipped out of the store like a shadow and watched from his car as I came out with my groceries. And two blogs later he described our encounter that morning on the on-ramp to the Palmetto Expressway in his usual riveting prose:

I was just crawling along in the usual bullshit morning traffic, going to my stupid fucking temp job, and driving "A"'s car to save on gas, and I'm looking at the cars around me, and boom—*I see that profile again. It's him, no fucking question, totally him. Just sitting there in his shitty little car like all the other wage slaves, just totally normal. And I can't make it* mean *anything, because everything around me is so fucking normal, like it is every day, but there's that face in a car right next to me, that same face I still see in my head surrounded by chopped-up body parts, and it's right there in traffic waiting to get up on the Palmetto. . . .*

And my brain is frozen, I can't think, and I'm staring, I guess thinking, like, Is he going to do something? I mean, flames shooting out, or make a cloud of bats come out or something? And I can see *it when he all of a sudden knows I am watching, and his head starts to turn toward me, just like that night in the house, and the same thing happens—I totally panic and hit the gas and I am gone before I even know what I am doing. And I think about it later, really, really pissed that I ran like that* again—*because I am* not *a fucking noth-ing and I know I should do something, but I was out of there before I could even think, which is totally not the real me.*

And I think, So, okay, what is the real me? And I realize I don't know. Because I have been pushing it away for so long, trying to make people happy with a fake version—the Priest, and my teach-ers, and "A," and even the asshole boss at my stupid temp job, who doesn't know an algorithm from his asshole, and he's telling me *about data mapping, the prick. Even him, all of them—I try harder to make them happy than I try to be Me, and that makes me think about who I am for a long fucking time, the whole rest of the drive to work.*

Okay, who am I? Make a list: First, I admit it; most people don't notice me. Second, I believe in following the rules, and it really pisses me off when nobody else does. Really good with computers. Eat healthy, stay fit. Um . . .

Is that it?

I mean, shouldn't there be more? There's not even enough to add up to anything except another wage slave so dumb I even pay my taxes.

And I think about Him. The guy with the knife.

Because it sure looks like he knows who He is. And he's being *it.*

And another thought hits me, and I wonder: Am I really run-ning from Him because I am scared of Him?

Or am I maybe more scared of what He makes me think about doing?

Fascinating stuff, all of it, but if he was half as smart as he seemed to think he was, he actually should be running from me. Because I could not remember ever wanting so badly to see someone taped to a table.

There was a great deal more, a new entry every few days. But before I could read any more I heard a clatter behind me. I reflexively brought my computer back to its home screen as Vince Masuoka came in, and the workday lurched off the blocks and onto its well-worn path of toil and drudgery. But through that whole long day I could think of nothing except that same awful, first sentence in the blog in my in-box. "And now I know your name." Somebody knew who and what I was, and whoever they were they were not kind and gentle and wanting only to reward my anonymous good works with flowers and the thanks of a grateful nation. At any moment he might attack, or decide to expose me so that my entire carefully crafted, beautifully fulfilling life would crash and burn and it would be Dexter Down the Drain.

Whoever he was, he knew my name. And I had no idea who he was, or what he was going to do about it.

THIRTEEN

THE THOUGHT STAYED WITH ME ALL DAY, AND THEN ALL the way home. After all, it was a fairly important subject, at least to me: the impending end of all that was Me, and Me completely helpless to stop it. I was barely aware of the rush-hour traffic and hardly noticed that I had made it home somehow, apparently on automatic pilot. And I am sure that many things happened when I arrived—there was probably some kind of interaction with the family, and a meal of some sort, and then an hour or so of sitting on the couch watching television. But I have no memory of any of it, not even of Lily Anne. My entire mind was focused on that one terrible thought: Dexter was Doomed, and there was no wiggle room.

I went to bed, my brain still churning, and somehow I managed a few hours of sleep. But at work the next day, it was even harder to maintain my disguise of cheerful and geeky competence. Nothing actually went wrong; no one shot at me or tried to put me in leg irons, but I felt cold breath on the back of my neck. At any moment my Shadowy Friend might decide it was time to stop dithering and Drop the Dime on Dexter, and here I was at work in the lion's den, the one place that would make it as easy as possible to slip the cuffs on my wrists and lead me away to Old Sparky.

But the day dragged on and nobody came for me. And then the next day followed, just like it was supposed to do, and still there was no howling of hounds in the distance, no heavy knock on my door, no jangle of chains in the hall. Everything around me stayed perfectly, maddeningly normal, no matter how hard I stared around me in complete ditherhood.

It would have been natural to expect that any move to take me down would be led by an enthusiastic Sergeant Doakes, but even he showed no sign of closing in, and there had been no repeat of the ominous encounter when I found him at my computer. I saw him glaring at me from a distance once or twice, and I had moments of paranoia when I was sure he *knew*—but he did nothing except watch me with his normal venom, just like always, which was no more than background radiation. Even Camilla Figg refrained from spilling more coffee on me. In fact, for several long and weary days, I didn't bump into Camilla at all. I overheard Vince teasing her about a new boyfriend, and the bright scarlet of her blush when it was mentioned seemed to indicate that it was true. Not all that interesting to me, but at least she was no longer sneaking up on me with dangerous beverages.

But somebody actually was sneaking up on me, and I could feel him circling around out there, staying downwind but moving closer all the time. And yet, I saw nothing, I heard nothing, I found no evidence that there was even anything to see or hear, no sign that anybody at work or at home had any sinister interest in me at all. Everyone else continued to treat me with the same casual disregard they always had, totally oblivious to my profound anxiety. All my coworkers and family members seemed remarkably, annoyingly contented. In fact, happiness blossomed all around me like flowers in the spring; but there was no joy in Mudville, for Mighty Dexter was about to strike out, and I *knew* it. The heavy feet of Armageddon were tiptoeing up behind me and at any moment they would crash into my spine and it would all be over.

But it is a truism of life that no matter how much we are suffering, nobody else cares—generally speaking, nobody even notices. And so even though I was spending all my time waiting for the abrupt end to absolutely everything, life went on around me; and as if to rub my nose in my own misery, life seemed to turn strangely jolly for everybody but me. Everyone else in Miami suddenly and mysteriously filled up with offensive good cheer. Even my brother, Brian, seemed infected by the dreadful light-headed jolliness that plagued the rest of the city. I knew this because when I got home on the third night after reading Shadowblog, Brian's car was parked in front of the house, and he himself was waiting for me inside, on the couch.

"Hello, brother," he said, flashing me his terrible fake smile.

For a moment, Brian's presence made no sense, because his routine was to come to our house for dinner every Friday night, and here he was on my couch on a Thursday night. And my badly damaged mental process was so completely occupied with my Shadow that I could not quite accept that Brian was really here, and I just blinked at him stupidly for several seconds.

"It's not Friday," I finally blurted, which seemed almost logical to me, but apparently he found it amusing, because his smile grew two sizes.

"That's quite true," he said, and before he could go on Rita rushed in with Lily Anne in one hand and a grocery bag clutched in the other.

"Oh, you're home," she said, which in my opinion topped my remark to Brian for obviousness. She dropped the grocery bag beside the couch, and to my great disappointment I saw that it contained a heap of papers instead of dinner. "Brian has a list," she said, smiling fondly at my brother.

But before I could learn what kind of list and why I should care, Astor's voice came down the hall, loud enough to crack glass. *"Mom!"* she yelled. *"I can't find my shoes!"*

"Don't be ridiculous— You just had them on— Here, Dexter," Rita said, thrusting Lily Anne at me and hurrying down the hall, presumably to keep Astor from yelling again and cracking the house's foundation.

I settled into the easy chair with Lily Anne and looked inquiringly at Brian. "Of course, it's always good to see you," I said, and he nodded, "but why are you here today? Instead of Friday."

"Oh, I'll be here Friday, too, I'm sure," he said.

"Wonderful news," I said. "But why?"

"Your lovely wife," he said, tilting his head down the hall toward Rita, probably to make sure I knew he meant Rita and not one of my other lovely wives, "Rita, has enlisted me to help you search for a new house."

"Oh," I said, and I remembered that she had said something about this recently—but, of course, it had slipped my mind, since I was dwelling so selfishly on my one little problem of being on the verge of death and dishonor. "Well," I said, more to fill the silence than anything else, and Brian agreed.

"Yes," he said. "No time like the present."

Before I could come up with a matching cliché, Rita stormed back into the room, still talking to Astor over her shoulder. "The sneakers are perfectly fine; just put them on; Cody, come on!" she said, picking up her purse from the coffee table. "Let's go, everybody!"

And so, swept along in the wake of Hurricane Rita, we went.

I really and truly did not want to go house hunting, not now, not when my entire world was creaking in preparation for falling apart. The only thing I wanted to hunt was my Witness, and I could not do that from the backseat of Brian's SUV. But I didn't see any choice. I had to go along and pretend to be interested in comparative lanais and relative shrubbery, while the whole time I could think of nothing but the vastly unpleasant fate that was certain to be circling closer and closer with every four-bedroom, two-and-a-half-bath ranch house we crawled through.

And we spent the next evening after work, and that whole long weekend, and then the first half of the following week riding around in Brian's SUV and looking at foreclosed houses in our area. My frustration and anxiety grew and ate away at me, and the houses we looked at seemed to be ominous symbols of my coming desolation. Every one of them was abandoned, with ragged shrubbery and lawns gone to weeds. They were all dark, too, their power shut off, and they seemed to loom over their forsaken yards like a bad memory. But they were all available cheap through Brian's connections from his new job, and Rita tore into each one of them with a savage intensity that my brother seemed to find soothing. And in truth, even though I kept looking over my shoulder, physically as well as mentally, Rita made the process so frantic and all-consuming that I began to experience

long periods of time when I forgot about my Shadow—sometimes
five or six minutes at a stretch.

Even Cody and Astor got into the spirit of things. They would
wander wide-eyed through the desolation of each abandoned house,
staring into the empty rooms and marveling that such opulent emptiness might soon be all theirs. Astor would stand in the center of
some pale blue bedroom with holes kicked in the walls, and she
would stare up at the ceiling and murmur, "My room. *My* room."
And then Rita would hustle in and herd everyone back out to the car,
spewing out staccato monologues about this being "the wrong school
district, and the tax base is way too high—the neighborhood has a
zoning change on appeal, and the whole house needs to be rewired
and repiped," and Brian would smile with genuine synthetic delight
and drive us to the next house on his list.

And as Rita found brand-new and increasingly absurd objections
to each house we looked at, the novelty wore off. Brian's smile grew
thinner and more patently phony, and I began to get very annoyed
every time we climbed into his car to see one more house. Cody and
Astor, too, seemed to feel that the whole thing was keeping them
away from their Wii far too long, and why couldn't we just pick a
nice big house with a pool and be done with it?

But Rita was relentless. For her, there was always one more house
to look at, and every single Next One was going to be *the* One, the
ideal location for Total Domestic Felicity, and so we would all race
grumpily on to another perfectly serviceable home, only to discover
that a leak in the sprinkler system in the backyard was almost certainly causing a sinkhole under the turf, or there was a lien on the second mortgage, or killer bees had been seen nesting only two blocks
away. It was always something, and Rita seemed unaware that she
had spun off alone into a deep neurotic fugue of perpetual rejection.

And even more tragically, since our evenings, and all day Saturday and Sunday, were spent on this endless quest, they were *not* spent
at home eating Rita's cooking. I had thought I could put up with the
house search as long as her roast pork turned up now and then, but
that was now no more than a distant memory, along with her Thai
noodles, mango paella, grilled chicken, and all else that was good
in the world. My dinner hour became a hellish maze of burgers and

pizzas, gobbled down in a grease-stained frenzy in between rushing through unsuitable houses, and when I finally put my foot down and demanded real food, the only relief I got was a box of chicken from Pollo Tropical. And then we were off into the endless cycle of negativity again, flinging away the chance to own another wonderful bargain, merely because the third bathroom had vinyl paneling instead of tile, and anyway the hot tub didn't leave any room for a swing set.

And although Rita seemed to be generating real bliss for herself with her constant rejection of everything that had four walls and a roof, the endless quest did nothing for me except add to my feeling that I was watching helplessly as impending disaster roared down at me. I went home from our house hunting hungry and numb, and I went to work the same way. I managed to cross off only three addresses on my Honda list, and although that was not nearly enough, I could do nothing but grind my teeth and carry on with my disguise as it all spiraled upward into dizzy heights of aggravated frustration.

It was first thing in the morning on Wednesday when the great pimple that was Dexter's Current Life finally came to a head. I had just settled in at my desk and begun to brace myself for another eight hours of wonder and bliss in the world of blood spatter, and I was actually feeling mildly grateful to be away from Rita's frenetic search for the perfect home. Why did everything seem to go wrong all at once? It may have been sheer self-flattery, but I thought I was pretty good at handling a crisis—as long as they came at me one at a time. But to have to deal with finding a house and living on awful fast food and Astor's braces and everything else while waiting for my unknown Shadow to strike in some unspecified way—it was starting to look like I would unravel long before I could handle anything at all. I had done so well for so long—why was it suddenly so hard to be me?

Still, I was apparently stuck with being myself, since nobody was offering me any better choices. So in a pitiful attempt to stop fretting and soldier on, I took two deep breaths and tried to put things in their proper perspective. All right: I was in a little bit of a bind, maybe several of them. But I had always found a way out of trouble before, hadn't I? Of course I had. And didn't that mean that I would somehow find a way out of the mess I was in now? Absolutely! That was who I was—a true champion who always came out on top. Every time!

And so even though I felt like a cheerleader for a team that wasn't even in the game, I pasted a horrible fake cheerful grin on my face and got right to work by opening my e-mail.

But of course, that was exactly the wrong thing to do if I wanted to maintain my artificial optimism. Because naturally enough, the very first e-mail waiting for my attention was titled, "Crunch." And there was absolutely no doubt in my mind who had sent it.

I have to say that my hand was not really trembling as I clicked it open, but that may have been only because of nervous exhaustion. And the e-mail was, in fact, exactly what I had thought: another note from my favorite correspondent. But this time it was brief and personal, rather than one of his long and rambling Shadowblogs. Just a few lines, but quite enough:

> *I have finally figured out that we are more alike than you might want to think, and that is not good news for you. I know what I am going to do, and I am going to do it your way, and that is even worse news for you. Because now you can guess what's coming but you can't guess when.*
>
> *It's crunch time.*

I stared at those few lines long enough to make my eyes ache, but the only thought that came to me was that I was still wearing my fake smile. I dropped it off my face and deleted the e-mail.

I don't know how I got through that day, and I have no idea what I did on the job until five o'clock, when I found myself sitting in my car once more and crawling through traffic toward home. And my blankness lasted through the first long stretch of homecoming and house hunting, until finally, after Rita had already rejected three very nice houses, I found myself looking out the window of Brian's car and realizing with growing horror that we were heading down a street that seemed vaguely familiar. And just as quickly I realized why: We were driving down the street toward the house where I had disposed of Valentine, and been caught in the act, the very place where all my misery and peril had begun—and just to make sure I collected my full share of unhappiness, Brian pulled the car over and parked it right in front of that exact house.

I suppose it made a certain sick sense. After all, I had chosen the house because it was foreclosed, and it was in the general area where we already lived, and in any case it was already clear that the Hand of Fate was working overtime to heap agony on poor undeserving Dexter. So I really should have expected it; but I hadn't, and here it was anyway, and once again I was reduced to doing nothing but blinking stupidly—because what, after all, could I say? That I didn't like this place because I had chopped up a clown here?

So I said nothing, and merely climbed out of the car and mutely followed the herd into that house of horror. And shortly I found myself standing in the kitchen right beside the counter that had been the very stage for Valentine's final performance. But instead of holding a knife I was clutching Lily Anne and listening to Rita babble on about the high cost of getting mold out of the crawl space under the roof, while Cody and Astor slumped to the floor with their backs against the butcher-block counter. Brian's eyes glazed over and his fake smile slid down his face and off the end of his chin; my stomach cleared its throat and growled a protest at the harsh treatment it had been getting lately, and all I could think about was that here I was in the one place I really and truly didn't want to be. I would soon be dead or in jail, and because I was standing in the very kitchen where things had started to go wrong, I couldn't think straight about anything at all. My stomach rumbled again, reminding me that I wasn't even getting a decent last meal before my certain demise. Life was no longer even a cruel mockery; it had turned into an endless, pointless piling on of petty torments. And just to ratchet things up one more unnecessary notch, Rita began to tap her toe on the floor, and, as I glanced reflexively at her foot, I saw what seemed to be a small dark stain—was it possible? Had I missed a spot of vile sticky clown blood in my frenzied hurried cleanup? Was Rita really tip-tapping her toe in a dried blotch of something I had overlooked?

The world shrank down to that one small spot and the metronomic beat of Rita's toe and for a long moment nothing else existed as I stared, and felt the sweat start, and heard my teeth begin to grind—

—and suddenly it was all too much and I could not stand another

moment of this eternally repeating melodramatic loop and something deep inside me stood up, flexed its wings, and began to bellow.

And as this wild roar rattled the glass of my inner windows the
mild and patient acceptance that had been my disguise for the last
few nights shattered and crashed to the ground in a heap of flimsy
shards. The real me kicked through the rubble to center stage and I
stood there liberated, Dexter Unbound. "All right," I said, and my
voice cut through the blather of Rita's never-ending objections. She
paused in midwhine and looked at me, surprised. Cody and Astor
sat up straight as they recognized the tone of Dark Command that
had come into my voice. Lily Anne shifted uneasily in my arms, but
I patted her back without taking my eyes off Rita. "Let's go home," I
said, with the sharp-edged firmness I felt growing in the depths of
my shadow self. "The old not-big-enough home."

Rita blinked. "But Brian has one more place for us to see tonight,"
she said.

"There's no point," I said. "The roof needs to be repiped and the
kitchen clashes with the zoning. We're going home." And without
pausing to enjoy her blank astonishment I turned from the room and
headed for Brian's car. Behind me I heard Cody and Astor scuffle
to their feet and charge after me, and as I reached the car they had
already caught up and started to argue about which game they were
going to play on the Wii when we got home. Moments later Rita trickled out, with Brian at her elbow urging her along with soothing pho-
niness and real eagerness.

A very puzzled-looking Rita climbed into the front seat, and
before she was even buckled in, Brian got behind the wheel, started
the engine, and took us home.

FOURTEEN

RITA WAS UNCHARACTERISTICALLY QUIET ON THE DRIVE back to our old too-small house. And when Brian dumped us at the curb and roared happily away into the sunset, she trudged slowly up to the front door behind the rest of us with an expression of puzzled concern on her face. As I put Lily Anne into her playpen and Cody and Astor settled down in front of the Wii, Rita disappeared into the kitchen. In my ignorance, I thought this might be a good thing—perhaps she would whip up a late dinner to wash away the accumulated grease of all our fast-food meals? But when I followed her a moment later I found that, instead of leaping into action at the stove, she had once again poured herself a large glass of wine.

As I came into the room, she sat at the table and slumped over. She glanced up at me quickly and then looked away and took a very healthy gulp of wine. Each of her cheeks sprouted a dull red spot, and I watched her throat muscles work as she took a second large sip before putting down the half-empty wineglass. I looked at her and knew I had to say something about what had just happened, but I had no idea what—obviously I could not tell her the real truth. She gulped more wine, and I tried to focus on how to tell her that her house hunting had lost a wheel and she was spinning in tight crazy circles in the ditch. But instead I felt another flush of deep irritation, and I heard once more the slow and careful rustling of hidden wings—wings quivering with an eagerness to unfold and hurl us up and into a warm dark sky—

"It has to be *right*," Rita said, frowning and still looking away from me.

"Yes." I nodded, not sure what I was agreeing to.

"It can't just be some *dump*, where somebody crapped in the tub and the crappy wiring will burn the house down."

"Of course not," I said, on much firmer ground now; we were talking about our vastly hypothetical new house. "But sooner or later we have to choose one, don't we?"

"How?" she said. "Because it's just— I mean the kids, and . . ." She stared at me and her eyes filled with moisture. "And *you*," she said, looking away from me. "I don't even know if . . ."

Rita shook her head and took another large sip of wine and gulped it down. She put the glass on the table and pushed back a strand of hair that had flopped onto her forehead. "Why is the whole thing so— And why is everybody *fighting* me?" she said.

I took a breath and felt satisfaction gleam inside. At last the chance had come, and I could tell her, simply and clearly, without the distraction of her maniacal full-bore scattershot jumping around, that she was driving us all off the edge of the map and into the tangled scenery of frustration and madness. I could feel the words forming on my tongue: cool and reasonable syllables that would lead her cheerfully away from her fugue of eternally berserk rejection and into a calm, enlightened place where we could all relax into a rational, methodical approach—something that included eating real food again—until we found an acceptable house. And as I opened my mouth to lay out my careful, compelling words in front of her, a terrible screeching sound came from the living room.

"Mom!" Astor shrilled in a tone of angry panic. "Lily Anne threw up on my controller!"

"Shit," Rita said, a very uncharacteristic word for her. She gulped the rest of her wine and lurched up out of her chair, grabbing a handful of paper towels as she hurried away to clean up. I heard her telling Astor in a scolding voice that Lily Anne should not have *had* the controller in the first place, and Astor saying firmly that her sister was more than a year old and they wanted to see if she could kill the dragon yet, and anyway they were *sharing* and what was wrong with that? Cody said, "Yuck," quite distinctly, Rita began muttering short and jerky instructions mixed with, "Oh, for God's sake," and, "Really, Astor, how can you even?" and Astor's voice slid up the scale into a rising whine of excuses combined with blame for everyone else.

And as the whole thing climbed the conversational stairs into absurd and pointless confrontation I let out my cool and careful breath and felt a new one rush in, hot and tight and full of dim red highlights; *this* was my alternative to exposure and prison? Squealing, squabbling, screaming, and the sour-milk vomit of endless emotional violence? *This* was the *good* side of life? The part that I was supposed to miss when the end came, at any minute now, to trundle me off into the dark forever? It was beyond endurance; just listening to it in the next room made me want to bellow, spit fire, crush heads—but, of course, that kind of honest expression of real emotion would only guarantee my reservation in prison. And so rather than steaming into the living room and laying about me with a club, as I so desperately wanted to do, I took a deep breath, stalked out through the turmoil of the living room, and went into my office.

My Honda list lay in its folder, practically growing cobwebs from the last few days of neglect. There was still time tonight to see a couple of addresses; I copied the next two entries from the list onto a Post-it and closed the folder. I went to the bedroom, changed into my running clothes, and headed for the front door. Once again I had to pass through the hideous bedlam at the front of the house, which had devolved into Astor and Rita grumbling at each other as they wiped almost everything around them with paper towels.

I had thought I might slip past them and out into the night without comment, but like all my other thoughts lately, that one was wrong, too. Rita's head snapped up as I hurried by, and even out of the corner of my eye I could see her face grow tighter, meaner-looking, and she stood up as I put a hand on the front door.

"Where are you going?" she said, and the tone of her voice still carried the edge she had used on Astor.

"Out," I said. "I need exercise."

"Is that what you call it now?" she said, and although her words might as well have been in Estonian, for all the sense they made, her tone was very clear, and it did not hold even the memory of anything pleasant.

I turned all the way around and looked at Rita. She stood beside the couch with her fists knotted at her sides—one of them held a clutch of soiled paper towel—and her face was so pale it was almost green, except for matching bright red patches on her cheeks. The sight of her was so odd, so completely different from the Rita I knew, that I just looked at her for a long moment. Apparently, that didn't soothe her; she narrowed her eyes at me even more and began to tap her toe, and I realized that I had not answered her question.

"What should I call it?" I said.

Rita hissed at me. It was so startling that I could do nothing but gawp, and then she threw the balled-up paper towels at me. They opened up in midair and fluttered to the floor a few feet away from me, and Rita said, "I don't give a damn *what* you call it." And she turned around and stomped into the kitchen, returning a moment later with more paper towels, and very pointedly ignoring me.

I watched a little longer, hoping for some clue, but Rita only ignored me even more thoroughly. I like a good puzzle as much as anybody else, but this one seemed much too abstract for me, and in any case I had more important answers to find. So I decided it was just one more thing I didn't understand about human behavior, and I opened the door and trotted out into the late afternoon heat.

I turned to the left at the end of my front walk and started jogging. The first name I had copied from the list was Alissa Elan: a strange name, but I took it as a good omen. Elan, as in zest, zeal, panache. It was exactly what I had been missing lately: Dexter's Deadly Dash. Perhaps I would rekindle it tonight when I saw Ms. Alissa's Honda. And as if there really was some kind of magic in that first name, "Alissa," I suddenly felt like I had been smacked on the head with something large, heavy, and wet, and I stopped dead in the middle of the street, and if there had been any traffic at all I wouldn't have noticed if it ran right over me because I had just realized that Alissa began with the letter "A."

My Shadow had blogged endlessly about the Evil Bitch known only as A, and yet until now I had not checked the list for "A's." I had obviously been watching too much TV—far too many gray cells had gone off-line and my once-mighty brain was in a sad state of decrepitude. But I did not linger and indulge myself in an appreciation of my own stupidity. Better late than never, and I had found it. This was it, I was sure of it, the one I had been looking for, and I let that surge of unreasonable glee push me into a trot, down the street and away into late-afternoon certainty.

The house was a little more than a mile away, but on the far side of U.S. 1. So far I had seen only the houses on my side of the highway, since crossing on foot in the evening was hazardous. But if I could get across safely, I could loop past it, turn north to see the second entry, and be home in less than an hour.

I ran for about fifteen minutes on the west side of U.S. 1, jogging slowly through an area that had never quite recovered from Hurricane Andrew. The houses were small and looked neglected, even the ones that were occupied, and on most of them it was very hard to see the address. The numbers were worn off, or covered with vegetation, or missing altogether. There were a number of older, battered cars lining the street, and many of them were abandoned wrecks. A dozen dirty kids were playing in and around them. More kids were kicking a soccer ball back and forth in the parking lot of a battered two-story apartment building. I watched the children as I jogged, wondering whether they might hurt themselves climbing all over the old and rusty cars, and I almost missed it.

I had just heard the thump of a well-kicked ball and turned my head to look as the soccer ball soared through the parking lot to the cries of, "Julio! *¡Aquí!*" But as I mentally applauded Julio's skill, the ball sailed past the front of the building and I saw the address above the door: 8834. The number I was looking for was 8837; I had let myself get distracted and almost gone right past.

I slowed my jog to a walk and then came to a stop in front of the apartment building, putting my foot up on a crumbling concrete block wall as if I was tying my shoelace. As I fiddled with the lace I glanced across the street—and there it was. Wedged in beside a huge and untrimmed hedge in front of the house across the street, there it really was.

The house itself was small, almost a cottage, and so overgrown that I couldn't even see the windows. A huge, knotted vine spread over the top of the house, as if it was holding the roof down so it wouldn't crumble and fall off. There was barely enough yard in front to park the Honda, and a rusted chain-link fence closed off the backyard. The nearest streetlight was half a block away, and with the row of untended trees along the street, anything that happened at the little house after dark would be almost invisible, which made me truly hope this really was it. The car was pulled in behind a large bougainvillea that took up half the yard and poured down across the roof of the house, and I could see only one small chunk of the rear section that stuck out from the shrubbery. But the certainty grew as I looked at the car.

It had probably started life as a neat little Honda with a metallic blue finish and bright chrome strips on the side. Now it was a mess: faded, dented, sagging slightly to one side, most of the chrome pulled off, the color battered away into a kind of uncertain medley of gray, blue, and primer.

And spread across that small section of the trunk there is a large rust stain, like a metallic birthmark, and my pulse bumps up a couple of notches as dark interior wings begin to flutter.

But far too many cars have rusty patches; I need to be sure, and so I push down the anticipation that is rising up inside. I straighten slowly and put my hands on my back, stretching as if I had run a little too hard, and I look casually at the tail end of the car. I can't see, can't be sure; the bougainvillea hides too much.

I have to get closer. I need some stupid excuse to move into the yard and peer behind the leaves and see if the taillight on the far side is the telltale dangling light I remember so well, but I can think of nothing. Very often in the past I have been The Man With The Clipboard, or The Guy With The Tool Belt, and this has gotten me as close as I ever needed to be. But tonight I am already Dude Jogging By; I can't change costumes now, and I am running out of excuses for lingering here. I put my foot up on the wall again and stretch the leg muscles, furiously rejecting a series of truly stupid ideas for going into the yard and peeking behind that horrible giant bougainvillea, until I have almost decided to risk the stupidest and most obvious—just step into the yard and look, and then jog away. Ridiculous, dangerous, and totally contrary to the picture I cherish of a somewhat more than clever Me, but I am out of time and have no better ideas—

Somewhere far away, sitting on a cloud perhaps, there must be some whimsical dark deity that really likes me, because just before I let frustration push me into stupidity, I dimly hear the voices of the soccer players, calling out in three languages to *look out, mister!* And before I can even realize that I am the only mister in the area, the soccer ball thumps into my head, bounces up into the air, and then rolls across the street.

I watch the ball roll, just a little dazed, not so much from the thump on the head, but from the sheer happy, improbable, stupidly lucky coincidence of it. And the ball rolls across the street, into the yard of the grubby little house, and comes to rest against the Honda's rear tire.

"Sorry, mister," I hear one of the kids say.

I look into the parking lot at where they stand in an uncertain knot, watching carefully to see if I will take the ball and run away, or perhaps even start shooting at them. So I give them a reassuring smile and say, "No problem. I'll get it."

I walk across the street and step into the yard where that wonderful, beautiful prince of all soccer balls has rolled to a stop. I loop to the left ever so slightly as I approach the Honda, trying not to look like I am staring at the car with feverish greed. Three steps into the yard, five, six—and there it is.

For a few long and delightful seconds I pause and just look at it and let the adrenaline flood into me. There it is, that telltale dangling left taillight, the same one I saw when I was seen, the same one that blinked at me as it raced away on the Palmetto on-ramp. There is no more doubt. This is the Honda I have been looking for. Deep inside the Dark Tower of Dexter there is a rumbling hiss of satisfaction, and I feel a shadowy tickle at the base of my spine that moves slowly up my back to my neck, and then settles across my face like a mask.

We have found our Witness.

And now he becomes our prey.

From inside the moldering, vine-covered house I hear voices rising in a very nasty argument, and then the front door slams. I tear my eyes away from that gorgeous dangling light and turn to look, just in time to see a man's back as he spins away and hurries back inside again to finish the fight. I feel a flutter of apprehension; he must have seen me—but the front door slams behind him; my luck has held, and his voice rises inside, hers answers, and I have found him and he doesn't know it and now it truly begins to end for my Witness. So I walk quickly the rest of the way across the grass to the Honda, pat it affectionately, and pick up the ball.

The soccer players are still standing in their insecure cluster, and I hold up the ball to them and smile. They look at it like it might be an improvised explosive device; they don't move. They watch me with great care as I throw the ball back to them. And then it bounces twice, one of the boys grabs it, and they all race away to the far end of the parking lot, and the game picks right back up where it left off.

I look fondly at the dirty little cottage and marvel at my luck. The overgrown yard, the street without lights—the setting is perfect, almost as if we have designed it ourselves as the ideal spot for an evening of dark-hearted fun. It is shrouded, tucked away in the shadows—the fussiest monster could not ask for a better playground.

A shiver of anticipation trembles the flagpoles of Castle Dexter. We have searched, we have found it, and there is suddenly a great deal to do, and very little time to do it. Everything has to be just right, exactly the way it should be, the way it always is, always *has* to be, so we can slide back here tonight—*tonight!*—back through the comfy dark to slice our way to blissful release and the promise of safety as we trim away this small and ugly blister that has been rubbing up against the heel of our comfort. And now the chafing unwanted threat was in our sights and as good as taped to a table, and soon all would be gleaming happiness once more. One, two, three, snicker-snee, and Dexter's life would return to its bright plastic case, all happy fake normal and human. But first—a program of careful but rapid preparation, and then a very sharp word from Our Sponsor.

A deep breath to beat down the rising tide of need and let shadowy balance back in; it must be done, but it must be done *right*. And slowly, carefully, casually, we turn our face away from the house and the Honda in its yard, and we jog back the way we had come. Home for now, but we would be back, very soon, as soon as it was dark.

And Dark is coming, with a capital "D."

It was a sweaty but very contented Dexter who jogged onto his street, slowed to a walk, and sauntered into his house. And that contentment surged to a level that might almost have been happiness when I went in the front door and saw my children gathered on the sofa, blissfully killing things with their Wii, because Astor looked up—it was Cody's turn in the game—and said, "Mom wants to see you. She's in the kitchen."

"That's wonderful," I said, and it really was. I had found my Witness, had an hour of healthful exercise, and now Rita was in the kitchen—it could be stir-fry, or roast pork again at last. Could life get any better?

But, of course, happiness is fleeting at best, and usually it's a hint that you haven't understood what's really happening. In this case it fled the moment I stepped into the kitchen, because Rita was not cooking at all. She was hunched over a large pile of papers and ledgers that spread over most of the kitchen table, and scribbling on a legal pad. She looked up as I came to a disappointed halt in the doorway. "You're all sweaty," she said.

"I've been running," I told her. There was still some tint of something in the way she looked at me that I didn't recognize, but she looked a little relieved, too, which was almost as strange.

"Oh," she said. "*Really* running."

I wiped a hand across my face and held it up to show her the sweat. "Really," I said. "What did you think?"

She shook her head and fluttered one hand at the heap on the table. "It doesn't— I have to work," she said. "This thing at work is completely— And now I have to . . ." She pursed her lips and then frowned at me. "My God, you're covered with— Don't sit down anywhere until— Damn," she said, as her cell phone started to chirp beside her on the table. She grabbed at it and said to me, "Could you order pizza? Yes, it's me," she said, turning away from me and speaking into her phone.

I watched her for just a moment as she rattled off a string of numbers to someone on the phone, and then I turned away and took my crushed hopes of a real meal down the hall and into the bathroom. When my mouth had been watering for a home-cooked meal, pizza was a bitter pill to swallow. But as I took a shower it began to seem like mere grumpiness. After all, I had Things to do tonight, Things that made even Rita's roast pork seem a trivial pleasure. I ran the water very hot, and scrubbed off the sweat from my run, and then I turned the shower to cold. I let the cool water run on the back of my neck for a minute, and felt icy glee return. I was going out tonight for a rare combination of necessity and true pleasure, and to make that happen I would gladly eat roadkill for a week.

And so I toweled off cheerfully, got dressed, and ordered a pizza. While I waited for it to arrive, I went to my office and prepared for my evening activities. Everything I needed fit easily into a small nylon shoulder bag, and I had packed it, then repacked it, just to be sure, by the time the pizza arrived a half hour later. Rita was completely occupied with her work, and the kitchen table was covered with her papers. So to the delight of the children, I served the pizza on the coffee table in front of the TV. Cody and Astor actually liked the stuff, of course, and Lily Anne seemed to catch their mood. She bounced happily up and down in her high chair and flung her mashed carrots at the walls with great skill and vigor.

I chewed on a slice of pizza, and luckily for me I barely tasted it, because in the dark corners of my mind I was already far away in a little house on a dingy street, placing the knife's tip *here* and the blade *there,* working slowly and carefully up to a blissful climax as my witness thrashes in his bonds, and I watch as the hope dies in his eyes and the thrashing grows slower and weaker and finally, at long loving last—

I could see it, almost taste it, practically hear the crackle of the duct tape. And suddenly hunger rolled away and the pizza was nothing but cardboard in my mouth, and the happy chomping of the children was an irritating artificial din and I could wait no longer to return to the reality waiting for me in the little house. I stood up and dropped the last third of my pizza slice back into the box.

"I have to go out," we said, and the chilly coiled sound of our voice jerked Cody's head around to face us and froze Astor open-mouthed in midchomp.

"Where are you going?" Astor said softly, and her eyes were wide and eager, because she did not know the "where" but she knew the "why" from the ice-cold edge of my voice.

We showed her my teeth and she blinked. "Tell your mother I had some work to take care of," we said. She and her brother goggled at us, moon-eyed with their own longing, and Lily Anne gave a short and sharp "Da!" that jerked at the corners of my dark cape for just a moment. But the music was swelling up in the distance and calling for its conductor, and we had no choice but to lift our baton and take the podium now.

"Take care of your sister," I said, and Astor nodded.

"All right," she said. "But, Dexter—"

"I'll be back," we said, and we grabbed our small bag of toys and were away out the door and into the warm and welcoming night.

FIFTEEN

I T WAS FULL DARK OUT NOW AND THE FIRST RUSH OF THE FREE
night air roared into my lungs and out through my veins, calling
my name with a thundering whisper of welcome and urging me
on into the purring darkness, and we hurried to the car to ride away
to happiness. But as we opened the car door and put one foot in, some
small acid niggle twitched at our coattails and we paused; something
was not right, and the frigid glee of our purpose slid off our back and
onto the pavement like old snakeskin.

Something was not right.

I looked around me in the hot and humid Miami night. The neighborhood was just as it had always been; no sudden threat had sprung
from the row of one-story houses with their toy-littered yards. There
was nothing moving on our street, no one lurking in the shadows of
the hedge, no rogue helicopter swooping down to strafe me—nothing.
But still I heard that nagging trill of doubt.

I took in a slow lungful of air through my nose. There was nothing to smell beyond the mingled odors of cooking, the tang of distant rainfall, the whiff of rotting vegetation that always lurked in the
South Florida night.

So what was wrong? What had set the tinny little alarm bells to clattering when I was finally out the door and free? I saw nothing, heard nothing, smelled nothing, *felt* nothing—but I had learned to trust the pesky whisper of warning, and I stood there unmoving, unbreathing, straining for an answer.

And then a low row of dark clouds rumbled open overhead and revealed a small slice of silvery moon—a tiny, inadequate moon, a moon of no consequence at all, and we breathed out all the doubt. Of course—we were used to riding out into the wicked gleam of a full and bloated moon, slicing and slashing to the open-throated sound track of a big round choir in the sky. There was no such beacon overhead tonight, and it didn't seem *right* somehow to gallop off into glee without it. But tonight was a special session, an impromptu raid into a mostly moonless evening, and in any case it must be done, *would* be done—but done as a solo cantata this time, a cascade of single notes without a backup singer. This small and wimpish quarter-moon was far too young to warble, but we could do very well without it, just this once.

And we felt the bright and chilly purpose close back around us; there was no lurking danger, only an absence of moon. There was no reason to pause, no reason to wait, and every reason to ride away into the velvet dark of a Bonus Evening.

We climb into the driver's seat of the car and start the engine. It is no more than a five-minute drive back to the neighborhood of the moldering apartment building and the small crummy house. We drive past it slowly and carefully, looking for any sign that things are not as they should be, and we find none. The street is empty now. The one streetlight half a block away flickers off and on, casting a dim blue glow rather than any real brightness. Other than that the only light in this tiny-mooned night comes from the windows of the apartment building, a matching purple halo from each window, a dozen televisions all tuned to the pointless, empty, idiotic unreality of the same reality show, everyone watching in vacuous lockstep as true reality cruises slowly past outside licking its chops.

The dirty little house shows one faint light in a front window half-covered with vines, and the old Honda is still there, tucked into the shadows. We drive past and circle halfway around the block and park in the darkness beneath a huge banyan tree. We get out, lock the car, and stand for just a moment, sniffing the breeze of this very dark and suddenly wonderful night. A light wind moves the leaves in the tree overhead, and far off on the horizon, lightning flickers in a huge black pillow of clouds. A siren wails in the distance, and a little closer a dog barks. But near at hand nothing stirs and we take a deep and cooling breath of the shadowy night air and let our awareness slide out and around us, feeling the stillness and the lack of any lurking danger. All is right, all is ready, all is just what it should be, and we can wait no longer.

It is time.

Slowly, carefully, casually, we slip our small gym bag over one shoulder and walk back to the crumbling house, just an ordinary guy coming home from the bus stop.

Halfway down the block, a large old car lurches around the corner and for just a second its headlights light us up. It seems to hesitate for half a second, leaving us uncomfortably illuminated, and we pause, blinking in the unwanted light. Then there is the sudden *bang* of a backfire from the car, accompanied by a strange rattling sound as a piston knocks in unison with a loose bumper, and the car speeds up and rolls past us harmlessly and disappears around the corner up ahead. It is quiet once more and there is no other sign of life in this fine dark night.

We stroll on and no one sees our perfect imitation of normal strolling, no one anywhere close is watching anything but the TV, and each step brings us closer to joy. We can feel the rising tide of wanting it, *needing* it, knowing it will be soon, and we very carefully keep our steps from showing our eagerness as we approach the house and stroll past it and into the darkness of the giant hedge that hides the Honda and now hides us.

And here we pause, looking out from our near-invisible spot beside the rusting car, and we think. We have wanted this so very much and now we are here and we will do it and nothing can stop that but—this is different. It is not just the lack of a moon that makes us hesitate and stand in the shadows and stare thoughtfully at the

awful little cottage. And it is no sudden change of heart or twinge
of conscience or any kind of doubt in the heartless, conscience-less
darkness of our purpose. No. It is this: There are two people inside
and we want only one. We need to, we must, we will, take and tape
our Witness and do to him all the many wonderful things that we
have waited too long to do to him but—

That second person. A. The ex-wife.

What do we do with her?

We cannot leave her to watch and then tell. But to tumble her
away, too, into the long forever night is against the Code of Harry,
against all the very reasonable well-deserved Wickedness we have
always done and hope to always do. This is unearned, unsanctioned,
messy, collateral damage. It is wrong, we cannot—but we must. But
we can't— We take a deep relaxing breath. Of course we must. There
is no other way. We will tell her we are very sorry, and we will make
it quick for her, but we must, just this one very naughty and regret-
table time, we absolutely must.

And so we will. We look carefully at the house, making sure that
all is right. One minute, then two, we do nothing at all except stand
and wait and watch, trickling all our senses out into the street around
us, the small yard of this dingy little house, watching and waiting for
any slight sign that we are being watched, and there is nothing. We
are alone in a world of dark longing that will very soon burst out into
bliss and carry us along to the happy and necessary ending of this
oh-so-lovely night.

Three minutes, five—there is no sign of danger, and we can wait
no more. And we take one more cool and steadying breath and then
we slide deeper into the shadows of the hedge, stalking back toward
the fence that blocks the backyard. A quick and silent vault over the
fence, a momentary pause to be absolutely sure that we are unobserved, and then we are cat-footing along the side of the house. Nothing can possibly see us except from the two small windows, one of
them up high on the wall and made of pebbled glass, a bathroom.
The other window is small and cranked open six inches and we stop
a few feet away from it and look inside.

There is a faint glow of light showing in this window, coming from some interior room, but there is no sound and no sign of any living thing. We open our bag, take out our gloves, and pull them on. We are ready, and we move on past the window and into the backyard.

The back edge of the yard is completely blocked by a fence that is overgrown with young bamboo. The shoots are slim, but already ten feet tall, and we cannot be seen from this side either and we breathe easier. On the back side of the house a little brick patio nudges up against a sliding glass door. Grass grows up shin-high between the bricks, and a rusted round grill is pushed to one edge, missing one wheel and tilting drunkenly over. Again we pause, staring into the house through the glass of the sliding door. Nothing moves inside, and a first gray finger of doubt pokes into our ribs; is anyone home? Have we come so far and been so very ready, all for nothing?

Slowly, carefully, we move closer onto the bricks and then up to the sliding glass door, where we wait, looking and listening and sniffing the air for anything at all—and there is nothing.

We put a hand on the metal rim of the door and push with carefully increasing pressure; the door moves. We slide it open an inch, six inches, two feet, taking half a minute to make sure there is no sound and no reaction from inside. Three feet open and we stop and wait one more cautious moment and again there is nothing and so we slip in through the door and tug it closed behind us.

We stand in a kitchen: a rusted refrigerator in the corner next to an old stove, a cracked Formica counter with a cupboard above it, a stained and dirty sink with a dripping faucet. The room is unlit, but through a doorway in the far wall we can see a faint gleam of light in the next room. A whispered tickle of warning begins to prickle up our spine and we know there is something there, something in that room in the light. And now all of our focus is forward, into that next room, and the nylon noose is in our hand as we glide slowly across the floor toward the light with a near-drool of anticipation and the glee surges up inside at the thought of what now must come as we stalk silently to the doorway and look carefully around the doorframe and into the next room at what is waiting in that one small halo of light and we pause and peek into the room and—

Everything stops.

No breath, no thought, no movement. Nothing but stunned and automatic denial.

This can't be. It just can't. No way, not here, not now, not this—we are not seeing this, not at all, we can't be seeing any such thing; it's impossible, wrong, not in the script—

But there it is. It does not move and it does not change and it is what it certainly is:

It is a table under a single dim hanging bulb. An old and unremarkable metal table from some thrift shop, with a chipped white finish. And spread across the tabletop in neat bundles is something that used to be a human being. The body has been carefully sliced and sectioned and stacked into orderly piles and it is all so very perfect and exactly as it should be and it spins me into an unreal moment of totally familiar and totally impossible comfort because I know just what it is—but it cannot possibly be that and I look and I look and it still is that, exactly that.

It is a body prepared for disposal after a long and lovely session with a knife and a need and it is familiar and comforting for the simplest of all possible reasons because this is precisely the way I do it myself. And that is not possible because I did not do it and there is no one else in the world who does it exactly the same way, not even my brother, Brian, but it is there and I blink at it and look again and it is still there and it has not changed.

And it is so impossible and so nightmare perfectly just what I was going to do that I cannot stop myself from stepping toward it through the doorway, pulled closer as if it was a giant magnet too strong to resist, and I move in without breath and without seeing anything else, step toward the thing that cannot be there even though it so clearly is: one step, two steps—

And on the far side of the table something steps toward me out of shadow and without a thought I whip out my knife and I jump forward at this new menace—

And *it* jumps forward at me with a knife in *its* hand.

And I crouch and freeze with my blade raised high—

And it crouches and freezes with its blade raised high.

And in an endless moment of total disoriented teeth-bared panic I look and I blink and I see it blink back. . . .

I slowly uncoil myself and stand up straight and stare and it does exactly as I do.

It cannot do anything else . . .

. . . because it is my reflection in a large, full-length mirror. It is *me* standing there looking back at *me* standing there looking back—

Once more I am frozen, unable to think or blink or do anything but stare at the image in the mirror, because this cannot be an accident, any more than the perfectly arranged body on the table is an accident. The mirror has been set up in this precise spot to do exactly what it has done and now here I am looking at me looking back at me over a body that only I could have done like that and I am almost certain I did not do it but there it is and I do not know what to do or what to think.

So I stand there in a dim tiny cone of unfeeling impossibility and I stare at something that someone has set up just for me—just so I will find it and do exactly what I am doing, which is nothing but looking at it and trying not to believe that it can be at all what it truly is.

And slowly, finally, one skittery little thought nudges up through the dumb muck that has poured all through my brain and it squeals at me just loud enough for me to hear it and I blink, take one shaky breath, and let the thought speak to me.

Who did this?

It is a good start, this tiny little thought, good enough to get one more thought to follow it up through the mist. Only my brother, Brian, knows my technique well enough to do this. For one flickering moment I wonder if he did; he still wanted to have some brotherly playtime with me. Could this be a small nudge in Dexter's ribs to encourage me?

But even as I think it I know that it is not possible. Brian would ask, he would urge, he would wheedle—but he would never do this. And other than Brian, there is no one else in the world who has seen my work and lived . . .

. . . except my Witness, of course. That one unknown Shadow who had seen me with Valentine and blogged his way to the head of my list, the self-same maddening blatherer I had come here to turn into an exact match of what I was looking at now. And as much as it made no sense, it had to be him that had done this. He had arranged this body in my pattern and placed a mirror on the far side of it, and there could be no other explanation, but that led to one more very urgent question:

Why?

I have no answer. I can still only think that this is impossible and yet it is out of the hypothetical and into the here and now and I am looking at it and it is as real as the knife in my hand. And I take one more slow and helpless step toward it, as if I could make it all go away if I could just get close enough—and on the far side of the table, the other me takes a step forward and I jerk to a stop again and look at me looking back at me.

There I am; I, Dexter. I raise a hand to touch my face, but it is the hand with the knife and I stop halfway as the wicked blade comes near my dumbly gaping face and I just look at me. Still life with knife and numbskull. The two faces of me, Dexter the Demon and Dexter the Dope. The face looks strange to me, like it belongs to somebody else—but it is my face, the one I have been wearing all these years. I stare for a long moment, frozen by the sight of me as I really am, both of me, as if I could stare hard enough to make the two faces come together into one real person.

I can't, of course. I let the hand with the knife drop to my side once more and look down at the table, stupidly hoping that the impossible thing there would be gone. But it is still there, still real, and still impossible. One more robot step forward and I am standing over it and looking down at what I have come to do and found already done. I stare at the disjointed leftovers, and for one idiot moment a tiny hope flutters up: Was it possible that this heap of flesh was not done by but instead done *to* my Shadow? Could someone else have somehow done the happy chore for me?

I look for some clue, and from this close I can see that there are small flaws that I would never have been guilty of. And then I see a breast and I realize this is female, my Shadow is male, and the small spider-footed hope scurries away and dies. This is not my Shadow; this is someone else, and most likely his ex-wife. I move closer. Up close I can see that this is not real quality work; right there, the left hand, so messy at the wrist, hurried, chopped instead of cut with Dexter-neat skill. I reach toward it with the point of my knife and poke it to test its reality—and as I do I pause.

I have been hearing a familiar sound this last minute and it is getting louder, and I can no longer ignore it, because it is a sound I know very well and one that I do not want to hear right now.

It is the sound of a siren and it is absolutely coming closer.

Once again I freeze into stupid unmoving thoughtlessness. A siren. Coming closer. To me. Here, now. To this dingy little house. Where I am standing above a chopped-up body. With a knife in my hand.

And finally a great sick air-raid siren of alarm begins to shriek from the ramparts of Castle Dexter, rumbling up from its lowest, earth-trembling note of warning and rising to a shattering scream of panic, and we spin away from the impossibly sliced and stacked trash on the table and in one rabbit-blink of an eye we are out the sliding door and into the night. Without a pause for thought we slam into and over the back fence and windmill our arms at the bamboo, tunneling frantically through the springy shoots and falling out face-first, into the backyard of the house on the far side. And we bounce up instantly and run at the full speed of complete panic, slashing through the yard and into the street beyond just as an outside light comes on in the yard where we were lying only seconds ago.

But we are gone now, safely away and out into the street, along a sidewalk that is just as dark and overgrown as we could wish, and we stroke down the screaming chorus of alarm and fear and force our legs to listen to the cool and soothing voice that says, *Slow down; act normal. We have escaped.*

We do slow down, we do try to act normal, but the approaching siren is right there on the next street now, in front of the cottage, and its high-pitched call is winding down again to say that it has arrived, and so in spite of the wise interior words of advice to go slow, we walk a little faster than we should until we turn the corner and come back to our car where it waits beneath the banyan tree.

And we slide gratefully into the driver's seat and start the engine and drive slowly away from the small and crumbling house of horrors, slowly and carefully back toward the refuge of normal life. We don't head straight home, though; we must try to think, and we must let the tremble leave the hands and the dry terror peel off from the mouth as the adrenaline fades away and we slowly morph back into something resembling a human shape before we head back to the company of real humans, and this takes much longer than it should. We drive south on U.S. 1, all the way down to Old Card Sound Road, trying to think and understand and make sense out of this surreal catastrophe of an evening—trying, and failing. Slowly the sick wet panic drains away, but the answers don't flow in to take its place, and all the way home there is only one single thought repeating endlessly through my numb and shattered brain, one thought that tumbles and echoes through the dark stone halls of Dexter's Dome. And no answer rises up to greet this thought and so it ricochets around in brittle confusion and repeats itself endlessly and as I finally park my car in front of my house I find that my lips are moving and repeating this same stupid single thought:

What just happened?

SIXTEEN

I T SHOULD NOT HAVE BEEN MUCH OF A SURPRISE, BUT I DID
not sleep very much that night. Eyes open or eyes shut, all I could
see or think about was that body in the small house, so very
nearly Dexter-right, and Dexter himself standing above it gaping at
his reflection, both of us drooling stupidly as the siren races closer
and closer—

It had all been a setup, a trap, flawlessly designed to catch nobody
but me, and it had so nearly worked. It had been perfectly baited,
drawing me in and then stunning me stupid with the body arranged
just as I might have done—I had seen so many bodies just like it, and
they had always brought me comfort, and it did not seem fair that
this one should steal my sleep, fill me with fear, slam nearly human
dread into all my thoughts. Was this what it was like to have a conscience? To roll around in bed all night with the thought that you
had done something terribly wrong and at any minute it was going
to rear up and crush you? I didn't like the feeling at all, and I liked
even less the thought that my Shadow had set me up so neatly and
very nearly got me.

But what could I do? What could I possibly come up with to
find and finish this awful lurking menace? Tracing the Honda had

been my best shot, my only shot, and I had fired it perfectly, only to find my Witness three steps ahead of me and looking back with a mocking grin. What was left for me now except to wait for his next move? Because there would be a next move; I did not doubt that for a moment. And I had no way to know what it would be, where it would come from—all I could know was that this first try had been very good, and the next one was bound to be better.

And so I rolled across the sheets all night, fretting and gnashing my teeth in helpless frustrated anxiety, finally dropping into blank and empty sleep around five thirty, and jerked right back out of it by the alarm clock at seven o'clock. I lay there for several stiff and numb minutes, trying to convince myself that it had all been a bad dream, but I was not nearly persuasive enough. It had happened. It was real—and I did not have even a tiny hint of what to do about it.

I stumbled into the shower and then into my clothes, and somehow I made it all the way to the table for breakfast, hoping to find some small relief there. And Rita rose to the occasion. She had filled the tabletop with the congenial clutter of blueberry pancakes and bacon. I collapsed into my chair and she thumped a steaming mug of coffee in front of me, and then she paused, hovering over me with that strange expression of half disapproval on her face until I looked up at her.

"You were out late," she said, a little more grimly than I was used to from her, and I wondered why.

"Yeah, sorry," I said. "I had some, um, tests to run. At the lab."

"Oh, tests," she said, "at the *lab*." And then Astor came in and slammed herself into a chair.

"Why do we have to have pancakes?" she said.

"Because they're *bad* for you and I want you to *suffer*," Rita snapped at her, and turned away to the stove. Astor watched her with an almost comical expression of surprise on her face, which vanished right away when she saw me looking at her.

"The blueberries get stuck in my *braces*," she mumbled grumpily at me, and then Cody came in and Lily Anne threw her spoon in a perfect arc to the back of Astor's head. Astor said, "Ow," Cody laughed, and then all pretense of calm and dignified behavior fled from the room as Astor jumped up, knocking her plate onto the floor, where it broke into three large pieces and a scattered pile of food. She ignored the mess and erupted into self-pitying rage while Rita cleaned up, gave her another plate, and scolded her. Lily Anne started to wail, and Cody simply sat and smirked and, when he thought no one was looking, took a piece of Astor's bacon.

I pulled Lily Anne out of her chair, partly to stop her crying and partly to protect her from Astor, and I held her on my lap with one hand while I sipped coffee with the other. It was several minutes before Astor stopped threatening her brother and sister and the uproar died away to the normal clangor of a weekday morning. I finished my pancakes and had a second cup of coffee; it didn't do a whole lot to get my brain moving, but by the time I finished it I was at least alert enough to drive, so with no other plan available to me besides following everyday routine, I put my mug in the sink and headed numbly in to work.

I could feel myself loosening up a little on the drive in. It wasn't because I had come up with any kind of Master Plan, or because I had realized that Things were not really That Bad; Things *were* that bad, and maybe worse. But as always, I found the vicious, backstabbing zest of Miami traffic kind of soothing, and on top of that I always take comfort in routine. By the time I arrived at work, my shoulders were no longer hunched up around my ears, and when I arrived at my desk I had actually unclenched my teeth. It didn't really make sense, but there it was. Unconsciously, I suppose I thought of work as some kind of refuge. After all, my little office was right there in police headquarters, surrounded by hundreds of hard-eyed men and women with guns who were sworn to protect and serve. But on this morning, when of all times I needed my job to be a snug and safe shelter from the storm, it turned out to be nothing but one more nail in the lid of Dexter's coffin.

I really should have seen it coming. I mean, I knew very well that my job involved going to crime scenes. And I knew just as well that a crime had been committed last night. It was a very simple equation of cause and effect, and it should not have been any kind of unpleasant shock to find myself standing once more in the dingy little room I had so recently fled, and looking down at the Dexter Duplicate mound of body parts.

But it was a shock, and it was very unpleasant, and it got even more so as the morning wore on through all the ordinary rituals of forensic magic. Each standard step of the process brought its own new jolt of panic. When Angel Batista began to dust for fingerprints, I sweated through several minutes of furiously trying to remember whether I had kept my gloves on the whole time. Just when I decided that I definitely had, Camilla Figg took her camera out into the yard and began to photograph footprints—my footprints! And I spent another five awful minutes stupidly reassuring myself that I was wearing different shoes this morning and I could get rid of the ones I'd worn last night as soon as I got home. And then, as if to prove that I really had descended into total idiocy, I spent several more minutes wondering if I could really afford the expense of throwing away a pair of perfectly good shoes.

I finished my own work fairly quickly; there was only a little bit of blood on the table with the body, and a few small traces on the floor underneath. I sprayed my Bluestar in a couple of likely spots in order to look diligent, but considering the funk I was in, I don't think I would have noticed anything smaller than a two-gallon spatter. All my attention was on my fellow crime scene wonks. Each procedure they performed sent a new spasm of anxiety through my system and another trickle of sweat down my back, until I was completely frazzled and my shirt was plastered to my body.

I had never before had such intense justification for anxiety, and yet even as I sweated and fretted it all seemed slightly unreal; only a few hours ago I had been right here in this same grungy room, confronting one of the great shocks of my long and wicked life. And now here I was again, in theory part of a team that was trying to find some trace of *me*, while the other me stood by watching the proceedings with frantic angst in case I really did. It was a nearly surreal clash of Dark Dexter with Dexter on Duty, and for the first time I wasn't sure I could keep the two parts of myself separate.

At one point I even caught sight of myself in the mirror in nearly the same position I'd been in last night—this time holding a bottle of Bluestar instead of a knife—and the two disconnected realities came crashing together. For a few minutes, the sounds of the surrounding forensic hustle faded completely away, and I was all alone with myself. It wasn't terribly comforting; I just stared at my image, trying to make sense of a picture that suddenly made no sense at all.

Who was I? What was I doing here? And most important, why wasn't I running for my life? The idiotic, pointless questions ran through my brain in a repeating loop until even the simple words seemed foreign to me and I just stood and looked at my suddenly unfamiliar image.

I probably would still be there if Vince hadn't finally jarred me out of my fugue.

"Very nice," he said, "and still very studly. Now get over yourself."

His face swam into focus in the mirror, suddenly right there beside the image of my own, and the sound track of the room came back on. I realized once more where I was, although none of Vince's words had registered. I jerked my head away from the mirror to face him.

"I'm sorry, what?" I said.

He snickered. "You've been staring at yourself in the mirror for, like, five minutes," he said.

"I, um, I was thinking about something," I said feebly.

Vince shook his head and looked very solemn. "Always a bad idea to cloud the brain, young Skywalker," he said, and he moved away to the other side of the room. I shook myself and went back to pretending to work. I floated through the rest of the morning in my cloud of adrenaline and alienation, the whole time feeling as if I might split apart at the seams at any minute.

But I didn't fall apart or burst into flames. Somehow, I survived. I know only too well just how fragile a human body is, but Dexter must be made of truly stern stuff, because I lived through that whole dreadful morning without suffering a stroke or a fatal heart attack, or even running out into the street with a shattered mind, yammering confessions and pleas for clemency. And in spite of their diligent and very practiced efforts, all the mighty labor of the forensics team failed to turn up even the faintest sign that I had been there the night before. Dexter had survived, against all the odds, and somehow he made it back to the office in one whole but badly jangled piece.

I slumped into my chair with real relief, and tried to concentrate on breathing normally for a little while, and it actually seemed to work. It does not speak well for my intelligence, but even with all the mounting evidence to the contrary, I still felt safe sitting at my desk. I closed my eyes and tried to make myself relax just a bit, trying to think things through in a calm and rational way. All right: I had been forced into the position of trying to catch myself. And I had almost been caught, but I'd gotten away. It had not been fun to return to the nightmarish scene in my role as Daytime Dexter, but I'd lived through that, too, and it didn't seem likely that anyone would find any evidence to connect me to the body on the table.

I slowly began to persuade myself that Things were really not as bad as they seemed, and through sheer pigheaded persistence, I very nearly convinced myself. And then I made the very grave mistake of taking one last deep breath, plastering a horrible fake smile on my face, and returning to the workday by dutifully checking my e-mail.

And when I did, all the carefully constructed artificial tranquillity flushed out of me like it had never existed at all as I saw that anonymous e-mail with the one-word title:

Closer.

I did not know what that word was supposed to mean, but I knew instantly who had written it and sent it to me and in that endless frozen moment of reading and rereading that one word I felt once more the awful churning panic and it crashed up higher and higher until I thought I would scream. . . .

I took a deep breath and tried to wrestle down the panic, but it had me pinned to the mat, and my hand was shaking as I clicked the mouse to open the e-mail. And as I read, a wild hissing rose up inside me and all calmness drained out of the world.

Like the others, this one started with the heading:

Shadowblog

But this time there was one startling difference. The shadow of the title, which had previously been a faint red, had grown to an enormous pool of what was absolutely meant to be blood. And now a small trail of blood-red footprints led from the heading down to the blog's one-word title, *Closer.* With a truly sick feeling of dread, I looked under the title and began to read.

I am learning so much about myself—and even more about you. For instance, I didn't know you were so fast on your feet. But you must be, because you got away somehow. You must have been quite a sight, racing through the night with your tail between your legs. Wish I'd been there with my camera.

I've learned a lot of other stuff about you, too. I've been watching you when you have no idea you're being watched—you, with your bags of groceries and your car seat, and on the job with that stupid spray bottle, trying to pretend you're just like everybody else. It's a pretty good act, and I ought to know. I've been acting my whole life, too. And when I said I am learning about myself? Guess what I can do now?

I know you've read my blogs. It's simple for me to know who comes to my page. I have to say I'm pretty good with computer stuff. You're finding that out. So you read my blog and you know I am just divorced and I don't like it. I was raised that divorce is not an option, and my wife? Let's just say she didn't think that way, or maybe at all. And I tried to reconcile, and I tried to show her divorce was wrong, and she just got bitchier and bitchier, and worse than that I began to realize that it wasn't just bitchy, it wasn't just lazy—she was amoral, evil, just as evil as if she'd killed somebody. And she is incurable, because she is a psychopath who sucks the life out of other people and contributes nothing but pain and misery, and she can't change so she had to be stopped.

Some people just don't have a sense of Right and Wrong. Born that way. Like you, for instance. And like my ex-wife. And when she is screaming at me to get the fuck out and never come back and fucking mail *the alimony check from now on—and I step outside and see* you *standing there in the yard . . .*

Hey, I'm pretty quick on my feet, too. You didn't see me, except maybe my back. And as I went back inside, and looked at her standing there with her mouth open, and thought about you standing outside and I know *you're thinking about coming back to get me—I guess I would say it just all came together and I knew who I am supposed to be now and what I am supposed to do. Old Me would have run for his life at the sight of you. But New Me saw how perfect this was, because it really is all about taking responsibility and suddenly I really understand for the first time just how far that goes and what I am supposed to do about it, which is . . . Get rid of her and you at the same time. Take out two Bad People with one stroke. It all adds up now. That's who I am. I was put here to deal with the rule breakers, the ones who have gone too far and can't come back. You. My very-ex-wife. And who knows who else? There's lots of 'em. I see 'em every day.*

So in a way I am becoming like you, right? The big difference is, I do it to stop people like you. I do it for Good. But hey, thanks for being a great role model. Maybe I should even thank you for my new girlfriend, except I don't think she's going to last too long.

I hope you don't think you are safe. I hope you don't think it's over. Because I know who you are and where you are and you don't know a thing about me. And think about this:

I am learning from you.

I am learning to do just exactly what you do, and I am going to do it to you. You will never know when or where. You can't know anything at all except that I am here and I am moving even closer.

Do you hear something behind you?

Boo. It's me.

Closer than you think . . .

I don't know how long I sat there without moving, thinking, or breathing. It probably wasn't as long as it felt, because the building where I sat had not crumbled into dust, and the sun had not turned cold and fallen from the sky. But it was still a very long time before a single jagged thought managed to penetrate the cold and empty vault between my ears, and when it finally did register I still couldn't do any more than take a large and sharp breath and let that thought echo around all alone.

Closer . . . ?

I read through the terrible thing again, desperately searching for some small clue that it was all a bad joke, some telltale word or phrase I might have overlooked the first time to show me I had misunderstood. But no matter how many times I read the lumpy, self-indulgent prose, it stayed the same. I found no hidden meaning, no invisible-ink message with a phone number and a Facebook page. Just the same wacky, annoying phrases, over and over, all adding up to the same vague and sinister conclusion.

He was moving closer and he thought he was just like me, and I knew very well what that meant, what he would try to do. He was circling around downwind and polishing his fangs and blending with the scenery of my life. At any moment—now, tomorrow, next week—he might spring out at me from anywhere at all, and there was not a single thing in the world I could do about it. I was fighting a shadow in a dark room. But this shadow had real hands, holding real weapons. He could see in this darkness, and I could not, and he was coming, whether from the front or from behind, from above or below; all I could know was that he wanted to do what I do just the way I do it and he wanted to do it to *me* and he was coming.

Closer . . .

SEVENTEEN

SHE WAS DIVORCED, LIVED THERE ALONE. HER NAME WAS Melissa. Fuck, wait a second," said Detective Laredo. He flipped open a folder and ran a thick finger down a paper inside it. "Yeah," he said. "It's *A*-lissa. With an 'A.' Alissa Elan." He frowned. "Funny name," he said.

I could have told him that right away, since I'd written that name on a Post-it only a day ago, but technically I wasn't supposed to know until he told us, so I held my tongue. And anyway, from what I knew of him, Laredo was not the kind of guy who liked to be corrected, especially not by eggheaded forensics geeks. But he was lead on the case of the chopped-up woman in the grubby little house, and we had all come together for his twenty-four, the session department policy mandated on a capital case twenty-four hours in. Since I was part of the team, I was there.

I probably would have found a reason to be there anyway, since I was desperate for any hint at all about who had done this awful thing. More than anyone else in the entire department—more than anyone else in the entire world of law enforcement, all across the globe—I wanted to find Alissa's killer and bring him to justice. But not the old, slow, feeble-witted whorish crone that is Miami's legal system. I wanted to find him myself and personally drag him down the steps to Dexter's Temple of Dark and Final Justice. So I sat and squirmed and listened as Laredo led us all through the sum total of what we knew, which turned out to be a little bit less than nothing.

There was no real forensic evidence, except for a few footprints from a New Balance running shoe, very common model and size. No prints, no fibers, nothing that might possibly lead to anything but my old shoes—and then only if Laredo hired a very good scuba diver to find them.

I contributed my dose of nothing on the topic of blood spatter, and waited impatiently until somebody finally said, "Divorced, right?" and Laredo nodded.

"Yeah, I put somebody on finding her ex-husband, guy named Bernard Elan," he said, and I perked up and leaned forward. But Laredo shrugged and said, "No luck. The guy died two years ago."

And he may have said more, but I didn't hear it, because in my own unobtrusive way I was reeling from the shock of hearing that Alissa's ex-husband had been dead for two years. I might wish with all my heart that it was true, but I knew very well that he was far from dead and he was trying very hard to make *me* dead instead. But Laredo was a pretty good cop, and if he said the man was dead, he had a very good reason for thinking it was true.

I tuned out the dull drone of routine cop talk and thought about what that meant, and I came up with only two possibilities. Either my Witness was not really Alissa Elan's ex-husband—or else he had somehow managed to fake his own death.

There was no reason on earth to make up an entire pretend life, complete with months of false blogs about "A" and his divorce from her. And he had, quite clearly, seen me there in her yard looking at the Honda—it had been his angry voice inside the house, and his back I had seen going inside. So I had to believe that this much was true: He really was Alissa's ex, and he really had killed her.

That meant he had fooled the cops into thinking he was dead.

The hardest part of faking your own death was fudging the physical evidence: You had to provide a realistic scenario, a true-to-life crime scene complete with compelling evidence and a convincing corpse. Very difficult to do with no mistakes, and very few people got away with it.

But:

Once you get past the first part of being dead, after you have cried at your funeral and buried your body, it gets a lot easier. In fact, by putting his death two years in the past, Bernard had turned the job into nothing more than paperwork. Of course, this is the twenty-first century, and paperwork nowadays means *computer* work. There were several basic databases you would have to hack and insert your false information—and one or two of them were fairly hard to get into, although I would rather not explain how I know that. But once past the various cyberdefenses, if you could just drop in one or two lines of new or altered information . . .

It could be done. Difficult—I thought I might be able to do it, but it was tricky, and my opinion of my Witness and his abilities with a computer went up several notches, which did not make me happy.

I was still unhappy when I left the meeting. I had come with a small faint hope of finding one tiny crumb that might lead to a bigger trail of bread crumbs I could follow to find my Witness. I left with even that small hope completely demolished. Once again I had absolutely nothing. Hope is always a bad idea.

Still, there was one very small lead, and I hurried to my computer to see where it went. I did a thorough search on Bernard Elan, and then Bernie Elan. Most of the official records were wiped clean, replaced with "Deceased." He had done a very complete job, whatever he might be calling himself now.

I did find a number of old articles about a Bernie Elan who played third base for a minor-league ball club in Syracuse, the Chiefs. Apparently he was a power hitter but never got the hang of the curveball, and never got called up to the majors, and after a season and a half he was gone. There was even a picture. It showed a man in a baseball uniform in profile, swinging at a pitch. The photo was grainy and a bit out of focus, and although I could tell he did have a face, I could not have said what it looked like, or even how many noses he had. There were no other pictures of Bernie anywhere on the Internet.

That was it; there was nothing else to find. I now knew my Witness had played baseball, and he was good with a computer. That narrowed it down to no more than a few million people.

The next few days went by in a sweat-stained blur, and not just because summer had really hit and turned the heat up a notch. Dexter was in a true dither, an all-time, all-star, all-out tizzy of near panic. I was jumpy, distracted, unable to focus on anything except the thought that someone I didn't know was coming my way to do Something I couldn't possibly prepare for. I had to be watchful, ready for anything—but how? What? Where would it come from, and when? How could I know what to do when I didn't know when, why, and to whom I would do it?

And yet, I had to be ready for it every moment of every day, waking and sleeping. It was an impossible task, and it had all my wheels spinning furiously without actually moving me anywhere but deeper into a funk. In my feverish paranoia, every step I heard was *Him,* sneaking up behind me with bad intentions and a Louisville Slugger.

Even Vince Masuoka noticed; it would have been hard not to, since I jumped like a scalded cat every time he cleared his throat. "My boy," he said at last, looking at me across the lab over his laptop screen, "you are seriously on edge."

"I work too hard," I said.

He shook his head. "Then you need to party even harder."

"I am a married man with three kids and a demanding job," I said. "I don't party."

"Listen to the wisdom of age," he said in his Charlie Chan voice. "Life is much too short not to get drunk and go naked now and then."

"Sage advice, Master," I said. "Perhaps I could try that tonight, at Cub Scouts."

He nodded and looked very serious. "Excellent. Teach them young, and they will truly learn," he said.

That night actually was our weekly Cub Scout meeting. Cody had been going for a year now, even though he did not like it. Rita and I had agreed that it was *good* for him and might help to bring him out of his shell. Naturally enough, I knew that the only way to *really* bring him out of his shell was to give him a knife and some living creature to experiment on, but that was a subject I thought best to avoid with his mother, and Cub Scouts was the best alternative. And

I really did think it would be good for him, by helping him to learn how to behave like a real human boy.

So that night I came home from work, rushed through a meal of leftover Pollo Tropical as Rita worked at the kitchen table, and hustled Cody into the car in his blue Scout uniform, which he put on every week with barely controlled hatred. He thought that the whole idea of a uniform involving short pants was not merely terrible fashion but also humiliating to anyone who was forced into wearing them. But I had persuaded him that the scouting experience was a valuable way to learn how to blend in, and I tried to make him understand that this part of his training was every bit as important as learning where to put leftover body parts, and he had gone along with the program for a whole year now without any actual open rebellion.

On this night we arrived at the elementary school where the meetings were held with a few minutes to spare, and we sat in the car quietly. Cody liked to wait until just before the meeting started before he went inside, probably because Blending In was still a very unpleasant strain for him. So most evenings we would sit together and do nothing except exchange a few words. He never said much, but his two- or three-word sentences were always worth hearing, and in spite of my great discomfort with clichés, I would have to say we had Bonded. Tonight, though, I was so busy looking for something sinister lurking in every shadow that I wouldn't have heard Cody if he'd recited the entire Kama Sutra.

Luckily, he didn't seem to feel talkative, and he did no more than watch studiously as the other boys climbed out of their cars and went in, some with a parent and some alone. Of course, I was watching them all just as carefully.

"Steve Binder," Cody said suddenly, and I jumped a bit reflexively. Cody looked at me with something like amusement, and nodded at a large unibrowed boy stalking past us and into the building. I looked back at Cody and raised an eyebrow; he shrugged. "Bully," he said.

"Does he pick on you?" I asked, and he shrugged again. But before he could answer in actual words I felt a small strange tickling on the back of my neck and a slight uncomfortable shifting of nonexistent bulk somewhere deep inside; I turned to look behind me. Several cars came into the parking lot and drove to nearby spaces. I could see nothing sinister about any of them, nothing unusual that would have caused the Passenger to stir as it had. Just a short string of minivans, and one battered Cadillac at least fifteen years old.

For one brief moment I wondered whether one of them was *Him*, my Shadow, somehow already moving *closer*—because something had sent a small electric twinge up from the Basement and into my conscious mind. Impossible—but I looked hard at each car as it rolled to a stop. For the most part they were generic suburban vehicles, the same ones we saw here every week. Only the Cadillac was different, and I watched as it parked and a stocky man got out, followed by a round young boy. It was a perfectly normal picture, exactly what you would expect to see. There was nothing odd or threatening about them, nothing at all, and they went inside to the meeting without throwing hand grenades or setting fire to anything. I watched them go, but the stocky man did not look at me or do anything except put a reassuring hand on the boy's shoulder and shepherd him inside.

Not him, not possibly anything at all except what it seemed to be, a man taking a kid in to Scouts. It would be lunacy to think that my Shadow could somehow know I would be here tonight, and then round up a boy on short notice, just to get close to me. I took a deep breath and tried to clear the Stupid out. It wouldn't happen here, whatever it was. Not tonight.

And so I resolutely pushed away the small and nagging warning flag that flapped in my face, and turned back to Cody—only to see that he was staring at me.

"What?" he said.

"Nothing," I said. And almost certainly it really was nothing, just a passing twitch of the radar, perhaps caused by sensing someone's anger at their favorite parking spot being taken.

But Cody didn't think so; he turned and stared around the parking lot, just as I had. "Something," he said positively. And I looked at him with interest.

"Shadow Guy?" I asked him. That was his name for his very own small Dark Passenger, planted in him courtesy of the repeated traumas he had received from his now-imprisoned biological father. If Cody and Shadow Guy had heard the same soft alarm bell ringing, it was worth paying attention.

But Cody just shrugged. "Not sure," he said, which very closely matched my feelings. We both looked around us at the parking lot for a moment, our heads swiveling in near unison. Neither of us saw anything out of the ordinary. And then the Cub Scout den leader, a large and enthusiastic man named Frank, stuck his head out the door and began to holler that it was time to start, and so Cody and I got out of the car and headed in with the other stragglers. I glanced over my shoulder one last time, noticing with something close to paternal pride that Cody did exactly the same thing at the same time. Neither of us saw anything more alarming than more boys in blue uniform shorts, so I shrugged it off and we went into the meeting.

This evening's den meeting was like most of the others: uneventful and even a little tedious. The only thing that broke the routine was the introduction of a new assistant leader, the stocky man I had seen getting out of the old Cadillac. His name was Doug Crowley. I watched him carefully, still feeling a little twitchy from my false alarm in the parking lot, but there was absolutely nothing about him that was even interesting, let alone threatening. He was about thirty-five years old and seemed dull, bland, and earnest. The round young boy he had brought in was a ten-year-old Dominican kid named Fidel. He wasn't Crowley's child; Crowley was a volunteer for the Big Brothers program, and he had offered to assist Frank. Frank welcomed him, thanked him, and then began some discussion of our upcoming camping trip to the Everglades. There was a report on the ecology of the area from two boys who were working on a badge project on the subject, and then Frank talked about how to practice fire safety when you were camping. Cody endured the whole tedious program with grim patience, and did not quite sprint for the door when it was over. And home we went, to our not-big-enough house with its table full of Rita's papers instead of food, with no sign along the way of anything more threatening than a bright yellow Hummer with a too-loud sound system.

The next day at work was endless. I kept waiting for some terrible something to hit me from any possible angle, and it kept not happening. And the day after that was no different, and the day after that. Nothing happened; no sinister stranger loomed up out of the shadows; no fiendish traps were sprung upon me. There was no deadly serpent hidden in my desk drawer, no assegais hurtling at my neck from a passing car, nothing. Even Deborah and her blistering arm punches were taking a holiday. I saw her and even spoke to her, of course. Her arm was still in a cast, and I would have expected her to call on me quite often for help, but she did not. Duarte was apparently picking up the slack, and Debs seemed content to live on a much lower dose of Dexter.

So life seemed to be slipping back into the ordinary rhythm of Dexter's Dull Days, hour plodding calmly into boring hour with no threat of any kind, no variation in routine, no sign of change at all, at work or at home. Nothing but more of the same. I knew *it* was coming, but every day that it did *not* come seemed to make it less likely that it would come at all. Very stupid, I know, but it was—dare I say it?—entirely human of me. No one can stay on high alert around the clock, endlessly, day after day. Not even the Ever-vigilant Dark Scout, Dexter. Not when ordinary synthetic reality was so seductive.

And so I relaxed, ever so slightly. Normal life: It's comforting exactly because it is dull and often pointless, and it slowly lulls us all into a state of waking slumber. It makes us fixate on stupid, meaningless things like running out of toothpaste or breaking a shoelace, as if these things were overwhelmingly significant—and all the while the truly important stuff we are ignoring is sharpening its fangs and slinking up behind us. In the one or two brief moments of real insight we get in our lives, we may realize that we are being hypnotized by irrelevant trivia, and we may even wish for something exciting and different to come along to help us focus and drive these stupid niggling trifles out of our minds. Because staying constantly alert is impossible, even for me. The more nothing happens, the more unlikely it all seems, until finally, I actually found myself wishing that whatever it was, it would just happen so it would all be over.

And, of course, one of the few great truths of Western thought is this: Be careful what you wish for, because you might get it.

And I did.

EIGHTEEN

I T WAS A HOT AND HUMID AFTERNOON AT AROUND THREE o'clock, and I had just gotten back to my office from a routine appearance at a rather dull crime scene. A man had shot his neighbor's dog, and the neighbor had shot him. The results were typical of the unfortunate mess that results so often nowadays from our modern obsession with large-caliber weapons. I tried to maintain a professional interest in separating the dog's blood from the man's, but there was so much of both I gave up. We had a confession, so it was clear who our killer was, and there didn't seem like much point in getting terribly worked up about it. Nobody else on the scene was having much luck staying focused, either. We had all seen this sort of thing many times before, cops and forensics wonks alike, and after all the recent hammer excitement, a normal garden-variety shooting homicide seemed irrelevant and a little bit dull.

So I wrapped up my part of the work rather quickly, and as I strolled into my office and slumped into my chair I was not thinking about the outraged dog owner who was now sitting in a cell at the detention center, nor even about the poor disemboweled pit bull he had avenged. Idiotically enough, I even stopped thinking about my Shadow, since I was in the safety of my own little nook, surrounded by the might of Miami-Dade's fearless police force. Instead, I was pondering a vastly more important question: how to persuade Rita to take one small evening off from working at home and cook us a real dinner. It was a touchy problem, and it would call for a rare and difficult combination of flattery and firmness, mixed with just the right touch of compassionate understanding, and I was certain it would be a real challenge to my skill as a Human Impersonator.

I practiced a couple of facial expressions that blended all the right things into a believable mask until I thought I had them right, and in one of those weird moments of self-awareness, I suddenly saw myself from the outside, and I had to stop. I mean, here I was, with a relentless invisible enemy laying siege to Castle Dexter, and instead of sharpening my sword and piling boulders on the battlements I was playing with my face in the hopes of getting Rita to make me a decent last meal. And I had to ask myself—did that really make sense? Was it truly the best way to prepare for what was certainly coming at me? And I had to admit that the answer was a very definite, *Probably not*.

But what actually *was* the best way to get ready? I thought about what I knew, which was almost nothing, and realized that once again I had let the uncertainty push me away from what I do best. I needed to drop my passive waiting and get back to being proactive. I had to circle back downwind, find something that told me more about my Shadow, and somehow track him back to his lair and let Dark Nature take its course once more. Thinking coldly, rationally, realistically, I knew that he was no match for me. I had been hunting people like him my entire adult life, and he was no more than a wannabe, a sheep in wolf's clothing, a poor sad clown trying to turn himself into a knockoff of the Very Real Deal that was Me. And I could oh-so-easily make that overwhelming truth very clear to him—all I had to do was find him.

But how? I no longer knew what kind of car he drove. I couldn't even be sure he was still living in the same area, down in South Miami near my house. It was very likely that he had gone somewhere else—where? I didn't know enough about him to guess where he might go to ground, and that was a problem. The first rule of being a successful hunter is to understand your prey, and I did not. I needed to get a better sense of how he thought, what made him tick, even if it was only background and not actually an address or a passport number. And the only window into his world I knew about was Shadowblog. I had read and reread that tedious, self-involved drivel a dozen times already, and I had not learned anything worth repeating. But I read through it once more anyway, and this time I tried to build a profile of the person behind the rant.

The biggest building block, of course, was his anger. At the moment it seemed to be directed mostly at me, but there was more than enough to go around. It started with the unfairness of the game of baseball that never gave him a fair shot at the majors, even though he did everything they asked and always played by the rules. It rambled on endlessly about Assholes who cut corners, cheated, committed crimes without punishment, and even more Assholes who thought hacking a Web site was *funny*. He certainly wasn't happy with his ex-wife, "A," either, or with the typical Miami drivers he encountered.

The anger clearly came from a rigid and overdeveloped sense of morality, and it had been there for a long time, burbling under the surface and waiting for some reason to boil over and become about something specific. He raged against everybody who didn't follow the rules as he saw them, and spoke longingly of "the Priest" and his teachings. Wonderful news, a real clue: I was looking for an angry Catholic, which narrowed it down to only about seventy-five percent of Miami's population. I closed my eyes and tried to concentrate, but it was no good. All I could think of was how badly I wanted to tape him down and teach him about True Penance, the kind that comes in the Dark Confession Booth at the Cathedral of Our Lady of Dexter's Knife. I could almost see him squirming, fighting helplessly against the duct tape that held him down, and I had just begun to savor the picture when Vince Masuoka stumbled into the room in a complete dither.

"Holy shit," he said. "Oh, my God, holy shit."

"Vince," I said, irritated because he had interrupted the first happy thoughts I'd had in days. "In traditional Western culture, we like to separate deity and feces."

He lurched to a halt and blinked at me and then, with truly annoying single-mindedness, he said, "Holy shit," again.

"All right, fine, holy shit," I said. "Can we move on to the next syllable, please?"

"It's Camilla," he said. "Camilla Figg?"

"I know who Camilla is," I said, still peeved—and then I heard a distant rustle of dark wings and I realized I was sitting up straighter in my chair and feeling a soft tendril of interest from the Passenger slide up my spine.

"She's dead," Vince said, and he gulped and shook his head. "Camilla is dead, and it's—Jesus—it's the same thing, with the hammer."

I felt my head move in an involuntary twitch of denial. "Um," I said. "Didn't everybody agree that Deborah caught the hammer guy?"

"Wrong," Vince said. "Your sister fucked up big-time and got the wrong guy, 'cause it happened *again*, the exact same, and now they won't let her near this one." He shook his head. "She fucked up *huge*, 'cause what happened to Camilla is the same damn thing that happened to the others." He blinked and swallowed, and looked at me with the most solemn and frightened expression I had ever seen from him. "She was *hammered* to death, Dexter. Just like the other guys."

My mouth went dry and a small tickle of electricity ran from the back of my neck straight down my spine, and although it is not terribly flattering to me, I was not thinking of Deborah and her apparent fall from grace. Instead, I was simply sitting, hardly breathing, as several waves of hot intangible wind fluttered across my face and sent dry leaves scuttering through the gutters of Castle Dexter. The Dark Passenger was up on point, hissing with more than casual concern, and I barely heard Vince as he stuttered on stupidly about what an awful thing this was and how terrible everybody felt.

I am sure that if I could feel at all I would have felt terrible, too, since Camilla was a coworker and I had labored beside her for many years. We had not really been close, and she had often behaved in ways that I found puzzling, but I was quite well aware that when Death visits a colleague, one must display the proper feelings of shock and awfulness. That was elementary, clearly stated in one of the first chapters of *The Olde Booke of Human Behavioure,* and I was sure that eventually I would work my way around to playing the part with my usual dramatic excellence. But not now, not yet. Right now I had far too many things to think about.

My first thought was that somehow, this was the work of my Shadow; he had written in his blog that he was going to do something, and now Camilla turned up dead, battered into jelly. But how did that affect me? Aside from forcing me to make grieving faces and mouth clichés about Tragic Loss, it didn't touch me at all.

So this was something else, something unconnected to my own personal conflict—and yet, something about it had caught the Passenger's attention, and that meant more than all the fake standardized emotions in the world. It meant that something was very off center here, wrong in a way that a Certain Shadowy Someone found extremely provocative, and *that* meant that whatever had happened to Camilla was far from being what it seemed to be—which in turn was an indication that, for some reason that was not at all clear at the moment, Dexter needed to pay attention.

But why? Aside from the fact that Camilla was a coworker and Deborah was in disgrace, why should this cause more than a mild flutter of passing interest from the Passenger?

I tried to shut out the blather of Vince and his annoying outpouring of emotion, and concentrate for just a moment on the facts. Deborah had been certain that she caught the right man. Deborah was very good at what she did. Therefore, either Deborah had made a huge and uncharacteristic mistake, or else—

"It's a copycat," I said, interrupting the flow of meaningless sound that was pouring out of Vince.

He blinked at me with eyes that seemed suddenly much too large and wet. "Dexter," he said. "There's never in *history* been anybody who did something like this hammer thing, not once ever before—and now you think there're *two* of them?"

"Yes," I said. "Has to be."

He shook his head vigorously. "No. No way. Can't be—it just can't. I mean, I know it's your sister; you gotta stick up for her, but hey," he said.

But once again his pointless drivel was contradicted by the far more compelling purr of reptile logic slithering out from the deep and shadowed stronghold of the Passenger's certainty, and I knew I was right. I still did not know why that should make the alarm bells ring—where was the threat to precious irreplaceable me? But the Passenger was almost never wrong, and the warning was clear. Someone had duplicated the Hammer Killer's technique, and aside from petty moral questions and copyright issues, something about that was *wrong*; some new threat was marching in too close for comfort, right up to the battlements of the Dark Lair, and I was suddenly deeply uneasy over what should have been no more than a routine opportunity to give another solid performance of Artificial Human Grief. Was the whole world out to get me? Was this really the new Model of how Things were going to be?

Nothing that happened in the next few hours made me feel any easier. Camilla's body had been found in a car parked in the far corner of the lot at a giant superstore located very close to headquarters. A lot of cops stopped at the store on their way home from work, and quite probably Camilla had, too. There were three plastic shopping bags with the store's logo scattered across the floor in the backseat of the car, and Camilla's body had been poured onto the seat above them. Just like the other two victims, she had been savagely hammered on every bone and joint until her body had lost its original shape.

But the car was not an official police vehicle, and apparently it was not even Camilla's, either. It was a five-year-old Chevy Impala, registered to a store employee named Natalie Bromberg. Ms. Bromberg had not had a great deal to say to the detectives so far, possibly because, since finding Camilla in her car, her time had been filled with screaming, crying, and finally accepting a large syringe filled with sedative.

Vince and I worked slowly through the area around the Impala, and inside it as well, and my sense that this was the work of a different hand grew steadily. Camilla's body was slumped half-on, half-off the seat, while the other two had been arranged a little more carefully. A small thing, but once again, it didn't fit the previous pattern, and it made me look a little closer.

I am not really an expert on blunt-force trauma, but the places on Camilla's body where she had been hit looked different from what I had seen in the two previous cases; Gunther's and Klein's impact points had visibly been made by the flat surface on the end of the hammer. These had a slight curve to them, a faint concave contour, as if the weapon had been rounded rather than flat, something like a pole, or a dowel, or . . . or maybe a baseball bat? The kind a former minor-league baseball player with anger-management problems might have lying around?

I thought about it hard, and it seemed like it fit—except for one small thing: Why would Bernie Elan want to kill Camilla Figg? And if for some reason he did want to kill her, why choose this difficult and repulsive method? It didn't add up, not at all. I was leaping to paranoid conclusions. Merely because somebody was after me, that didn't mean he would do this. Ridiculous.

I worked around the outside of the car, spraying Bluestar in the hopes of finding some telltale blood spatter. I found a very faint bloody impression from the toe of a running shoe on the white line separating the Impala's parking spot from the one next to it. And there were no taco wrappers inside the car, either, which was hardly conclusive. But there was a large patch of blood on the seat under the body that had leaked out from a savage wound on the left side of Camilla's head. Head wounds are notorious gushers—but this one had merely trickled onto the seat, meaning that she had been killed somewhere else and then dumped here soon after. The killer had probably parked close to the Impala and quickly slid the body out of his vehicle and into the Chevy's backseat, and it was my guess that blood from the head injury had made the partial footprint.

There was another smaller wound on Camilla's arm, where the bone of the forearm was actually poking up through the skin. It had not leaked nearly as much as the head wound, but to me it was significant. Neither of the other victims' bodies had bled at all, and this one had been thumped open twice. It was not quite enough evidence to swear out a warrant and arrest somebody, but to me it was a very important point, and in keeping with my position as a responsible adult in the law enforcement community, I immediately brought it to the attention of the detective in charge, a man named Hood.

Detective Hood was a large guy with a low forehead and a lower IQ. He had a permanent leer and he liked put-downs, sexual innuendo,

and hitting suspects to encourage them to speak. I found him standing a few feet away from the Impala's owner, waiting impatiently for
the sedative to kick in a little so she could understand his questions
without shrieking. He was watching her with his arms crossed and
a very intimidating expression on his face, and Ms. Bromberg would
probably need a second shot if she glanced up and saw him staring.

I knew Hood slightly from working with him in the past, so I
approached him with chummy directness. "Hey, Richard," I said; his
head jerked around toward me and his expression darkened a notch.

"What do *you* want?" he said, and he made no attempt to match
my cordial tone. In fact, he sounded almost hostile.

Every now and then I find that I have misjudged a situation and
used an incorrect phrase or expression; clearly I had done so now. It
always takes a moment to adjust and pick a new one, particularly if
I am not sure what I did wrong. But a blank stare and a long pause
seemed unsuitable, so I filled the gap as best I could. "Um," I said.
"Just, you know—"

" 'You *know*'?" he said, with a mean mimicking tone. "You wanna
hear what I *know*, dickless?"

I didn't want to hear, of course; Hood couldn't possibly know anything beyond the third-grade level, except possibly about pornogra-
phy, and that sort of thing is not really interesting to me. But it didn't
seem politic to say so, and in any case he didn't wait for me to answer.

"What I *know* is, your half-ass Hollywood sister shit the bed," he
said, and, completely untroubled by the fact that this image did not
really make sense, he repeated it. "She shit the fucking bed," he said
again.

"Well, maybe," I said, trying to sound meek yet confident, "but
there's actually some evidence that this might be a copycat killer."

He glared at me, and his jaw bulged out on the sides. It was a
very big jaw, and it looked quite able and willing to bite a large chunk
of flesh out of me if it had to. "Evidence," Hood said, as if the word
tasted bad. "Like what."

"The, um, wounds," I said. "The body is bleeding from two places,
and on the other two the skin wasn't even broken at all."

Hood turned his head a quarter of an inch to the side and spit.

"You're fulla shit," he said, and he turned away from me, back to facing Ms. Bromberg. He recrossed his arms, and his upper lip twitched. "Just like your half-ass sister."

I looked down at my feet, just to be sure his glob of spit had really missed my shoe, and was very happy to see that it had. But it was clear that I would get nothing from Detective Hood except saliva and scatology, so I decided to leave him to his lowbrow musings and go back to looking at all that was left of Camilla Figg.

But as I began to turn away from Hood, I felt a dry, seismic rumble pushing up from a deep and shadowy corner inside, a sharp and urgent shock of warning from the Passenger that Dexter stood in the crosshairs of some hostile scope. Time slowed to a crawl as I froze midturn and searched around me for the threat, and as I looked to the side, off by the yellow tape guarding our perimeter, a bright flash went off and the Passenger hissed.

I blinked, bracing for a bullet, but none came. It was nothing but some gawker taking a photograph. I squinted through lingering blindness from the flash, and saw only the blur of a thick man in a gray T-shirt lowering a camera and turning away to blend back into the crowd. He was gone before I could see his face, or anything else about him, and there wasn't any visible reason why he had set off my silent alarm. He was not a sniper, not a terrorist with an exploding bicycle. He couldn't possibly be any real danger at all, nothing but another one of the many unwashed feeding a queasy curiosity about death. Now I was truly being stupid; I was seeing Shadows everywhere, even where they made no sense. Was I slipping completely out of the world of reason and into kaleidoscopic paranoia?

I watched the spot where the photographer had disappeared for a few more moments. He didn't come back, and nothing came roaring out to kill me. It was just nerves, nothing more, and not my Witness, and I had work to do.

I went back to the Impala, where Camilla's battered body lay in its final untidy heap. She was still dead, and I couldn't lose the feeling that somewhere, somebody was watching me, licking his lips, and planning to make me dead, too.

NINETEEN

I T WAS VERY LATE WHEN I GOT HOME, ALMOST MIDNIGHT, AND
out of pure reflexive habit I went into the kitchen and looked to
see if Rita had left some food for me. But no matter how hard
I looked, there were no leftovers, not even a single slice of pizza. I
searched carefully, all in vain. There was no Tupperware container
on the counter, nothing on the stove, no covered bowl in the refrigerator, not even a Wendy's bag on the table. I searched the entire kitchen,
but I found no sign of anything edible.

I suppose it was not really a tragedy, comparatively speaking.
Worse things happen every day, and one of them had just happened
to Camilla Figg, someone I had known for years. I really should have
been grieving a little bit. But I was hungry, and Rita had left me nothing to eat; to me that seemed vastly more saddening, the death of
a great and sustaining tradition, a violation of some unspoken but
important principle that had nurtured me through my many trials.
No food for Dexter; All was Utterly Lost.

I did, however, find a chair pulled out from the kitchen table at a
sloppy angle, and Rita's shoes flung haphazardly down beside it. Her
work was once again piled up on the table, and her blouse hung mess-

ily from the back of the chair. Across the room I saw a yellow square stuck to the refrigerator and I went over to look; it was a Post-it note, presumably from Rita, although the scrawled words did not look like her usual neat handwriting. The note was stuck to the freezer door and it said, "Brian called—where were *you*!?!" It had taken her two tries to write the "B" in "Brian," and the last word was crookedly underlined three times; the point of the pen had gone all the way through and made a small tear in the paper.

It was only a small yellow note, but something about it made me pause, and I stood there by the refrigerator for a moment, holding the Post-it and wondering why it troubled me. It was surely not the slap-dash handwriting; no doubt Rita was simply tired, frazzled by rush-ing out of work after a long tense day of fighting her annual crisis at work, and then hustling three kids through the hot and crowded Miami evening and into a burger joint. It was enough to make any-body tense up, grow weary, and . . .

. . . and lose the ability to make the letter "B" properly?

That didn't make any sense at all. Rita was a precise person, neu-rotically neat and methodical. It was one of the qualities I admired in her, and mere fatigue and frustration had never before dimmed her passion for doing things in an orderly way. She had faced many hard-ships in her life, like her disastrous first marriage to the physically abusive drug addict, and she had always dealt with the violent disor-der of life by making it stand up straight, brush its teeth, and put its laundry in the hamper. For her to scrawl a messy note and leave her shoes and clothing scattered across the floor like this was very much out of character, and a clear indication that, um . . . what?

Last time it had been a spilled glass of wine—had it spilled because she'd had more than one? And done the same thing again tonight?

I went back over to the kitchen table and looked down at where Rita had sat and left her shoes, and I looked at it as a trained and highly skilled forensics technician. The angle of the left shoe showed a lack of motor control, and the sloppily hanging blouse was a defi-nite indication of lessened inhibition. But just for the sake of scientific confirmation I walked over to the big covered trash can by the back door. Inside the can, underneath a scattering of paper towels and junk mail, was an empty bottle that had recently contained red wine.

Rita was enthusiastic about recycling—but here was an empty bottle stuffed into the trash can and covered over with paper. And I did not remember seeing the bottle when it was full, and I am usually very familiar with what is in my kitchen. This was a whole bottle of merlot, and it should have been visible almost anywhere in the kitchen. But I hadn't seen it. That meant that either Rita had gone to some trouble to hide it—or else she bought the bottle tonight, drank it all in one sitting, and forgot to recycle.

This was not a glass of wine while she worked and I ordered pizza. This was a whole bottle—and worse, she drank it when I was out of the house, leaving the children unwatched and unprotected.

She was drinking far too much, and far too often. I had assumed that she was just sipping a little wine as a way of dealing with the temporary stress—but this was more than that. Had some other unknown factor suddenly changed Rita into an emerging lush? And if so, wasn't I supposed to do something about it? Or should I wait until she began to miss work and neglect the children?

From down the hall, as if on cue, I heard Lily Anne begin to cry, and I hurried into the bedroom to her crib. She was kicking her feet and waving her arms around, and when I lifted her out of her little bed it was obvious why. Her diaper was bulging out against her sleepy suit, full to overflowing. I glanced at Rita; she was facedown on the bed, snoring, one arm flung up and the other pinned under her. Clearly, Lily Anne's fussing had not penetrated the fog of her sleep, and Rita had failed to change the baby's diaper before she went to bed. It was not at all like her—but then, neither was secret and excessive wine drinking.

Lily Anne kicked her feet harder and moved the volume of her crying up a few notches, and I took her over to the changing table. Her problem was clear and immediate and it was something I could deal with simply. Rita would take some thought, and it was too late at night for thinking. I got the baby changed into a dry diaper and rocked her until she stopped fussing and went back to sleep. I put her back in the crib, and went over to my bed.

Rita lay there in the exact same position, sprawled unmoving across two-thirds of the bed. She might have been dead, except for the snoring. I looked down at her and wondered what was going on in that pleasant-looking blond head. She had always been totally reliable, completely predictable and dependable, never deviating even one small step from her basic pattern of behavior. It was one of the reasons I had decided it was a good idea to marry her—I almost always knew exactly what she would do. She was like a perfect little toy railroad set, whirring around the same track, past the same scenery, day after day without change.

Until now—clearly she had gone off the tracks for some reason, and I had the unpleasant idea that I was supposed to deal with it in some way. Should I stage an intervention? Force her to go to an AA meeting? Threaten to divorce her and make her keep the kids? This was all foreign turf to me, ideas that were in the syllabus for Advanced Marriage, a postgraduate course in the area of human studies, and I knew almost nothing about it.

But whatever the answer might be, I was not going to figure it out tonight. After the long workday, dealing with Shadowblog and whimpering coworkers and Detective Knucklehead, I was bone-tired. A thick and stupid cloud of fatigue had spread over my brain and I had to sleep before I did anything else.

I rolled Rita's limp body over to her side of the bed and climbed under the sheet. I needed sleep, as much as possible, and right now, and almost as soon as my head hit the pillow I was unconscious.

The alarm woke me up at seven, and as I slapped it off, I had the entirely unreasonable feeling that everything was going to be all right. I had gone to bed with the worry bin full: Rita and Shadowblog and Camilla Figg—and during the night something had come along and swept away all my fretting. Yes, there were problems. But I would deal with them; I always had before, and I would this time. It was entirely illogical, I know, but I was filled with relaxed confidence instead of the bone-tired anxiety of last night. I have no idea why the change had happened; maybe it was the effect of deep and dreamless sleep. In any case, I woke up into a world where unreasonable optimism seemed like common sense. I am not saying I heard birds

singing in the golden sunlight of a perfect dawn, but I did smell coffee and bacon coming from the kitchen, which was a far better thing
than any singing bird I have ever heard. I showered and dressed, and
when I got to the kitchen table there was a plate of sunny-side-up
eggs waiting for me, with three crisp strips of bacon on the side, and
a mug of hot and strong coffee on the table next to it.

"You were out awfully late," Rita said as she cracked an egg into
the skillet. For some reason, it sounded almost like she was accusing
me of something, but since that made no sense, I decided it was just
the residual effect of too much wine.

"Camilla Figg was killed last night," I said. "The woman I work
with?"

Rita turned from the stove, spatula in her hand, and looked at me.
"So you were *working*?" she said, and once again that too-much-wine-
last-night edge was in her voice.

"Yes," I said. "They didn't find her until late in the day."

She watched me for a few seconds, and then finally shook her
head. "That would explain it, wouldn't it," she said, but she kept looking at me as if it didn't explain anything.

It made me a bit uneasy; why was she staring like that? I glanced
down to make sure I was wearing pants, and I was. When I looked up
again, she was still staring.

"Is something wrong?" I said.

Rita shook her head. "Wrong?" she said. She rolled her eyes
toward the ceiling. "Is something *wrong*, he wants to know?" She
looked at me with her hands on her hips and tapped one toe impatiently. "Why don't *you* tell *me* if something's wrong, Dexter?"

I looked back at her with surprise. "Um," I said, wondering what
the right answer was, "as far as I know, nothing is wrong. I mean,
nothing out of the ordinary . . . ?" It seemed like a sadly inadequate
answer, even to me, and Rita clearly agreed.

"Oh, good, nothing's wrong," she said. And she just kept looking
at me, raising one eyebrow and tapping her toe like she was expecting more, even though what I had already said was so very feeble.

I glanced behind her to the stove; smoke was rising from the pan,
where fragrant steam should have been. "Um, Rita?" I said carefully.
"I think something's burning?"

She blinked at me, and then, as she understood what I had said, she whipped around to the stove. "Oh, shit, look at that," she said, leaping forward with the spatula raised. "No, shit, look at the *time*," she added in a voice that was rising with what must have been frustration. "Damn it, why can't it— There's just never any— Cody? Astor? Come get your breakfast! Now!" She scraped two eggs out of the pan, threw in a pat of butter, and broke two more eggs into the pan in a series of motions so rapid that it seemed like one move. "Kids? Now! Come on!" she said. She glanced at me again—and then hesitated for just a moment, looking down at me. "I just— We need to . . ." She shook her head, as if she couldn't think what the words might be in English. "I didn't hear you come in last night," she said, the end of the sentence trickling off weakly.

And I might have said that last night she wouldn't have heard the Queen's Own Highland Regiment marching through the house with bagpipes skirling, but I had no idea what she wanted me to say, and why ruin a lovely morning trying to find out? Besides, my mouth was full of egg yolk, and it would have been rude to talk through the food. So I just smiled and made a dismissive sound and ate my breakfast. She looked at me expectantly for a moment more, but then Cody and Astor trudged in, and Rita turned away to hurry their breakfast onto the table. The morning went on in its perfectly normal way, and I was once more feeling the feebleminded glimmer of unfounded hope I woke up with as I drove in to work through the crawling traffic.

Even in the early morning, Miami traffic has an edge to it that you don't find in other cities. Miami drivers seem to wake up faster and meaner than others. Maybe it's because the bright and relentless sunlight makes everyone realize that they could be out fishing, or at the beach, instead of crawling along the highway to a boring, soul-crushing, dead-end job that doesn't pay them anything near what they are really worth. Or maybe it's just the added jolt we get from our extra-strong Miami coffee.

Whatever the reason, I have never seen a morning drive without a full edge of homicidal mania, and this morning was no exception. People honked, yelled threats, and waved middle fingers, and at the interchange for the Palmetto Expressway an old Buick had rear-ended a new BMW. A fistfight had broken out on the shoulder, and everyone else slowed down to watch, or to shout at the fighters, and it took an extra ten minutes for me to get past the mess and in to work. That was just as well, considering what was waiting for me when I got there.

Since I was still feeling stupidly bright and chipper, I did not stop for a cup of the lethal coffee that might, after all, kill the buzz—or even me. Instead I went directly to my desk, where I found Deborah waiting for me, slumped into my chair and looking like the poster girl for the National Brooding Outrage Foundation. Her left arm was still in a sling, but her cast had lost its clean and bright patina, and she had leaned it against my desk blotter and knocked over my pencil holder. But nobody is perfect, and it was such a happy morning, so I let it go.

"Good morning, sis," I said cheerfully, which seemed to offend her more than it should have. She made a face and shook her head dismissively, as if the goodness or badness of the morning was irritating and irrelevant.

"What happened last night?" she said, in a voice that was harsher than usual. "Was it the same as the others?"

"You mean Camilla Figg?" I said, and now she very nearly snarled.

"What the fuck else would I mean?" she said. "Goddamn it, Dex, I need to know—was it the same?"

I sat down in the folding chair opposite my desk, which I thought was quite noble of me, considering that Debs was in my very own chair and this other one was not terribly comfortable. "I don't think so," I said, and Deborah hissed out a very long breath.

"*Fuck* it; I *knew* it," she said, and she straightened up and looked at me with an eager gleam in her eye. "What's different?"

I raised a hand to slow her down. "It's nothing really compelling," I said. "At least, Detective Hood didn't think so."

"That stupid asshole couldn't find the floor using both feet," she snapped. "What did you get?"

"Well," I said, "just that the skin was broken in two places. So there was some blood at the scene. Uh, the body wasn't arranged quite right, either." She looked at me expectantly, so I said, "The, um, I think the trauma wounds were different."

"Different how?" she said.

"I think they were made with something else," I said. "Like, not a hammer."

"With what," she said. "With a golf club? A Buick? What?"

"I couldn't tell," I said. "But probably something with a round surface. Maybe . . ." I hesitated for a half-second; even saying it out loud made me feel like I was being paranoid. But Debs was looking at me with an expression of eagerness-ready-to-turn-cranky, so I said it. "Maybe a baseball bat."

"Okay," she said, and she kept that same expression focused on me.

"Um, the body wasn't really arranged the same," I said.

Deborah kept staring, and when I didn't say anything else she frowned. "That's it?" she said.

"Almost," I said. "We'll have to wait for the autopsy, to be sure, but one of the wounds was on her head, and I think Camilla was unconscious or even dead when the wounds were made."

"That doesn't mean shit," she said.

"Deborah, there was no blood at all with the others. And the first two times the killer was incredibly careful to keep them awake the whole time—he never even broke the skin."

"You'll never sell that to the captain," she said. "The whole fucking department wants my head on a stick, and if I can't prove I got the right guy locked up, he's going to give it to them."

"I can't *prove* anything," I said. "But I know I'm right."

She cocked her head to one side and looked at me quizzically. "One of your *voices*?" she said carefully. "Can you make it tell you anything more?"

When Deborah had finally found out what I really am, I had tried to explain the Dark Passenger to her. I had told her that the many times I'd had "hunches" about a killer were actually hints from a kindred spirit inside me. Apparently I'd made a clumsy mess of it, because she still seemed to think I went into some kind of trance and chatted long-distance with somebody in the Great Beyond.

"It's not really like a Ouija board," I said.

"I don't care if it's talking tea leaves," she said. "Get it to tell us something I can use."

Before I could open my mouth and let out the cranky comeback that was lurking there, a massive foot clomped at the doorway, and a large dark shadow fell over the shreds of my pleasant morning. I looked around, and there, in person, was the end of all happy thoughts.

Detective Hood leaned against the doorframe and gave us his very best mean smile. "Looka this," he said. "Wall-to-wall loser."

"Looka that," Debs snapped back at him. "Talking asshole."

Hood didn't seem terribly hurt. "Asshole in charge to you, darling," he said. "Asshole who will find the *real* cop killer, instead of fucking around on *Good Morning America*."

Deborah blushed; it was a very unfair remark, but it hit home anyway. To her very great credit, though, she came right back with a zinger of her own. "You couldn't find your own dick with a search party," she said.

"And it would be a pretty small party anyway," I added cheerfully; after all, family has to stick together.

Hood glared at me, and his smile got bigger and meaner. "You," he said, "are off this thing altogether as of right now. Just like your Hollywood sister."

"Really," I said. "Because I can prove you're wrong?"

"Nope," he said. "Because you are now"—Hood paused to taste the words, and then let them out in a slow, obviously delicious trickle—"a person of interest to the investigation."

I had been all set to whip another witty and stinging remark at him, no matter what he said, but this took me totally by surprise. "Person of interest" was police code for, "We think you're guilty and we're going to prove it." And as I stared at him in numb horror I realized that there was no clever response to being told that you're under investigation for murder—especially when you didn't even get to commit one first. I felt my mouth open and close a couple of times in what must have looked like a really good imitation of a grouper pulled up out of deep water, but no sound came out. Luckily, Deborah jumped right in for me.

"What kind of brain-dead bullshit are you pulling, Richard?" she said. "You can't chase him for this just because he knows you're a moron."

"Oh, don't worry about that," he said. "I have a really *good* reason."

And as he spoke you would have thought he was the happiest man in the world—until you saw the next man who came into my office.

And that next man came in like he'd been waiting his whole life for just the right cue line to his dramatic entrance. I heard a stiff and rhythmic clumping in the hall as Hood's last two words still hung in the air, and then the *real* happiest man in the world came in.

I say "man," but in truth it was really no more than three-fourths of a flesh-and-blood Homo sapiens. The prosthetic clatter of his steps revealed that the living feet were gone, and twin metal pincers gleamed where his hands should have been. But the teeth were still human, and every single one of them was showing as he stumped in and gave a large manila envelope to Hood.

"Thanks," Hood said, and Sergeant Doakes just nodded and kept his eyes fixed on me, his supernaturally happy smile stretching across his face and filling me with dread.

"What the fuck is this?" Deborah said, but Hood just shook his head and opened the envelope. He pulled out what looked like an eight-by-ten glossy picture and twirled it onto my desk.

"Can you tell me what this is?" he said to me.

I reached over and picked up the photo. I did not recognize it, but as I looked at it I had a brief and unsettling moment of feeling that I had lost my mind as I thought, *But that looks like me!* And then I took a steadying breath, looked again, and thought, *It is me!* Which made absolutely no sense, no matter how reassuring it was.

It was me. It was a picture of Dexter: shirtless, half turned away from the camera, and stepping away from a body sprawled on the pavement. My first thought was, *But I don't remember leaving a body there. . . .* And it doesn't really say good things about me to admit it, but my second thought, as I looked at my bared torso, was, *I look good!* Muscle tone excellent, abs in good shape—no sign of the very slight spare tire that had been settling around my waist lately. So the picture was probably a year or two old—which did not explain why Doakes was so pleased with it.

I pushed away my narcissistic thoughts and tried to focus on the picture itself, since it apparently represented a very real threat to me. Nothing occurred, no hint of where it had been taken or who had taken it, and I looked up at Hood. "Where did you get this?" I asked.

"Do you recognize the picture?" Hood said.

"I've never seen it before," I said. "But I think that's me."

Doakes made a kind of gurgling sound that might have been laughter, and Hood nodded as if a thought was actually forming in his bony head. "You think," he said.

"Yes, I do," I said. "And it really doesn't hurt; you should try it sometime."

Hood pulled another photo out of the envelope and flipped it onto the desk. "What about this one?" he said. "You think that's you, too?"

I looked at the picture. This one showed the same setting as the first, but now I was a bit farther away from the body and pulling on a shirt. Something new had come into the field of focus, and after a moment of study I recognized it as the back of Angel Batista's head. He was bending over the body on the ground, and the little lightbulb over my head finally went on.

"Oh," I said, and relief flooded in. This was not a picture of Dexter caught in the act of shuffling off somebody's mortal coil; it was Dexter on Duty, a mere workaday nothing. I could explain it simply, even prove it, and I was off the hook. "Now I remember. This was like two years ago, a crime scene in Liberty City. Drive-by shooting—three victims, very messy. I got blood on my shirt."

"Uh-huh," Hood said, and Doakes shook his head, still smiling fondly.

"Well," I said, "it happens sometimes. I keep a clean shirt in my bag just in case." Hood kept staring at me; I shrugged. "So I changed into the clean shirt," I said, hoping he would understand at last.

"Good idea," he said, nodding as if he approved of my solid common sense, and he threw one more picture onto the desk. "What about this one?"

I picked it up. It was me again, very obviously me. It was a close-up shot of my face, in profile. I was looking off into the distance with an expression of noble longing that probably meant it was time for lunch. There was a slight dusting of beard stubble on my face, which hadn't been there in the first pictures, so this one had been taken at a different time. But because it was so very tightly focused on my face, I couldn't make out anything at all that would tell me more about the picture, or when it had been taken. On the plus side, that meant there was no way it could be used to prove anything against me, either.

So I shook my head and flipped the picture back onto my desk. "Very nice picture," I said. "Tell me, Detective, do you think a man can be *too* handsome?"

"Yeah," said Hood. "I think he can be too fucking funny, too." And he flipped one last photo onto the desk. "Laugh this one off, funny boy."

I picked up the picture. It showed me again, but this time standing face-to-face with Camilla Figg. There was an expression of startled adoration on her face, a look of such fond longing that even a dolt like Hood could read it without help. I stared, scanning for clues, and finally recognized the background. This had been taken at the Torch, where Officer Gunther had been found. But so what? Why was this large and stupid thug showing me pictures of me, nice as they were?

I flipped the photo back onto the desk with the others. "I had no idea I was so photogenic," I said. "Do I get to keep them?"

"No," Hood said. He leaned over me to the desk and the odor of unwashed detective overlaid with cheap cologne almost made me gag. Hood scooped up the photos and straightened as he stuffed them back into the envelope.

With Hood a few feet away from me once more, I managed to breathe again, and since my curiosity was coming to a boil, I used the breath for something practical. "They're all very nice pictures," I said. "But so what?"

"So what?" Hood said, and Doakes made another one of his tongueless but joyful sounds; there were no actual words to it, but the garbled syllables had a distinct overtone of *gotcha* that I did not like at all. "Is that all you got to say about your girlfriend's photo collection?"

"I'm married," I said. "I don't have a girlfriend."

"Not anymore you don't," Hood said. "She's dead." And as if they were wired together and controlled from offstage, Hood and Doakes showed all their teeth in unison in a blinding display of enamel and carnivorous happiness. "These were in Camilla Figg's apartment," Hood said. "And there's hundreds more of 'em."

He pointed a finger the size of a banana right between my eyes. "All of you," he said.

TWENTY

SOMEWHERE IN THIS WORLD IT IS QUITE POSSIBLE THAT children laughed without a care and played with unworried joy. Somewhere, gentle breezes probably blew across a field of grass as innocent young lovers held hands and strolled through the sunlight. And somewhere on this grubby little globe it is even remotely possible that peace, love, and happiness were abounding in the hearts and minds of the righteous. But right now, in the present location, Dexter was Deep in the Doo-doo, and happiness of any kind was a bitter, mocking fable—unless your name was Hood or Doakes, in which case you were in the best of all possible worlds. See the funny Dexter? See him squirm? See the sweat pop out on his forehead? Ha, ha, ha. What a funny, funny guy. Oh, look—his mouth is moving, but nothing is coming out except meaningless vowels. Sweat, Dexter. Stutter and sweat. Ha, ha, ha. Dexter is funny.

I was still struggling to find a consonant when my sister spoke up. "What the fuck are you trying to pull here, shithead?" she said, and I realized that those were the exact words I had been searching for, so I closed my mouth and nodded.

Hood raised his eyebrows, and his forehead was so low they

almost merged with his hair. "Pull?" he said with exaggerated innocence. "I'm not pulling nothing. I'm investigating a murder."

"With a couple of bullshit pictures?" Deborah said with heart-
warming scorn.

Hood leaned toward her and said, "Couple?" He snorted. "Like
I said, there's *hundreds* of 'em." He shoved his gigantic finger toward
my head again. "Every one of 'em a picture of laughing boy here," he
said.

"That doesn't mean *shit*," Deborah said.

"Framed and hanging on the walls," Hood said relentlessly.
"Taped to the refrigerator. Stacked on the bedside table. In boxes in
the closet. In a binder on the back of the *toilet*," he said with a leer.
"Hundreds of pictures of your brother, sweetheart." He took a half
step toward Debs and winked. "And I may not get to go on the *Today*
show to talk about it, like some losers who arrest the wrong guy?"
he said. "But I am in charge of this investigation now, and I think all
those pictures *do* mean shit, and maybe a lot more than shit. I think
they mean he was banging Camilla, and I think she was going to
tell his pretty little wifey, and he didn't want her to. So lemme ask
this one more time real polite and official," he said, stepping back
from Debs. He leaned over me now, and as he spoke the smell of his
unwashed armpits mingled with his rotten breath and made my eyes
water. "You got anything you want to tell me about these pictures,
Dexter?" he said. "And maybe about your relationship with Camilla
Figg?"

"I don't know anything about the pictures," I said. "And I didn't
have any relationship with Camilla except that I worked with her. I
barely knew her."

"Uh-huh," Hood said, still bent over and in my face. "That all you
got to say?"

"Well," I said, "I'd also like to say that you really need to brush
your teeth."

He didn't move at all for a few long seconds, made even longer by
the fact that he exhaled again. But finally he nodded, straightened up
slowly, and said, "This is going to be fun." He nodded at me, and his
nasty smile got bigger. "As of five o'clock today, you are suspended,
pending the results of this investigation. If you wish to appeal this

decision, you may contact the administrative coordinator for personnel." He turned to Sergeant Doakes and nodded cheerfully, and I felt a cold knot form in my stomach even before he added the inevitable clincher. "That would be Sergeant Doakes," he said.

"Of course it would," I said. Nothing could be more perfect. The two of them smiled at me with genuine, heartfelt happiness, and when Hood had done all the smiling his system could stand without melting, he turned away and stepped to the door. He spun around there, and pointed his finger at Deborah, making a clicking sound as he dropped his thumb like he was shooting her. "See you later, loser," he told her, and he sauntered out, smiling like he was going to his own birthday party.

Sergeant Doakes hadn't taken his eyes off me the whole time, and he didn't now. He just smiled at me, clearly having more fun than he'd had in a very long while, and then finally, just as I was thinking about throwing a chair at his head, he made his horrible, gargling, tongueless-laughing sound, and followed Hood out into the hall.

There was silence in my office for what seemed like a very long time. It was not by any means a peaceful, contemplative silence. It was, instead, the kind of quiet that comes right after an explosion, when the survivors are looking around at all the dead bodies and wondering if another bomb is going to go off, and the eerie silence did not end until Deborah finally shook her head and said, "Jesus Christ." That seemed to sum things up pretty well, so I didn't say anything, and Deborah said it again and then added, "Dexter—I have to know."

I looked at her with surprise. She seemed to be very serious, but I couldn't imagine what she was thinking. "Know what, Debs?" I said.

"Did you sleep with Camilla?" she said.

And now it was my turn to say it. "Jesus Christ, Debs," I said, and I was genuinely shocked. "Do you think I killed her, too?"

She hesitated half a second too long. "No-o," she said, and it was not very convincing. "But you gotta see how it looks."

"To me it looks like you're playing Pile On Dexter," I said. "This is crazy—I barely spoke twenty words to Camilla in my entire life."

"Yeah, but come on," Deborah said. "All those fucking pictures."

"What about them?" I said. "I didn't take them, and I don't see what you think they mean."

"I'm just saying they mean a lot to a brainless shit-bag like Hood—and he's going to run with it, and he might even make it stick," she went on, recklessly mixing her metaphors. "It's perfect for him—married guy bangs chick at work, then kills her to keep his wife from finding out."

"*That's* what you think?" I said.

"I'm just saying," she said. "I mean, you gotta see how it would look like that. It's totally believable."

"It's totally *un*believable to anybody who knows me," I said. "That's just completely . . . How can you even think that for a second?" And I was actually feeling authentic human emotions of hurt, betrayal, and outrage. Because for once, I was totally innocent—but even my very own sister didn't seem to believe that I was.

"All right, Jesus," she said. "I'm just saying, you know."

"You're just saying I'm up Shit Creek and you won't hand me a paddle?" I said.

"Come on," she said, and to her great credit she squirmed uncomfortably.

"You're saying you want to know if it's all right if they arrest your brother," I said, because I can be relentless, too. "Because you know he's secretly the kind of guy who smashes his coworkers with a hammer?"

"Dexter, for fuck's sake!" she said. "I'm sorry, okay?"

I looked at her another second, but she actually did seem sorry, and she wasn't reaching for her cuffs, so I just said, "Okay."

Deborah cleared her throat, looked away for a moment, then looked back at me. "So you never banged Camilla," she said, and with a little more conviction she added, "And you totally never beat anybody to death with a hammer."

"Not yet," I said, with just a touch of warning.

"Fine," she said, holding up her good hand, as if she wanted to make sure she was ready if I really did try to smack her with a hammer.

"And seriously," I said. "Why would anybody want even *one* picture of me?"

Deborah opened her mouth, closed it again, and then looked like she'd thought of something funny, although I certainly didn't see anything to laugh about. "You really don't know?" she said.

"Know *what*, Debs?" I said. "Come on."

She still seemed to think something was comical. But she shook her head and said, "All right. You don't know. Shit." She smiled and said, "I shouldn't be the one to tell you, your sister, but hey." She shrugged. "You're a good-looking guy, Dexter."

"Thank you, you're not so bad yourself," I said. "What's that got to do with anything?"

"Dexter, for Christ's sake, don't be dense," she said. "Camilla had a *crush* on you, asshole."

"On *me*?" I said. "A *crush*? Like, a romantic infatuation crush?"

"Shit, yeah, for *years*. Everybody knew about it," Deborah said.

"Everybody but me."

"Yeah, well," she said, shrugging. "But all those pictures, it looks more like a total obsession."

I shook my head, as if I could make the idea go away. I mean, I don't pretend to understand the clinically insane human race, but this was a bit much. "That's crazy," I said. "I'm married."

Apparently that was a funny thing to say. In any case, it was funny to Deborah; she snorted with amusement. "Yeah, well, getting married didn't make you ugly," she said. "Not yet, anyway."

I thought about Camilla and how she had behaved toward me over the years. Just recently, while we were working on the site where Officer Gunther's body had been dumped, she had taken a picture of me, and then stammered out something lame and incoherent about the flash when I looked at her. Maybe her inability to speak in complete sentences only happened when she was in my presence. And it was true that she had blushed every time she saw me—and come to think of it, she had tried to kiss me in a drunken stupor at my bachelor party, instead only managing to pass out at my feet. Did all this add up to a secret obsession with little old me? And if so, how did a crush get her crushed?

I have always prided myself on my ability to see things as they really are, without any of the hundreds of emotional filters humans put between themselves and the facts. So I made a conscious effort to clear away the bad air, real and metaphorical, that Hood had left behind. Fact one: Camilla was dead. Two: She had been killed in a very unusual way—and that was actually more important than fact one, because it was an imitation of what had been done to Gunther and Klein. Why would somebody do that?

First, it made Deborah look bad. There were people who would want that, but they were either in jail or busy running a murder investigation. But it also made *me* look bad—and that was more to the point. My Witness had made the threat, and then Camilla turned up dead and I was the main suspect.

But how could he have known that Camilla had all those pictures? A stray wisp of memory wafted by, some snippet of office gossip. . . .

I looked at Deborah. She was watching me with one eyebrow raised, as if she thought I might fall off my chair. "Did you hear that Camilla had a boyfriend?" I asked her.

"Yeah," she said. "You think he did it?"

"Yes," I said.

"Why?"

"Because he saw her photo gallery of me," I said.

Debs looked dubious and shook her head. "So, what?" she said. "He killed her because he was jealous?"

"No," I said. "He killed her to frame me."

Deborah stared at me for several seconds, with a look on her face that said she couldn't decide whether to smack me or call for medical assistance. She finally blinked, took a deep breath, and said, with obviously artificial calm, "All right, Dexter. Camilla's new boyfriend killed her to frame you. Sure, why not. Just because it's totally fucking crazy—"

"Of course it's crazy, Debs. That's why it makes sense."

"Uh-huh," she said. "Very logical, Dex. So what kind of psycho asshole would kill Camilla just to drop you in the shit?"

It was an awkward question. I knew what psycho asshole had done it. My Witness had said he was moving closer, and he had; that had been *him* watching me at the crime scene and taking pictures. And he had killed Camilla Figg, purely as a way to get at me. It really was remarkably wicked, killing an innocent person merely to cause me inconvenience, and it would have been very tempting to pause and ponder the absolute depths of callous perfidy that this act revealed. But there really wasn't a lot of time to ponder at present, and in any case worrying about moral turpitude is best left to those with morals.

The real question at this point, and it was an awkward one, was how to tell Deborah that all this was happening because somebody had seen me in flagrante delicto. Debs had accepted me for the monster I am, but that was not at all the same thing as sitting in police headquarters and hearing about an actual example of my hobby. Aside from that, I really find it a bit uncomfortable to talk about my Dark Dabbling, even to Debs. Still, it was the only way to explain things.

So without giving her too many embarrassing details, I told her how I had been seen at play by an unhinged blogger who was now taking it all personally. As I stumbled awkwardly through my tale of woe, Deborah took on her stonefaced I-am-a-cop expression, and she said nothing at all until I finished. Then she sat quietly a little longer and looked at me as if she was waiting for more.

"Who was it," she said at last—a statement rather than a question, and it didn't quite make sense to me.

"I don't know who it is, Debs," I said. "If I did we could go get him."

She shook her head impatiently. "Your victim," she said. "The guy he saw you doing. Who was it."

For a moment I just blinked at her; I couldn't imagine why she would focus on such an unimportant detail when my precious neck was halfway into the noose. And she made it sound so tawdry, just saying it right out like that. "Victim" and "doing," in that flat cop tone of voice, and I didn't really like thinking about it that way. But she kept staring, and I realized that explaining to her that it really wasn't like that would be a great deal harder than simply answering her question. "Steven Valentine," I told her. "A pedophile. He raped and strangled little boys." She just stared, so I added, "Um, *at least* three of them."

Deborah nodded. "I remember him," she said. "We pulled him in twice, couldn't make it stick." About half the frown lines vanished from her forehead, and I realized with surprise why she had wanted to know who my playmate had been. She had to be sure that I had followed the rules set down by Harry, her demigod father, and she was now satisfied that I had. She knew Valentine fit the bill, and she accepted the justice of his unorthodox end with satisfaction. I looked at my sister with a real fondness. She had certainly come a long way from when she first found out what I am, and had needed to fight down the desire to lock me up.

"All right," she said, jolting me out of my doting reverie before I could sing "Hearts and Flowers." "So he saw you, and now he wants to take you down."

"That's it," I said. Deborah nodded and continued to study me, pursing her lips and shaking her head as if I was a repair problem beyond her ability to fix.

"Well," I said at last, when I had gotten tired of being stared at. "So what do we do about it?"

"There's not a whole shitload we *can* do, at least officially," she said. "Anything I try is going to get me suspended—and I can't even ask somebody off the record, because it's my *brother* under investigation—"

"It's not actually my fault," I said, mildly peeved that she made it sound like it was.

"Yeah, well, so lookit," she said, waving that off. "If you really are innocent—"

"Deborah!"

"Yeah, sorry, I mean, *because* you're really innocent," she said. "And Hood is a brain-dead bag of shit who couldn't find anything even if you were guilty, right?"

"Is this going somewhere?" I said. "Maybe someplace far away from me?"

"Listen," she said. "I'm just saying, in a couple of days, when they got nothing at all, we can start looking for this guy. For now, just don't get too worked up about Hood and his bullshit. Nothing to worry about. They got nothing."

"Really," I said.

"Just stay cool for a couple of days," my sister said with complete conviction. "It *can't* get any worse."

TWENTY-ONE

I F WE ARE CAPABLE OF LEARNING ANYTHING AT ALL IN THIS
life, we very quickly discover that anytime somebody is absolutely certain about something, they are almost always absolutely
wrong, too. And the present case was no exception. My sister is a very
good detective and an excellent pistol shot, and I'm sure she has several other praiseworthy qualities—but if she ever has to make a living as a fortune-teller, she will starve to death. Because her words of
reassurance, *It can't get any worse,* were still echoing in my ears when
I discovered that actually, things *could* get worse by a great deal, and
they already had.

Things were not great to start with: I had crawled through the
entire rest of the day at work with everyone avoiding me, which is
much more difficult than it sounds, and it resulted in several moments
of classic comedy, as people scrambled to escape my presence while
pretending that they hadn't seen me. For some reason, however, I had
a bit of difficulty in appreciating the comic effect, and by six minutes
of five o'clock I was feeling more worn-down than I should have as I
slumped into my chair to watch the clock tick away the last few minutes of my career, and possibly my liberty.

I heard a noise in the lab and turned to watch as Vince Masuoka came in, saw me, and stopped dead. "Oh," he said. "I forgot, um." And he spun around and raced out the door. Clearly, what he forgot was that I might still be there and he would have to say something to a coworker under investigation for the murder of another coworker, and for someone like Vince that would have been too uncomfortable.

I heard myself sigh heavily, and I wondered if this was really how it all ended; framed by a brainless thug, shunned by my colleagues, stalked by a whining computer nerd who couldn't even make it in minor-league baseball. It was well beyond ignoble, and very sad—I'd shown such tremendous early progress, too.

The clock ticked; two minutes of five. I might as well get my things together and head for home. I reached for my laptop, but as I put my hand on the screen to close it up a small and ugly thought crawled across the floor of my brain and I clicked on my in-box instead. It was really not even definite enough to call a hunch, but a soft and leathery voice was whispering that after I found the Dexter-ized body in the grubby little house he had sent an e-mail and now Camilla was dead and maybe, just maybe . . .

And as I opened my in-box, maybe turned to certainly as I read the subject line of my most recent e-mail. It said, "If you can read this, you're not in jail!"

With no doubt at all in my mind about who had sent this, I clicked it open.

At least, not yet. But don't worry—if your luck stays this good, you'll be there soon, which is anyway better than what I have in mind for you. It's not enough for me just to put you in the ground. I want people to know what you are first. And then . . . Well, you've seen what I can do now. And I am totally getting better at it, just in time for your turn.

She really liked you—I mean, all those pictures? They were everywhere! It was really sick, an obsession. And she let me in to her apartment on like the second date, which you have to say, she wouldn't do if she was a Good person. And when I saw your face plastered all over the place, I knew what I was supposed to do about it, and I did it.

Maybe I was a little hasty? Or maybe I'm just getting to like

*doing this, I don't know. Ironic, huh? That trying to get rid of you,
I'm becoming more and more like you. Anyway, it was too perfect to
be an accident, so I did it, and I am not sorry, and I am just getting
started. And if you think you can stop me, think again. Because you
don't know anything about me except that I can do exactly what you
do and I am coming to do it to you and you don't even know when
except it's soon.*

Have a nice day!

On the plus side, it was nice to see that I was not having paranoid
delusions. My Shadow really had killed Camilla to get at me. On the
minus side, Camilla was dead and I was in deeper trouble than I had
ever been.

And of course, things got even worse, all because Deborah said
they couldn't.

I headed home in a state of numb misery, wanting only a little bit
of quiet comfort from my loving family. And when I arrived, Rita was
waiting for me by the front door—but not in a spirit of tender welcome.
"You son of a bitch, I *knew* it," she hissed at me in greeting; it was as
shocking as if she had flung the couch at my head. And she wasn't
done yet. "God*damn* you, Dexter, how *could* you?" she said, and she
glared at me, with her fists clenched and a look of righteous fury on
her face. I know very well that I am guilty of a great many things that
might make many people unhappy with me—even Rita—but lately it
seemed like everyone was finding me guilty of all the wrong things:
things that I hadn't done and couldn't even guess at. So my normally
rapid wit did not respond with the kind of clever, brainy comeback
for which I am so justly famous. Instead, I just goggled at Rita and
stammered, "I could . . . How . . . What do I . . . ?"

It was almost unforgivably feeble, and Rita took advantage of it.
She socked me on the arm, right smack in the middle of the tender
bull's-eye that was Deborah's favorite target, and said, "You fucking
bastard! I knew it!"

I glanced past her to the couch; Cody and Astor were completely
hypnotized by the game they were playing on the Wii, and Lily Anne
was in her playpen next to them, happily watching them slay monsters. They hadn't heard any of Rita's naughty words, not yet, but if it

went on much longer, even mesmerized children would wake up and notice. I grabbed Rita's hand before she could hit me again and said, "Rita, for God's sake, what did I do?"

She yanked her hand away. "Bastard," she repeated. "You know goddamned well what you did. You *fucked* that pasty-faced bitch, god damn you!"

Every now and then we find ourselves living through moments that make no sense at all. It's almost as if some omnipotent film editor has snipped us out of our familiar everyday movie and spliced us into something completely random, from a different time and genre and even from a foreign country and partially animated, because suddenly you look around you and the language is unknown and nothing that happens has any relationship to what you think of as reality.

This was clearly one of those moments. Mild-mannered, Dexter-Devoted Rita, who never lost her temper and never, *never* said bad words, was doing both at the same time and directing it all at her innocent-just-this-once husband.

But even though I didn't know what movie I was in, I knew it was my line, and I knew I had to take control of the scene quickly. "Rita," I said as soothingly as I could. "You're not making any sense—"

"*Fuck* making sense and *fuck* you!" she said, stamping her foot and raising her fist to hit me again. Astor's head came up and she looked at us—it was Cody's turn in the game—and so once more I took Rita's hand and pulled her away from the front door.

"Come on," I said. "Let's take this into the kitchen."

"I'm not going to—" she started to say, and I raised my voice over hers.

"Away from the kids," I said. She glanced at them guiltily, and then followed along as I led her through the living room and into the kitchen. "All right," I said, pulling out my chair and sitting at the familiar table. "Using words that are simple, clear, and not outlawed in Kentucky, will you please tell me what the hell you're talking about?"

Rita stood on the far side of the table and glared down at me with an unchanging look of righteous fury on her face and her arms crossed. "You are so fucking smooth," she said through her teeth. "Even now, I almost believe you. Bastard."

I actually *am* smooth, in fact; Dexter is almost *all* smooth, icy control, and it has always served him well to be just that way. But right now I could feel the cool and the smooth melting away into a warm pudding of frustration, and I closed my eyes and took a deep breath in an effort to get things back to a more comfortable temperature. "Rita," I said, opening my eyes and giving her a very authentic look of patient long suffering. "Let's pretend for just a minute that I don't have any idea what you're talking about."

"You bastard, don't you try—"

I held up a hand. "You don't need to remind me that I'm a bastard; I remember that part," I said. "It's the other part I'm having trouble with—*why* I'm a bastard. Okay?"

She glared a little more, and I heard her toe tapping the floor, and then she uncrossed her arms and took a deep breath. "All right," she said. "I'll play your little game, you son of a bitch." She pointed at me, and if her finger had been loaded I would have died right then and there. "You had an affair with that bitch from work—a *detective* called me!" she said, as if a *detective* calling her proved everything beyond a doubt. "And he said did I know anything about her and the *affair* you had and were there any more *pictures*! And then it was on the news that she's *dead,* and Jesus Christ, Dexter, did you *kill* her, too, so I wouldn't find out?"

I am pretty sure that some level of my brain was still working, because apparently it reminded me to breathe. But all the higher mental functions seemed to be completely shut down; little fragments of thought scuttled past but none of them seemed able to pull themselves together into anything I could actually think or say. I felt another breath come in and then go out and I was dimly aware that a certain amount of time had passed and that the silence was getting uncomfortably long—but I really couldn't bring together enough of the scurrying pieces of thought to make up a real sentence. Slowly, painfully, the wheels turned, and finally single words came back to me—*bastard . . . kill . . . detective*—and at last, with that third word, a picture floated up out of the scampering neurons and rose to the top of my swirling nonthoughts—a glowering, knuckleheaded portrait of a human ape with a low brow and a mean smile, and at last I had one entire syllable that made sense. "Hood," I said. "He called you?"

"I think I have a right to know my husband killed somebody," Rita said. "And he's *cheating* on me?" she added, as if killing might be overlooked, but *cheating* was something truly despicable. It was not quite the proper order of our society's priorities as I had come to understand them, but this was not the time to debate contemporary ethical concepts.

"Rita," I said, with all the calm authority I could muster. "I barely knew this woman. Camilla."

"Bullshit," she said. "Richard said—the detective said there were pictures of you *everywhere*!"

"Yes, and Astor has pictures of the Jonas Brothers," I said; and I thought it was a pretty good point, but for some reason Rita didn't agree.

"Astor is eleven years old," Rita said venomously, as if I was totally vile even to try this argument and she would never let me get away with something that low. "And *she* doesn't stay out all night with the Jonas Brothers."

"Camilla and I worked together," I said, trying to break through the cloud of unreason. "And sometimes we have to work late. In *public*. With lots of cops all around us."

"And did all of the *cops* have *pictures* of you?" she demanded. "In a binder? On the back of the *toilet*?! Please. Don't insult my intelligence."

I very badly wanted to say that I had to find it before I could insult it, but sometimes we have to sacrifice a very good line for the larger purpose at hand, and this was almost certainly one of those times. "Rita," I said. "Camilla took pictures of me." I put the palms of my hands up to show that I was man enough to admit an awkward fact. "Lots of them, apparently. Deborah says she had a crush on me. I can't control any of that." I sighed and shook my head, to let her see that the full weight of an unjust world lay comfortably on my broad shoulders. "But I have never, *ever* cheated on you. Not with Camilla, not with anyone else."

I saw a first small flicker of doubt on her face—I really am very good at portraying a real human being, and this time I had the advantage of telling something that was very close to the truth. It was a genuine Method Acting Moment, and Rita could see that I was being sincere.

"Bullshit," she said, but with less conviction. "All those nights when you just leave the house? With some stupid excuse about work? As if I was supposed to believe . . ." She shook her head and gathered steam again. "Goddamn it, I *knew* it was something like this. I just *knew* it, because— And now you *killed* her?"

It was a very uncomfortable moment, even more so than when she had first accused me. "All those nights" in question, I actually *had* been up to something: not quite an affair, and certainly nothing involving Camilla—just the quiet pursuit of my hobby, which was relatively innocent, at least in the present context. But I couldn't tell her that, and of course, there was no proof of this innocence—at least, I hoped not; I mean, I was sure I'd always cleaned up quite thoroughly. Worst of all, though, was realizing that I had just assumed she hadn't really noticed when I slipped "casually" out of the house, which made me look incredibly stupid, even to me.

But surviving in this life almost always means making the best of bad situations, and if a small moment of creativity is called for, I am usually up to the task—especially since I am not burdened by any compulsion to tell the truth. And so I took a breath and let my giant brain lead me out of the woods. "Rita," I said. "My work is important to me. I help to catch some really bad people—not even people. They're *animals*. The kind of *animal* that's a real threat to all of us—even . . ." And I paused shamelessly for dramatic effect. "Especially the kids. Even Lily Anne."

"And so you leave the house at night?" she said. "To do *what*?"

"I, um," I said, as if I was a little bit embarrassed. "Sometimes I get an idea. About something that, you know. Might help break the case."

"Oh, come on," Rita said. "That's incredibly— I mean, I'm not naive enough, for God's sake—"

"Rita, damn it, you're the same way—obsessed with your job," I said. "You've been working nights lately, and . . . I mean, I thought you understood when I did, too."

"I don't slink out of the house at night to go to the office," she said.

"But you don't *have* to," I said, and I felt myself gaining a little bit of momentum. "You can do your work in your head, or on a piece of paper. I need the equipment in the lab."

"Well, but, I mean," she said, and I could see the doubt creeping into her eyes. "I just assumed that— I mean, it makes more sense that, you know."

"It makes more sense that I would cheat on someone as beautiful as you?" I said. "With somebody as drab and shapeless as Camilla Figg?" I know it isn't considered proper to speak ill of the dead, and doing so puts you at risk of some kind of divine retribution. But as if to prove that God does not really exist, I bad-mouthed dear dead Camilla and yet no bolt of lightning crashed through the ceiling to turn Dexter into chitlins, and Rita's expression even softened a bit.

"But that's not . . ." she said, and to my great relief she was slipping back into her normal speech pattern of partial sentences. "I mean, Richard said— And you never even, all those late nights." She blinked and fluttered one hand in the air. "How can it just—with all those pictures?"

"I know it looks bad," I said, and then I had one of those wonderfully happy inspirations that only a totally empty, wicked, hollow mockery of a person could ever have the gall to actually use—which, of course, made it just perfect for me. "It's looks bad to Detective Hood—*Richard*," I said, and gave her a bitter shake of the head to show I had noticed she was on a first-name basis with the enemy. "So bad that I'm in a lot of trouble," I said. "And to be honest, I thought you were the one person I could count on to stand by me. When I really need somebody in my corner."

It was a perfect punch, a true body blow, and it took the wind out of her so completely that she collapsed into a chair as if she was an inflatable doll and somebody had just punctured her. "But that's only . . ." she said. "I didn't even— And he *said*," she said. "I mean, he's a *detective*."

"A really *bad* detective," I said. "He likes to beat up suspects to make them talk. And he doesn't like me."

"But if you didn't do anything . . ." she said, trying one last time to convince herself that I actually did.

"People have been framed before," I said wearily. "This is Miami."

She shook her head slowly. "But he was so *sure*— How could he even . . . ? I mean, if you didn't."

There comes a time when repeating your arguments starts to sound like you're only making excuses. I knew this very well from the hours of daytime drama I had watched over the years, and I was pretty sure I was at that point now. Luckily, I had seen this exact situation so many times on TV that I knew precisely what to do to. I put both hands on the table, pushed upward, and stood. "Rita," I said, with truly impressive dignity, "I am your husband, and there has never been anybody else but you. If you can't believe me now, when I really need you—then I might as well let Detective Hood take me away to jail." I said it very sincerely, and with such conviction and pathos that it nearly persuaded even me.

It was my last round of ammunition—but it was a bull's-eye. Rita bit her lip, shook her head, and said, "But all those nights when you— And the *pictures* . . . And then she's *dead. . . .*" For just a second a last small doubt flickered across her face and I thought I had failed; and then she closed her eyes tightly and bit her lip and I knew I had won. "Oh, Dexter, what if they believe him?" She opened her eyes and a tear rolled out of the corner and down across one cheek, but Rita brushed it away with a finger and pursed her lips. "That *bastard*," she said, and I realized with great relief that she no longer meant me. "And he's supposed to— But he can't just . . ." And she slapped a hand on the table. "Well, we won't let him," she said, and then she stood up and ran around the table and grabbed me. "Oh, Dexter," she said into my shoulder. "I'm so sorry if I— You must be so . . ."

She snuffled, and then pushed herself away to arm's length. "But you have to understand," she said. "And it wasn't just— It's . . . for a while now. And then lately, you've been so . . . kind of . . ." She shook her head slowly. "I mean, you know," she said, but in fact I didn't know, or even have a guess. "It just all made *sense,* because sometimes it seems lately like . . . I don't know— And it isn't just the house," she said. "The foreclosures? It's everything, all of it." She kept shaking her head, faster now. "So many nights, when you— I mean, that's how . . . *men* act. When they're doing that— And I have to, with the kids here, and all I can do about it is just . . ."

She turned half away from me and crossed her arms again, placing the knuckle of one finger between her teeth. She bit down and a tear rolled down her cheek. "Jesus, Dexter, I feel so . . ."

It may be that I really am becoming more human, slowly but surely, but I had a sudden moment of insight of my own as I watched

Rita hunch her shoulders and drip tears onto the floor. "That's why you've been drinking so much wine," I said. Her head jerked back around toward me and I could see the muscles of her jaw tighten down even more on her poor helpless finger. "You thought I was sneaking out to have an affair."

"I couldn't even . . ." she said, and then she realized she was still chewing her finger and dropped it from her mouth. "I wanted to just— Because what else can I do? When you are just so— I mean, sometimes . . ." She took a deep breath and then stepped closer. "I didn't know what else to do and I felt so . . . *helpless.* Which is a feeling I really— And then I thought it was probably *me*—because right after a new baby? And you never seem to . . ." She shook her head vigorously. "I've been such an idiot. Oh, Dexter, I'm so sorry."

Rita leaned her forehead against my chest and snuffled, and I realized it was my line again. "I'm sorry, too," I said, and I put an arm around her.

She raised her head and looked deep into my eyes. "I'm an *idiot,*" she said again. "I should have known that— Because it's you and me, Dexter," she said. "That's what matters. I mean, I *thought* so. Until just suddenly, it seemed like . . ." She straightened suddenly and gripped my upper arms. "And you didn't sleep with her? Really?"

"Really and truly," I said, greatly relieved to have a sentence fragment with a complete thought behind it that I could react to at last.

"Oh, my God," she said, and she put her face down onto my shoulder and made wet noises for a minute or two. And from what I know about people, it's possible that I should have felt a little guilt about the way I had manipulated Rita so completely. Or even better, maybe I should have turned to the camera to show my true villainy with a leer of wicked satisfaction. But there was no camera, as far as I knew, and I had, after all, manipulated Rita with the truth, for the most part. So I just held on to her and let her soak my shirt with tears, mucus, and who knows what else.

"Oh, God," she said at last, raising her head. "I can be so *stupid* sometimes." I did not rush in to disagree, and she shook her head and then wiped at her face with a sleeve. "I never should have doubted you," she said, looking at me closely. "I feel like such a— And you must be so totally . . . Oh, my God, I can't even *begin* to— Dexter, I am *so* sorry, and it isn't just— Oh, that bastard. And we need to get you a lawyer, too."

"What?" I said, trying to switch gears rapidly from following her mental leaps with bemusement to dealing with an alarming new idea. "Why do I need a lawyer?"

"Don't be simple, Dexter," she said with a shake of her head. She sniffled, and began to brush absentmindedly at my shoulder where she had leaked all over it. "If this man Rich—Detective Hood," she went on, pausing just a second to blush. "If he's trying to prove you killed her, you need to get the best possible legal advice and— I think Carlene, at work? She said her brother-in-law . . . And anyway the first consultation is almost always free, so we don't have to— Not that money is any— So I'll ask her tomorrow," she said, and clearly that was settled, because she stopped talking and looked at me searchingly again, her eyes jerking from left to right. Apparently she didn't find what she was looking for on either side, and after a moment she just said, "Dexter—"

"I'm right here," I said.

"We really have to talk more."

I blinked, which must have been startling to her at such close range, and she blinked back at me. "Well, sure, I mean . . . talk about what?" I said.

She put her hand on my cheek and for just a second she pressed so tightly that I wondered if she was trying to stop a leak in my face. Then she sighed and smiled and took her hand away and said, "You can be such a *guy* sometimes," and it was difficult to disagree with that, since I had no idea what it meant.

"Thank you?" I tried, and she shook her head.

"We just need to *talk*," she said. "It doesn't have to be *about*— Because that's where this whole thing has gone so completely— And it's probably my fault," she said. Again, it was very tough to argue with the conclusion, since I hadn't understood anything leading up to it.

"Well," I said, feeling remarkably awkward, "I'm always happy to talk with you."

"If I had only said," she told me sadly. "Because I should *know* you wouldn't— I should have *said* something *weeks* ago."

"Um," I said, "we didn't know any of this until today."

She gave her head one brief, irritated shake. "That isn't the point," she said, which was a relief, even though I still didn't know what the point was. "I just mean, I should have . . ." She took a deep breath and shook my shoulders slightly. "You have been very, *very*— I mean, I should have known that you were just busy and working too hard," she said. "But you have to see how it looked to me, because— And then when he called it all seemed to make sense? So if we only just talk more often . . ."

"All right," I said; agreeing seemed a little easier than understanding.

It was clearly the right thing to say, because Rita smiled fondly and then leaned forward to give me a big hug. "We'll get through this," she said. "I promise you." And then, maybe oddest of all, she leaned back slightly from our embrace and said, "You didn't forget that this weekend is the big summer camping trip? With Cody and the Cub Scouts?"

I hadn't actually forgotten—but I also hadn't remembered it in the context of playing out a dramatic scene of domestic anguish, and I had to pause for just a second to catch up with her. "No," I said at last. "I didn't forget."

"Good," she said, putting her head back down onto my chest. "Because I think he's really looking forward— And you could use some time away, too," she said.

And as I patted Rita's back with absentminded little thumps, I tried very hard to feel good about that thought—because, thanks to a Neanderthal detective and a copycat murder, I was going to get some time away whether I wanted it or not.

TWENTY-TWO

THE NEXT DAY WAS FRIDAY, AND OUT OF NOTHING MORE than pure reflex I lurched upright in bed at seven o'clock. But as consciousness flooded in to my brain, unpleasant reality came back in with it, and I remembered that I had nowhere to go and no reason to get up: I was suspended from work while a man who didn't like me investigated me for the murder of somebody I hadn't had sex with and hadn't even killed, and my only appeal lay through someone who absolutely hated me—Sergeant Doakes. It was the kind of near-perfect trap we would all love to see a comic book villain wedged into, but I could not see the justice of cramming Dashing Dexter into it. I mean, I know I am not without my little flaws, but really; why me?

I tried to look at the bright side: At least Hood had not persuaded the powers-that-be to suspend my pay, too. That might be important if Rita really did find us a new house; I would need every penny. And here I was at home, saving even more money by not using gas, or buying lunch; lucky me! In fact, if I thought about it the right way, it was almost like having an extra vacation—except for the possibility that this little holiday might end with me in jail, or dead. Or even both.

Still, here I was, suspended, and at the moment there seemed to be very little I could do about it, so there was no reason for me to leap out of bed and fret. And if I had been the logical and rational creature that I often like to think I am, I would have seen that even this unhappy situation had a very real upside—I didn't have to get up!—and I would have gone right back to sleep. But for some reason, I found that I could not; at my first memory of what had happened yesterday, sleep had run screaming from the room, and in spite of the fact that I lay there frowning and threatening it for several minutes, it would not come back.

So I lay stubbornly in bed and listened to the sounds of morning at Dexter's house. The sounds had not changed, even though it was summer and school was out. The kids were enrolled in a day-care program at the park where they went for after-school care during the school year, and Rita still had to be at work at the regular time, so the morning program had not changed. I could hear Rita in the kitchen; the smells wafting down the hall told me she was making scrambled eggs with cheese, and cinnamon toast on the side. She called Cody and Astor to come and get it twice before I finally admitted that I was not going back to sleep, and I slumped into my place at the kitchen table just as Cody was finishing his breakfast. Lily Anne was in her high chair, creating a magnificent apple-sauce mural across its tray and her face. Astor sat with her arms crossed, apparently more inter-ested in scowling than eating.

"Good morning, Dexter," Rita said, thumping a cup of coffee down in front of me. "Cody had seconds, so I have to make— Astor, honey, you have to eat something." She went briskly back to the stove and began cracking eggs into the pan.

"I can't eat," Astor hissed. "It gets stuck on my *braces*." She said the word with enough venom to drop an elephant, and she bared the bright silver bands so we could all share her horror at the hideous disfigurement.

"Well, you still have to eat," Rita said, stirring the eggs. "I'll get you some yogurt, or you can—"

"I *hate* yogurt," Astor said.

"You liked it yesterday," Rita said. •

"Ooohhhh," Astor said through clenched teeth. She slammed

her elbows onto the table and leaned angrily onto them. "I'll eat the eggs," she said, as if she was nobly agreeing to do something vile and dangerous.

"Wonderful," Rita said, and Lily Anne tapped her spoon on the tray with sisterly encouragement.

Breakfast ended and led to the shouting, slamming, foot-stomping ritual of teeth-and-hair brushing, dressing, and finding socks, changing Lily Anne and packing her bag for the day, and finally, with five separate slams of the front door, they got all the way out to the car, Rita and Astor still arguing about whether pink socks went with a red shirt. Astor's voice faded into the distance, I heard the car doors thunk shut, and suddenly the house was unnaturally quiet.

I got up and turned off the coffee machine, pouring the last of the brew into my cup. I sat back down and sipped it, wondering why I bothered; there was no reason for me to be awake and alert. I had all the leisure time a man could want—I was suspended from work, and being stalked by somebody who thought he was turning himself into me. And if he somehow missed me, I was still under investigation for a murder I hadn't committed. Considering how many I had gotten away with, that was probably very ironic. I tried a hollow, mocking laugh at myself, but it sounded too spooky in the sudden silence of the empty house. So I slurped coffee and concentrated on self-pity for a while. It came surprisingly easily; I really was the victim of a gross miscarriage of justice, and it was a simple matter for me to feel wounded, martyred, betrayed by the very system I had served so long and well.

Luckily, my native wit trickled back in before I began to sing country songs, and I turned my thoughts toward finding a way out of my predicament. But in spite of the fact that I finished the coffee—my third cup of the morning, too—I couldn't seem to kick my brain out of the glutinous sludge of misery it had fallen into. I was reasonably sure that Hood could not find anything and make it stick to me; there was nothing there to find. But I also knew that he was very anxious to solve Camilla's murder—both so that he would look good to the department and the press and, just as importantly, so he could make Deborah look bad. And if I added in the uncomfortable fact that he was obviously aided and abetted by Sergeant Doakes and his toxic tunnel vision, I had to conclude that the outlook was far from rosy. I didn't really believe they would manufacture evidence merely in order to frame me, but on the other hand—why wouldn't they? It had happened before, even with an investigating officer who had a whole lot less on the line.

The more I thought about it, the more worried I got. Hood had his own agenda, and I was tailor-made for the starring role. And Doakes had been looking for a way to make me legally guilty of something for a very long time—almost anything would do, as long as it ended with Dexter in the Dumpster. There was no reason for either of them to discard a perfectly good opportunity to put me in the slammer just because it was fiction. I could even see the path their reasoning would take: *Dexter was guilty of something; we can't prove it but we are certain of it. But if we cut a few corners here and there, we can make this thing fit him, and put him where he really belongs anyway—in the pokey for a very long time. No real harm is done, and society is much better for it—why, indeed, not?*

It was perfect Bent-cop Logic, and the only question was whether Hood and Doakes were bent enough to follow it and make up a few small details that would convince a jury of my guilt. Were they both so twisted and so determined to get me that they would go through with it? I thought about the synchronized display of dental work they had shown in my office, the truly vicious glee they so clearly felt at having me in their clutches, and a cold and acrid lump grew in my stomach and murmured, *Of course they would.*

So I spent the first half of the day slouching around the house, trying out nearly every chair in the place, to see if perhaps a glimmer of hope might flare up if only I could find the right piece of furniture. None of them seemed to work better than any other. The chairs in the kitchen didn't do a thing to stimulate my cerebral process, and neither did the easy chair by the TV. Even the couch was a mental dead zone. I could not drive away the image of Hood and Doakes pronouncing my doom with such joy, their teeth gleaming with identical feral smiles, which matched perfectly the tone of my Shadow's last note. Everyone seemed to be showing me their teeth, and I could not come up with a single thought that might help me shut their jaws or wiggle off their hooks. I was trapped, and there was not a piece of furniture in the world that could get me out of it.

I spent the rest of the day fretting, wondering what I would say to Rita and Debs when Hood and Doakes finally came for me. It would be hard on Rita, of course—but what about Deborah? She knew what I was, and knew I deserved whatever punishment I got. Would that make it easier for her to accept? And how would my arrest affect her career? It can't be easy for a homicide cop to have a brother in the slammer for murder. People would certainly talk, and the things they said would not be kind.

And what about Lily Anne? What terrible damage would it do to such a bright and sensitive child, growing up with a famous monster for a father? What if it pushed her off the edge and into a life on the Dark Side, along with Cody and Astor? How could I live with the knowledge that I had destroyed such a potentially beautiful life?

It was far too much for any human being to bear, and I was very glad that I wasn't one. It was hard enough dealing with my own colossal irritation and frustration—I am sure that if I'd had normal emotions I would have torn my hair, wailed, and gnashed my teeth, all of which were probably counterproductive.

Not that a single thing I did that day produced anything of value, either. I couldn't even come up with a decent farewell speech to give in the courtroom, after the jury pronounced me Guilty on All Counts, as they certainly would. What could I possibly say? "It is a far, far darker thing I have done—and loved every minute of it."

I made a sandwich for lunch. There were no leftovers in the refrigerator, and no cold cuts. There was also no bread left, except for two half-stale heels, so I ended up with the perfect meal to fit this day: a peanut-butter-and-jelly sandwich on stale bread crusts. And because it is so important to match the beverage to the meal, I washed it down with tap water, relishing the succulent chlorine bouquet.

After lunch I tried to watch television, but I found that even with two-thirds of my brain focused on fretting about my coming demise, the remaining third of my intellect was a little too smart to put up with the bright and brainless daytime drivel on all the channels. I turned off the set and just sat on the couch, letting one tense and miserable thought chase another, until finally, at half past five, the front door burst open and Astor stormed in, flung her backpack on the floor, and rushed to her room. She was followed by Cody, who actually noticed me and nodded, and then Rita, carrying Lily Anne.

"Oh," Rita said, "I'm so glad you didn't— Could you take the baby, please? She needs a fresh diaper."

I took Lily Anne away from Rita and held her, wondering again if this was the last time. Lily Anne seemed to sense my mood, and tried very hard to cheer me up by poking me in the eye and then gurgling with amusement. I had to admit it was very clever, and I very nearly smiled as I took her down the hall to the changing table with one eye half-closed and leaking tears.

But even Lily Anne's sly wit and cheerful antics were not enough to make me forget that my head was in the noose, and some very eager hands were pulling it closed around my throat.

TWENTY-THREE

HALF-BRIGHT AND MUCH TOO EARLY THE NEXT MORNING, Cody and I stood in the parking lot of the elementary school where the Cub Scouts met. Frank, the pack's leader, was already there with an old van that had a trailer hitch on the back. With him was his new assistant, Doug Crowley, along with Fidel, the boy Crowley sponsored through the Big Brothers program. As Cody and I arrived they were pushing the den's trailer toward the hitch. I parked my car as three other boys were dropped off by mothers in several different stages of Saturday-morning undress and unawake. We all climbed out of our cars into the heavy humid heat of the early summer morning and watched as more boys arrived, shoved from their cars with their gear, and shuffling from one foot to the other as they watched their moms drive quickly and gratefully away for a weekend of boyless bliss.

Cody and I stood together, waiting as the other Scouts trickled in. I had a large helping of Rita's coffee in a travel mug, and I sipped it and wondered why I ever bothered to go anywhere on time. It was clear that I was the only one in Miami who actually understood what those numbers on the face of the clock really meant, and I spent far too much of my dwindling liberty waiting for people who couldn't quite grasp the notion of time. It should have stopped bothering me long ago—after all, I grew up here, and I was very familiar with Cuban Time, an immutable law of nature stating that any given hour for a rendezvous actually means, "plus forty-five minutes."

But this morning I was finding the tardiness particularly irritating. I could feel Dexter's Doom closing in, and I felt that I should be exploding into focused action, doing something clever and dynamically proactive, and not just standing in an elementary school's parking lot sipping coffee and watching Cuban Time unfold. I hoped that whoever came to arrest me would be working on Cuban Time—or even Double Cuban. I could probably make my getaway while they finished a *cafecita*, played a game of dominoes, and finally strolled around to get me.

I sipped. I glanced down at Cody. He was staring thoughtfully across the parking lot, his lower lip twitching slightly, at where Frank and Doug were pushing at the trailer. Cody never seemed to get bored or impatient, and I wondered what he was thinking that kept him occupied so contentedly. Since I knew very well that he was like me inside, with his Shadow Guy and its Dark Longings, I could guess which direction his thoughts were moving. I just had to hope I could be half as good at steering him away from acting on them as Harry had been with me. Otherwise, Cody would probably celebrate his fifteenth birthday in jail.

As if he could feel my thoughts, Cody looked up at me and frowned. "Something wrong?" I asked him. But he just shook his head, still frowning, and went back to watching Frank and Doug play with the trailer. I slurped coffee and watched, too, which turned out to be the closest thing to real entertainment the day had offered so far. Frank was winding down the jack stand on the trailer, and as it took on the full weight of the trailer, it snapped and the trailer's yoke thumped hard onto the pavement.

I could think of several very choice words that might have been appropriate, but of course, Frank knew he was surrounded by innocent ears, so he merely put both hands over his face and shook his head. Crowley, though, bent over and grabbed the yoke with both hands and, with a grunt that was audible all the way across the parking lot, he straightened, lifting the trailer up with him. He took two small steps toward the van, dropped the yoke onto the trailer hitch, and dusted off his hands.

It was impressive as well as entertaining. From the way it had dropped when the jack stand broke, it was clear that the trailer was quite heavy. Yet Crowley had lifted it and pulled it all by himself. Maybe that was why Frank had made him assistant leader.

Unfortunately, that was the last act of entertainment on the morning's program, and forty minutes after our scheduled departure time we were still waiting for three final Cubs to arrive. Two of them arrived together as I finished my coffee, and then finally, with a cheerful and unconcerned wave from his father, the last boy climbed out of a new Jaguar and sauntered over to where Frank was standing. Frank waved his arm at the rest of us and we all gathered around for orientation.

"All right," Frank said. "Drivers?" He looked around at the entire group with raised eyebrows, perhaps thinking that one or two of the boys might be driving. But none of them seemed to be holding car keys; maybe that was asking a bit much of a Cub Scout, even in Miami. Instead, I raised my hand, as did Doug Crowley and two other men I didn't know.

"Okay," Frank said. "We are going to Fakahatchee State Park." One of the boys snickered and repeated the name, and Frank looked at him wearily. "It's a *Native American* name," he said ominously, looking at the smirking boy for a long moment until the kid felt the full weight and power of confronting something Native American while wearing a Cub Scout uniform. Frank cleared his throat and went on. "So, uh . . . Fakahatchee State Park. We'll meet at the ranger station, in case, you know. If we get separated or whatever. Now," he said, raising his eyes up above the boys to adult level, "we're gonna leave the cars, and the trailer, right there at the ranger station. It's perfectly safe; the rangers are right there. And then we hike in two miles to the campsite." He smiled, looking like a large and eager dog. "It's gonna be a great hike, just the right distance, and we'll have lots of time to get those pack straps right so they don't chafe, okay? And the rangers will give us all a book that tells us all the cool things to look for along the path. Because if you keep your eyes open you will definitely see some great stuff. And if we're really lucky, we *might* even see"—Frank paused very dramatically and looked around the circle, his eyes gleaming with excitement—"a *ghost orchid*."

The boy who had been last to arrive said, "What's that? Like a flower that's a ghost?"

The boy next to him shoved him and murmured, "Idiot," and Frank shook his head.

"It's one of the rarest flowers in the world," Frank said. "And if we see one you have to be very careful not to touch it. Don't even *breathe* on it. It is so delicate, and so *rare*, that hurting one would be a true crime." Frank let this sink in, and then gave them a small smile and went on. "Now remember. Besides the orchids. We are going into an area that has been kept just the way the Calusas left it."

He lowered his eyes to the boys' level and nodded at them. "We talked about this, guys. This is a primitive area, and we need to respect its purity. Leave nothing behind except footprints, right?" He glanced at each boy to make sure they were properly serious; they were, so he nodded and smiled again. "Okay. We're gonna have a *great* time. Let's get going."

Frank assigned each boy to one of the cars. Along with me and Cody, I had room for two; one of them turned out to be Steve Binder, the boy Cody had said was a bully. He was a big kid with a single eyebrow and a low hairline—he might have been Detective Hood's child, if you could only believe that any woman alive would have the poor taste to submit to Hood, and then keep the result.

My other passenger was a cheerful kid named Mario, who seemed to know every scouting song ever written, and by the time we got halfway to the park he had sung all of them at least twice. Because I had to keep both hands on the steering wheel, I couldn't really turn around and strangle him, but I didn't interfere when Steve Binder, at the point in the song when there were still eighty-two bottles of pop left on the wall, finally gave Mario a hard elbow and said, "Cut it out, stoopit."

Mario sulked for a full three minutes, and then started babbling happily about Calusa shell mounds and how you could make water-tight shelters with palmetto palm fronds and the best way to start a fire in the swamp. Cody stared straight ahead through the windshield from his place of honor in the front seat, and Steve Binder glow-

ered and twitched in the backseat and every now and then glared at
Mario. But Mario babbled on, apparently without noticing that everyone else in the car wanted him dead. He was bright and cheerful and
well-informed and almost everything a Cub Scout should be, and I
would not have objected too much if Steve Binder threw him out the
window of the car.

By the time we got to the ranger station at the park I was gritting
my teeth and clutching at the steering wheel so hard my knuckles
showed white. I pulled in and parked next to one of the other dads
who had gotten there first, and we all got out and released Mario
into the unsuspecting wild. Steve Binder stomped away to find something to break, and once again Cody and I found ourselves standing
in a parking lot and waiting for people to show up.

Since I no longer had any coffee to sip while I waited, I used the
time to pull our gear out of the trunk and make sure it was all carefully packed into our backpacks. My pack held our tent and most of
our food, and it was already starting to look much bigger and heavier
than it had when I first packed it at home.

It was a good half hour before the last car arrived at the ranger
station—the battered old Cadillac filled with Doug Crowley and his
group. They had stopped for a pee break and to buy some MoonPies.
But ten minutes after that we were all on the trail and hiking off to
our Wonderful Adventure in the Wild.

We didn't see a ghost orchid along the trail. Most of the boys were
able to hide their bitter disappointment, and I kept my mind off my
shattered hopes of seeing the rare flower by adjusting Cody's pack
straps until he could stand up straight enough to walk. The trick, as
we had learned in one of our den meetings, was to get the weight onto
the hip strap, and then keep the shoulder straps tight, but not so tight
that they cut off circulation and made your arms go numb. It took a
couple of tries to get it just right as we hiked along the trail, and by
the time Cody nodded at me that he was comfortable, I realized that
my arms had gone numb, and we had to start all over again. Once the
feeling came back into my arms and we could walk normally, I began
to feel a burning pain on my heel, and before we were even halfway
to the campsite I had a wonderful new blister on my left heel.

Still, we staggered in to the campsite in good shape and relatively high spirits, and in no time at all Cody and I had our tent set up under a shady tree all snug and comfy. Frank organized the boys for a nature walk, and I made Cody tag along. He wanted me to go, too, but I refused. After all, the whole purpose of getting him involved in scouting was to help him learn how to act like a real boy, and he could not study that hanging out with me. He had to get out there on his own and figure out how to cope, and this was as good a time as any to start. Besides, my blister hurt, and I wanted to take off my shoes and sit in the shade for a while, doing nothing more than rubbing my feet and exercising my self-pity.

And so I sat there, back against a tree trunk and bare feet stretched out in front of me, as the voices faded into the distance; Frank's eager baritone calling out fascinating nature facts over the higher-pitched sound of the boys joking around, and the overriding noise of Mario singing "There's a Hole in the Bucket." I wondered whether anyone would think to feed him to an alligator.

It got very quiet, and for a few minutes I sat there and enjoyed it. A cool breeze blew through the trees and over my face. A lizard ran by me and up the tree at my back; halfway up he turned to face me and puffed out his throat, the crimson skin rolling out as if he was daring me to stand and fight. Overhead a large heron flew past, muttering to himself. He was a little awkward-looking, but perhaps that was deliberate, a kind of camouflage to lull his prey into underestimating him. I had seen his kind on the job in the water, and they were lethal and lightning-fast when they went to work on the fish. They would stand very still, looking cute and fluffy, and then slash down into the water and come up with a fish impaled on their beak. It was a great routine, and I felt a certain kinship with herons. Like me, they were predators in disguise.

The heron disappeared into the swamp, and a flock of cattle egrets went by in its place, wings rattling. Almost as if it was caused by the birds' passage, the wind riffled through the trees and blew over me again, and it felt very good on my face and my feet. The blister on my heel stopped throbbing, I started to relax, and even all my troubles with Hood and Doakes and my Shadow faded into the background just a little. After all, it was a beautiful day in the primeval forest, in the middle of wonderful, eternal nature, complete with birds. This had not changed in thousands of years, and it might very well stay just like this for another five or six years, until somebody wanted to build condos. Beautiful wild things were killing each other all around me, and there was something soothing about sitting here and feeling like I was a part of a process that went on practically forever. Maybe there really was something to this whole Nature business after all.

It was relaxing and wonderful and lasted almost five whole minutes, and then the nagging worries began to seep back in and batter at me until all the lush feathered scenery might as well have been painted on a ratty old postcard. What did it matter if the forest was timeless? Dexter was not. My time was ticking away, draining off forever into the Long Dark Night—what good was a tree if it grew in a world with no Dexter? Even as I sat here admiring birds in the wild, my Goose was being Cooked back in the real world. With luck and skill, I might just survive the attack by Hood and Doakes—but without luck and some inspired cleverness, it was all over for me. So unless I could find a way to defuse them, I was going to end my days in a cell.

And even if I dodged their bullet, my Shadow was still lurking with unknown menace. I tried to recapture the sense of quiet confidence I'd woken up with the other day. So much had happened since, and instead of handling it with the sure-footed competence I used to display routinely, I was sitting under a tree in the swamp and watching birds, without a single thought about what to do. I didn't have a plan. To be honest, I didn't even have a glimmer of real thought that might turn into a plan. But there should have been some small comfort in knowing I was out here in Nature, where predators are respected, which really ought to count for something.

Sadly, there wasn't any comfort, none at all. I could see nothing ahead of me except pain and suffering, and far too much of it was going to be mine.

"Hey, you didn't go either, huh?" said a cheerful voice behind me, and it startled me so badly I almost threw a shoe. Instead, I merely turned around to see who had so rudely interrupted my reverie.

Doug Crowley leaned against my tree, looking a little too casual, as if he was trying to learn this position but wasn't quite sure he'd gotten it right yet, and his eyes behind his wire-rimmed glasses seemed a little too wide to be really nonchalant. He was a man of about my age, with a square, slightly soft-looking body, and the stubble of a trimmed-short beard on his face that was probably supposed to hide a weak chin, but didn't quite. And somehow, in spite of his size, he had snuck up behind me silently and I had not heard him, and I found that almost as irritating as his chummy good cheer.

"On the walk," he said hopefully. "You didn't go on the nature walk. Either." A poor fake smile flickered on and off his mouth. "Neither did I," he added, quite unnecessarily.

"Yes, I can see that," I said. It was probably not very gracious of me, but I was not feeling particularly chummy, and his efforts at being friendly were so clearly artificial that he offended my sense of craft; I had put a great deal of time and work into learning to fake everything. Why couldn't he?

He stared down at me for a long and awkward moment, forcing me to crane my neck up to stare back. His eyes were very blue and seemed a little too small, and something was going on behind them, but I couldn't tell what, and frankly, I didn't really care.

"Well," he said. "I just wanted to, you know. Say hi. Introduce myself." He pushed off the tree, and then lurched down at me with his hand held out. "Doug Crowley," he said, and I reluctantly took his hand.

"Pleased to meet you," I lied. "Dexter Morgan."

"Yes, I know," he said. "I mean, Frank said. Nice to meet you, too." And then he straightened up and just looked at me for what seemed like several long minutes. "Well," he said at last. "This your first time in the 'Glades?"

"No, I used to go camping a lot," I said.

"Oh, uh-huh. Camping," he said, in a very odd tone of voice that seemed to indicate he thought I might be lying.

So I added, "And *hunting*," with just a little bit of emphasis.

Crowley shuffled backward a half step and blinked, and then finally nodded. "Sure," he said. "I guess you would." He looked at his feet, and then looked uncertainly around, as if he thought someone might be hunting him. "You didn't bring any . . . I mean, you weren't planning to . . . you know. This trip?" he said. "I mean, with all the kids around."

It came to me that he was asking if I was planning on hunting right now, in the middle of a flock of wild Cub Scouts, and the thought was so stupid that for a moment I could do no more than cock my head to one side and look at him. "Noooo," I said at last. "I wasn't actually *planning* on it." And just because he was being so irritatingly dumb, I shrugged and added, "But you never know when the urge may strike, do you?" And I gave him a happy smile, just so he could see what a really *good* fake looked like.

Crowley blinked again, nodded slowly, and shifted from one foot to the other. "Riiiight," he said, and his cheap artificial smile flickered on and off again. "I know what you mean."

"I'm sure you do," I said, but I was really only sure that I wanted to see him burst into flames. And after all, putting him out would be a great exercise for the boys.

"Uh-huh," he said. He shifted his weight back onto his other foot and looked around him again. There was no help coming, so he looked back at me. "Well," he said. "I'll see you later."

"Almost certainly," I said, and he gave me a slightly startled look, freezing where he stood for just a moment. And then he nodded his head, flashed me one more brief and unconvincing smile, and turned away to wander back to the far side of the camp. I watched him go; it had been an incredibly awkward performance, and it made me wonder how he hoped to be assistant den leader without having the Cub Scouts beat him up and take his lunch money. He seemed so awkward and helpless, I couldn't see how he had reached such an advanced age without being pecked to death by angry pigeons.

I knew very well that there are far more lambs in the world than wolves—but why was I always the one they came bleating to? It seemed terribly unfair that way out here, in the middle of the savage woods, I could still be assailed by twinkies like Crowley. Shouldn't there be a park regulation against them? Or even an open season? They certainly weren't an endangered species.

I tried to shake off the irritation at this uncalled-for interruption, but my focus had fled. How could I concentrate on wiggling out of a trap when I was constantly tormented by pointless interruptions? Not that I'd come up with any thoughts on creative wiggling anyway. I'd pounded away at the mental rock pile for two full days and was still totally clueless. I sighed and closed my eyes, and as if to confirm that I really was stupid, the blister on my heel began to throb again.

I tried to think soothing thoughts, picturing the heron spearing a large fish, or pecking at Crowley, but the picture wouldn't stick. I couldn't see anything but the painfully happy faces of Hood and Doakes. Dull gray despair curdled in my guts, gurgling a mean and scornful laugh at my blockheaded attempts to get out of the trap. There was no escape, not this time. I was besieged by two very determined and dangerous cops who really and truly wanted to arrest me for something—anything—and they needed only a little fake evidence to put me away forever, and on top of that a completely unknown person with an obscure but probably very dangerous threat was circling closer. And I thought I could fight them all off by sitting in a Cub Scout tent and admiring herons? I was like a little boy playing war, yelling, *Bang, bang! Gotcha!,* and looking up to see a real Sherman tank rolling right at me.

It was pointless and hopeless, and I was still clueless.

Dexter was Doomed, and sitting barefoot underneath a tree and being rude to a ninny was not going to change that.

I closed my eyes, overwhelmed, and as the full-throated chorus of *Pity Me* echoed across the emptiness inside me, I apparently fell asleep.

TWENTY-FOUR

I WOKE UP FROM A GRUMPY DOZE TO THE SOUNDS OF THE Nature Hike stomping back into the camp, with two or three boys' voices calling out to each other, Frank yelling something about lunch, and Mario's voice rising above it all with a very instructive lecture on what alligators do with their prey and why it was a bad idea to give them anything to eat, even that awful Mystery-Meat stuff they serve in the school cafeteria, which would probably make even an alligator throw up.

It was a very strange way to come back to consciousness from the totally dead and dopey sleep I'd been lying in, and at first the sounds didn't make sense to me. I blinked my eyes open and tried to force the noise to add up to something approaching consensus reality, but the leaden stupidity of my nap would not leave me, so I just lay there in a blank stupor at the base of my tree, frowning and clearing my throat and trying to rub the sand out of my eyes, until at last a small shadow moved into my line of sight and I looked up to see Cody. He stared down at me very seriously until I finally pulled myself up to a sitting position, cleared my throat one last time, and somehow remembered how to make real words come out of my mouth.

"Well," I said, and to my heavy-headed ears even that one syllable sounded stupid, but I plowed on. "How was the nature hike?"

Cody frowned and shook his head. "Okay," he said.

"What kind of nature did you see?"

For a moment I thought he might actually smile, and then he said, "Alligator," and there was a slight edge in his voice that could almost have been excitement.

"You saw an alligator?" I asked, and he nodded. "What did it do?"

"*Looked* at me," he said. Something about the way he said it added up to a whole lot more than three small words.

"And what happened then?" I asked him.

Cody glanced around and then lowered his already soft voice to make sure no one else could hear him. "Shadow Guy *laughed*," he said. "At the alligator." It was a very long speech for him, and to make it even more notable, he really did smile then, just a brief flicker across his small and serious face, but there was no mistaking it. Shadow Guy, Cody's Dark Passenger, had made an emotional connection with the honest and savage spirit of a real live predator, and Cody was delighted.

So was I. "Isn't nature wonderful?" I said, and he nodded happily. "Well, what now?"

"Hungry," he said, which actually made sense, so I unzipped the fly of our tent and got our lunch. It was in Cody's pack, because I had wanted him to carry less weight coming home, in case the ordeal of camping made him tired.

We did not have to do a great deal of preparation for this meal; Rita had packed us a premade lunch consisting of bologna salad sandwiches and a baggie full of carrot spears and grapes, followed by a final course of a medley of cookies from the grocery store's bakery. Hiking and fresh air are said to make food taste better, and it may be true. In any case, there were no leftovers.

After lunch, Frank called everybody together again, and then organized us into teams, each with an Important Job. Cody and I were assigned to the firewood-collecting group, and we stood by the fire circle and listened dutifully as Frank lectured us thoroughly about making sure we gathered only deadwood, and remember that sometimes it could *look* dead but it wasn't, and that to injure a living tree in this area was not only bad for the planet but an actual *crime*; and don't forget to be very careful about poison oak, poison ivy, and something called manchineel.

I realized that it was very hard to be careful about something if you had no idea what it was, so I made the mistake of asking about manchineel. Unfortunately, this was just the excuse Frank needed to launch himself into a full-blown Nature Lecture. He gave me a very happy nod. "You *have* to watch out for that one," he said brightly. "Because it is *deadly*. Even just touching it will burn your skin. I mean, blisters and everything, and you will definitely require medical attention. So watch for it—it's a tree, and the leaves are kind of oval and waxy, and it's got, um—the fruit looks kinda like apples? But Do Not Eat It! It will absolutely *kill* you, and even *touching* it is dangerous, so—"

This was obviously a subject close to Frank's heart, and I wondered if I had misjudged him. Anyone with such a passion for lethal vegetation couldn't be all bad. He had a lecture five full minutes long just on the manchineel tree, and that was only the start.

It was very instructive: Manchineel, apparently, had been used by the Aboriginal Peoples of the Caribbean for poison, torture, and several other worthwhile purposes. Even sitting under the tree during a rainstorm could be deadly. In fact, the Carib Indians had actually tied their prisoners to the trunk of the tree when it rained, because the water dripping off the leaves made an acid bath strong enough to eat through human flesh. And arrows dipped in the sap could cause painful death; clearly it was wonderful stuff. But Frank's main point—avoid the manchineel!—was very plain long before he wound up his lecture with a few halfhearted warnings about poison oak. And then, just when I thought we could make our getaway, one of the boys said, "What about snakes?"

Frank smiled happily; on to lethal animals! He took a deep breath, and he was off again. "Oh, it's not just snakes," he said. "I mean, we talked about the rattlesnakes—diamondback and pygmy—and coral snakes! They are Absolute Killers! Don't confuse them with the corn snake— Remember? 'Red touches yellow'?"

He raised his eyebrows, and the whole group dutifully finished the rhyme, chanting, "You're a dead fellow." Frank smiled and nodded at them.

"That's right," he said. "Only coral snakes have red bands that touch their yellow bands. So keep clear of those. And don't forget the cottonmouth, too, by the water. Not as deadly as coral snakes, but they'll come after you. One bite probably wouldn't kill you, but there's usually a whole bunch of them all together, and they come at you like bees, and you get five or *six* bites, that's more than enough to kill you. Okay?"

I really thought that might be it, and I actually had one foot raised to make my getaway when Mario cheerfully called out, "Hey, the guidebook says there's bears, too!"

Frank nodded and pointed a finger at him and we were off again. "That's right, Mario. Good point. We have black bears in Florida, which are not as aggressive as the brown ones, and they're not as big, either. Kind of puny next to a grizzly, only around four hundred pounds."

If he was hoping we would all heave a sigh of relief at the petite size of the black bear, he was disappointed; a four-hundred-pound bear seemed plenty big enough to play jai alai with my head, and judging by the wide eyes of the boys all around me, I was not the only one who thought so.

"Just remember, they may be small, but they can be very cranky if they have a cub? They run *very* fast, and they can climb trees. Oh! So can panthers—which are very rare, an endangered species. So we probably won't see one, but if we do—remember this, guys: They are basically like lions, and . . . you know. We talk about how cool they are, and how we need to help protect panthers and their habitat—but they are still very dangerous animals. I mean, *most* of the animals out here. Let's remember they are *wild*. So give them room; respect their habitat, because you are in their space, and it's— Even raccoons, okay? I mean, they get into everything, and they look awful cute. They might even come right up to you. But they can have rabies, which you can get from them just from a little scratch, so stay away."

Once again, I made some small movement in the direction of escaping, and just as if he was a prison guard nailing a fleeing prisoner with his sniper's rifle, Frank whipped up his finger, pointed right at me, and said, "And don't forget the insects, because there are *so many* venomous insects. Not just fire ants, which you all know about?" The boys nodded solemnly; we all knew about fire ants. "Well, out here you got wasp mounds, too, and Africanized bees are possible—and scorpions? The black scorpion can really sting you good—and there are some spiders to watch out for, too, the brown recluse, the black widow, the *brown* widow. . . ."

I had always thought that Miami was a dangerous place, but as Frank rambled on through his recital of the countless forms of hideous death awaiting us in the woods, Miami began to pale in comparison to the rapacious bloodlust of Nature. There was an endless list of things that could kill us, or at least make us very unhappy, and while the thought of murderous ravening Nature truly did have its charms, I began to think it might not have been such a good idea to come to a place that was so crammed full of lethal plants and animals. I also wondered if we would escape Frank before nightfall, since his list of the Terrors of the Wild was still unfolding after fifteen minutes, and he seemed quite capable of talking at length on each and every one of them. I looked around me for a way to escape, but it seemed that every single direction was blocked by lurking terror. Apparently almost everything in the park was just waiting for a chance to murder us, or at least cause fits of bloody vomiting.

Frank finally wound down with a few words of caution about alligators—and don't forget the American crocodile! Which has a pointier nose and is much more aggressive! He finished with a final reminder that Nature was Our Friend, which seemed a little delusional, considering the long and deadly census of the park he had just completed. At any rate, Cody was impressed enough that he insisted on going back to the tent and getting his pocketknife. I stood at the head of the trail and waited for him, watching as the other work parties got busy with their jobs. Doug Crowley was leading a trio of boys around the camp in a quest for litter, and I watched them for a moment, until he abruptly stood up with a crushed and faded Dr Pepper can in his hand and turned to look back at me.

For a long moment Crowley just stared, his mouth hanging slightly open. I stared back, although my mouth was closed. The moment stretched on and I wondered why we didn't both simply look away. But then one of Crowley's crew shouted something about an indigo snake, and he turned quickly away. I watched his back for a few more seconds, and then I turned away, too. On top of being a total nonentity, Crowley was quite clearly far more socially inept than I had ever been; he had no idea how to relate to other people, and his awkwardness made me a little uncomfortable. But it would be easy enough to avoid him once this expedition into deadly horror was over, assuming I survived. A minute later, Cody came back with his pocketknife and he and I finally managed to tiptoe off into the venomous forest in search of a few combustible twigs that would not kill us.

We moved slowly and carefully; Frank had done a wonderful job of convincing us that we would only survive by a miracle of random chance, and I could tell that Cody felt danger and violent death breathing down his neck with every cautious step he took. He crept along the path with his pocketknife open in his hand, approaching each leaf and twig as if it might leap up and sever his jugular. Still, after an hour or so we had managed to collect a decent pile of deadwood, and miraculously enough, we were still alive. We took our wood back to the fire circle at the campsite, and then slunk back to the relative safety of our tent.

The tent's flap was open, although I had definitely closed it. Clearly Cody had left it open when he went back for his pocketknife. This was doubly annoying, since we now knew that the whole area was swarming with terrifying creatures that were absolutely trembling with eagerness for a chance to slip into our tent to poison, torture, and devour us. But the whole purpose of the trip was to have quality time with Cody, and scolding him for his carelessness would probably not be a bonding experience in the best sense of the words, so I just sighed and crawled watchfully into the tent.

Dinner that night was a communal affair, with everyone gathered around the fire circle and happily eating traditional wilderness food, just like the Calusas ate—beans and wieners. Afterward, Frank pulled out a small and battered guitar and launched into a program of campfire songs, and by the end of the second song he had worn down the boys' resistance enough that they began to sing along. Cody stared around him with a look of appalled disbelief on his face, which grew even bigger when I finally joined in on "There's a Hole in the Bottom of the Sea." I nudged him to get him to sing, too—after all, we were trying to teach him to fit in. But this was too much for his finer nature, and he just shook his head and watched with disapproval.

I had to set an example, of course, and show him how simple and painless it could be to pretend to be human. So I plowed on grimly through "Be Kind to Your Web-footed Friends," "Davy Crockett," "Cannibal King," the Cubs' version of "Battle Hymn of the Republic," and dozens of other touching and funny reminders that America is a nation with a song in its heart and a hole in its head.

Cody sat and looked around him as if the world had gone mad and exploded into a hideous caterwauling din, and he was the only one left with a clear head and a sense of decency. Even when Frank finally put down his guitar the fun was not over. The magical evening wound on through a series of terrifying ghost stories. Frank seemed to get real enjoyment out of telling them, and he had a knack for horrific detail that made his listeners slack-jawed with fear. We listened with growing dread to "The Hook," "The Terrible Smell," "The Quiet Thump in the Next Room," "The Dark Sucker," "The Viper," and many more, until the fire died down to a red glow, and Frank finally released us to stagger away and crawl stunned and trembling into our snug little sleeping bags, with visions of supernatural terror now mingling with our thoughts of snakes and spiders and bears and rabid raccoons.

And as I finally drifted off into sleep, I vowed to myself that if I lived through the night, I would never go camping again without a flamethrower, a bag of dynamite, and some holy water.

Ah, wilderness.

TWENTY-FIVE

IT MAY BE THAT I WILL HAVE TO RETHINK THE POSSIBILITY OF a kind and caring Deity, because I did live through the night. This did not come without a price, however. Frank's nearly endless list of the terrors of the wild had included dozens of lethal insects, and yet he had left out one of the most common—the mosquito. Perhaps upset at being left off the list, the mosquito hordes had gathered their vast army inside our tent, and they spent the night making sure that I would never forget them again. When I woke up, much too early, my face and hands, which had been exposed all night, were covered with bites, and as I sat up I was actually a little bit dizzy from the loss of blood.

Cody was in slightly better shape, since he had been so worried about rabid alligators and zombies with metal hooks that he had wiggled all the way down inside his sleeping bag and left only his nose sticking out. But the tip of his nose was crowded with red dots, as if the insects had held a competition to see how many bites they could fit onto the smallest area of exposed skin.

We crawled weakly out of the tent, scratching ourselves vigorously, and somehow staggered over to the fire circle without fainting. Frank already had a cooking fire going, and I perked up a little when

I saw he had some water boiling in a kettle. But because the Universe was clearly set on punishing Dexter for all his real and imagined sins, no one had brought any kind of coffee, not even instant, and the boiling water was all used to make hot chocolate.

The morning crawled on through breakfast and into Organized Activities. Frank started the boys on a snipe hunt, which was mostly intended to humiliate the new Cubs who had not been camping with the pack before. Each of these Newbies was given a large paper bag and a stick and told to beat the bushes with the stick and yodel until the snipes ran out and jumped into the bag. Luckily, Cody was too suspicious to fall for this hoax, and he stood beside me and watched the hilarity with a puzzled frown, until a giggling Frank finally called off the game.

After that, everyone got out their nature booklets, and we all wandered into the Lethal Forest again to see how many different things from the booklet we could identify before one of them killed us. Cody and I did very well, finding many of the birds, and almost all the plants. I even discovered some poison ivy. Unfortunately, I found it in a very direct way. I saw what I thought was a black scorpion crawling away, and when I carefully pushed aside some foliage to show it to Cody, he pointed at the plant I was holding and held up his booklet.

"Poison ivy," he said. He pointed to the illustration, and I nodded; it was a perfect match. I was actually holding poison ivy in my unprotected hands. Since they were already covered with mosquito bites, it seemed redundant, but clearly I was in for an epic itch. Now if only an endangered species of eagle would attack me and claw out my eyeballs, my Wilderness Adventure would be complete. I scrubbed with soap and water and even took an antihistamine, but my already itchy hands were throbbing and swelling up by the time we hiked back to our cars for the drive home.

Other campers who had not had such wonderful luck encountering Our Lethal Forest Friends milled around and called to each other happily, while I cradled my hands and waited for everyone to arrive in the parking lot and find their assigned vehicle. For some reason, possibly just one more mean trick on me by a positively cranky Fate, Doug Crowley's group all arrived together, got into the beat-up old Cadillac, and drove away for home while Cody and I were still waiting for

Mario. I watched the old car cruise past and head out of the parking lot and then turn right onto the highway. The car gave a funny lurch and backfired once, causing a strange rattling sound as the piston knocked at the same time the loose front bumper shook. Then the old Caddy accelerated and was gone down the road, and I turned away and leaned on my car, watching the trailhead for any sign of Mario.

Mario did not appear. A fly began to circle my head obsessively, searching for whatever it is that flies always want. I didn't know what it was, but I was evidently full of it, because the fly found me overwhelmingly attractive. It circled, darted in toward my face, and circled some more, and it would not give up and go away. I swatted at the fly, but I couldn't touch it, and my flailing didn't seem to discourage it. I wondered whether the fly was poisonous, too. If not, I would certainly be allergic to it. I swatted again with no luck, maybe because my hands were swollen from the poison ivy and mosquito bites. Or maybe I was just getting old and slow. I probably was, just when I needed all my reflexes at peak ability to deal with the threats coming at me, known and unknown.

I thought about Hood and Doakes, and wondered what they had been doing to frame me while I was busy infecting myself with plant and insect venom. I hoped that the lawyer Rita was arranging would help, but I had a very bad feeling that he wouldn't. I have been in and around the law my whole life, and it's always seemed to me that when you need a lawyer it's already too late.

Then I thought about my Shadow, and I wondered how and when he would come at me. It sounded so melodramatic, right out of an ancient comic book. The Shadow is coming. Mooo-hahaha. Goofy rather than dangerous, as far as the sound was concerned, but then sounds can be misleading. Like the sound of Crowley's car backfiring—it sounded like the car was about to fall apart, but obviously the old thing made it here safely. And I had heard that sound before.

I blinked. Where had that thought come from?

I swatted at the fly again and missed. I was certain I had heard that distinctive clattering backfire not too long ago, but I couldn't remember when. But so what? Not important. Just more clutter in my overloaded mental works. Funny sound, though, very singular, and

I was sure I'd heard it before. *Bang, rattle-rattle.* But my brain stayed blank; perhaps the poor ravaged thing was collapsing into premature senility. Quite likely an inevitable side effect of the recent combination of peril and frustration and loss of blood from the mosquitoes. Even the one time I had slipped out for a little amusement had gone wrong; I played that evening back mentally, once again remembering the horrible surprise in the grubby little house. And it had started out with such a promising feel to it, from the dark and deserted street outside when I felt so eager, ready, unstoppable even, when I had been unexpectedly lit up by a passing car—

Without realizing what I was doing I found myself standing up straight and staring out at the highway. It was a stupid thing to do; Crowley's car was long gone. I stared after it anyway, for a very long time, until I finally became aware that Cody was jerking on my arm and saying my name.

"Dexter. Dexter. Mario's here. Dexter, let's go," he said, and I became aware that he had said it more than once, but it didn't matter, because I was also aware of something much more important.

I knew when I had heard that backfire before.

Bang. Double rattle.

Dexter stands there bathed in the light of an old car's high beams, holding his gym bag filled with party favors and blinking at the light. Just standing on the sidewalk, wrapped in the cool cocoon of my Need-filled disguise, and as the car turns the corner I am suddenly lit up like I am on center stage and singing the title song of a Broadway show—and whoever is in that car can see me as clearly as if it is a bright summer afternoon.

Just that one frozen moment of perfect illumination; then the car speeds up:

Bang. *Double rattle.*

And it hurries away, around the next corner and into the night and away from the grubby little house on the dark street, away from the neighborhood where Dexter has found his Witness's Honda.

And Dexter thinks no more about it and goes on into the house, and is still staring at the Almost-familiar Thing on the table when the sirens begin to wind closer . . .

. . . because someone had known exactly *when I went in, and timed their call to 911 perfectly . . .*

. . . because he had seen me outside, lit up in his high beams, and when he was sure it was me he had put his foot down hard on the accelerator to get away and make his call—

Bang. *Double rattle.*

Away into the night while Dexter slipped inside for his gaping and drooling lesson.

And now he has told me he is coming Closer, to mock me, to punish me, to become *me—*

And he has come closer, all the way up to my face.

Doug Crowley is Bernie Elan; my Shadow.

I had thought it was self-indulgent nonsense, blather from a deranged doofus, and I would be more than a match for whatever he could come up with. But then Camilla turned up dead and I was blamed for it. . . .

And just like he had promised, I looked very bad all of a sudden.

He had gotten into Camilla's apartment and seen all the pictures of me, and even left one of his own—Camilla and me face-to-face, the final clinching shot in his collage, the ideal way to set me up and take me down. And he had killed Camilla to push all the suspicion on to me. It was very neat; whether I was ever actually arrested or not didn't matter. I was pinned in the spotlight, under constant scrutiny, and therefore completely helpless to do *anything*. One small part of me actually paused and admired the way he had worked it. But it was a very small part, and I crushed it quickly and felt myself begin to smolder. *Closer than you think,* he had said, and he had done exactly that. His stupid, awkward attempt at conversation that I had found so irritating; I had wondered why he wouldn't go away and leave me alone. And now I knew why. He had been riding up into my face and touching me to say, *This could have been your death, and you are too slow and stupid to stop me.*

Boo.

And he was right. He had proved it. I hadn't suspected anything, felt nothing but irritation as he had goggled down at me and blathered nonsense and then walked away, no doubt lit up inside like the Fourth of July sky. And I didn't even know it until right now.

Bang. Double rattle.

Gotcha.

"Dexter?" Cody said one more time, and he sounded a little worried. I looked at him frowning at me and tugging at my arm. Mario and Steve Binder stood behind him, watching me and looking uncomfortable.

"Sorry, guys," I said. "I was just thinking about something." And it is a tribute to my long years of diligent training that even though my brain was screaming at me to run to action stations and open fire with all guns, I still managed to maintain my cheerful disguise and get all three boys into the car and start driving, and I even remembered the right direction to take us all home.

Happily for us all, Mario was much quieter on the long ride back. He had stumbled onto a wasp mound and gotten three or four stings before he escaped, which just proves that insects are a lot smarter than we give them credit for. The other boy, Steve Binder, just sat silently beside him in the backseat, frowning. Every now and then he would turn and stare at Mario's wasp stings, poke one with a finger, and smirk when Mario jumped. Even in my profound mental funk, I began to warm up to Steve Binder just a little.

Other than those few interruptions, the drive home was quiet, and I used the relative silence to think, which was something I desperately needed to do right now. With a few minutes of reflection I pulled myself off high alert and began to sort through things calmly and rationally. All right: The Caddy's sound was distinctive, but that was not conclusive proof of anything. Sounds like that might come from any old car. And to think of Crowley as being dangerous in any way took some hard work. He was so completely soft, inept, his presence almost intangible . . .

. . . which the writer of Shadowblog had made a point of saying about himself. It was where the name Shadowblog came from. *I walk into a room and it's like they can't even see me, like I'm no more than a fucking shadow.* A perfect description of Crowley, if shadows could be annoying.

But to think of it as a disguise, the same kind as mine? Ridiculous—it was *too* good, maybe even better than mine, which I did not want to admit at all. And it was impossible that it could be good enough to fool *me*—and fool the Passenger, too. Nobody was that good—especially nobody who had so much trouble faking a real-looking smile. To think that anything with an appearance that soft and insubstantial could hammer Camilla Figg to death—it was absurd. It made no sense at all. . . .

I remembered my admiration of the heron back in the swamp: so cute and fuzzy, and so very deadly. Was it possible that Crowley was not a bland doofus at all, but was actually another of Nature's great achievements, something like the heron, which looked so tame and pleasant that it got right on top of you and got its beak into you while you were still admiring the plumage?

It was possible. And the more I thought about it, the more I thought it was likely, too.

Crowley was my Shadow.

He had stalked me, framed me, and then come right up to me to gloat about it. And now he was going to push me out of my life and into the Dark Forever, where I had sent so many deserving friends. And then what would he do, take my place? Become the new Dark Avenger? Turn himself into Dexter Mark II, a double with a new look, softer and more harmless-looking? Lure his victims in with the appearance of bland and annoying Normality and then *bang!* Speared and swallowed, just like the heron's prey.

Maybe it should have been comforting to think that someone wanted to continue my Good Works after I was gone, but I was not comforted, not at all. I liked being me and doing what I did, and I was not done yet, not by a long shot. I planned to go on being Dexter for a very long time, finding the wicked and sending them on their way, and I had one very immediate candidate in mind. It had become personal. I knew that was a bad thing, against the Harry Code and everything I knew to be right and true, but I wanted Doug Crowley, or Bernie Elan, or whoever he wanted to be. More than I had ever wanted anything, I wanted to get my hands on him and tape him to a table and watch him squirm and see his eyes bulge out with terror and smell the fear sweat as it broke out all over him and then slowly, very slowly, raise up a small and very sharp blade and as his eyes go red with knowing that the agony is coming I will smile and I will begin his very own end. . . .

He thought he was so clever, coming right up to my face and mumbling stupidly, while all the while he was playing his game, touching me lightly instead of killing me. He had been counting coup on me, that ancient game of the Plains Indians. It was the ultimate insult if you were a Lakota, a failure of manhood so shameful it could actually end a warrior's life when it happened, to be touched by an enemy while you stood helpless—but I was not a Native American. I was Dexter, the One, the Only, and Crowley had overlooked one important thing:

The Lakota lost.

They rode off into the history books with their honor intact, but they lost the war and everything else because they came up against people who preferred to kill and didn't even know that they had been insulted—and that was also a very good description of me. I did not play those kindergarten games. I came, I duct-taped, I conquered. That was who I am.

And he dared to think he could be me? And start off with such a lousy job of it? He had no idea what being Me really meant—he had missed the point completely. But he was about to find out that Dexter's Point is on the end of a knife, and Dexter has no equal and no competition, and no one was ever going to take his place, least of all a chinless geek who had to steal my methods because he didn't even have his own personality. Crowley was going to learn firsthand why there could never be a Dexter Double, and that lesson would be his very last and his most painful, and he would take it with him into the red darkness and as he spun away into All Over Forever he would know he had been taught the Ultimate Lesson by the Old Master.

Doug Crowley was going to go the way of all flesh, and as quickly as possible I would find him and flense him and send him off to the ocean's floor in four neat and separate garbage bags, and I would do it before he could write another taunting drivel-filled blog bragging about his insult to me. I would tape him and teach him what it truly meant to be Me, and I would make him wish he had chosen someone else to fill out his shadow, and the only question at all was a very simple one-word query:

How?

TWENTY-SIX

IT WAS A LONG DRIVE HOME, BUT NOT LONG ENOUGH FOR ME
to come up with any answers. I had to find my Shadow, and
quickly, but how? The only hint I had was the name he was using
now, Doug Crowley. From the skill with computers he had shown
already—faking his own death had been impressive—I was certain
he would not use a name that did not have documentation and a
convincing background. It wasn't much, but I had access to several
search engines that left Google far behind in the dust, and I could
certainly find a few hints about him and where he might be. It was
a starting point, and I felt a little bit better about things by the time I
dropped off Mario and Steve Binder and headed for home.

The female section of my little family was sitting on the couch
when we arrived. Rita had a cup of coffee in one hand and was sipping it as she watched TV. She looked up at us, frowned, and then did
a double take and leapt to her feet and slapped the coffee cup down
onto the table. "Oh, my God, look at you!" she said, hurrying over
to us and looking from Cody's large red nose to my large speckled
hands and face. "What on earth happened to— Cody, your nose is
completely— Dexter, for God's sake, didn't you take any bug spray?"

"I took some," I admitted. "I just didn't use it."

She gave me an appalled shake of her head. "I don't know what you were thinking, but that's— Oh, just look at the two of you! Cody, stop scratching."

"It's itchy," he said.

"Well, if you scratch it, it's just going to get worse— Oh, for the love of . . . Dexter, your hands, too?"

"No," I said. "That's mostly poison ivy."

"Honestly," she said, with obvious disgust at my bungling. "It's a wonder you weren't eaten by a bear."

There was very little I could say to that, especially since I agreed, and in any case Rita gave me no chance to say anything. She immediately jumped into action and began bustling around us, applying calamine lotion to my face and hands and pushing Cody into a hot bath. Lily Anne started crying, and Astor sat on the couch smirking at me. "What's so funny?" I asked her.

"Your face," she said. "You look like you got leprosy."

I took a step toward her. "Poison ivy is contagious," I said, raising my hands at her.

Astor flinched away and grabbed at Lily Anne, lifting her up and holding her between us like a protective shield. "Stay away; I'm holding the baby. There, there, Lily Anne," she said, slinging her sister onto one shoulder and patting her back with a series of rapid thumps. Lily Anne stopped crying almost at once, possibly stunned by the force of Astor's patting, and I left them there and went to take a shower.

The hot water running over my swollen hands was an amazing sensation, unlike anything I had ever felt before, and truthfully, not something I was eager to experience ever again. It was somewhere between an immensely powerful itch and searing agony, and I almost yelled out loud. I got out of the shower and put more calamine on my hands, and the throbbing died down to a kind of background torment. My hands felt numb and clumsy, and I had some trouble using them to get dressed. But rather than ask for help with the zipper and my shirt's buttons, I fumbled my clean clothes on all by myself, and soon I was seated at the kitchen table with a very welcome cup of coffee of my very own.

I held the coffee cup between the palms of my swollen and throbbing hands. The backs of my hands pulsed with the warmth of the cup, and I wondered what I could possibly hope to do with two such useless appendages. I felt like I needed all the help I could get, and not just because my hands were out of commission. For some reason, I had been two steps behind the whole way, almost as if Crowley was reading my mind. Knowing what I now knew about him, I couldn't believe it was because he was so amazingly clever—he wasn't. It had to be me. I was off my game, sliding into the muck of mediocrity, all the way down the long slope from my usual lofty perch of supreme excellence, and I wondered why that was.

Maybe I was just not as sharp and gleefully wicked as I used to be. It might well be, I realized, that Crowley really was a match for the Me I was nowadays. I had gotten too soft, allowed my new role as Daddy Dexter to make me a bit too human. One little problem had turned me all mushy and helpless. Although to be accurate, it was two problems, and neither of them was all that little, but the point was the same.

I thought of the other Me, the one that matched the picture of myself I had hanging on the back wall of my self-esteem: Dexter the Dominant. Clever, sharp, fit, and ready for anything, eager to be off on the hunt and always alert and able to sniff out the potential perils that might lie along any small fork in the game trail. And comparing that hallowed portrait to what actually stared back at me from the mirror of this present moment, I felt a sense of loss—and of shame. How had I lost this other me, the ideal Dexter of my dreams? Had I let easy living bring me so far down?

Clearly I had. I had even thrown it away cheerfully, eager to become something I could never really be. And now, when I needed to be Me more than ever before, I had gone all squishy at the edges. My own fault—things had been too comfortable for me lately and I had come to like it that way. The placid ease of married life, the softening influence of having Lily Anne to care for, the routine of home and hearth and homicide—it had all become too comfortable. I had turned soft, smug, self-satisfied, lulled to sleep by my cushy lifestyle and the easy availability of the game in these pastures of plenty I had been hunting in for so long. And the first time a real challenge came along I had behaved like all the other sheep in the pen. I had bleated and dithered, unable to believe that any real threat could actually be aimed at *me,* and I was still simply sitting here, waiting for it to swoop down and get me, and doing no more to stop it than hoping it would go away.

Was this really who I had turned into? Had I truly lost my edge? Had common Humanity snuck into the very fiber of my being and turned me into a marshmallow-souled hobbyist, a part-time monster too bone-idle, sluggish, and dumb to do anything but gawp at the ax as it fell on my neck and cry, *Alas, poor Dexter*?

I sipped the coffee and felt my hands throb. This was getting me nowhere. I was simply digging myself deeper into the Pit of Despair, and I was in quite far enough already. It was time to claw my way out, stand up straight, and climb back up the mountain to my right-ful position as King of the Heap. I was a tiger, but for some reason I had been acting like a house cat. This had to stop, and right now, and I finally had a small handle on how to stop it. I had a name to search and a computer to search it with, and all I had to do was to get busy and do it.

So I finished my coffee, stood up, and went down the hall to the little room that Rita calls Dexter's Study. I sat and fired up my lap-top, and as it started up I closed my eyes, took a deep breath, and tried to get back in touch with my Inner Tiger. Almost immediately I felt it stretch and purr and rise up to rub against my hand. Nice kitty, I thought with gratitude, and it showed me its fangs in a happily wicked smile. I smiled back, opened my eyes, and we went to work.

First I checked the credit card records, and to my infinite joy I got immediate results. "Doug Crowley" had used his Visa card to buy gasoline at a station on the Tamiami Trail, between Miami and the Fakahatchee Park, Saturday morning, the day we all drove down there for the camping trip.

If there was a working credit card, there was a billing address. However he had managed it, he had become Doug Crowley, a solid citizen with a good credit record and a home, and if he was using the credit card, he was confident that its owner wouldn't complain. That probably meant that the house was available, too, since I knew very well now how my Shadow liked to solve his personnel problems. The real Doug Crowley was dead, so his house was available, and *my* Doug Crowley would almost certainly be there. And wonder of wonders, it was even convenient; the address was on 148th Terrace, only about two miles from where I was sitting.

I stared suspiciously at the computer; could it really be this easy? After everything that had happened, was it really going to be so simple? Just find the address, saunter over, and spend some quality bonding time with my formerly anonymous admirer? It didn't seem nearly complicated enough, and for a moment or two I glared at the address as if it had done something very wrong.

But the Passenger stirred impatiently, and I nodded; of course it was this simple. I had not known what name Crowley was using before now, and he had tried to keep me from learning it. Now that I knew, there was no reason to doubt that I had found his lair. I was merely being cynical and paranoid—and after all, who had a better right? I absentmindedly rubbed my swollen hands and thought about it, and felt certainty flow slowly back in. This was him; it *had* to be. And as if to add the Seal of Dread Approval, the Passenger gave a contented purr of agreement.

Splendid: I had found him. Now all I had to do was think of a way to take care of him without using my hands.

But I could muddle through with poison ivy, and in any case I couldn't wait. The end was in sight, and speed was essential; Crowley had been far too slippery so far, and I couldn't give him any time to prepare. I would do it tonight, as soon as it was dark, swollen hands or not. The mere thought of it made me feel better than I had for a very long time, and I wallowed in the excited anticipation I felt burbling up in the darkest corners of Dexter's Basement. I was going to go once more into that good night, and I was not going gentle.

The rest of the day passed pleasantly enough. And why shouldn't it? Here I was, a man with a plan, nestled in the bosom of my happy family. I sat with Lily Anne on my lap and watched as Cody and Astor slaughtered their animated friends on the Wii.

Rita had vanished into the kitchen; I assumed she was working through another grocery bag full of mind-numbing charts and figures from her job. But gradually I became aware that the aroma seeping out of the kitchen was not ink and calculator tape but something far more succulent. And lo and behold, at six o'clock the kitchen door swung open, releasing an overwhelming gush of delicious steam that had me drooling. I turned to look, and there stood a radiant Rita, clad in apron and oven mitts, face flushed with her righteous efforts. "Dinner," she told us. Even the children looked up at her, and she blushed just a little more. "I just thought . . ." she said, looking at me. "I mean, I know that lately it hasn't really— And you've been so . . ." She shook her head. "Anyway," she said. "So I made something— And it's ready now. Mango paella," she added with a smile, and happier words were never spoken.

Mango paella was one of Rita's better recipes, and it had been a very long time since Rita had cooked at all. But the time off had not diminished her skill, and she had done it proud. I plowed into the steaming, fragrant mass with a will. For a good twenty minutes I had no thoughts at all more complicated than, *Yum!*, and to be brutally frank, I ate too much. So did Cody—and even Astor lost her grumpiness as she tucked into her dinner, and when we were all blissfully bloated and pushed our chairs back from the table there were no leftovers.

Rita looked around at her food-numbed family with an expression of true contentment. "Well," she said, "I hope that was— I mean, it wasn't as good as usual. . . ."

Astor rolled her eyes and said, "Mo-om, you always say that. It was o-*kay.*"

Cody looked at his sister, shook his head, and then turned to Rita. "It was *good.*"

Rita beamed at him, and, knowing a cue when I heard one, I added my part. "It was a work of art," I said, stifling a contented belch. "Very *great* art."

"Well," said Rita. "That's very— Thank you. And I just wanted to— I'll get the dishes," she said, blushing again and bouncing up to begin clearing the table.

And wrapped in a cloud of complete contentment, I staggered off to Dexter's Study and made my modest preparations for dessert: duct tape, filet knife, nylon noose—just a few simple accessories to round off a lovely evening with my favorite confection. When everything was checked and rechecked and then zipped carefully into my gym bag, I rejoined the children in front of the Wii. I sat on the couch and watched the happy mayhem, and I could actually feel some of the tension of recent events seeping out of me. And why not? I had a gym bag full of toys and a friend picked out to share them with; Normal Life was finally returning, and Rita had made it wonderfully official with a memorable meal.

So I sat and waited for it to get dark outside, thinking smugly of the Thing I would do just a little later, and content to do nothing else for the moment except digest the unreasonable amount of paella I had eaten. It was pleasant labor, relatively undemanding, and I believe I was doing a very good job of it when somehow, I fell asleep.

I woke up unsure of where I was and what time it was, blinking stupidly around me in a semidark room. I am not ordinarily given to naps, and this one had snuck up and sandbagged me and left me feeling slow and dopey. It was a full minute before I remembered that I was on the couch in my living room and there was a clock beside the TV. Summoning all my superhuman strength, I rolled my eyeballs in the right direction and stared at the clock; it was ten forty-seven. This was more than a nap; it was hibernation.

I blinked and breathed for another minute, trying to climb back into a state of eager readiness for what I had planned for the rest of this night. But the fat-headed feeling stayed with me. I wondered what Rita had put into the paella: some kind of sleep-inducing herb? Kryptonite? Whatever it was, it had knocked me out as efficiently as if it had been roofies. I actually spent a good two minutes thinking that it might be a good idea to go back to sleep and let Crowley wait for tomorrow. It was late, I was tired, and surely there was nothing so urgent that it couldn't wait one more day. . . .

Just in time a small dash of common sense trickled in and reminded me that no, in fact, it couldn't wait, not at all. The danger was immediate; the solution was at hand—and probably even therapeutic. I had to act now, right away, without delay. I repeated that to myself a few times; it was not enough to bring back my complete and eager edge, but at least it got me moving. I stretched and stood up, waiting for full consciousness to return. It didn't, so I went down the hall anyway and got the gym bag I had packed after dinner.

Before I left, I peeked into my bedroom; Rita was asleep, snoring softly, and Lily Anne was peacefully at rest in her crib. All quiet on the home front, and time for Dexter to steal away into the night.

But as I slipped out the front door of the house, a huge yawn creaked out of me, instead of the icy awareness I was used to. I shook my head in a vain effort to get the blood flowing again. What was wrong with me? Why couldn't I seem to get going? I had a pleasant and rewarding chore to take care of, and there was no point in doing it if I was going to sleepwalk through it on automatic pilot. I gave myself a stern pep talk: *Focus, Dexter. Get your head back in the game.*

By the time I slid behind the wheel of my car and cranked it up, I was starting to feel a little more alert. I put the car in gear and eased out onto the street, thinking that a slow drive through Miami traffic would almost certainly get the adrenaline flowing again. And it worked even better than I had hoped—because before I had gone even a hundred feet my entire allowance of adrenaline for the month came roaring into my system when I glanced casually into the rearview mirror. Behind me, at the vacant lot half a block from my house, a pair of headlights clicked on and another car nosed out into the street to follow me.

I stared into the mirror, trying to make the following headlights into a hallucination. But they kept coming, sliding up the street behind me, and I nearly ran into a tree before I remembered I had to watch the street ahead, too. And I tried to do that, but my eyes kept flicking back to the mirror and the headlights bobbing along in my wake.

This is nothing, a mere coincidence, I told myself firmly, fighting down the alarm that began to clang in my brain. Of course I was not being followed; some neighbor had merely parked randomly at the vacant lot for some reason and was now randomly taking off on a random late-night jaunt. Or perhaps a drunk had pulled over to sleep off too many Cuba Libres. There were many sane and sober explanations, and just because somebody started up their car at the exact time I did and then drove along right behind me, it didn't mean I was being followed. Reason said it was pure chance and nothing more.

I turned right at the stop sign and motored along slowly, and, a moment later, so did my unwanted companion, and my interior alarm clanged a little louder. I tried to muffle it by thinking logical thoughts: Of course he turned right, too. That was the way out of the neighborhood, the shortest route to Dixie Highway and its conve-

nience marts and the Farm Store for a midnight quart of milk. Everything that might take somebody out onto the streets at this hour was
at the end of this road. It was the only way to go, and the fact that
somebody was going there right behind me was complete happenstance, and nothing more. Just to prove it, I turned right at the next
stop sign, away from brightly lit Dixie Highway and all its commercial pleasures, back into the darker streets lined with houses, and I
watched in the mirror for the car behind me to turn left.

It didn't.

It turned right, the same way I had gone, and it followed along
behind me like an unwanted shadow. . . .

And as that word trickled into my brain, a jolt of near panic jerked
me up straight in my seat: *shadow?* Was it possible? Could Crowley
have gotten the drop on me once again?

It took almost no thought at all to figure that out. Of course it was
possible; more than possible, it was likely, since he had been outthink-
ing me every step of the way. He knew where I lived. He knew what
my car looked like. He knew everything about me. He had already
told me that he'd been watching, and he'd said that he was coming for
me. And now here he was, snuffling along my trail like a hellhound.

Unconsciously I sped up; the car behind me matched my pace
and then began to close the gap between us. I turned right, left, right,
on random streets. The other car stayed with me, edging ever closer,
while I fought furiously against the impulse to mash down the gas
pedal and roar away into the night. But through all my twists and
turns he stayed with me, slowly gaining on me until he was only
about thirty feet back.

I turned left again, and he followed. It was useless. I had to outrun
him or confront him. My battered little car was not going to outrun
anything faster than a three-speed bicycle, so clearly confrontation
was the option.

But not here, not on these semidark residential streets, where he
could do whatever he had in mind with no worry that he would be
seen. If there was going to be a face-off, I wanted it to happen under
the bright glare of the lights along Dixie Highway, someplace where
security cameras and convenience store clerks would see everything.

I turned the car back the way I had come, back toward Dixie

Highway, and a moment later the other car swung in behind me, once more moving a little closer. And he edged even nearer as I hurried up to the highway, turned right into traffic, and then pulled into the first open gas station. I parked in the brightest area of light, right in front of the window, clearly in view of the clerk and the security camera. I put the car in park and waited, engine idling. A moment later the car that had followed me all the way from my house slid to a stop next to me.

It was not the battered old Cadillac Crowley had been driving before. Instead, it was a newish Ford Taurus. It looked like a car I had seen before—a car I had seen frequently, even daily, and as its driver opened up his door and stepped out into the bright orange glare of the security lights, I realized why that was.

And so instead of exploding out of my car to bludgeon Crowley with my swollen hands, I simply sat behind the wheel and rolled down the window as the other driver approached. He came right up to my car, looked down at me, and smiled: a beautiful, blissful smile that revealed hundreds of shiny, sharp teeth, and in the face of such complete happiness there was only one thing I could say.

"Sergeant Doakes," I said, with a very good imitation of mild surprise. "What on earth are you doing here at this hour?"

TWENTY-SEVEN

FOR A LONG AND UNEASY MOMENT, SERGEANT DOAKES DID not answer. He just looked down at me and smiled his bright predator's smile until I began to feel like the lack of conversation was turning a bit uncomfortable. Even more disquieting than the sergeant's toothy silence, I remembered the gym bag on the floor of the backseat, right behind me. The contents of that bag would be difficult to explain to someone with a nasty, suspicious mind—someone, in other words, exactly like Doakes—and if he were to open the bag and see my collection of innocent toys it could well make for a few very awkward moments, since I was under Official Suspicion for using just such items.

But Dexter was raised on danger and bred on bluff, and this was exactly the kind of crisis that brought out the very best in me. So I took the initiative and broke the ice.

"This is an amazing coincidence," I said brightly. "I was just out for some antihistamines." I showed him my swollen hands, but he didn't seem interested. "Do you live around here somewhere?" I paused for his reply; he didn't give me one, and as the silence grew I had to fight down the impulse to ask whether the cat had his tongue, before I realized that he was not carrying his speech synthesizer. "Oh,

I'm sorry," I said. "You don't have your talking machine, do you? Well, then, I'll cut this short. Nothing worse than a one-sided conversation." And, reaching to roll up the window, I added a cheery, "Good night, Sergeant!"

Doakes leaned forward and put both his shiny prosthetic claws on the top of my window and pushed down. He was not smiling now, and the muscles in his cheeks flexed visibly as he leaned down and kept my window from closing. I wondered briefly what would happen if his pressure broke the glass: Was it possible that a shard of broken window would spear up past his silver claws and slice his wrists open? The thought of Doakes bleeding out in the parking lot beside my car was very appealing—but of course, there was also the possibility that the horrible wet blood would spurt out of him, into the car, and cover me in awful sticky red mess, which was an image that made my skin crawl. Not just the nasty appalling blood, but *Doakes's* vile blood; it was a thought so revolting that for a moment I couldn't breathe.

But car windows are made of safety glass. They do not shatter into shards. They explode into a pile of small pebbles, and it would take a great deal of ingenuity to use them to kill Doakes, unless I could persuade him to eat them. That didn't seem likely, so with a philosophical shrug, I stopped cranking the window and returned the good sergeant's stare. "Was there something else?" I asked politely.

Sergeant Doakes had never been known for his skill as a conversationalist, and having his tongue removed had done nothing to add to his talent in that area. And so while it was clear that there was a great deal on his mind, he did not share it with me. He just stared, and his cheek muscles continued to bulge out even though he was no longer pushing down on the window. Finally, when a lesser man than Dexter would have cracked under the strain, Doakes leaned in even closer to me. I looked back at him. It was very awkward, but at least he didn't smell as bad as Hood, and I managed to endure it without collapsing into tears and confessing.

And finally Doakes must have realized that, in the first place, there was quite literally nothing he could say and, in the second, I was not going to break down and admit that I was exactly what he thought I was, and out on a mission to do precisely what he suspected. He straightened up slowly, never taking his eyes off me, nodded a couple of times, as if to say, *All righty then*. Then he showed just the front row of his impressive set of teeth, a feral half grin that was much more troubling than the full smile, and he made that clichéd macho gesture we have all seen in so many movies: two fingers pointed at his own eyes, and then one pointed directly at me. Of course, since he had no fingers, he had to point with his bright and shiny prosthetic claw, and it took a little extra imagination on my part to decipher the signal. But the message was very clear: *I'm watching you*. He let that sink in for a moment, just pointing the claw and glaring at me without blinking. Then he turned abruptly away, strolled back around to the driver's side of his car, opened the door, and got in.

I waited for a moment, but Doakes did not put his car in gear. He just sat there, half turned to watch me, even though I was doing nothing more interesting than sweating. Clearly, he was going to be very literal-minded in carrying out his threat. He would *watch* me, no matter what I did or did not do. He was watching me now, and I remembered that I was supposed to be buying some antihistamine, and he was very intently watching me not buy it. And so, after a few more awkward moments, I got out of my car and went inside the convenience mart. I grabbed a box of something I had seen a commercial for, paid for it, and went back to my car.

Doakes was still watching. I put my own car in gear, backed out of the parking spot, and began the drive back to my house. I didn't need to look in the rearview mirror to know that Doakes was following along right behind.

I drove slowly home, and the headlights of Doakes's car stayed in the exact center of my rearview mirror the whole way, never wavering and never dropping back more than thirty feet. It was a wonderful textbook example of following somebody with what is called an open tail, and I really wished that Doakes was off at Detective College teaching the technique, instead of bedeviling me with it. Just a few minutes ago I had been so very nearly happy, filled with paella and purpose, and now I was right back on the horns of my dilemma. I absolutely *had* to take care of Crowley, and as soon as possible—but "soon" and "possible" were both far, far out of reach as long as Sergeant Doakes stayed welded to my bumper.

And even worse than the teeth-grinding frustration was the growing awareness of my own inept stupidity. It wasn't just Crowley who was running rings around me; Sergeant Doakes was, too. I should have known. Of *course* he would be watching me. He had waited for years to have me in this exact predicament. It was what he lived for, and he would not need to eat or sleep or polish his prosthetics as long as he had Dexter squirming in his crosshairs.

I was trapped, well and truly snookered, and there was no way out. If I didn't get Crowley, he would get me. If I tried to get him, Doakes would get me instead. Either way, Dexter was Got.

I turned it every way I could, but it always came out the same. I had to do something and I couldn't do anything—the perfect puzzle, and Miss Marple was nowhere around to help me solve it. By the time I parked the car in front of my house I had ground a layer of enamel off my teeth, smacked my swollen hands on the steering wheel with surprisingly painful results, and almost chewed through my lower lip. None of those things had provided an answer.

I sat behind the wheel with the engine off for a minute, too completely frustrated to move. Doakes drove slowly past, turned around, and parked where he had before, with a perfect view of me and my house. He switched off his engine and his headlights and he sat and watched me. I sat and ground my teeth some more, until they began to hurt almost as much as my hands. It was no good; I could sit here until I found a way to injure all my body parts, or I could accept the fact that I was stuck, go in the house, and snatch a few hours of troubled sleep. Maybe an answer would blossom in my subconscious mind while I slept. Just as likely, maybe a meteor shower would fall in the night and crush both Doakes and Crowley.

I decided on sleep anyway. At least I would be well rested when the end came. I got out of my car, locked it, and went in to bed.

And to my very great surprise, strangely, amazingly, wonderfully, an answer actually did come to me while I slept. It did not appear to me in a dream; I almost never have dreams, and on the rare occasions when I do they are shameful little things, full of obvious and embarrassing symbolism, and I would never listen to any word of advice they might offer.

Instead, when I opened my eyes to the early morning sounds of

Rita in the bathroom, a single clear image was floating in my fore-brain: the cheerful, synthetically smiling face of Brian, my brother. I closed my eyes again and wondered why I should wake up think-ing of him, and why the mental picture of his artificial grin should make me feel so happy. Of course, he was family, and having family should naturally be a source of bliss for us all. But there was a great deal more to it than that. Beyond sharing my DNA, Brian was also the one and only person in the whole wide world who could play the music for Dexter's Dark Dance nearly as well as I did. And even bet-ter, he was also the one and only person in the world who might play a request.

I lay in bed with a nearly real smile growing on my own face, and I thought about it as Rita bustled back into the bedroom, got dressed, and hurried away into the kitchen. I tried to frown the idea away, thinking of all that might be wrong with it. I told myself I was merely clutching at straws, lying in a sleep-induced cloud of dunderheaded hope. It couldn't possibly work; it was too simple, too effective, and ten seconds of clear and alert consciousness would almost certainly prove to me that this was no more than a stupidly optimistic pipe dream.

But alertness grew, and no negative epiphany grew with it, and the smile kept returning to push away my great frown of logic.

It just might work.

Give Crowley's address to Brian, explain the problem to him, and let nature take its course.

It was an elegant solution, and the only real problem with it was that I would not get to do away with Crowley in person. I wouldn't even get to watch, and that seemed terribly unfair. I had really, *really* wanted to do this myself: to watch the miserable self-inflated creature sweat and squirm and try to twist away as I slowly, carefully, fondly, took him farther and farther away from any taste of hope and closer to the dark circle at the end of his bright quick moment of light—

But a large part of learning to be an adult is admitting to yourself that nothing is ever perfect. We all have to sacrifice small indulgences from time to time in order to achieve our larger goals, and I would just have to behave like a grown-up and accept that the results were more important than my petty personal gratification. The essential thing here was to send Crowley off on his merry way into deep dark eternity, and it didn't really matter whether he got there without my help, just as long as he actually got there, and quickly.

I got out of bed, showered, dressed, and sat at the table in the kitchen, and I could find nothing wrong with my idea. Certainty grew as I ate a very good breakfast of waffles and Canadian bacon, and by the time I pushed away the empty plate and poured myself a second cup of coffee, it had grown into a full-size plan. Brian would help me; he was my brother. And it was exactly his kind of problem, something that played to his strengths and at the same time gave him a chance to enjoy himself—and even help his only sibling. It was neat and efficient and satisfying and I actually found myself ruminating on how good it was to have a big brother. It's true what they say: Family really is the most important thing in life.

By the time Rita cleared away the breakfast dishes, I was filled with smug good cheer and a truly annoying fondness for life as well as waffles, as I now found it was nudging me close to singing out loud. The problem was as good as solved, and I could get back to dealing with the other blip on my radar: Doakes and Hood and their attempt to rain on my parade. But I felt so very good about the solution to my Shadow, some of the optimism spilled over, and I began to believe that I would find a way out of that problem, too. Perhaps I could go back to sleep and simply wait for another idea to burble out of my unconscious mind.

My family's morning preparations clattered around me, rose to a climax, and then, just before the part where I knew from experience that the front door would begin to slam and go on slamming at least four times, Rita came in and gave me a kiss on the cheek. "Two thirty," she said. "I forgot to tell you last night because you fell asleep? And before that I just wanted, you know—because the paella really takes time?"

Once more I had the sensation of being in the middle of a conversation that had started a few minutes ago without me. But on a morning so full of bright hope, I could be patient. "It was very good paella," I said. "What did you forget to tell me?"

"Oh," she said. "Just that at two thirty. I mean, today? And I'll meet you there. Because I made the appointment while you and

Cody? And then when you both came home so completely— Anyway, it went right out of my head."

Several brilliantly funny remarks crowded into my mouth and fought for space on my tongue, but once again I somehow made myself stay focused on the larger point, which was that I still had no idea what Rita was talking about. "I'll be there at two thirty," I said. "If you promise to tell me where it is and why I'm going there."

Astor yelled, "Mom!" and the front door slammed once and Rita frowned and shook her head. "Oh," she said. "Didn't I . . . ? But Carlene at work, like I said. Her brother-in-law? He's the lawyer," she said, and turning her head toward the front door she yelled, "Just a minute, Astor!"

It might be only that I was getting used to her disjointed conversations, but I actually understood what Rita was saying after only a few seconds of struggling to put the pieces together. "We have an appointment with a lawyer?" I said.

"Today at two thirty," Rita said, and she leaned down and kissed me again. "The address is on the refrigerator, on the blue Post-it." She straightened up and said, "Don't forget," and then she vanished into the living room calling for Astor. Their voices rose together into a complicated and pointless squabble about the dress code, which didn't apply because it was summer, and anyway the skirt wasn't *that* short, so why should she have to wear shorts under it, and after only a few minutes of hysteria the front door slammed three more times and a sudden quiet descended. I sighed with relief, and I believe I could almost feel the whole house do the same.

And even though I do not like having someone else manipulate my schedule, and I don't like dealing with lawyers even more, I got up and took the blue Post-it from the fridge. It said, *Fleischman, 2:30,* and below that was an address on Brickell Avenue. That didn't tell me much about how good a lawyer he might be, but at least the address meant he would be expensive, which really ought to be some consolation. It wouldn't hurt to go see him and find out if he could help me out of my trouble with Hood and Doakes. It was time for me to think about getting the full weight of the law off my back—especially since my other problem was one quick phone call away from being solved.

So I tucked the Post-it into my pocket and went to get my phone, and as I punched in Brian's number it occurred to me that this was not the sort of lighthearted chitchat that was truly appropriate for a cell phone. I had heard enough taped conversations to know better. Even the standard evasions, like, "Did you see the guy with the thing about the stuff?" sounded highly suspicious when played back to a jury. Cell phones are wonderful devices, but they are not actually a secure form of communication, and if Doakes was going to all the trouble of tailing me, he might very well have access, legal or not, to anything I said on the phone. And so, thinking that "Better safe than sorry" was an excellent motto for the day, I arranged to meet Brian for lunch at Café Relampago, my favorite Cuban restaurant.

I spent the morning puttering around the house and tidying up things that were really at least half-tidy already, but it was better than sitting on the couch again and trying to convince myself that watching daytime TV was better for me than slamming my head against a brick wall. I unpacked my gym bag and put everything away with loving care. *Soon,* I told my toys.

At twelve thirty I locked up the house and got into my car. As I nosed it into the street, Sergeant Doakes pulled out behind me and followed along; all the way across the city on the Palmetto Expressway he stayed right behind me, and when I got off by the airport and wound my way to the strip mall that held Café Relampago, he was still on my tail. I parked in front of the café and Doakes parked a few spots to my left, between me and the parking lot's only exit. Happily for me, he did not follow me inside. He simply sat in his car, motor idling, staring at me through the windshield. So I gave him a cheery wave and went in to meet my brother.

Brian was sitting in a booth at the back, facing the door, and he raised his hand in greeting when I came in. I slid onto the seat facing him. "Thank you for meeting me," I said.

He raised his eyebrows in pretend surprise. "Of course," he said. "What's family for?"

"I'm still not sure," I said. "But I do have a suggestion."

"Do tell," he said.

But before I could, in fact, tell him, the waitress rushed over and slapped two plastic menus onto the table in front of us. The Morgan family had been coming to Café Relampago my whole life, and this waitress, Rose, had served us hundreds of times. But there was no flicker of recognition in her face as she dropped the menus in front of me and, as Brian opened his mouth to speak to her, hurried away again.

"Charming woman," Brian said, watching Rose disappear back into the kitchen.

"You haven't seen anything yet," I told him. "Wait till you see how she puts a plate on the table."

"I can hardly wait," he said.

I could have made small talk, or told Brian the secret Morgan family technique for getting Rose to bring the bill in under five minutes, but I felt events pressing in on me, so I cut right to the chase. "I need a little favor," I said.

Brian raised his eyebrows. "Of course, I grew up in foster care," he said, and he began to play with a sugar packet on the tabletop. "But in my experience, when a family member asks for a 'little favor,' that always means it's huge, and probably painful." He flipped the sugar from one hand to the other.

"I hope it will be very painful," I said. "But not for you."

He stopped flipping the sugar packet and looked up at me with a faint gleam of something dark stirring at the back of his eyes. "Tell me," he said.

I told him. I stumbled through a rather clumsy explanation of how Crowley had seen me at play. I'm not sure why I felt so awkward telling it. It is true that I never really like to talk about Those Things; but beyond that, I think I was embarrassed to admit to my brother that I had been so childishly careless and allowed myself to be seen. I felt my cheeks get hot, and I had trouble meeting his eyes, which had locked onto me as I began to talk, and stayed locked on me until I faltered to a finish.

Brian did not say anything at first, and I thought about reaching over and grabbing a sugar packet of my own to play with. In the silence, Rose appeared suddenly and slammed two glasses of water in front of us, scooped up the menus, and vanished again before either of us could speak.

"Very interesting," Brian said at last.

I glanced at him; he was still looking at me, and the faint shadow was still there in his eyes. "Do you mean the waitress?" I asked.

He showed me his teeth. "I do not," he said. "Although her performance has certainly been diverting so far." He finally looked away from me, glancing over his shoulder at the kitchen door, where Rose had disappeared. "So you find yourself with this little problem," he said. "And naturally you come to your brother for help . . . ?"

"Um, yes . . ."

He picked up the sugar packet again and frowned at it. "Why me?"

I stared at Brian, wondering if I had heard him wrong. "Well," I said, "I don't really know too many people who can do this kind of thing."

"Uh-huh," he said, still frowning at the sugar, as if he was trying to read the tiny print on the packet.

"And like I said, I'm being watched," I said. "Sergeant Doakes is out in the parking lot right now."

"Yes, I see," he said, although he wasn't actually seeing anything but the sugar packet in his hands.

"And you're my brother?" I added hopefully, wondering why he had suddenly gone all vague. "I mean, the whole family thing?"

"Yeeeesss . . ." Brian said doubtfully. "And, ah . . . that's really all of it? An inconsequential favor from your favorite family member? A small gift-wrapped project for big brother, Brian, because little Dexie is in time-out?"

I had no idea why Brian was acting so strangely, and I really was counting on his help, but he was getting more annoying with each syllable and I'd had enough. "Brian, for God's sake," I said. "I need your help. Why are you being so weird?"

He dropped the sugar packet onto the table, and the small sound it made seemed much louder than it really was. "Forgive me, brother," he said, and he looked up at me at last. "As I said, I grew up in foster care. It's given me a rather nasty, suspicious turn of mind." He showed me his teeth again. "I'm sure you have no ulterior motives at all here."

"Like what?" I said, genuinely puzzled.

"Oh, I don't know," he said. "I can't help thinking that it might be some kind of setup?"

"What?"

"Or that you might want to use me as a kind of cat's paw, just to see what happens?"

"Brian," I said.

"It's the sort of thing that naturally occurs to one, isn't it?" he said.

"Not to me," I said, and because I could think of nothing more compelling, I added, "You're my brother."

"Yes," he said. "On the other side, there is that." He frowned, and for a moment I was terrified that he would pick up the sugar packet again. But instead, he shook his head, as if overcoming a large temptation, and looked me in the eye. For a long moment he simply stared, and I stared back. Then his face lit up with his terrible fake smile. "I would be delighted to help you," he said.

I exhaled a very large cloud of anxiety, and inhaled even more relief. "Thank you," I said.

TWENTY-EIGHT

THE LAW OFFICES OF FIGUEROA, WHITLEY AND FLEISCHMAN were on the fourteenth floor of a high-rise building on Brickell Avenue, just on the edge of the area where office space starts to get pricey. The lobby was deserted when I walked in at two fifteen, and as I stood next to the elevator and scanned the building's directory, I noticed that very few of the floors had any tenants at all. Like many of the newer buildings in Miami's cluttered skyline, this one had apparently been built during the wild optimism of the last real estate boom, when everyone was certain prices would keep going up forever. Instead, prices had collapsed like a punctured balloon, and half of the glittering new buildings in downtown Miami had turned into shiny and very overpriced ghost towns.

Rita was not in the waiting room when I stepped off the elevator, so I sat down and thumbed through a copy of *GOLF* magazine. There were several articles on improving my short game that would have been much more interesting if only I played golf. The large golden clock on the wall said it was exactly two thirty-six when the elevator doors slid open and Rita stepped out. "Oh, Dexter, you're here already," she said.

I never really know what to say to that kind of painfully obvious remark, even though it seems to be very popular, so I just admitted that I was, in fact, right here in front of her, and she nodded and hustled over to the receptionist. "We have an appointment with Larry Fleischman?" she announced breathily.

The receptionist, a cool, stylish woman of around thirty, cocked her head at the appointment book and nodded. "Mrs. Morgan?"

"Yes, that's right," Rita said, and the receptionist smiled and dialed a number on the phone on her desk.

"Mr. and Mrs. Morgan," she said into the phone, and a few moments later we were ushered into an office halfway down the hall, where a serious-looking man of about fifty with badly dyed black hair sat behind a large wooden desk. He looked up as we entered, and then stood and held out his hand.

"Larry Fleischman—you must be Rita," he said, taking her hand and staring deep into her eyes with well-practiced and totally fake sincerity. "Carlene has told me so much about you." His eyes flicked down to the front of her blouse and Rita blushed and gently tried to disengage her hand. Larry looked up at her face and reluctantly dropped her hand at last, and then he turned to me. "And, uh . . . Derrick?" he said to me, holding out his hand just far enough away that I had to lean over to shake it.

"Dexter," I said. "With an 'X.' "

"Huh," he said thoughtfully. "Unusual name."

"Almost bizarre," I said, and then, just to keep things on an even footing, I added, "And you must be Leroy Fleischman?"

He blinked and dropped my hand. "Larry," he said. "It's *Larry* Fleischman."

"Sorry," I said, and for a moment we just looked at each other.

Finally, Larry cleared his throat and looked back at Rita. "Well," he said, frowning. "Sit down, won't you?"

We sat facing the desk in matching chairs, battered wooden things with worn fabric seats, and Larry sat back down behind his desk and opened a manila folder. It had only one sheet of paper in it, and he picked that up and frowned at it. "Well," he said. "What seems to be the problem?"

Our problem was apparently not written on the paper, and I wondered whether there was anything written on it at all, or if it was just a prop for Larry's I-am-a-real-lawyer act, and the folder was as phony as his hair color. To be honest, I was beginning to wonder whether Larry could possibly be any help at all. If I was going to fight off a determined and dishonest attack by Hood and Doakes, I needed an attack dog, a lawyer who was sharp and eager and very aggressive and ready to snap the leash and maul that vile old whore, Justice. Instead I was looking at a middle-aged poser who clearly didn't like me, and would probably decide to help them throw me in the slammer so he could hit on my wife.

But we were here, after all, and Rita seemed to be impressed. So I sat and let her burble her way through our tale of woe. Larry stared at her and nodded, occasionally tearing his eyes off her cleavage and looking over at me with an expression of dull surprise.

When Rita finally finished, Larry leaned back in his chair and pursed his lips. "Well," he said. "First of all, I want to reassure you that you've done exactly the right thing by coming here to consult me." He smiled at Rita. "Too many people wait to consult an attorney until things have gone too far for me to be really helpful. Which you haven't done, in this case." He seemed to like the sound of that, and he nodded a few times in the direction of Rita's breasts. "The important thing," he told them, "is to have some good legal advice at the very beginning of this thing. Even if you are innocent," he said, turning to look at me with an expression that said he didn't really think I was. Then he turned back to Rita and gave her a condescending smile. "The American legal system is the finest in the world," he told her, which didn't seem remotely possible, since he was part of it. But he said it with a straight face and went on. "However, it is an adversary system, which means that it's the prosecutor's job to get a conviction any way he can, and it's *my* job to stop him and keep your husband out of jail." He looked at me again, as if he was wondering whether that was such a good idea after all.

"Yes, I know," Rita said, and Larry snapped his head back around and looked at her attentively. "I mean, that's exactly— And I don't even know . . . Have you had, you know. A lot of experience? With, um, this kind of . . . I mean, we understand that criminal law and corporate law are very much— And Carlene said, your sister-in-law? So it might be important."

Larry nodded at Rita as if everything she'd said made sense, which was one more clue that he wasn't actually listening. "Yes," he said, "that's an important consideration. And I want you to know that I will leave no stone unturned and do absolutely everything in my power to help you beat this thing. But," he said, showing her the palms of his hands and smiling confidently, "that will take some work. And you need to know that it may turn out to be expensive." He glanced at me again, then back to Rita. "Not that you can really put a price on freedom."

I was pretty sure that, in fact, Larry could and would put a price on freedom, and it would turn out to be exactly ten dollars more than we had in the bank. But before I could think of a diplomatic way to tell him that I would rather spend twenty years in the penitentiary than ten more minutes in his company, Rita began to reassure him that she understood completely and money was no object, because Dexter, that is, her husband, and anyway, so that was fine and we were very grateful. And Larry smiled and nodded thoughtfully at Rita's breasts until she finally ran out of oxygen and blathered to a gasping halt. And as she paused to inhale he stood up behind his desk and held out his hand.

"Terrific," he said. "And let me reassure you that I will do everything I can, so I want you to stop worrying." He beamed at her, and I have to say that it was a far shoddier effort than even Brian's fake smile. "And I want you to call me if I can help with anything." He nodded slowly. "Anything at all," he said, with a little too much emphasis.

"Thank you, that's really very— We will, and thank you," Rita said, and a few moments later we were in the waiting room again and the receptionist was handing us a stack of forms and telling us that if we could please just fill these all out for Mr. Fleischman he would appreciate it very much.

I looked back down the hallway to the door of Fleischman's office. He was standing there, looking around the half-closed door. I was pleased to see that at least he was no longer looking at the front of Rita's blouse; instead, he was staring at the seat of her skirt.

I turned back to the receptionist and took the forms from her. "We'll mail them in," I said. "My parking meter is about to expire." And as Rita frowned at me and opened her mouth to say something,

I took her firmly by the arm and led her into the elevator. The doors slid mercifully closed, shutting out the nightmare world of Figueroa, Whitley and Fleischman for what I devoutly hoped would be the very last time.

"You could have parked in the building and they validate?" Rita said. "Because I don't even see— Dexter, I didn't know there were any parking meters at all in this part of—"

"Rita," I said, pleasantly but very firmly, "if I have a choice between watching Larry stare at your cleavage and going to prison, I think Raiford looks like a good idea."

Rita blushed. "But that isn't even— I mean, I know, my God, he must think I'm blind or else— But, Dexter, if he can help at all? Because this is still very serious."

"Too serious to trust it to Larry," I said, and the elevator gave a muffled *ding!* and the doors slid open and spilled us out onto the ground floor.

I walked Rita to her car. Following her own excellent advice, she had parked it in the building's garage, although she had failed to get her ticket validated because I had rushed her out before she could ask the receptionist.

I reassured her that the extra ten dollars would not really send us plummeting into bankruptcy, promised her I would ask around for another lawyer, and watched her drive away into the traffic on Brickell Avenue. Rush hour was already starting, and I wondered how Rita ever managed to survive Miami traffic. She was not a good driver; she drove the way she talked, with lots of stops and starts and sudden changes, but she made up for that by being the luckiest driver I had ever seen, and she'd never had even a small fender-bender.

I got into my car and started the tedious drive home, south again on Brickell for a few blocks, and then west and up onto I-95 until it ended and dumped me down onto Dixie Highway. I found myself pondering as I drove, which is never a great idea in Miami's rush-hour traffic, and at the intersection of Le Jeune I very nearly plowed into a Jaguar whose driver had made the perfectly reasonable decision to turn left from the center lane. I swerved around it at the last second, earning myself a loud and operatic chorus of horns and bad words in three languages. I supposed it served me right for criticizing Rita's driving.

Somehow I made it home without smashing into a tanker truck and being consumed by a giant fireball, and I had just enough time to make a pot of coffee and pour myself a cup when Rita burst into the house, with Lily Anne in her arms and the other two children following along in her wake.

"You're home!" she said as she rushed through the front door. "Because I have some wonderful news, and I have to— Cody, don't just throw your jacket there; hang it up on the— Astor, for God's sake, don't slam the door like that. Here, take the baby," she said to me, thrusting Lily Anne in my direction and turning away again so rapidly that I had to lurch forward to grab the baby, spilling a quarter of a cup of coffee as I did.

Rita put her keys into her purse and the purse on the table by the front door as she continued. "Brian just called me, your brother?" she said, in case I had forgotten who Brian was. "And anyway, he told me— What, dear?" she said, turning to Cody, who was at her elbow asking her something in his soft voice. "Yes, you can play the Wii for an hour now— So, Brian? When he called?" And she came back over to me where I stood juggling Lily Anne and my cup, with one foot in a pool of spilled coffee. "Oh," she said, frowning at the small puddle on the floor. "Dexter, you spilled your coffee. I'll get it," she said, and rushed into the kitchen, hurrying back out again almost instantly with a wad of paper towels. She squatted down and began to blot up the coffee.

"What did Brian say?" I asked the top of Rita's head, and she glanced up at me with a radiant smile.

"We have to go to Key West," she said, and before I could ask her why we *had* to go, or why Brian could order us around like that, and why that made her so happy, Rita leaped to her feet and ran for the kitchen with the wet paper towels clutched in her hand. "Honestly," she said over one shoulder, "nobody else around here ever even—" And she was gone through the kitchen door, leaving me to marvel at the fact that I somehow managed to survive in this house without ever knowing what was going on around me, or even what I was talking about.

But Lily Anne reminded me of the futility of trying to understand the harsh conditions of our bleak existence; she gave me a clout on the nose that brought tears to my eyes, topped it with a hearty chuckle as I blinked at her through the haze of pain, and then Rita whisked back into the room and snatched the baby from my arms.

"She needs a change," Rita said, and hurried away toward the changing table before I could add that I did, too. But I followed along behind her, hoping for some kind of clarity.

"Why did Brian say we have to go to Key West?" I asked her back.

"Oh," Rita said. "It's about the house? Brian said that they're all going to be there— Stop fussing now, silly Lily," she told the baby as she began to change the diaper. "And so if we go there, too? It's a very good opportunity for— And with Brian's connections? We could get a really good deal, too. There you go, little sweetie," she said as she put the fresh diaper on Lily Anne. "So if you promise to call around about the lawyer? Tonight? Because we would have to leave tomorrow morning."

Rita turned to me with Lily Anne in her arms, and I had to believe that the expression of excited pleasure on her face had nothing to do with the amazingly rapid diaper change she had performed. "It's just a chance," she said, "but it's a *wonderful* chance. And Key West! It's going to be so much fun!"

In every man's life there comes a time when he must stand up, assert himself, and be a *man*. For me, that time had come. "Rita," I said firmly, "I want you to take a deep breath, and then slowly, carefully, and *clearly* tell me what the hell you are talking about." And to underline just how serious I was, Lily Anne smacked her mother's cheek and told her, "Blap!" in a clear and commanding voice.

Rita blinked, possibly from pain. "Oh," she said. "But I said—"

"You said Brian is forcing us to go to Key West, whether we want to or not," I said. "And you said all the houses will be there. Other than that, you might as well be speaking Etruscan."

Rita opened her mouth, and then closed it again. She shook her head and said, "I'm sorry. I thought I said— Because sometimes it seems so clear to me."

"I'm sure it is," I said.

"I was in the car, picking up the kids?" she said. "And Brian called me. On the phone," she added. The thought of her talking on the phone in the course of her already erratic driving made me very glad

I was off the roads already. "And he said . . . He told me that, you know. The real estate company he works for? They're about to file Chapter Eleven and they need to raise as much cash as they can." She gave me another very warm smile. "Which is *wonderful* news," she said.

I am not really a financial maven, but even I had heard of Chapter 11 before, and I was reasonably sure it had something to do with bankruptcy. But if that was true I couldn't see why that would be wonderful news, except for any business rivals Brian's employers might have. "Rita," I said.

"But don't you see?" she said. "That means they have to sell off all their houses for whatever they can get, so they're having an auction!" she said triumphantly. "This weekend! And it's in Key West, because you can get a convention rate? And anyway more people will come to the auction if they have it there. Which is why we have to go down there and try? I mean, to get one of them—the houses? At the auction? And so Brian is bringing us a complete list, so this is really a great chance for us to get the new house! Dexter, this could really, really be exactly— Oh, I'm so excited!" she said, and she lurched forward and tried to give me a hug. But since she was still holding Lily Anne it was more of a lean against my chest, which sandwiched the baby in between us. Lily Anne was never one to waste an opportunity, and she began to kick at my stomach vigorously.

I took a step back from the onslaught and put my hands on Rita's shoulders. "An auction in Key West?" I said. "Of all the foreclosed houses in our area?"

Rita nodded, still beaming. "In Key West," she said. "Which we haven't even been to together before."

For a moment I tried very hard to think of something to say, and I failed. Events seemed to be spinning away from me. I felt like I was being pushed off my feet and rolled along the floor toward something wildly irrelevant, weird, and foreign. I know that in theory I am not actually the center of the universe, but I had some very important and immediate concerns right here in Miami, and to go rushing off to Key West to buy a house that was right here in South Miami, and at a time like this? It seemed just a little bit frivolous, and, well . . . not at all about Me, which didn't seem quite right.

But aside from my petty desire to stay home and save my own hide, I couldn't think of any real reason not to go—especially in the face of Rita's near-hysterical enthusiasm. And so five minutes later I found myself sitting down in front of my trusty laptop to make hotel reservations for a three-night stay in Key West. I turned it on and waited. It seemed to start up a bit slower lately. I was usually pretty good about keeping the hard drive clean, but I had been a little distracted. In any case, computer cookies and spyware get more sophisticated every day, and I was not absolutely up-to-date. I made a mental note to spend a little time catching up when things settled down again.

The computer finally finished turning itself on, and I went online to find a hotel room for our visit to the Southernmost City. Travel arrangements for the family was my job—in part because I was much better at navigating the Internet, and in part because in her excitement, Rita had sprinted away for the kitchen to make some kind of celebratory meal, and even in my completely understandable grouchiness I didn't want to interfere with that.

I flipped through the usual Web sites that offered travel bargains. My mood did not improve as I learned that hotel rooms were difficult to come by this weekend because this was the climactic weekend of Hemingway Days, an ancient festival featuring bearded fat guys celebrating all possible forms of human excess. I could not find a reasonably priced hotel room, but I did get a very good deal at the Surfside Hotel for a suite. It had enough room for all of us at a price we could easily pay off in ten years or so, which wasn't too bad, considering that it was in Key West and the town was founded by rapacious pirates. I gave them a credit card number and registered the Morgan family for three nights in room 1229, starting tomorrow night, and turned off my computer.

I spent a good five minutes staring at the laptop's darkened screen and thinking even darker thoughts. I tried to tell myself that everything was going to be fine—I could trust Brian to do a thorough job of taking care of Crowley, even if I didn't get to watch. And Hood's noncase against me would almost certainly collapse. It had to; there was no trace of evidence against me, not anywhere in the world, and after all, I had Deborah watching my back. She would be watching

him and Doakes closely, and she would stop them from cutting corners. It was all no more than the proverbial tempest in a teapot.

And best of all, taking a quick trip to the Keys would completely
derail Doakes. He would either have to drop tailing me, or spend an
exorbitant amount of his own money on gasoline to follow me all the
way down to Key West.

Thinking about that made me feel a little better. The image of
Doakes standing at a gas pump and watching the dollar total spin
higher and higher while he gnashed his teeth was very pleasing, and
for a little while I was satisfied with that. Costing Doakes some cash
was not really payback on the epic scale I preferred, but it would have
to do for now. Life is hard and uncertain, and sometimes a small vic-
tory has to be enough.

TWENTY-NINE

THE REST OF THE EVENING WENT BY IN A MAD FRENZY OF activity. My last calm moment came when I called Deborah and asked her to recommend a lawyer. She said she had a buddy in Professional Compliance and would get me the name of the guy they all hated most to come up against. And then Rita called out, "Dinner!" and the doorbell rang, and at the same time Astor started yelling at Cody to stop cheating and Lily Anne began to cry.

I went to the front door and opened it. Brian stood there, dressed in dark clothing, and for once, the smile he gave me did not seem completely synthetic. "Hello, brother," he said happily, and the tone of his voice made the hair rise on the back of my neck, and in the Deep Downstairs the Dark Passenger hissed and uncurled in uneasy anticipation.

Brian's voice seemed deeper, colder than normal, and there was a smoldering Something flickering in his eyes, and I knew very well what all that added up to.

"Brian," I said. "Are you . . . Did you . . . ?"

He shook his head and his smile got wider. "Not yet," he said. "On my way now." I watched him with something very like jealousy while his smile grew bigger and even more real. "Here," he said, and he held out several pages of paper stapled together and completely covered with closely written entries that seemed to be mostly numbers.

For one wild second I thought the paper was somehow connected to what we both knew he was about to do, and I took the paper from him without really looking at it. "What is it?" I asked him.

"It's your list," he said, and when I didn't answer he added, "The list of houses. For the auction. I told your lovely wife I would bring it by."

"Oh. Right," I said, and I finally looked at the top sheet. One glance was enough to see that it was indeed a list of Miami addresses, with columns for square footage, number of rooms, and so on. "Well," I said. "Thank you. Um . . . have you had dinner?" I held the door open wider to invite him in.

"I have . . . other plans for the evening," he said, and there was no mistaking the edge in his voice. "As you know," he added softly.

"Yes," I said. "I guess I just . . ." I looked at him in his dark clothes and darker purpose and now it truly was envy that roiled through me, but there was in truth only one thing I could say and so I said it. "Good luck, brother."

"Thank you, brother," he said, and he nodded at the list in my hands. "You, too." And his smile might have had just a touch of mockery to it as he added, "With your houses." Then he turned and hurried away to his car and drove off into the growing darkness as I could only watch and wish I was going along with him.

"Dexter?" Rita called from the kitchen, snapping me out of my wistful funk. "It's getting cold!"

I closed the door and went to the table, where the meal was already in full and frantic swing. And things did not calm down all through dinner. It seemed like a near felony to rush through Rita's stir-fried pork, but we did. I tried to eat calmly and actually taste things, but the kids were totally wound up about the sudden trip to Key West, and Rita was far above us all and cranked to the pitch of a hummingbird's hyperrhythmic fluttering. In between each mouthful of food, she would snap out a list of things that each of us absolutely had to do right after we finished eating, and by the time the dishes were all in the sink I found that I had caught the frantic rhythm, too.

I left the table and hurried through packing my clothes. There really wasn't a great deal to the job, in spite of the fact that Rita spent several all-consuming hours at it. For my part, I grabbed a swimsuit and a few complete changes of clothing and chucked them into a gym bag, while Rita sprinted back and forth between the closet and the bed, where her enormous suitcase sat gaping open and empty. When I was finished I took my bag and put it beside the front door, and then went to check on Cody and Astor.

Cody was sitting on the bed with a full backpack beside him, watching his sister as she stared menacingly into her closet. She took out a shirt, held it up, made a horrible face, and put it back. I watched, fascinated, as she repeated the procedure twice. Cody looked at me and shook his head.

"Are you all packed, Cody?" I asked him.

He nodded, and I looked at Astor. She jiggled in place, chewed on her lip, and stomped her foot, but other than that she seemed to be making very little progress. And so, thinking that it was the correct fatherly thing to do, I took the very great risk of trying to speak to her. "Astor?" I said.

"Leave me *alone!*" she snarled over her shoulder. "I am trying to *pack*! And I have *no clothes at all!*" And she flung a handful of objectionable stuff that was apparently not really clothing off the hangers and onto the floor and kicked it.

Cody raised an eyebrow at me. "Girls," he said.

He was probably right that it was a gender thing, because Astor's high-strung performance was almost identical to the one Rita gave me a few moments later when I went back into the bedroom. Rita was holding a sundress in her hand and staring at it like it had killed Kennedy, and there was a pile of dresses and blouses on the floor beside the bed—slightly neater than Astor's furiously flung heap, but very much the same kind of thing. "How are you doing?" I asked Rita cheerfully.

She snapped her head around and looked at me with the expression of a startled and rather angry deer, as if I had interrupted her in the middle of some intense and private meditation. "What?" she said, and gave me a shake of her head and a very cranky frown. "Oh, Dexter, *please* not now," she said. "Honestly, you don't even— Can't you go put gas in the car or something? I have to— This is *repulsive!*" she said, flinging the sundress onto the pile beside the bed.

I left Rita to her high-octane dithering, and put my suitcase and Cody's backpack in the car. I checked the gas gauge and saw that it was nearly full. And then I stood beside the car and thought about what my brother was doing right now, as I did no more than shuffle around carrying luggage. If everything had gone well he would have started by now. It didn't seem fair that he got to have all the fun, when I was the one who'd had to put up with Crowley all this time. But at least that was over. By the time I went to sleep tonight, Crowley would have gone the way of the dodo and the balanced budget. My troubles were winding down to a wicked ending, and that was all good, even if every cell of my body was pleading with me to follow Brian off to Playtime.

But I would have to content myself with standing in the moonlight and trying to picture my brother's happy activities. And just in case I needed a reminder of why that was, one glance up the street to the vacant lot was enough. The Ford Taurus containing the ever-vigilant Sergeant Doakes was still parked there, and I imagined I could see his teeth gleaming at me through the windshield. I sighed, waved at him, and went inside.

Rita was still flinging clothing around and muttering rapidly under her breath when I went to bed. I closed my eyes and tried very hard to sleep, but it's a very difficult thing to do when you are in the middle of a minor cyclone. Time and again I would drift into slumber, only to be jerked awake by the sound of coat hangers clashing angrily, or hundreds of shoes cascading onto the closet floor. Occasionally Rita would say some very surprising things under her breath, or rush out of the room altogether and then hurtle back in again a moment later clutching some arcane object that she would then cram into the bulging suitcase.

Altogether, it made wooing Morpheus a great deal more difficult than usual. I napped and woke up, napped and woke up, until finally, around two thirty, Rita closed her suitcase, thumped it onto the floor, and crawled in beside me, and I dropped off into deep, wonderful sleep at last.

In the morning, we raced through breakfast at high speed, and actually got the car loaded and ready at a very reasonable hour. Everyone climbed in as I folded up Lily Anne's stroller and threw it into the back and we were good to go. But as I started the car and put it in gear, a Ford Taurus pulled in and blocked us.

There was no great mystery about who might be driving the other car. I got out and, as I did, the Ford's passenger door opened and Detective Hood stepped out and gave me a good-morning sneer.

"Sergeant Doakes said you were packing your car," he said.

I looked past him to the Ford; Doakes's happy face was just visible behind the glare on the windshield. "Did he?" I said.

Hood leaned in toward me until his face was only a few inches from mine. "I don't want you thinking you can run away from this, sport," he said, and his breath smelled like low tide at the fish cannery.

I am a very good imitation, but I am not really a good person. I have done many very bad things, and I hope to live long enough to do many more. And to be completely objective, I almost certainly deserve all the things Hood and Doakes wanted to do to me. But while I wait for the long arm of the law to grab me by the neck, I also deserve to breathe air that is not fouled with the stench of unwashed and rotting dental apocalypse.

I put a stiff index finger into Hood's sternum and pushed him away. For a moment he thought he was going to tough it out—but I had chosen my spot well, and he had to back off.

"You can arrest me," I told Hood, "or you can follow me. Otherwise, get out of my way." I pushed a little harder and he had to take another step back. "And for God's sake, brush your teeth."

Hood slapped my hand away and glared at me. I glared back; it takes very little energy, and I could do it all day if that was what he wanted. But he got tired of our staring match first. He looked over his shoulder at Doakes, then back at me. "All right, sport. I'll be seeing you." He stared a moment longer, but when I didn't melt he just turned away, climbed back in beside Doakes, and the car backed away about fifty feet down the street.

I watched them for a moment to see if they would do anything, but they were apparently happy just to watch me. So I got back in our car and began the long drive south.

Doakes stayed right behind us almost all the way to Key Largo. But when it became clear even to his limited reasoning faculties that I was not going to leap out of my car and onto a seaplane and escape to Cuba, he pulled off, turned around, and then drove back toward Miami. After all, there was only one road in and out of the Keys, and I was on it. A few phone calls and they would probably even turn up my reservation in Key West if they wanted to. Fine, I wasn't doing anything I wouldn't do in front of them. I put them out of my mind and concentrated on the traffic, which was already getting worse.

The drive from Miami down to Key West has never been a pleasant one if you are interested in actually getting there. On the other hand, if what you really want to get out of the trip is a nice, slow, meandering crawl through an endless column of bumper-to-bumper traffic that winds through a garish wonderland of T-shirt stores and fast-food joints, and you like to stop in the middle of the road now and then so you can gape at some roadside sign and memorize the words to tell all your friends back in Ohio, while everyone in all the cars behind you swelters in the July sun that no air-conditioning can ever overcome, and all the drivers of those other cars stare anxiously at the needle on the temperature gauge of their car as it climbs steadily into the red and they snarl at you through the blinding glare of the windshield and wish you would simply burst into flames and disappear from the face of the earth even though there are a thousand cars filled with people just like you on the road ahead waiting to take your place and start the whole hideously slow crawl all over again—if that is your idea of a dream vacation in the Promised Land, come to the Keys! Paradise awaits!

It really should be a two- or three-hour drive. I have never made it in less than six, and this time it was seven and a half hours of sweltering road rage before we finally pulled into the parking lot of the Surfside Hotel in downtown Key West.

A remarkably skinny black man in a dark uniform leaped in front of our car and opened the door for me, then raced around to the other side of the car and held the door for Rita as she clambered out, and we all stood there for a moment, dazed and blinded by the merciless heat of July in Key West. The guy in the uniform trotted back to stand in front of me. Apparently he didn't feel the heat—or perhaps he was so thin he simply had nothing in his system that could make sweat. In any case, his face was bone-dry, and he was jumping around in a dark jacket without showing any sign at all that the very air we were all breathing was so hot and humid you could hold an egg in your hand and watch it boil.

"Checking in, sir?" the man said, with the heavy lilt of some Caribbean island in his voice.

"I hope so," I said. "Especially if you have air-conditioning."

The man nodded his head as if he heard this all the time. "Every room, sir. May I help you with your bags?"

It seemed like a very reasonable request, and we all watched as the man piled our bags onto a cart—except for Cody, who would not let go of his backpack. I don't know whether he was suspicious of the uniformed man, or he had something in the pack he didn't want anyone else to see; with Cody, either was possible. But it didn't seem as important as getting into the cool, dark lobby of the hotel as quickly as possible, before the soles of our shoes melted and we stuck to the pavement and sagged helplessly in place while all the flesh melted off our bones.

We followed Captain Skinny inside, and as we stepped into the lobby the cool air hit me with a force that numbed my lips and made time slow down. But we all made it over to reception somehow without slipping into hypothermic shock. The man at the desk inclined his head at us with great gravity and said, "Good afternoon, sir. Do you have a reservation?"

I nodded back and said we had, in fact, reserved a room—and Rita leaned in front of me and blurted out, "Not a room, it's a suite? Because it's supposed to be, I mean, and anyway when we got it—online? And Dexter said—my husband. I mean, Morgan."

"Very good, ma'am," the clerk said. He turned to his computer, and I left Rita to go through all the little rituals of registration while I took Lily Anne and followed Cody and Astor over to a large rack holding pamphlets for all the many charming and glamorous attractions this Magic Isle held for even the most jaded traveler. Apparently, one could do almost anything in Key West—as long as one had a couple of major credit cards and an overwhelming urge to buy T-shirts. The kids stared at the dozens of brightly colored brochures. Cody would frown and point to one, and Astor would pull it from its slot. Then their two heads came together over the pictures as they studied the page, Astor whispering to her brother and Cody nodding and frowning back at her, and then their eyes would snap up and they'd go back to the rack to pick another one. By the time Rita had us registered and came to join us, Astor held at least fifteen brochures.

"Well," Rita said, as breathlessly as if she'd just run all the way from Miami. "We're all set! Shall we go up to our room? I mean our *suite*—because we're here and it's— Oh, this hotel is just so— This is going to be so much fun!"

Perhaps I was just tired from grinding my teeth in traffic for seven and a half hours, but I found it hard to match Rita's high-spirited enthusiasm. Still, we were here, and more or less intact. So I followed along behind her as she led us to the elevator and up to our room—I mean our suite.

The suite consisted of a large bedroom, a living area with a kitchenette and a foldout couch, and a tiled bathroom with a shower and a Jacuzzi. The entire suite had a faint smell to it, as if somebody had deep-fried a bag of lemons in a vat of toxic cleaning fluids. Rita rushed in and opened the curtains, revealing a beautiful view of the back side of the neighboring hotel. "Oh," she gushed, "this is just so— Dexter, get the door; it's the man with our bags— Look at this, Cody, Astor! We're in Key West!"

I opened the door. As advertised, it was the man with our bags. He put them in the bedroom and then smiled at me so aggressively that I almost felt guilty giving him a mere five-dollar bill. But he accepted it without any kind of tantrum and vanished out the door. I barely had time to sit down before a second knock came on the door—this time another uniformed man, who wheeled in a crib, set it up for us, and gravely accepted another five dollars for his labors.

When he was gone I sat again, with Lily Anne bouncing in my lap. She and I watched as the other members of our little family scuttled through the suite and explored it, opening doors and cupboards and calling to each other with each new discovery. It all felt a little bit unreal. Of course, Key West always does, but it seemed a bit more so this time. After all, I really shouldn't have been here at all, and it made no sense to me that I was—yet here I sat in this bright and shiny tourist mecca, in an expensive hotel room—I mean *suite*—while only a few hours away some very serious and very bent cops were working overtime to frame me for murder. And on the other side of Miami, my brother was lounging around in the afterglow of a playdate that should have been mine. Those two things were immediate, important, and tangible to me in a way that our trip to this surreal oasis of greed never could be, and it was difficult to believe that I was trapped in a glitzy time-out while real life whirled away without me just a few hours north.

Rita finally finished opening all the cupboards and closets, and came to sit beside me. She reached over and took Lily Anne from my lap and sighed heavily. "Well," she said, sounding utterly content. "Here we are."

And as unlikely as it seemed to me, she was right. Here we were, and for the next few days, whatever happened in Real Life would have to happen without me.

THIRTY

SINCE OUR REAL ESTATE AUCTION DID NOT TAKE PLACE UNTIL tomorrow, we had a long afternoon and evening of what Rita called free time, which seemed like a very misleading thing to call something that cost so much. We all followed Rita through the streets of Old Key West buying bottled water—at airport prices—and then ice cream and a five-dollar cookie and sunglasses and sunscreen and hats and T-shirts and genuine Key West sandals. I began to feel like a portable ATM. At the rate I was tossing away cash, we would be dead broke by bedtime.

But there was no slowing down Rita. She was obviously set on forcing us all into a delirium of high-priced bankruptcy, and just to make sure I lost my last inhibitions about saving enough money to buy gas for the trip home, she even dragged us all to a very loud bar that opened onto the sidewalk. She ordered two mai tais and two virgin piña coladas, and when the bill came it was really no more than dinner for eight at a good restaurant. I sipped from the plastic cup, nearly poking out my eye with the little paper umbrella that was shoved into the bright pink slush, while Rita gave Astor her cell phone and made her snap a picture of the two of us standing in front of a large plastic shark with our mai tais raised.

I finished my drink without discovering any actual alcohol in it, and got a brief but blinding headache from slurping the frozen slop too fast. We trudged on up Duval Street, finding ever more ingenious ways to throw away money. Then we hurried back down the other side of Duval Street to Mallory Square and got there just in time to participate in a more free-form style of wasting money, the legendary sunset celebration. Rita handed dollar bills to Cody and Astor and urged them to fling them at the vast collection of jugglers, fire-eaters, acrobats, and other freeloaders—all climaxing when Rita herself dropped a ten-dollar bill into the outstretched hands of the man who forced a collection of domestic cats to leap through flaming hoops by screeching at them in a high-pitched voice with a strange foreign accent.

We had dinner at a charming place that claimed to serve the freshest seafood in town. It was not air-conditioned, so I hoped it really was fresh. Even with the ceiling fans whirling it was stiflingly hot, and after sitting at the large picnic-style table for five minutes I found that I was stuck to the bench. But the food came after only forty-five minutes, and the grease it had been cooked in was only a few days old, so I couldn't really object when the bill came and the total was no more than the down payment on a new Mercedes.

Through it all the heat never let up, the crowd noise grew louder, and my wallet got much lighter. By the time we staggered back to the hotel I was soaked with sweat, half-deaf, and I had three new blisters on my feet. It was altogether a great deal more fun than I'd had in a long time, and as I slumped into a chair in our hotel room—*suite*—I remembered again why I really don't like having fun.

I took a shower and when I came out, clean but very tired, Cody and Astor had settled down in front of the TV to watch a movie. Lily Anne was sound asleep in the crib, and Rita was sitting at the desk with the list of houses for tomorrow's auction, frowning and scribbling in the margins. I went to bed and slid immediately into sleep, visions of dollar bills dancing in my head. They were all waving good-bye.

It was still half-dark when I opened my eyes the next morning. Rita sat at the desk, again—or still—flipping through the list of houses and scribbling on a legal pad. I looked at the clock on the bedside table. It said five forty-eight.

"Rita," I said, in a voice that was somewhere between a croak and a gargle.

She didn't look up. "I have to figure them all at the thirty-year fixed rate," she said. "But if we finance it through Ernesto's brother it's a lower rate? But we pay closing."

It was a little too much information for me in my barely awake state and I closed my eyes again. But I had just started to slide back into sleep when Lily Anne started to fuss. I opened one eye and looked at Rita; she was pretending she didn't hear Lily Anne, which is Married Person Code for, *You do it, dear.* So I bade a fond farewell to the whole idea of slumber and got up. I changed Lily Anne's diaper and made her a bottle of formula, and by the time I was done she had made it clear that she was awake and that was all there was to it.

The sign in the hotel's lobby had said that breakfast was served starting at six a.m. If I was going to be awake, I decided I should do it right and have some coffee and an assembly-line Danish. I got dressed and, with Lily Anne under one arm, headed for the door.

But two steps into the living room a small blond head popped up from the tangle of blankets on the foldout couch. "Where are you going, Dexter?" Astor said.

"Breakfast."

"We wanna come, too," she said, and she and Cody both exploded up out of the bedding and onto the floor as if they had been loaded into a torpedo tube and waiting for me to swim by.

By the time they were dressed, Rita had come out to see what all the fuss was about, and decided to come with us. So ten minutes after I had taken my tentative step toward the door and coffee, the entire troupe was on the march for the dining room.

There were only two other people there: a couple of middle-aged men who looked like they were on their way out to go fishing. We sat down as far from the TV as possible and tore into a surprisingly good buffet, considering it was just $19.95 per person.

I sipped a cup of coffee that tasted like it had been made at my office last year, frozen, and shipped down to Key West in a barrel of bait. Still, it definitely got my eyes open. I found myself thinking of Brian and what he had almost certainly finished by now. I was a little jealous; I hoped he'd taken his time and had a little fun.

I thought about Hood and Doakes and wondered whether they had followed me down here after all. I was sure they'd want to—but technically that would be a little bit outside the rules, wouldn't it? Still, Doakes had never let regulations dampen his zeal. And I didn't think Hood could actually understand the rules, since many of them had words in them with more than one syllable. I was pretty sure they'd turn up sooner or later.

My train of thought was derailed when Rita slapped the list onto the table and spoke very definitely. "Five," she said, frowning heavily and tapping one of the entries with a pencil.

"Excuse me?" I said politely.

She looked up at me blankly. "Five," she said again. "Five *houses.* The others are all . . ." She vigorously shook her hand, the one with the pencil, and went on in a brittle and rapid voice. "Too big. Too small. Wrong area. Bad zoning. High tax base. Old roof and maybe—"

"So there are five possible houses to bid on that might work for us?" I said, because I have always believed that both people in a conversation should know what they are talking about.

"Yes, of course," Rita said, frowning again, and then smacking the paper with her pencil. "This one, on a Hundred and Forty-second Terrace, this would be the best, and it's not that far from the house we're in now, but—"

"Do we have to talk about all that boring house stuff?" Astor interrupted. "Can't we go to the aquarium, and then just buy a house later?"

"Astor, no, we can't—don't interrupt," Rita said. "This is extremely important and I— You have no idea how much we still have to do, just to be ready by three o'clock."

"But we don't *all* have to do it," Astor said in her very best reasonable whine. "We wanna go to the aquarium." She looked at Cody, and he nodded at her, and then at his mother.

"That's impossible," Rita said. "This is one of the most important decisions— And your future! Because you will be living there for a very long time."

"Aquarium," Cody said softly. "Feed the sharks."

"What? Feed the— Cody, you can't feed the sharks," Rita said.

"You can so feed the sharks," Astor said. "It says in the brochure."

"That's crazy; they're *sharks*," Rita said with emphasis, as if Astor had used the word wrong. "And the auction is only— Oh, look at the time." She began to flutter in place on her chair, stuffing the pencil into her purse and waving the list of houses to summon the waiter. And I, sensing that there are certain forms of tedium that are best endured without me, looked at Cody and Astor, and then turned to Rita.

"I'll take the kids to the aquarium," I said.

Rita looked up at me, startled. "What? Dexter, no, don't be— We have to go through this whole list, let alone the five—and then register with the— No, there's too much," she said.

Once again, my extensive background watching daytime drama told me the right move to make, and I reached across to put my hand on top of hers—not an easy thing to do, since the hand was in constant motion. But I snared it and pinned it to the table and then, leaning over as close to her as I could get, I said, "Rita. This is something you know more about than the rest of us combined. More important, we trust you to do it right."

Cody and Astor are not slow, and they knew a dramatic cue when they heard one. Cody nodded rapidly and Astor said, "Totally, Mom, really."

"Besides," I said, "they're kids. They're in a strange new place, and they want to see new and exciting things."

"Feed the sharks," Cody said stubbornly.

"And it's educational!" Astor almost shouted, which I thought might have been overkill.

But apparently the shot went home, because Rita no longer seemed so certain when she said, "But the list, and Dexter, really, you ought to . . . you know."

"You're right," I said, which was at least possible. "But, Rita—look at them." I nodded at the kids, who both instantly put on beaten-puppy faces. "And I really do trust you to do the right thing. Completely," I added, giving her hand a little squeeze for emphasis.

"Well, but really," Rita said feebly.

"Pleeeeeeeeeease?" Astor said, and Cody added, "Sharks, Mom."

Rita looked from one to the other, chewing rapidly on her lip until I was afraid she would chomp it right off. "Well," she said. "If it's just . . ."

"Yay!" Astor called out, and Cody nearly smiled. "Thanks, Mom!" Astor added, and she and her brother both jumped up from the table.

"But you brush your teeth first!" Rita said. "And, Dexter, they have to put on sunscreen—it's on the desk up in our room, our suite."

"All right," I said. "Where will you be?"

Rita frowned and looked around the room until she found the clock. "The auction office opens at seven—that's ten minutes. I'll take Lily Anne over there and ask them— And Brian said they have pictures, too, better than the ones— But, Dexter, really . . ."

I reached across and patted her arm comfortingly.

"It's going to be fine," I said again. "You're really good at this."

Rita shook her head. "Don't let them get too close to the sharks?" she said. "Because after all."

"We'll be careful," I assured her, and as I walked out to join Cody and Astor, Rita was lifting Lily Anne out of the high chair and wiping apple sauce from her face.

Astor and Cody were out in front of the hotel, watching in dumbstruck awe as several clusters of stocky bearded men headed past, hurrying down Duval Street and glaring suspiciously at each other.

Astor shook her head and said, "They all look alike, Dexter. They even dress the same. Are they gay or something?"

"They can't all be," I said. "Even in Key West."

"So then what's up?" she said, as if it was my fault that the men looked the same.

I was about to tell her it was a strange cosmic accident, when I remembered that it was July and this was, after all, Key West. "Oh," I said. "Hemingway Days." They both looked at me blankly. "The men are all Hemingway look-alikes," I told them.

Astor frowned and looked at Cody. He shook his head.

"What's Hemingway?" Astor said.

I watched the crowd of look-alikes milling around on the sidewalk, jostling each other and slurping beer. "A man who grew a beard and drank a lot," I said.

"Well, I wouldn't want to look like that," she muttered.

"Come on," I said. "You have to brush your teeth."

I herded them in and over to the elevator, just in time to see Rita heading out the door. She gave us a big wave and called out,

"Don't get too close— I'll call you when I— Remember, be there at two o'clock!"

"Bye, Mom!" Astor called back, and Cody waved to her.

We rode up to our floor in silence, and trudged down the hall to our room. I put the key card into the lock on our door, pushed the door open, and held it for Cody and Astor. They hurried inside and, before I could follow them in and close the door, they stopped dead in their tracks.

"Whoa," Astor said.

"Cool," Cody added, and his voice seemed louder and sharper than normal.

"Dex-ter," Astor called in a happy singsong tone. "You'd better come look."

I pushed past them into the room for a look, and after one quick glance, looking was all I could do. My feet would not move, my mouth was dry, and all coherent thought had fled me, replaced by the single syllable "but," which repeated itself in an endless loop as I just stared.

The foldout couch where Cody and Astor had slept was pulled out and neatly made up, with pillows fluffed and blanket turned down. And nestled snugly onto the bed was a rigid lump of something that had once been a human being. But it didn't look like one now; where a face should have been there was a shallow, flattened crater with a smear of crusted blood around it where some large, hard object had come in contact with flesh and bones. A few stubs of gray teeth showed in the middle, and one eyeball, popped out of its socket by the force of the blow, dangled down one side of the mess.

Somebody had hit that face with appalling force, with something like a baseball bat, crushing it out of shape and probably killing it instantly, which almost seemed too bad. Because even without a shape, and in spite of the fact that I was shocked nearly thoughtless by finding it here, I recognized the cheap suit and enough of the squashed features to know who this scabby lump had once been.

It was Detective Hood.

THIRTY-ONE

I HAD NEVER LIKED DETECTIVE HOOD, AND I LIKED HIM A LOT less now. He had been enough of an annoyance alive; turning up dead in my hotel room was much worse, violating even the most basic standards of etiquette and decency. It was just plain wrong, and I almost wished he was still alive, so I could kill him again.

But beyond this severe breach of decorum there were other implications, infinitely more troubling. And although I would like to say that my high-powered brain immediately kicked into top gear and began to compute them all, the truth is sadly otherwise. I was so busy being angry at Hood's final offense against good taste that I did not think at all until I heard Astor say, "But, Dexter, what's it *doing* here?"

And as I opened my mouth to snap some angry dismissal at her, it hit me that this was a very important question. Not why Hood was in Key West; he had clearly followed me to make sure I didn't steal a boat and run for Cuba. I had half expected that. But someone else had followed along, too, and killed Hood in this very distinctive way, and that was far more troubling, because theoretically, it was impossible. Because unless I was willing to accept the idea that a monstrous coincidence had led a complete stranger to kill Hood for some whimsical reason, and then by miraculous happenstance chose to dump him randomly in my suite, there was only one person in the world who could have done this.

Crowley.

Of course, he was supposed to be dead, which should have kept him too busy to do anything like this. But even if he was still alive somehow . . . how had he found me here? How had he discovered not only that I was in Key West, but that I was here, in this hotel, in this exact room? He had known every move I was going to make before I had made it, and now even my room number. How?

Cody tried to push past and get a closer look, and I pushed him firmly back toward the door. "Stay back," I said, and I reached for my phone. If I couldn't figure out how Crowley had stayed ahead of me the whole time, at least I could find out if he was really dead. I dialed. There were three short rings and then a dreadfully cheerful, "Hello!"

"Brian," I said. "Sorry if this is an odd question, but, um . . . did you take care of that thing you were going to do the other night?"

"Oh, yes," he said, and even through the phone I could hear the very real happiness in his voice. "And a good time was had by nearly all."

"You're sure?" I said, staring at the lump that had been Hood.

"You're right; that really is an odd question," Brian said. "Of course I'm sure, brother; I was there."

"And there was no mistake?"

There was a pause on the line, and I wondered whether the connection had dropped. "Brian?" I said.

"Well," he said after a moment, "it's just funny that you should ask that. The, um . . . the gentleman in question? He used that word a lot. He kept saying I was making a terrible mistake. Something about identity theft, I think? I wasn't really listening."

Something nudged me from behind. "Dexter," Astor said, pushing harder. "We can't *see*."

"Just a minute," I snapped at her, pushing them back again. "Brian," I said into the phone. "Can you describe the, um, gentleman in question?"

"Before or after?" he said.

"Before."

"We-e-ellllll," he said. "I would say about forty-five, maybe five-foot-ten and a hundred and sixty pounds? Blond hair, clean shaven, with little gold-rimmed glasses."

"Oh," I said. Crowley was probably thirty pounds heavier than that, younger, and he had a beard.

"Is everything okay, brother? You sound a little out of sorts."

"I'm afraid that everything is not quite okay," I said. "I think the gentleman in question was right."

"Oh, dear," Brian said. "There was a mistake?"

"It sure looks like it from here," I said.

"Oh, well," Brian said. "*Qué será.*"

Astor nudged me again. "Dex-ter, come *on*," she said.

"I have to go," I told Brian.

"I'd love to know what I did," he said. "Call me later?"

"If I can," I told him. I put away the phone and turned to face Cody and Astor. "Now," I said, "you two go wait in the hall."

"But, Dexter," Astor said, "we didn't get to see anything, not really."

"Too bad," I said firmly. "You can't go any closer until the police are done."

"Not fair," Cody said, with a major-league pout.

"Tough. This is what I do for a living," I told him—meaning crime scene work, of course, and not the actual crime. "We have to leave the room without touching anything and go call the police."

"We just wanna look; we won't *touch* anything," Astor said.

"No," I said, pushing them toward the door. "Wait in the hall. I'll just be a minute."

They didn't like it, not at all, but they went, trying all the way to get one more look at the thing on the foldout sofa. But I hustled them into the hall and shut the door and went to take a closer look of my own.

No one would ever have called Hood a handsome man, but as he was now he was positively repulsive. His tongue stuck out between the broken teeth, and the eye that wasn't hanging out of the socket had gone red. This had clearly been the result of one tremendously powerful blow, and I didn't think Hood had suffered for very long, which didn't seem fair.

I knelt down beside the bed and looked underneath. There were no hastily dropped keys or monogrammed handkerchiefs to tell me who had done this, but they weren't needed. I knew who had done it. But I still needed to know *how*. On the far side of the bed I saw something, and I went around to the other side and poked it out just far enough so I could see it. It was a large souvenir pirate hat, the kind with the black rubber eye patch molded onto it so it hangs down the front. Stuffed inside was a red bandanna. Even without touching it, I could see blood on the bandanna. A disguise for Hood? Probably to cover the wounds long enough to get him into the hotel.

I stood up and, just to be thorough, I went into the bedroom to see if anything was amiss. But everything looked fine—no one was lurking in the closet, Rita's suitcase seemed undisturbed, and even my laptop was still sitting on the desk, apparently untouched. When I thought about it, that seemed a little odd. After all, Crowley boasted about his mastery of computer lore; why hadn't he taken two minutes to look at my computer and learn my secrets?

And from somewhere deep inside Dexter's Dungeon there came a soft flex of wings and a gently whispered answer:

Because he didn't need to.

I blinked. It was a painfully simple answer, and it made me feel stupider than I could ever remember feeling.

He didn't need to learn my secrets.

He already knew them.

He had stayed a step ahead of me because he had *already* hacked into my hard drive, and every time I powered on to find his address or read my e-mail or make a hotel reservation, he was there with me. There were plenty of programs that could do that. The only question was how he had put it on my hard drive. I tried to remember if I had left my computer alone anyplace but home or work—I hadn't. I never would. But, of course, you didn't need to touch a computer to hack into it. With the right worm, wi-fi would work fine. And with that thought I remembered sitting in front of my computer and opening an e-mail pitching the new Web site "Tropical Blood." There had been a burst of fancy flash graphics and then a slow crawl of blood—perfect for distracting me for just a moment while the program wormed onto my hard drive and started telling Crowley everything about me.

It made sense; I was sure I was right, and with two minutes on the computer I could know for sure—but a rapid pounding came on the door, followed by Astor's muffled, anxious voice calling my name. I turned away from my computer. It didn't matter. Even without finding Crowley's worm, I knew it was there. Nothing else was possible.

The knocking came again, and I opened the door and went out into the hall. The two of them tried to peer around me and see Hood's body, but I pulled the door closed.

"We just wanted one last look," Astor said.

"No," I said. "And that's another thing. You have to pretend to be grossed out and scared. So people think you're just ordinary kids."

"*Scared?*" Astor demanded. "Scared of what?"

"Scared of a dead body, and thinking that a killer was right here in your hotel room."

"It's a suite," she said.

"So put on your frightened faces for the cops," I said, and I got us all into the elevator. Luckily, there was a mirror in the elevator, and all the way down to the lobby they practiced looking scared. Neither one of them was completely convincing—it really does take years of practice—but I hoped nobody would notice.

I have been at hundreds of crime scenes in my career, and many of them were in hotels, so I was quite well aware that the management, generally speaking, does not consider dead bodies in the rooms a major selling point. They prefer to keep such things quiet, and in the spirit of polite cooperation, I went to the front desk and asked to see the manager.

The desk clerk was a nice-looking African-American woman. She smiled with genuine sympathy and said, "Of course, sir. Is there a problem?"

"There's a dead body in our suite," Astor said.

"Hush," I told her.

The desk clerk's smile twitched and then faded as she looked from me to Astor. "Are you sure about that, young lady?" she asked Astor.

I put a restraining hand on Astor. "I'm afraid so," I told the clerk.

She just gaped for several seconds. "Oh, my God," she said at last. "I mean . . ." She cleared her throat and then made a very visible effort to pull her official clerk face back together. "Wait right here," she said formally, and then she thought again and added, "I mean . . . please come with me?"

We followed her through the doorway behind the desk and waited while she called the manager. The manager arrived, and we waited some more while he called the police. And then we waited even longer while the police and local forensics team went up to our suite. A woman arrived and stared at us while she talked to the clerk. She seemed to be about forty-five, with graying hair, and loose skin hanging from her neck like crepe paper. She looked like she had been one of the party girls who came to Key West and hung out in the bars, until one day she woke up and realized the party was over and she had to get a real job. It didn't seem to agree with her; she had a look of permanent disappointment etched onto her face, like there was a bad taste on her tongue and she couldn't get rid of it.

After a quick and quiet conversation with the desk clerk she came over and spoke to me. "Mr. Morgan?" she said formally, and I recognized the tone right away. Her next words proved that I was right. "I'm Detective Blanton," she said. "I need to ask you a few questions."

"Of course," I said.

"First I'd like to make sure your children are okay?" she said, and without waiting for an answer from me she crouched down beside Cody and Astor. "Hi," she said to them, in a tone of voice usually reserved for clever puppies or human idiots. "My name is Detective Shari. Can you talk about what you saw upstairs in your room?"

"It's a suite," Astor said. "And anyway, we didn't get to see hardly anything because Dexter made us leave the room before we could really look at it."

Blanton blinked with her mouth hanging open. This was clearly not quite the reaction she'd been expecting. "I see," she said, and she looked up at me.

"They're very frightened," I said, putting a little emphasis on the word so they would remember that they were scared.

"Of course they are," Blanton said. She looked at Cody. "You gonna be okay, buddy?"

"Fine," he said softly, and then he glanced at me and added, "Really scared."

"That's totally normal," Blanton said, and Cody looked very pleased. "How about you, sweetheart?" she continued, turning back to Astor. "You doing all right?"

Astor made a visible effort not to snarl at being called "sweetheart" and instead managed to say, "Yes, I'm fine, thank you, just scared."

"Uh-huh," Blanton said. She looked back and forth between the two of them, apparently searching for some clue that they might be slipping into shock.

My phone rang—it was Rita. "Hello, dear," I said, turning half away from Blanton and the children.

"Dexter, I just went past the aquarium? It doesn't open until almost— And so, where are you? Because it's a couple of hours."

"Well," I said. "We got a little sidetracked. There's been a little incident here at the hotel—"

"Oh, my God, I knew it," she said.

"Nothing at all to worry about," I said, raising my voice over hers. "We're all fine; it's just something that happened and we were witnesses, so we have to make a statement, that's all."

"But they're just children," Rita said. "It isn't even legal, and they have to— Are they all right?"

"They're both fine; they're talking to a very nice policewoman," I said, and thinking it was best to cut things short, I said, "Rita, please, you go right ahead with the auction. We'll be fine."

"I can't possibly— Because, I mean, the *police* are there?"

"You have to do the auction; it's what we came for," I said. "Get us the place on a Hundred and Forty-second Street."

"It's terrace," she said. "A Hundred and Forty-second Terrace."

"Even better," I said. "And don't worry; we'll be there in plenty of time."

"Well, but," she said, "I just think I should be there—"

"You need to get ready for the auction," I said. "And don't worry about us. We'll finish up here and then go see the sharks. This is just a minor inconvenience."

"Mr. Morgan?" Blanton said behind me. "There's somebody here who wants to talk to you."

"Get that house," I said to Rita. "I have to go now." And I turned to face Blanton, and saw that my minor inconvenience had just grown a few sizes.

Gliding into the room, teeth first, was Sergeant Doakes.

I have been in many police interrogation rooms, and truthfully, the one in the Key West police station was fairly standard. But it did look a little different this time, since I was on the wrong side of the table. They hadn't handcuffed me, which I thought was very nice of them, but they also didn't seem to want me to go anywhere. So I sat there at the table while first Blanton and then several other detectives came and went, snarling the same questions, and then disappearing again. And each time the door swung open, I could see Sergeant Doakes standing in the hall outside the room. He was not smiling now, although I'm sure he was very happy, since I was right where he wanted me, and I knew he'd think it was worth losing Hood to put me here.

I tried very hard to be patient and answer the four standard questions the Key West cops kept asking, no matter how many times they asked, and I tried just as hard to remember that this one time I really was completely innocent and I had nothing to worry about. Sooner or later they would have to let me go, no matter how many ways Doakes managed to invoke professional cooperation.

But they seemed in no hurry, and after an hour or so in which they didn't even offer me coffee, I thought perhaps I should encourage them. So when the fourth detective came in and sat down opposite me, and informed me for the third time that this was a very serious matter, I stood up and said, "Yes, it is. You are holding me here for no reason, without filing a charge, when I have done absolutely nothing wrong."

"Sit down, Dexter," the detective said. He was probably about fifty and looked like he'd been beaten up a few times, and I felt very strongly that one more time would be a good idea, because he said my name like he thought it was funny, and although I am normally very patient with stupidity—after all, there's so much of it—this was the last straw.

So I put my knuckles on the table and leaned toward him, and I let fly with all the righteous indignation that I actually felt. "No," I said. "I will not sit down. And I will not answer the same questions over and over anymore. If you aren't going to file a charge and aren't going to let me go, I want an attorney."

"Look," the guy said, with world-weary chumminess. "We know you're with the Miami-Dade department. A little professional cooperation wouldn't hurt you, would it?"

"It would not hurt me at all," I said. "And unless you release me immediately, I plan to cooperate as much as possible with your Internal Affairs department."

The detective drummed his fingers on the table for a few seconds and looked like he thought he might tough it out. But instead he slapped the table softly, stood up, and walked out without another word.

It was only another five minutes before Blanton came back in. She didn't look happy, but maybe she didn't know how. She was holding a manila folder in one hand and smacking it against the other one, and she looked at me like she wanted to blame me for the federal budget deficit. But she didn't say anything; she just looked, smacked the folder a few times, and then shook her head. "You can go," she said.

I waited to see if there was anything else. There wasn't, so I walked through the door and into the hall. Naturally enough, Sergeant Doakes was standing there waiting for me. "Better luck next time," I told him.

He didn't say anything, and he didn't even show me his teeth. He just stared at me with that hungry-jackal look of his that I knew so well, and since I have never been the sort who enjoys uncomfortable silence, I turned away from him and stuck my head back into the interrogation room that had been my home for the last ninety minutes.

"Blanton," I said, rather proud of myself for remembering her name. "Where are my children?"

She put the folder down, sighed, and came over to the doorway. "They've gone to be with their mother," she said.

"Oh, all right," I said. "Did they get to ride over in a patrol car?"

"No, we could get in trouble for that," she said. "We got budget problems, you know."

"Well, you didn't just stick them in a taxicab all alone, did you?" I said, and I admit I was getting irritated with her, and the entire Key West Police Department.

"No, of course not," she said, with a little more spirit than she'd shown so far. "They left with an authorized adult."

I could think of only one or two people who might be considered authorized, and for a moment I felt a brief glimmer of hope; perhaps Deborah had arrived and things were looking up at last. "Oh, good," I said. "Was it their aunt, Sergeant Deborah Morgan?"

Blanton blinked at me and shook her head. "No," she said. "But it's okay; your son knew him. It was his Cub Scout leader."

THIRTY-TWO

I HAD SPENT FAR TOO MUCH TIME LATELY BEMOANING THE
decline of my once-stunning mental powers, and so it was a
great relief to realize that the gray cells were coming back online,
because I did not think, even for a second, that "Cub Scout leader"
meant Frank, the big-bellied, ghost story–telling *real* leader of the
pack. I knew instantly who had taken Cody and Astor.

It was Crowley.

He had come right into the station, a building filled with police-
men who were looking for *him*, even though they didn't know it, and
he had bluffed his way into possession of my children and walked
out with them, and while a very small part of me admired the absolute brazen nerve of it, the rest of me was in no mood to hand out
compliments.

He had taken *my* kids. Cody and Astor were *mine*, and he had
snatched them from under my nose. It was a special, personal affront,
and it filled me with a rage larger and brighter and more blinding than
anything I had ever felt before. A red mist came down and covered
over everything I saw, starting with Detective Blanton. She was gog-
gling at me like some kind of awful, stupid, droopy fish, just gawking

and mocking me for getting caught and for losing the children—and it was all her fault. All of it—she had listened to Doakes and brought me here and taken *my* kids away, only to give them to the one person on earth I didn't want anywhere near them—and she was standing right there in front of me making stupid faces and I wanted very badly to grab her around her saggy little neck and shake her until the crepe-paper wrinkles on her neck rattled and then squeeze until her eyes popped and her tongue flopped out and her face turned purple and all the small and delicate bones in her throat crunched and splintered in my hands—

Blanton must have noticed that my reaction was a little more than a polite thank-you and a carefree nod of the head. She took a step away from me, back into the interrogation room, and said, "Uh, that was okay, wasn't it, Mr. Morgan?" And even though it was a step up from being called by my first name, it did not pacify me, not at all. Without realizing what I was doing I took a step toward her and flexed my fingers. "Your boy *knew* him," she said, starting to sound a little desperate. "It was . . . I mean, the Cub Scouts? They all have to pass a background check—"

Just before I got my hands on her throat, something very hard and metallic grabbed my elbow and jerked me back a half step. I turned toward it, ready to rip it into small pieces, too—but of course, it was Sergeant Doakes, and he did not look at all rippable, even through the red mist. He had latched onto my arm with one of his prosthetic claws, and he was looking at me with an expression of amused interest, as if hoping I would really try something. The red mist dropped away from my vision.

I pried his claw from my arm, which was harder than it sounds, and I looked one more time at Detective Blanton. "If anything has happened to my children," I told her, "you will regret it for the rest of your short, stupid, miserable little life."

And before she could think of anything to say to that, I turned away, pushed past Doakes, and walked away down the hall.

It was not really a very long walk back to the center of town. There aren't any long walks in Key West. Everything you read about the place tells you it is a small island, no more than a few square miles tucked snugly away at the end of the Florida Keys. It's supposed to be a comfy little town stuffed full of sun and fun and relentless good times that never end. But when you step into the smothering heat of Duval Street trying to locate one specific man and two children, there is nothing small about it. And as I finally hit the center of town and stared around me in my angry panic, that came home to me with a force that nearly took the wind out of me. I was looking for the tip of a needle in a field full of haystacks. It was far past futile, beyond hopeless; there was not even a place to begin that made any sense.

Everything seemed to be stacked against me. The streets were overflowing with people of all sizes and shapes, and I couldn't even see half a block in any direction. A trio of Hemingways walked past me, and it rubbed my nose in the fact that even looking for Crowley was ridiculous. He was a stocky guy with a beard, and the streets of Key West were crammed full of stocky guys with beards. I stared wildly around, but it was useless, pointless, hopeless; they were everywhere. Several more stocky bearded men pushed past; two of them held children by the hand, kids about the size and shape of Cody and Astor, and each time I felt a sharp stab of hope, and each time the faces were wrong and the crowd closed around them and surged along Duval and left me stewing in a dark gray cloud of despair. I would never find them. Crowley had won and I might as well go home and wait for the end of all things.

The hopelessness came flooding in like a spring tide and I slumped against a building and closed my eyes. It was easier to do nothing while resting in one place than to do the same nothing galloping around with no idea where to go or what to look for. I could just stay here, leaning in the shade and wrapped in defeat. And I might have stayed there placidly for a much longer time—except that one very small bright idea swam upstream through the gray tide and wiggled its tail at me.

I watched it swim in its lazy slow circles for a moment, and when at last I understood what it was saying I grabbed it by the fins and held it up to look at it. I turned it over and looked at all sides, and the more I did, the more right it seemed. I opened my eyes and stood up slowly and deliberately and looked at the wiggly little thing one more time, and I knew it was right.

Crowley had not won—not yet.

I don't mean that my thought brought some flicker of idiot hope, or that it had told me where Crowley had gone with Cody and Astor. It had told me a much simpler, more compelling truth:

The game was not over.

Crowley had not yet done what he needed to do. Taking Cody and Astor was not the Endgame, because we were not playing Capture the Kids. We were playing Let's Demolish Dexter. He didn't want to hurt them—his overdeveloped sense of right and wrong wouldn't let him hurt innocent children. No, he wanted to hurt *me,* to punish *me* for the wicked things I had done. So until I was dead or at the very least in leg irons, Crowley was not done playing.

Neither was I. I was just getting started.

He'd had it all his way so far, kept me off balance, stepping in to deliver his nasty little jabs and then dancing away before I could react, and he thought he was winning and I was no more than a dull punching bag, a broad and simple target, easy to find and slow to react, and he had pushed me and slapped me and jabbed me into a corner until he thought he had me on the ropes and I would be easy to finish off.

He was wrong.

He hadn't faced *me* yet. He had no idea what it meant to try to put me down in person. He had not stood toe-to-toe with the champ, Dexter the Destroyer, facing *me* in the flesh with the certainty of Death in each hand and the dark wind howling around us—that was my home turf, and he had not set foot on it yet, and until he did the fight had not even started.

But Crowley had rung the bell for the final round when he snatched Cody and Astor. He believed I was weakened and he was ready, and he had made his move. And he had not taken the kids to taunt me, to show me he was very clever and I was a helpless fool. No, he had taken them so I would come after them. They were the bait for his trap, and a trap can't catch anything at all unless the prey knows where it is.

He was waiting for me to find him. And that meant that somehow, some way, he would have to let me know where he was. There would be a broad and obvious hint somewhere, an actual invitation to the dance. He would not want to wait too long, and he would not leave it to chance. I knew I was right. He had slapped me with a glove, and someplace near and obvious he had dropped it for me to find.

My phone rang, and I glanced at it; it was Rita. I almost answered it out of mere habit—but before I could push the button and speak, I heard a different, interior bell chime softly and I *knew*.

Of course. This whole thing had been centered around computers and Crowley's conceited belief that he was King of the Internet. He would not just leave a hint somewhere—he would send it to me in an e-mail.

The phone was still ringing insistently, but now I had a much more important use for it than talking to Rita, and I hit the disconnect button. I tapped the icon to get to my e-mail and it seemed to take hours before the screen finally showed my in-box. But it did at last, and there, at the top, was a note from Shadowblog. I opened it.

Very good, it said. *You finally found my real name and address.*

Something bumped me and I flinched into alertness. A rowdy group of young men that looked like a fraternity party turned bad roiled past me, shouting and slopping beer from plastic cups. I pushed through them and sat down on the edge of a low wall in front of a restaurant, and went back to reading the e-mail.

> *You finally found my real name and address. Too bad it isn't my real name and address. Did you really think it would be that easy? But thanks anyway—you solved a problem for me. The guy was my ex-boss, a real douche bag. And "Doug Crowley" is a lot safer to use now that there's nobody to complain. I get to use his car now, too.*
>
> *You and me are just about done. You have to know that. There's just one last piece of work, and you know what that is, too.*
>
> *You and me.*
>
> *You have to pay for what you have done. I have to make you pay. There is no other way and you know you got it coming and you have to do this; I have your kids. I probably won't hurt them, unless you don't show up.*
>
> *This time it's on my terms. I get to set up and wait for you to walk right into it. I picked the place, and I picked a good one. Really witty, in a kind of dry way. Hurry down—don't be a turtle.*
>
> *They seem like really nice kids.*

That was it. I read it again, but there was no more.

My jaw hurt. I wondered why. Nobody had actually hit me. Had I been grinding my teeth a lot lately? It seemed like I had. I was probably wearing all the enamel off. That wasn't good. I would get cavities. I wondered if I would live long enough to get to the dentist. Or, if things went better than I thought they could possibly go, if the dental program would cover it in Raiford Prison.

Of course, if I stood here any longer thinking about my teeth, it would probably be best if I just pulled them all out myself.

Somewhere Crowley, or Bernie, or whatever name he liked, was waiting for me. But right here, in Key West? Unlikely; you didn't play this game in Party Central. He would find someplace off the beaten path, even a little isolated—and he would tell me about it in some clever way, so I could figure it out eventually, but not too soon. But in his own way he was just as anxious to get it done as I was, so it had to be someplace that wasn't too far away. He wouldn't take them to Zanzibar, or even Cleveland.

I read the e-mail one more time, looking for my clue. It was all relatively straightforward—except at the end, where he said "witty, in a kind of dry way," and then, "Don't be a turtle." That made no sense at all. It was a clunky way to say it, and it wasn't his style. And how could a location be witty? Even if it was, why didn't he just say, *I think it's funny; hurry*? Nothing else in the note stuck out; these lines had to be telling me where to go. Perfect; if I could only think of a funny place and hurry there, I would almost certainly find him.

"Funny." There were several cabarets in town, and a comedy club, all within walking distance, so I could get there quickly. But funny wasn't really the same thing as witty—and why was it so important to hurry?

I realized I was grinding my teeth again. I stopped and took a deep breath. I reminded myself that I was really very clever, much smarter than him, and anything he came up with to taunt me I could certainly decode and shove down his throat. I just had to think positive thoughts and concentrate a little.

It made me feel a lot better. I started over from the top:

Witty. It did nothing for me.

Don't be a turtle. Even worse. Nothing at all came to me. It was wonderful to see the power of positive thinking.

All right, I was missing something. Maybe it was the word "witty." Perhaps some awful pun—there was a White Street only a few blocks away. But that was stretching it too far. Was there a Whitt Key? I'd never heard of it. What about "turtle" then? There was Turtle Kraals down by the water. But he said *"don't* be a turtle," so that didn't make sense. That couldn't be it, and I was clearly not as clever as I thought I was.

A trio of men walked past, arguing in Spanish. I made out the word *pendejo,* and I thought it was probably appropriate. I was a *pendejo,* a complete dolt, and I deserved to lose everything to an even bigger *pendejo,* whether in Spanish or English. Crowley probably couldn't even speak Spanish. I could, and it hadn't helped me find him so far. In fact, it had never helped me do anything except order lunch. It was a useless language, as useless as I was, and I should probably move away someplace where I would never hear it spoken again. Find a small island somewhere and just . . .

Far, far away, I heard crowd noise and music playing, and the clanging bell of the Conch Train as it rattled through the streets, and all the sounds of drunken, brainless revelry I had found so annoying only moments before. And somewhere up above me the July sun was still beating down without mercy and scorching everything under its glare. But Dexter was no longer hot and bothered; Dexter felt a cool and gentle breeze blowing, and Dexter heard only a soft and soothing melody, the delightful symphony of life as it played its stately and wonderful song. Key West really was an enchanted place, and Spanish was actually the emperor of all languages, and I blessed the day I had decided to learn it. Everything was new and marvelous and I was not a *pendejo* at all, because I had remembered one simple Spanish word and everything made sense.

The Spanish word for "turtle" is *tortuga.*

The cluster of islands sixty miles south of Key West was called the Tortugas—in fact, the *Dry* Tortugas, as in Crowley's dry wit. There's a park there, and an old fort, and several ferries every day to take you there, and I knew where Crowley had taken Cody and Astor.

There was a hotel across the street from where I sat. I ran across the street and into the lobby. Right inside the door, just where it should have been, stood a wooden rack stuffed with brochures for all the attractions in Key West. I scanned them rapidly, found one with a bright blue heading that said, CONCH LINE, and plucked it from the rack.

Our superfast, ultramodern fleet of high-tech catamarans, it read, *make a high-speed run to Fort Jefferson in the Dry Tortugas twice a day!*

The boats left from a dock about half a mile from where I stood right now, and the second and final boat left at ten a.m. I looked around the lobby and found a clock over the desk; it was nine fifty-six. Four minutes to get there.

I sprinted out of the lobby and down Duval. The crowds were even larger and jollier now; it was always Happy Hour in Key West, and trying to run through the mobs of revelers was nearly impossible. At the corner I turned right on Caroline Street and the flock thinned out immediately. Half a block up, four bearded men sat on the curb with a bottle of something in a paper bag. They were not Hemingways; their beards were long and matted, and they watched me with dead faces and then cheered sloppily as I ran past. I hoped there would be something to cheer about.

Three more blocks. I was sure it had been more than four minutes already. I told myself that nothing ever left on time. I was soaked with sweat, but the water was in sight now on my left, between the buildings, and I picked up my pace as I galloped into the large parking area at the docks. More people now, music coming from the waterfront restaurants, and I had to dodge a couple of slow and wobbly bicycles before I came out on the old wooden pier and pounded out past the dockmaster's shack, out onto the battered planking of the wharf—

And there it was, the Conch Line's superfast ultramodern high-speed catamaran, leaning away from the dock and slowly, ponderously, slipping out into the harbor. And as I crashed to a halt on the last eight inches of the dock it was not really very far away across the water, not far at all, only about fifteen feet from me—just far enough to be too far.

Just far enough to see across the widening gap as Cody and Astor stood at the rail, looking anxiously back at me. And right behind them, wearing a floppy-brimmed hat and a triumphant smirk, Crowley. He put one hand on Astor's shoulder, and he raised the other to wave at me, and I could do nothing but watch as the boat pulled away from the pier, picked up speed, and vanished past Sunset Key and then south into the deep and empty blue of the Atlantic Ocean.

THIRTY-THREE

A LOT OF PEOPLE DO NOTHING IN KEY WEST. IT'S A GOOD place for that. You can watch everyone moving along Duval Street and wonder what strange alien race they belong to. Or you can go down to the water and look at the pelicans, watch the boats bobbing at anchor or racing past in the harbor, crowded with sunburned partiers, and if you look up you can see the planes flying low overhead towing their banners.

For five minutes, that's all I did. I slumped right into the national pastime of the Conch Republic and I did nothing. I just stood on the dock and watched the water, the boats, the birds. There didn't seem to be a whole lot more I could do. The boat with Cody and Astor was gone, speeding away across the ocean. It was already more than a mile away and I couldn't call it back and I couldn't run after it across the water.

So I did nothing. And it seems a little bit ironic, but apparently there is actually one place in Key West where you can't do that, and I had found it. I became aware that people were pushing past me, briskly moving coils of rope and hoses and two-wheeled carts stuffed with baggage, food and ice, and dive gear. And judging by the irritated glances they sent me, I was in their way.

Finally one of them stopped beside me, dropping the handles of a cart filled with scuba tanks and straightening up to face me. "Say there, Captain," he said in a bluff and friendly voice. "Wonder if you could move off to the side a bit? We got to load the boat for a dive trip."

I turned away from the water and looked him in the face. It was a friendly and open dark brown face, and just in case I might be a potential customer, he added, "Right out to the reef, it's absolutely beautiful. Oughta see it sometime, Captain."

A tiny little gleam of hope flickered deep in the dark corners of my brain. "You don't go anywhere near Fort Jefferson, do you?"

The man laughed. "Tortugas? No, sir, you just missed the last boat down there. Next one's tomorrow morning."

Of course—as always, hope was a stupid waste of time. My one small flicker hissed out and the gray fog rolled back in. And because people always insist on talking to you when you want to be alone with your quiet despair, the man went on babbling at me with his cheerful huckster's patter.

"Now, Tortugas are worth seeing, too, you know. You can't believe Fort Jefferson till you *see* it. Maybe the best way to see it, by air? Got a brochure over here . . ." He trotted five steps to his right and rummaged in a dock locker, then came back and handed me a glossy, brightly colored pamphlet. "Here ya go," he said. "My girlfriend works for them. They fly down there four times a day? Beautiful, coming in low over the fort, and then you splash down, very cool, very exciting . . ."

He thrust the brochure into my hand and I took it. It said, Alba-tross Airlines! across the top—and suddenly it really was exciting, the most exciting thing in the world. "It's a seaplane?" I said, staring at the pictures.

"Sure, has to be, no landing strip down there," he said.

"It would be a lot quicker than the boat, wouldn't it?" I said.

"Oh, yeah, absolutely. Conch Lines boat takes a good three hours, maybe a little more. This'll have you there in like forty minutes. Great trip, too."

It didn't matter to me if the trip was great. If it got me to the Dry Tortugas before Crowley got there, before he could set his Dexter-Smashing Trap, it could be the most miserable trip of all time

and I would still want to hug the pilot. "Thank you," I said, and I
actually meant it.

"Sure thing," he said. "Uh, so if you wouldn't mind . . . ?" He gestured to one side of the dock and raised his eyebrows to help me find
my way out of his path, but I was already gone, sprinting down the
dock, past the shops and restaurants and into the parking lot, where
for once luck was with me and a bright pink Key West taxi was just
disgorging its load of pale overweight passengers, and I jumped in as
the last of them paid the driver.

"Hiya, bud," the driver said. She was about fifty, with a square
face that had been savaged and turned to old worn leather by the sun,
and she stretched it into a brief professional smile for me. "Where to?"

It was a fair question, and I realized I didn't know the answer.
Luckily, I was still clutching the pamphlet, so I opened it up and
scanned it rapidly. "Airport," I said, as I found it on the page. "And as
quickly as possible."

"You got it," she said, and we were off, out of the parking lot,
across the island, and out on the far side on Roosevelt. My phone
rang; it was Rita again. I turned my phone off.

The cab rolled past Smathers Beach. A wedding party clustered
on the sand, the bride and groom standing at the edge of the water
under a white canopy, the kind they use in Jewish weddings—a hoo-
poe? No, that was a bird. Something like that. I couldn't think of the
word. That didn't seem as important as the fact that we were finally
turning off the beachfront road into the airport.

I jumped out of the cab and flung money at the driver without
counting it or waiting for change, and as I ran into the terminal I
thought, *Chuppah.* That was the name of the Jewish wedding canopy.
Remembering the word pleased me a whole lot more than it should
have, and I made a mental note to think about why that mattered
some other day.

I found Albatross Airlines down at the far end of the terminal. A
woman in a brown uniform stood behind the counter. She was about
fifty, with a leathery face that looked like my cab driver's twin. I wondered if she was the girlfriend of my new friend on the dock. For his
sake, I hoped not.

"Can I help you?" she said in a voice like a very butch raven.

"I need to get to the Dry Tortugas as fast as possible," I told her.

She nodded at the sign on the back wall. "Our next flight is at noon," she cawed.

"I need to get there *now*," I told her.

"Noon," she said.

I took a very deep breath and told myself that caving in somebody's head is not always the best solution. "It's an emergency," I said.

She snorted. "A *seaplane* emergency?" she said with heavy sarcasm.

"Yes," I said, and she blinked in surprise. "My kids are on the boat down to the Dry Tortugas," I said.

"Nice trip," she said.

"They're with somebody—a man who might hurt them."

She shrugged. "You can use my phone, call the cops," she said. "They'll call the ranger station down there."

"I can't call the cops," I said, hoping she wouldn't ask me why.

"Why not?" she said.

I thought quickly; clearly the truth was not an option here, but that has never been much of an obstacle for me. "Um," I said, waiting for something plausible to slide into the out-box. "He's . . . he's my brother-in-law. And, you know. It's family. And if the cops get involved it would break my sister's heart. And my mother would . . . you know. It's a family thing, and, uh, she has a heart condition."

"Uh-huh," she said dubiously.

I was clearly getting nowhere with her, in spite of my wonderful creativity. But I did not despair. I had been to Key West before, and I knew how to get things done here. I reached for my wallet.

"Please," I said, counting out a hundred dollars. "Isn't there something we can do?"

The money vanished before I finished my sentence. "I don't know," she said. "Lemme ask Leroy."

There was a door on the back wall under the schedule and she went through it. A minute later she came back out, followed by a man in a pilot's uniform. He was about fifty, with hard blue eyes and a boxer's flattened nose.

"What's up, Skipper?" he said.

"I need to get to the Tortugas as fast as possible," I said.

He nodded. "Jackie said," he told me. "But our next scheduled flight is in two hours, and we have to keep the schedule. Nothing I can do. Sorry."

No matter how sorry he might have been, he didn't leave, and that meant he wasn't refusing—he was negotiating. "Five hundred dollars," I said.

He shook his head and leaned on the counter. "Sorry, bud, I just can't do it," he said. "The company has a policy."

"Seven hundred," I said, and he shook his head. "It's my children; they're young and helpless," I said.

"I could lose my job," he told me.

"A thousand dollars," I said, and he stopped shaking his head.

"Well," he said.

Those of us who are fiscally responsible look with scorn and condemnation on profligates who max out their credit cards. But the hard-eyed buccaneer behind the counter very quickly dropped me into exactly that financial hot water. It took two of my cards, but when I had finally sated his unholy lust for my money, it took only five minutes more and I was buckling myself into the passenger seat of his aircraft. Then we lumbered down the runway, gathering speed, until we finally waddled up into the sky.

The man on the dock, and the brochure he had given me, had assured me that the flight down to the Dry Tortugas was beautiful and memorable. If it was, I don't remember it. All I saw was the hand on my watch crawling forward. It seemed to be moving much slower than normal: Tick. Long pause. Tick. Another. This was taking too long—I had to get there first. How long had it been since the boat pulled away from the dock? I tried to put the numbers together in my head. It shouldn't have been hard, but for some reason all my concentration was on grinding my teeth and I couldn't think about the time.

Luckily for my teeth, I didn't have to. "There she is," the pilot said, nodding out the window. It was the first thing he'd said since we were airborne, and I stopped grinding my teeth for a moment and looked at him. He nodded again. "The boat," he said. "With your kids."

I looked out the window. Below us I could see the bright white deck of a large, fast-moving boat, trailing a long wake behind it. Even from our height I could see a few people on the deck, but I couldn't tell if any of them were Cody and Astor.

"Relax," the pilot told me. "We'll get in a good forty-five minutes before they do."

I didn't relax, but I felt a little better. I watched as we passed over the boat and left it behind us, and finally, just as it dropped out of sight, the pilot spoke again. "Fort Jefferson," he said.

The fort began to take shape as we got closer, and it was impressive. "It's big," I said.

The pilot nodded. "You could fit Yankee Stadium inside with room to spare," he said. And although I couldn't think of any reason why someone might want to try that, I nodded anyway.

"Very nice," I said.

I shouldn't have encouraged him; he began to ramble, a long blather about the Civil War and the assassination of Lincoln and even something about a missing hospital on a nearby sandbar, and I tuned him out and concentrated on the fort. It really was huge, and if I let Crowley get loose on the inside, I might never find him. But on the far side of the fort there was a pier jutting out, and as far as I could see it was the only one attached to the island.

"The boat has to dock there, right?" I said. The pilot glanced at me, with his mouth half-open. I had interrupted him in the middle of a story about a lighthouse that was just visible a mile or so across the water from the fort.

"That's right," he said. "But you see some of the people get off it, you wish they'd just dump 'em out there." He nodded at the stretch of dark blue water between the fort and the lighthouse. "Leave 'em for the Channel Hog."

"The what?"

He smirked at me. "Channel Hog," he said. "Biggest goddamned hammerhead shark known to man. Over twenty feet long, and always hungry. I truly would not recommend taking a swim out there, buddy."

"I'll keep it in mind," I said. "When do we, um, splash down?"

He looked a little peeved that I had failed to appreciate his wit, but he shrugged it off. After all, he had enough of my money to take the sting out of such a small snub.

"Right about now," he said, and he banked the plane, bringing it in low over the Channel Hog's front hall. The plane's pontoons smacked down, sending up showers of clean and fresh-looking salt water, and the noise of the engine rose up to a higher pitch for a moment as we slowed and turned toward the fort. It really was huge, and it stuck up out of the flat expanse of water around it, looking very imposing and out of place, with its enormous redbrick walls looming up over a few palm trees. Closer up I could see a row of gaping holes across the upper part of the fort, probably unfinished gun ports. They had a haunted look to them, as if they were the empty eye sockets of some gigantic skull leering down at me, and it gave the place a slightly spooky appearance.

The pilot slowed the plane a little more, and we bumped through the small waves past some pilings from a vanished jetty and turned into a very nice little harbor. A cluster of yachts was anchored at the far side, and a smaller boat with a National Park Service logo on the side was tied at the dock. We slowed, turned, and slid in next to it.

I walked off the dock and onto the brick path that led into the fort, looking for the perfect place to wait for Crowley—someplace where I could see him without being seen, and take him before he knew I was anywhere near. I do love a surprise, and I wanted to give Crowley one of my best.

The sun was still hot and blindingly bright, and I didn't see any good places to lurk on the outside. The brick path led to a wooden bridge over a moat, where a few people stood. They were dressed in shorts and flip-flops and they all had earbuds crammed into their ears, each of them swaying slightly to a different beat as they stared at a sign that said:

FORT JEFFERSON
DRY TORTUGAS NATIONAL PARK

It was only six words, and it shouldn't have taken very long to read, but maybe they couldn't concentrate with their music blasting directly into their skulls. Or maybe they were just slow readers. In any case, I didn't think the sign would make a good hiding place, even without the postliterate witnesses.

I moved past them and crossed the bridge. At its other end, directly underneath an American flag flying from the top rampart, a large and dark gateway led inside the walls. Even crossing the moat, I couldn't see what was inside, except for a circle of daylight on the far side. I went through the square marble arch and stepped in, and I paused, because I couldn't see anything at all in the sudden gloom. It was like stepping into midnight, and I had to blink for a moment as my eyes adjusted.

And as I stood there squinting in the darkness, a small light came on in the deeper darkness between my ears, and I actually heard myself murmur, "Aha."

This was the place. This was where I would wait for Crowley. I could see out, all the way to the dock where the ferry would tie up, but he could not see me here, nestled in the shadows. And he would come off the boat, thinking that I was sixty miles behind him, and he would walk up the path, across the moat, and into this archway, where he would be temporarily blinded, as I had been. And then he would take that one last step, right into the True Darkness of Dexter's Delight. It was perfect.

Of course, it left me with the problem of what to do next. I could easily surprise Crowley, overpower him before he knew what was happening—but what then? I had none of my special party favors with me: no noose, no duct tape, nothing. And I was in a very public place. It would be easy enough to knock him out—but then I would have a large and unconscious body to cope with, never an easy assignment, even without the assorted tourists who might be dawdling nearby. I could drag the body somewhere, but then I would certainly be observed, which would leave me with nothing but some truly lame excuse like, "My friend is drunk." Or I could finish him off quickly right here in the dark gateway and simply leave him, making a rapid but nonchalant exit with the kids. If we got most of the way to the dock before we were seen, we just might get away with it.

I bit my lip so hard I nearly broke the skin. This whole thing was all "if" and "hope," and I hated that. There were people wandering around all over, and if only one of them saw what I did it was too many. There was going to be a dead body, and I was going to be seen with it before it died. And since I was already under police scrutiny for two murders, I didn't think they would buy the good old standby of saying it was an accident.

But there really was no choice. I had to do this, I had to do it now, and this dark archway gave me my best chance. I just had to hope I would get a small break. I'd never relied on luck before, and it made me very unhappy to do so now. I didn't believe in it. It was too much like praying for a new bicycle.

A middle-aged man and woman walked into my shadowy retreat from the interior of the fort. They held hands and ambled past me, hardly seeing me, their flip-flops slapping on the hard stone floor, and then they disappeared out the other side toward the dock. I thought it through again, and it didn't get any better. But I didn't think of any other choices either. My best new thought came when I remembered that technically, Crowley had kidnapped Cody and Astor. If I was truly cornered, I could claim I had been defending them and throw myself on the mercy of the court. I was pretty sure there wasn't a lot of that in any Florida court, and I didn't think much of it would be reserved for me, but it didn't really matter. This was my only shot, and I would just have to take it and let things sort themselves out later.

In any case, I really wanted to do this. I wanted Crowley dead, and I wanted to do it myself, and nothing else was quite as important as that. If that meant a long vacation behind bars, so be it. I probably deserved it.

I looked at my watch. The boat should arrive in about half an hour. I couldn't lurk here in the shadows the whole time without somebody wondering what I was doing. So I continued on through the gateway and walked into the fort.

It seemed even bigger on the inside. The walls folded around a huge green lawn speckled with trees and crossed by a few pathways that led away to the far side, which seemed to be very far away. There were a few buildings, probably where the park rangers lived. To the right was a sign that read, VISITOR CENTER, and beyond it on the top of the wall a black lighthouse stuck up into the bright blue sky.

The top story of the high brick wall gaped in an endless chain of large openings, a series of huge doorways with no doors. The bottom floor echoed this pattern, with smaller, squatter doorways leading into blank darkness inside the walls. It was a vast arena of dark and secluded spots, so many of them over such a huge area that the 10th

Mountain Division could not have covered it all, let alone a small handful of park rangers, and I could see why Crowley had chosen it. It was the perfect setting for a recreational murder, followed by a haunting.

I went to the right, past the doorway into the Visitor Center and along the wall, peering into dark and empty rooms. Underneath the lighthouse I found a stairway leading up to the top of the wall, and I climbed it, coming out on top into the bright sunlight again. I squinted and looked around, and the intensity of the light hurt my eyes. I wished I'd brought sunglasses. But I also wished I'd brought a bazooka, or at least a baseball bat, so the glasses seemed a little bit trivial.

I went to the edge of the wall and looked down. Below me the moat came right up to the wall, and beyond that there was a sandy roadway between the fort and the beach. A fat man in a tiny bathing suit walked by on the sand, following a large black dog. Beyond him was a sliver of beach and several large boats moored just a few yards out from the sand. Someone on the deck of one of the yachts yelled something, and there was a brief blare of music.

I turned to my left, walking along the top of the wall in the direction the ferry would be coming from, picking my way through sand and tufts of grass, past a big black cannon where three kids were playing pirate. Beyond them I saw a chunk of loose brick lying in the sand. It had split in three pieces and fallen out of its slot in the wall. I glanced around me casually; the pirates were on the far side of their cannon, and there was no one else in sight. I stooped and picked up a piece of the brick and slid it into my pocket. It wasn't quite a bazooka, but it was better than nothing.

It was a five-minute walk across the top of the wall to the far side of the fort. When I finally got there I was soaked in sweat and I had a slight headache from the sun's sharp glare. I stood there and looked back toward Key West, squinting through the reflected gleam of light off the water. I waited for ten minutes or so, doing no more than scanning the horizon. Three more people walked past me, two middle-aged women chattering away in deep harsh voices, and one old man with a bandage on the side of his head. And then a small white speck appeared in the distance, even brighter than the blaze of sunlight off the water, and I watched as it grew bigger and brighter, and in only a few minutes it was big enough to be sure. It was the ferry, bringing me Cody and Astor and an end to the threat of Crowley. They were almost here, and it was time.

I hurried back to the staircase and went down to the gateway to wait.

THIRTY-FOUR

I STOOD IN THE SHADOWS INSIDE THE FORT'S GATEWAY, HALF-hidden behind the stone arch, and I watched as the large catama-ran slid up to the dock and tied off. Many times in my sad short life I have waited in ambush and cuddled my wicked thoughts, but this was different. This was no deliciously private rendezvous on a carefully chosen night of silvery moonlight. This was a public execu-tion in a crowd of strangers, a perversion forced on me by necessity, and it seemed like I was doing everything for the very first time. I felt stiff, clumsy, amateurish. I did not hear the sweet wing-rustle and whisper of encouragement from the Dark Passenger, and I did not hear the music of the Dance Macabre, and there was no delicious cool rush of power and certainty flowing out through my fingertips. My mouth was dry and my still-swollen hands were sweaty and I could hear my heart pounding rapidly in my ears and this was not wonderful wicked me lying in wait in complete control, not at all, and it made me fidgety and unhappy in a way that was almost painful.

But there was no choice, no way out, no direction but forward, and so I waited and watched as the ferry's steel ramp slammed down onto the dock, and the crowd of gawkers surged off the boat and onto

Dry Tortugas National Park, home of Fort Jefferson and Dexter's Last Stand.

There were about sixty people on the boat, and most of them had come down the ramp and begun to amble around the outside of the fort before I saw Astor's unmistakable blond head through a gap in the parade. A moment later the crowd parted again and there they were, all three of them. Cody and Astor held hands and Crowley walked very close behind them, herding them forward off the dock and onto the brick path toward the fort.

I tensed and slid deeper into the shadow of the stone gate. I flexed my fingers. They felt cramped and stupid, incapable of anything but knotting up. I made and unmade a fist several times, and when my hands felt as lively as they were going to get I reached into my pocket and took out my chunk of brick. It didn't make me feel much better.

I waited. My throat was so dry that swallowing hurt, but I swallowed anyway and took a deep breath and tried to force icy calm into my veins. It didn't work. My hands were shaky and the brick felt slippery in my grip. I took half a peek around the stone arch and for a few frozen seconds I didn't see them anywhere. I eased out of the shadows a little more; there they were, standing stupidly in front of the sign, staring around them. I could see Astor's mouth moving in what was clearly a tirade of irritation, and Cody's small face was set in a scowl. Crowley had a duffel bag slung over one shoulder, and he wore an idiotic mask of pleasant anticipation, as if he really was on an enchanted holiday with two wonderful children.

But they didn't move away from the sign. I wondered what Crowley had told them to keep them docile. It must have been good. They had no reason to distrust him if he had a plausible enough lie, but these were not ordinary, well-behaved children. Behind their pleasant and youthful features, throbbing inside their delightful tousled heads, dark and wicked flowers were blooming. Crowley could not possibly suspect it, but these were Dexters-in-Training, and they were, in every sense of the word, little Monsters. I felt a surge of affection for the two of them.

A clump of tourists stomped onto the drawbridge and came between me and Crowley. I stepped all the way back inside and pretended to be examining the stonework, but they didn't even see me as they sauntered on through the gateway, chattering in Spanish and vanishing out the far side into the interior of the fort. When they were out of sight I eased my head around the arch and peeked out at the sign again.

They were gone.

Panic ripped through me and for a moment I couldn't think anything at all. I just stared at the spot where they had been and squeezed my brick until my fingers hurt. Where could they be? And if they had to go somewhere, why weren't they at least strolling over the drawbridge and into my ambush?

I leaned out farther and looked left; I saw nothing. I came a full step out of the archway and looked right—there they were, sauntering away on the sandy path to the far side of the island, toward the campground and away from my trap. Irritation boiled up inside me; what pointless stupidity were they performing? Why wasn't Crowley bringing his fat head into the gateway and under my brick like he was supposed to do?

I watched as they ambled by a line of picnic tables and then past a clump of stunted trees that grew just before the beach, and then they were hidden by the branches and I couldn't see them anymore.

I heard a hissing sound and realized it was me, blowing angry breath out between my teeth, and that was even more annoying. If that was the best I could do, I might as well go home now. I pried my fingers open and put the brick chunk back in my pocket, and, thinking very dark thoughts, I stepped into the sunlight and followed.

A family of five sat at one of the picnic tables. They were eating lunch, and they looked so happy I wanted to use the brick to bash in their heads. But I left them to their sandwiches and stalked down the path to the back side of the grove of scrub trees.

I paused for a moment, uncertain. The foliage screened me from Crowley, but it also hid him from me. He could very well be lurking just beyond the branches, watching his back trail for any Dexters that might be sniffing along behind him. Elementary predator's caution would tell him to be sure no one was following. So, deciding that safe was very much better than sorry, I moved to my left, skirting along the back side of the tree line through even more picnic tables and ducking under a clothesline until I came to a break in the trees. I moved carefully around one last picnic table and into scrub. I pushed through the sand and the branches and stopped behind the last tree and slowly parted the leaves with my hand.

I should have seen them to my right, no more than thirty feet away. I didn't. I pushed the branches farther apart, and there they were, standing stupidly on the sand and staring at the swimming area. If I slipped carefully back through the trees and came out behind them— But no. Crowley put one hand on each small shoulder and urged them back the way they had come, and the little trio slowly turned and trudged back into the scrub trees and headed toward the dock. It was obvious that he was scouting, making sure everything was just the way he wanted it to be, before he went to his special place to wait for me, the place where he would surprise me.

But, of course, I was already here, and I was going to surprise him first, if I could just stay close behind and watch for my chance—but how? There was very little cover between the trees and the dock, no more than one white metal building close to where the ferries tied up. Other than that, nothing but the fort, the water, and the thin sandy path leading around the tall redbrick walls. If I stepped out from the trees and followed I would be extremely visible. But I couldn't let them just ramble away.

I looked in front of me on the beach. There were about half a dozen towels thrown around, with flip-flops and beach bags stacked beside them. The nearest towel was bright orange, and right beyond it there was a big white one. The towels' owners were apparently all in the water.

At the far end of the beach, a large middle-aged woman sat in a fold-up canvas chair, watching a group of very loud children splashing around in the shallows. No one else was in sight, except for the people swimming farther out, toward the buoys marking the edge of the swimming area. I looked right again, and saw that Crowley and the kids were still strolling away around the fort.

A small idea popped into my head, and before I could think about how lame it was, I acted. Looking as casual as possible, I stepped out onto the beach, grabbed the white towel, and then strolled back into the cover of the trees. I took off my shirt and tied it around my waist, and then I draped the towel over my head like a bedouin headdress, clutching my half brick in one corner of the towel. I left the trees and walked through the picnic area. *Look at me; I have been swimming and I have wet hair which I am now drying, and I am perfectly normal and not Dexter at all.*

They were walking toward the far side of the fort now, past the dock and onto the sandy access road, and I followed. Suddenly, Cody stopped and turned around. He looked back toward the dock, then turned and looked at the fort, and then he frowned. I could see his lips move briefly, and he pointed at the drawbridge. Crowley shook his head and once more put a hand on his shoulder to urge him on, but Cody jerked away and pointed stubbornly at the drawbridge. Crowley shook his head and reached for Cody, who jumped away from him, and Astor stepped in between them and started talking.

I took advantage of their halt to get closer. I had no clear idea of how I was going to do this, but if I could get within half a brick length of Crowley I was ready to cave in his head and take my chances. Closer—and when I was only ten feet away I distinctly heard Astor say that this was all a bunch of bullcrap, and where was Dexter anyway? I raised my hands up and began to towel my head vigorously. I was actually within four big steps of them when Astor broke off her tirade, stared right at me, and said, "Dexter! You're really here!"

I froze in place: stupid, I know, but I really was not my abnormal self. Crowley didn't have that problem, and he wasted no time trying to see under the towel to confirm my identity. He dropped his duffel bag, yanked Astor off her feet, tucked her under one arm, and ran for the dock. She immediately began to wiggle frantically and yell at the top of her lungs, but without even slowing, Crowley punched her on the side of the head, hard, and she went limp.

I dropped the towel and jumped after them, paused for one second, and looked at Cody. "Go inside the fort," I said. "Find the park rangers and tell them you're lost." And without waiting to see whether he would obey, I turned and sprinted after Crowley.

He had a good head start, but he was slower because he was carrying Astor, and I was closing fast when he pounded out to the end of the dock. A forty-five-foot sportfishing boat was backing in to tie up, and Crowley jumped onto the deck, where a woman in a bikini stood gaping at him and clutching the stern line. Crowley shoved her hard, and she went backward into the water, still holding the rope. An elderly man on the flybridge yelled, "Hey!" in a hoarse voice as Crowley dropped Astor to the deck. She slid up against a cooler and lay motionless, and Crowley lunged up the ladder to the flybridge. The old man yelled, "Help!" in a strangled self-conscious way, and then Crowley punched him in the gut and took the controls. The old man bent over and fell to his knees and the boat began to move away from the dock.

I was almost close enough to leap onto the deck when Crowley shoved the throttle forward and twirled the wheel hard over. The boat spun sluggishly around and began to move out toward the channel. And for once in this whole miserable adventure I did not hesitate or pause to think and bemoan. I ran the last few feet as fast as I could, and I jumped.

It was a good jump, very athletic, a nice arc to it and a near-perfect trajectory, and it was just good enough to splash me into the water three feet behind the boat. I went under and floundered to the surface again, just in time to see the boat start to accelerate. The prop wash boiled back at me, pushing me away and filling my mouth with water. And as I swallowed water and tried without hope to swim through the wake and grab the boat, something thumped me hard in the back and shoved me underwater again.

I had a horrible moment of panic as I remembered what the pilot had said about the Channel Hog, the largest hammerhead shark known to man—but the thing that had hit me felt too smooth to be a shark. I grabbed on to it and felt it pull me to the surface, and as I sucked in a breath and blinked the water out of my eyes I saw that I was holding a human leg. Even better, it was still attached to somebody—the bikinied woman Crowley had dumped into the water, and she was grimly clutching the stern line and dragging along behind the boat.

The boat began to pick up speed, and the wake foamed up around us, making it nearly impossible to see, and difficult to hold on. Very shortly I was sure it would be too much for the woman whose leg I was holding. She would let go, and then Crowley would be gone, taking Astor and all my hopes with him, probably for good this time. I could not let that happen.

And so, throwing caution and good manners to the wind, I grabbed higher up. My fingers clamped on to the band of fabric at the woman's waist and I pulled myself forward—and suddenly I was sliding backward again as the bikini bottom shimmied off and down her legs, taking me with it.

I grabbed again, this time clamping on to her knee and then reaching up around her waist with both hands, and pulled upward until I got a hand on her shoulder. And just as I got one hand on the rope, the woman finally let go. Her body bumped against me, hard, and she scrabbled for a grip along the whole length of my body. For a moment I didn't think I could hold on. But then she whirled away in the foamy white wake and I got my other hand on the rope and began to work my way toward the boat.

Slowly, hand over hand, fighting the turbulence every inch of the way, I jerked closer to the transom. I could see it clearly, tantalizingly close, bright blue letters spelling out its name and home port: REEL FUN, ST. JAMES CITY. And finally, after what seemed like hours but was probably no more than a minute or two, I got close enough to grab on to the boat's dive platform, a narrow wooden shelf jutting out from the transom, and I clambered onto it, shoulders aching, breathing hard.

I flexed my hands; they were stiff and knotted up—and why not? After all they had been through the last few days I should have been grateful that they had not withered and fallen off. But they would have to perform one last good deed, and so I sent them ahead of me up the chrome ladder and I climbed into the cockpit of the boat.

I could just see Crowley's head and shoulders above me; he stood on the flybridge, ten feet higher than the cockpit, looking forward and steering the boat out into the channel. Good—he didn't see me, had no idea I was on board, and hopefully he wouldn't until it was too late.

I hurried across the deck. The old man lay to one side, cradling his forearm and moaning softly. Crowley had clearly dumped him off the bridge and he had probably broken his arm in the fall. Very sad, but it didn't really matter to me. I stepped past him to the ladder that led up to the flybridge. Astor lay at its foot, crumpled into a small untidy heap next to a cooler. The lid had bumped open, revealing ice and cans of beer and soda. I bent down beside Astor and felt for a pulse in her neck; it was there, steady and strong, and as I put a hand on her face she frowned and made soft and grumpy sounds. She would probably be all right, but there was nothing I could do for her right now.

I left her there and slithered up the ladder, pausing when my head came up just over the top step. I was looking at the back of Crowley's legs. They looked spry, surprisingly muscular for someone I had thought of as doughy. I had misjudged him every step of the way, underestimated what he was capable of doing, and it made me hesitate now as a very un-Dexter thought came over me.

What if I couldn't do this? What if I really had met my match, and he was just too much for me to handle? What if this was it, and the Dexter Show was about to end?

It was a truly horrible moment, and it got even worse when I realized what it was—real live human uncertainty. I really had fallen low. I'd never before doubted myself or my ability to perform routine executions, and this was a terrible time to start.

I closed my eyes for just a second, reaching out for the Passenger in a way I never had before, pleading for one last charge of the Dark Brigade. I felt it grumble, sigh, and rustle its wings—not really encouraging, but it would have to do. I opened my eyes and climbed quickly and quietly the rest of the way up the ladder onto the flybridge.

Crowley stood with one hand on the wheel, guiding the boat through the channel and away from the fort, and I hit him with my whole body as hard as I could. He slammed forward into the controls, bumping the throttle. The boat lurched forward, coming to top speed as I put my arm around Crowley's throat and choked him with all my strength.

But he really was stronger than he looked. He dug his fingers into my forearm and pivoted, lifting me off the floor and bashing me into the side of the cockpit. My head bounced off the console; I saw stars, and Crowley slipped out of my grip.

Before I could throw off the dizziness he was on me, thumping me in the stomach, and although it took my breath away, at least it cleared my head, and I dropped to one knee and then punched sideways, connecting solidly with his kneecap. He said, "Oog," very distinctly, and threw an elbow at my head that would have decapitated me if it had landed. But I ducked under it and scrambled to the other side of the bridge, jumping to my feet and turning shakily to face Crowley.

He straightened and faced me and we stood for a strange frozen instant, looking at each other. Then he took a step forward, feinted with his right hand, and, as I dodged, reached out with his left and yanked the boat's throttle all the way back. The boat staggered to a stop, and I staggered with it, hitting the console with my hip and tipping toward the windscreen, struggling to regain my balance.

Crowley didn't need to struggle; he had been braced for the sudden stop, and he was on me before I could recover. He hammered a knee into my midsection, and then he put both his hands on my throat and began to squeeze. Things quickly began to grow dim around me, and everything started to slow down.

So this was how it ended. Strangled by a Cub Scout leader—and not even the leader, merely an assistant. There didn't seem to be a whole lot of glory in it. I got my hands onto Crowley's wrists, but things were fading around me and it was getting very hard to stay interested.

And look there—I was already hallucinating houris in Paradise. Or was that really Astor coming up the ladder? It *was* her, and she was holding a can of soda from the cooler in the cockpit. Very thoughtful—my throat was hurting, and she had brought me a cool drink. It was unlike her to be so considerate—but now she was shaking the can as hard as she could. That was more like it. She was going to prank me with a spray of soda. A last sticky bath before dying.

But Astor stepped quickly around to Crowley's side and pointed the can at his face. She screeched, "Hey, asshole!" And when Crowley turned to face her she pulled the tab. There was a very satisfying explosion and a great brown gout of soda shot out, right into Crowley's eyes. Then she threw the can as hard as she could. It hit him squarely in the nose, and without a pause Astor stepped in and kicked him in the crotch.

Crowley staggered sideways under this unexpected onslaught, grunting with pain and taking one hand from my throat to wipe at his eyes, and as the pressure on my throat let up, a small trickle of light seeped back into my brain. I put both hands on the fingers remaining on my throat and I pried up hard. I heard one finger snap, and Crowley made a weird gargling noise and let go of me. Astor kicked his crotch again, and he took a drunken half step away from her and slouched over the railing.

And I, never one to waste an opportunity, hurtled forward and put my shoulder into him. He went right over, and there was an ugly *thud-splash* as he hit the gunwale below us and then flopped into the water.

I looked over the side. Crowley was bobbing in the water face-down, drifting slowly past us as the boat moved forward at idle speed.

Astor stood beside me, looking at Crowley as he bobbed away into our wake. "Asshole," she said again. Then she gave me a wonderfully fake smile and said sweetly, "Is it okay to use that word, Dexter?"

I put an arm around her shoulders. "This time," I said, "I think it's okay."

But she stiffened and lifted her arm to point. "He's moving," she said, and I turned to look.

Crowley had raised his head up out of the water. He was cough-ing, and there was a trickle of blood running down his face, but he paddled feebly away across the channel toward a nearby sandbar. He was still alive—after Astor and I beat him, kicked him, broke his hand, flung him from the bridge, drowned him, and even sprayed him with soda, he was still alive. I wondered if he was related to Rasputin.

I took the wheel of the boat and spun us around to point back to where Crowley was dog-paddling steadily toward safety and escape.

"Think you can drive this thing?" I asked Astor.

She gave me a look that very clearly said, *Duh*. "Totally," she said.

"Take the wheel," I told her. "Steer real close to him, slow and steady, and don't run into the sandbar."

"Like I *would*," she said. She took the wheel from me and I hurried down the ladder.

In the cockpit the old man had straightened up into a sitting posi-tion, and his moaning had gotten louder. Clearly he would be no help at all. More interesting, however, was that there was a boat hook beside him in a set of clamps. I pried it out and hefted it: about ten feet long, with a heavy metal tip. Just the thing. I could smack Crowley in the temple with the tip, then hook his shirt with it and hold his head under for a minute or two, and that really should be an end to it.

I stepped over to the railing. He was in the water right ahead of us, thirty feet away, and as I raised the boat hook in preparation, the boat's motors suddenly roared up the scale and we surged forward. I stumbled back and grabbed at the transom, regaining my balance just in time to hear something *thump* against the hull. The engines wound back down to idle and I looked up at Astor on the bridge. She was smiling, a real smile this time, and looking back into our wake.

"Got him," she said.

I went back to the transom and looked. For a moment there was no sign of Crowley, and I could not see under the water in the foam of our wake. Then there was a slow, heavy swirl under the surface. . . . Was it possible? Was he still alive?

And with breathtaking speed and violence, Crowley's head and shoulders broke the surface. His mouth was stretched into an enormous expression of unbelievable pain and surprise as he rocketed upward until the top half of his body was all the way out of the water. But there was an alien shape clamped around his middle and thrusting him upward, a colossal gray thing that seemed to be all teeth and malice, and it shook him with incredible force: once, twice, and then Crowley simply fell over from the waist, sliced neatly in two, and the top half of his body sank from sight and the gigantic gray thing swirled after him into the deep, leaving nothing but a small red whirlpool and the memory of unbelievably savage power.

It had all happened so fast that I couldn't be sure I had really seen it. But the image of that great gray monster was burned into my brain as if it had been etched there with acid, and the foam in our wake had a faint pink tint to it now. It had happened, and Crowley was gone.

"What was that?" Astor said.

"That," I said, "was the Channel Hog."

"Sweeeet," she said, drawing out the word. "Totally. Flippin'. *Sweeeeeeet.*"

THIRTY-FIVE

AS IT HAPPENED, THE OLD MAN IN THE COCKPIT HELPED out a great deal after all. He had apparently broken his collarbone when Crowley rolled him off the bridge, and even better, he was an extremely rich and important old man, who did not mind making himself the center of attention and letting everyone know that he was a very influential person, and demanding that everyone in the immediate vicinity drop whatever they were doing and focus on giving him their absolute and devoted care.

He yelled in pain, and raved about the madman who had savagely attacked him and stolen his boat, threatening to sue the parks department, pausing only to point at me and say, "If not for that brave, wonderful man!" which I thought hit just the right note and made the whole crowd look at me with admiration. But they didn't look long, because the important old man was far from done. He hollered for morphine and an airlift and ordered the rangers to secure his boat at once and call his attorney, and he made vague threats involving the legislature or even the governor, who was a personal friend, and he made himself completely, rivetingly annoying. Altogether he turned himself into such a perfect spectacle that nobody even noticed his female companion, who was standing there wrapped in a towel to hide the fact that she was naked except for her bikini top.

And nobody noticed when that brave wonderful man, Darling Dashing Dexter, took his two wayward imps by the hand and led them away from the hurly-burly and back to the relative calm and sanity of Key West.

When we got to our hotel, we were informed that our suite was still sealed by order of the police. I should have anticipated that. I had sealed enough crime scenes myself. But as I was about to sink wearily onto the cold marble floor and weep away my life of care, the desk clerk reassured me that they had moved us to an even nicer suite, one that had an actual view of the water. And just to confirm that at last everything had turned around and living was once more worth all the trouble and mess, she went on to inform me that the manager was so deeply sorry for all the unpleasantness that he had refunded our entire deposit, thrown away our bill, and hoped we would accept a complimentary dinner in the restaurant, beverages not included, which was not meant to suggest that the hotel or its staff and management were in any way responsible for the unfortunate accident, and the manager was sure we would agree and enjoy the rest of our stay, which was extended an extra night, too, and if I would only sign one small piece of paper acknowledging that the resort had no liability?

Suddenly I was very tired. And yet, with the fatigue came an unreasonable sense of well-being, a vague suggestion burbling up around the edges that the worst really was over and everything was actually going to be all right. I had been through so much, and failed miserably at dealing with most of it, and yet I was still here, all in one piece. In spite of my terrible performance and my unquestionable iniquity, I was being rewarded with dinner and a free vacation in a luxury suite. Life really was a wicked, awful, unjust thing, and that was exactly as it should be.

So I gave the clerk my very best smile and said, "Throw in banana splits for the kids and a bottle of merlot for my wife, and you've got a deal."

Rita was waiting for us in our new improved suite. It really did have a wonderful view of the harbor, and it was much easier for me to appreciate the postcard prettiness of the water than it had been just a few hours ago, when I stood on the dock and watched the catamaran pull away. Rita had apparently been enjoying the view from the balcony for some time—even more so since she'd opened the minibar and mixed herself a Cuba Libre. She jumped to her feet when we came in and rushed over to us, fluttering like the absolute Avatar of Dither.

"Dexter, my God, where have you been?" she said, and before I could answer she blurted out, "We got the house! Oh, my God, I still can't— And you weren't here! But it's the one, you remember you said? On a Hundred and Forty-second Terrace, just a mile and a half from our old house! With a pool, my God, and it was only— There was one other bidder, but they dropped out right before— It's ours, Dexter! We have a new house! A big, wonderful house!" And she sniffled and then sobbed, and one more time she said, "Oh, my God."

"That's wonderful," I said, although I was not completely convinced that it was. But I said it with as much reassurance as I could muster, since she was crying.

"I just can't believe it," she said, sniffling again. "It's just exactly perfect, and I got us a mortgage at four and a half— Astor, did you get a sunburn?"

"Only a little," Astor said, though she'd gotten quite a bit more than a sunburn. The side of her face, where Crowley had hit her, was red, and I was sure it would soon turn purple, but I was also confident we could bluff our way through Rita's questions.

"Oh, look at your poor face," Rita said, laying a hand on Astor's cheek. "It's swollen, and you can't even— Dexter, what in the world happened?"

"Oh," I said, "we went for a little boat ride."

"But that's— You said you were going to feed the sharks," she said.

I looked at Cody and Astor. Astor looked back at me and snickered. "We did that, too," I said.

Our complimentary dinner that evening was really quite nice. I have always found that free meals taste just a little bit better, and after two days of the rapacious greed of the Key West economy, this was succulent indeed.

And the flavors were just a little bit more delicious when, three minutes into the entrée, my sister, Sergeant Deborah Morgan, blew into the dining room like a category-four hurricane. She came in so fast that she was actually sitting at our table before I knew she was there, and I am quite sure I heard the sonic boom catch up to her a moment later.

"Dexter, what the fu—what the, um, heck have you been doing?" she said, with a guilty glance at Cody and Astor.

"Hi, Aunt Sergeant, " Astor said, with visible hero worship. Debs got to carry a gun and boss large men around, and Astor found that intoxicating.

Debs knew it; she smiled at Astor and said, "Hi, honey. How are you doing?"

"Great!" Astor gushed. "This is the best vacation *ever*!"

Deborah raised an eyebrow at that, but just said, "Well, good."

"What brings you down to old Key West, sis?" I said.

She looked back to me and frowned. "They're all saying that Hood followed you down here and turned up dead—in your room, for Christ's sake," Debs said. "I mean, Jesus."

"Quite true," I said calmly. "Sergeant Doakes is around somewhere, too," I said.

Deborah's jaw bulged out; it was quite clear that she was grinding her teeth, and I wondered what had happened to the two of us in our childhood to turn us both into molar manglers. "All right," she said. "You better tell me what happened."

I looked around the table at my little family, and although I was very happy to have my sister here to share my tale of woe, I realized that there were quite a few details that might not be appropriate for sensitive ears—I mean Rita's, of course. "Would you join me in the lobby, sis?" I said.

I followed Debs out to the lobby, where we found a soft leather couch. We sank into the low cushions together, and I told her. It was surprisingly pleasant to be able to tell it all, and it was even more gratifying to hear her reaction when I finished.

"You sure he's dead?" she said.

"Deborah, for God's sake," I said. "I saw him bitten in half by a giant shark. He's dead and digested."

She nodded. "Well," she said. "We just might get away with it."

It was very nice to hear her say "we," but there were still some worrisome details that were more "I, Dexter" than plural. "What about Hood?" I said.

"That asshole got what was coming to him," she said. It was a shock to hear her speak approvingly of a brother officer's death; perhaps she had noticed his terrible breath, too, and was relieved that it was gone forever. But it also occurred to me that his brief attack on Deborah's reputation might have done some real professional harm.

"Are you okay with the department again?" I asked.

She shrugged and rubbed her cast with her good hand. "We got my psycho in a cell. Kovasik," she said. "Once I get back on it, I know I can make it stick. He did it, and Hood can't change that. Especially now he's dead."

"But don't the Key West cops still think I killed Hood?" I asked.

She shook her head. "I talked to Detective, um, Blanton?" she said, and I nodded. "That bag he dropped on the dock in the Tortugas had a baseball bat in it, among other things," she said.

"What kind of things?" I said; after all, if he'd come up with something new, I really wanted to know about it.

Deborah made an irritated face and shook her head. "I don't know, fuck," she said. "Duct tape. Clothesline. Fishhooks. A carpenter's saw. *Things*," she said, clearly cranky now. "What matters is the bat. There's some blood, tissue, and hair on it that they think will probably match up to Hood's." She shrugged and then, oddly, smacked my arm, hard, with her fist.

"Ouch," I said, thinking about the fishhooks—some very interesting possibilities . . .

"Which kind of lets you off the hook," Deborah said.

I rubbed my arm. "So they're just going to drop it? I mean, as far as I'm concerned?"

Deborah snorted. "Actually, they're kind of hoping you'll just go away and not make any fuss about them handing your children to a kidnapper. Right out of their own front door, too. Fucking idiots."

"Oh," I said. Oddly enough, I hadn't even thought of that. It really did seem like the sort of thing they might hope would just disappear. "So they're happy with Crowley, even though he's gone?"

"Yeah," Debs said. "Blanton may not look like much, but she knows her job. She found a hotel maid who saw somebody and got a description. Thirties, stocky, short beard?"

"That's him," I said.

"Uh-huh. So this guy was helping his drunk friend out of the service elevator on your floor. Except the maid said he looked a little *too* drunk—like *dead* drunk—and he had one of those pirate hats covering his face, like they found in your room?"

"Suite," I said reflexively.

She ignored me and shook her head. "The maid didn't want to say anything; she's from Venezuela, scared to lose her green card. But she gave a good description. And two of the cooks saw them coming in from the loading dock, too. Also, the waiter at breakfast confirms that you were with your family in the dining room at the time, so . . ."

I thought about it, nursing a tiny spark of hope as it grew into a glimmer. It was unlike Crowley to be so sloppy, but I suppose he had been surprised by Hood and had to improvise. I had a quick mental picture of the two of them trying to follow me at the same time and tripping over each other; comic hijinks result, leading to the hilarious bludgeoning death of Detective Hood. Maybe Crowley had panicked, maybe he had just been riding his luck and feeling invincible. I would never know, and it didn't really matter. Somehow, he had gotten away with it. Nobody had seen him kill Hood, and nobody had stopped him when he moved the body into my room. But of course, people see only what they expect to see, and precious little of that, so the only surprise was that anybody had noticed anything at all.

But the true marvel was that I could see a real live light at the end of what had been a very long, very dark tunnel. I breathed a tentative sigh of relief and looked at my sister, and she looked back. "So I'm off the hook in Key West?" I said.

She nodded. "It gets better," she told me. "Fucking Doakes really shit the bed this time."

"I hope it was his own bed," I said.

"He's supposed to be in Admin, not out working a case," she said. "Plus, here he is in Key West, which is way out of his jurisdiction. And," she added, raising her good hand, the one with no cast, in the air and making a very sour face, "the Key West cops have made a formal complaint. Doakes tried to bully them into holding on to you, and he intimidated witnesses, and . . ." She paused and looked off into the distance for a moment. "Fuck," she said at last. "He used to be a pretty good cop." She actually sighed, and it pained me to see her feeling sorry for someone who had spent so much time and effort making me miserable.

But there were, after all, more important matters at hand. "Deborah," I said. "What about Doakes?"

She looked up at me with an expression I couldn't quite read. "Suspended, without pay, pending investigation by Professional Compliance," she said.

I really couldn't help myself, and I blurted out, "That's wonderful!"

"Sure," Deborah said, a little sour. She continued her silent funk for a few more seconds and then shook herself out of it. "What the hell," she said.

"What happens back home?" I said. "Am I still a person of interest to the investigation?"

Deborah shrugged. "Officially you are," she said. "But Laredo has taken over the case, and he's not a dope. You'll probably be back at work in a few days." She looked at me. It was a hard look, and there was clearly something on her mind, but whatever it was she didn't say it. She just looked, and then finally turned away to stare at the front door. "If only," she said, "there was . . ." She hesitated, cleared her throat, and went on slowly. " . . . just a little bit of evidence, so . . . Then you'd be home free." A fat man in plaid shorts came in the front door, followed by two small blond girls. Deborah seemed to find them interesting.

"What kind of evidence, Debs?" I said.

She shrugged and watched the fat man. "Ah, I dunno," she said. "Maybe something that showed that Hood was bent. You know. So we can see he was not clean, not really a good cop. And maybe why he tried to put it on you."

The fat man and his entourage disappeared down the hall, and Deborah looked at the cast on her broken arm where it lay in her lap. "If we could find something like that," she said, "and keep your name out of the thing in the Tortugas, who knows." She looked up at me at last, with a small, very strange smile. "We just might get away with it."

Perhaps there really is some kindly, doting Demigod of Darkness that watches over the truly wicked, because we actually did get away with it—at least the first part. The Thing in the Tortugas caused a little fuss in the press, and there was some mention of the anonymous hero who had saved the old man's life. But nobody actually knew the hero's name, and witnesses' descriptions of him were so vague they could have been six different randomly selected strangers. It was too bad, because it turned out that the old man really was important, and he owned several TV stations and quite a few state legislators.

There was some confusion about what had happened to the very bad man who had attacked the old guy. The woman who lost her bikini gave a good description of Crowley, and it matched up with what the Key West cops had, so it was clear that this terrible felon had killed a Miami cop and then tried to steal a boat and flee, probably to Cuba. Whether he had ended up in Havana or someplace else was not clear, but he was gone. He was listed as officially missing, wanted, and he went onto a few assorted lists. But no one really missed the missing person, and these are hard times, with dwindling budgets, so there was not a great deal of money and effort spent trying to find him. He was gone, nobody cared, and The Thing in the Tortugas was soon pushed out of the news by a triple nude decapitation involving a middle-aged man who had once been a child star on TV.

We really were getting away with it. If only one last small miracle could somehow discredit Hood, my coworkers would welcome me back to work with open arms and joyous smiles, and life would return to its wondrous banal predictable everyday boring bliss. And the day after I returned from Key West, Deborah called to inform me that a forensics team would be going to Hood's house the next morning. We just had to hope that something helpful might turn up.

And it might. It very well might. It *might* be something so very helpful that the entire case would vanish in a puff of malodorous smoke, and Dexter would go from a shabby felon slinking out of his office, to a real live martyr, a victim of gross injustice and wicked defamation of character.

But was it really possible that something like that might turn up?

Oh, yes, quite possibly it might. In fact, it *might* be a great deal of Something Like That, things that *might* be so very damning that they cast doubt not just on the case against me, but on Detective Hood himself, and his right to wear Our Proud Uniform, and to walk among the Just, so absolutely damning that the department would want the whole thing to disappear quickly and quietly, rather than risk a huge and stinking blemish on its proud reputation.

In fact, it *might* be that the forensics team will come into the vile, smelly little hovel where Hood had lived, and stare around in disgusted wonder at the heaps of garbage, dirty dishes, filthy discarded clothing, and they will marvel that a human being could actually live like this. Because the place just *might* be a truly nauseating mess—why, I can almost picture what it *might* look like.

And I can almost picture my coworkers' disgust as it turns slowly to shock, and then grim but total condemnation as they find kiddie porn on the hard drive of Hood's computer—I mean, they *might* find it, along with a series of torrid love notes written to Camilla Figg and her reply that she never wanted to see him again because of his sick thing about children, and anyway his breath was so horrible. It would be easy to conclude that Hood had killed her out of rage at the breakup and then tried to cover his ass by pinning it on poor guiltless Dexter—especially since he found all her pictures of me, and these hypothetical notes *might* reveal that he had never liked me anyway.

And at some point in this remarkable train ride into Hood's inarguable guilt and shame, someone could very well pause and say, "But isn't this all just a little *too* perfect? Isn't there almost *too much* evidence against Detective Hood, who is no longer here to defend himself? Why, it's almost as if somebody snuck into this foul shanty and planted fabricated evidence, isn't it?"

But this pause will be a short one, and it will end with a disapproving shake of the head and a return to belief in the evidence, because it's all there, right before their eyes, and the thought that someone might have planted it is too wacky for words. After all, who would ever do such a thing? And even more, who *could* do it? Might there really be one person who has the amazing combination of talents, cunning, and moral emptiness to pull off such a complete destruction of Detective Hood's posthumous character? Was there really one person who might know enough about the case to manufacture just the right evidence, and have enough knowledge of police procedure to make it airtight? Who?

And Who *might* slide through the night like a darker part of the shadows and slither unseen into Hood's house to plant it? And once inside, Who *might* have the computer know-how to take all this evidence off a flash drive—for example—and put it onto Hood's little computer in such a way that it is utterly convincing? And Who, on top of all that, *might* do all this not merely so well but with such a truly clever, original, naughty sense of humor?

Is there really any Who anywhere who *might* be that good at all these dark and different things—and more important, wicked enough to do them? In all the world, *might* there possibly be anybody so wonderfully just like that?

Yes.

There *might* be.

But only one.

DEXTER™

SEASONS 1-5

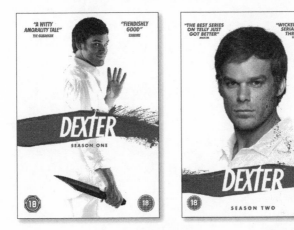

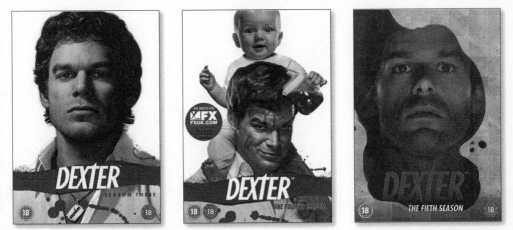

UK only artwork

AVAILABLE ON DVD / BLU-RAY NOW